PARABOLIC, MAGNETIC KEY

MOLISIA
BAUSTIC MOUNTAINS
GAROBANSUROV
RIFTOLEN
DEEPW
HOF
INFERTI
DESERT
N
W
E

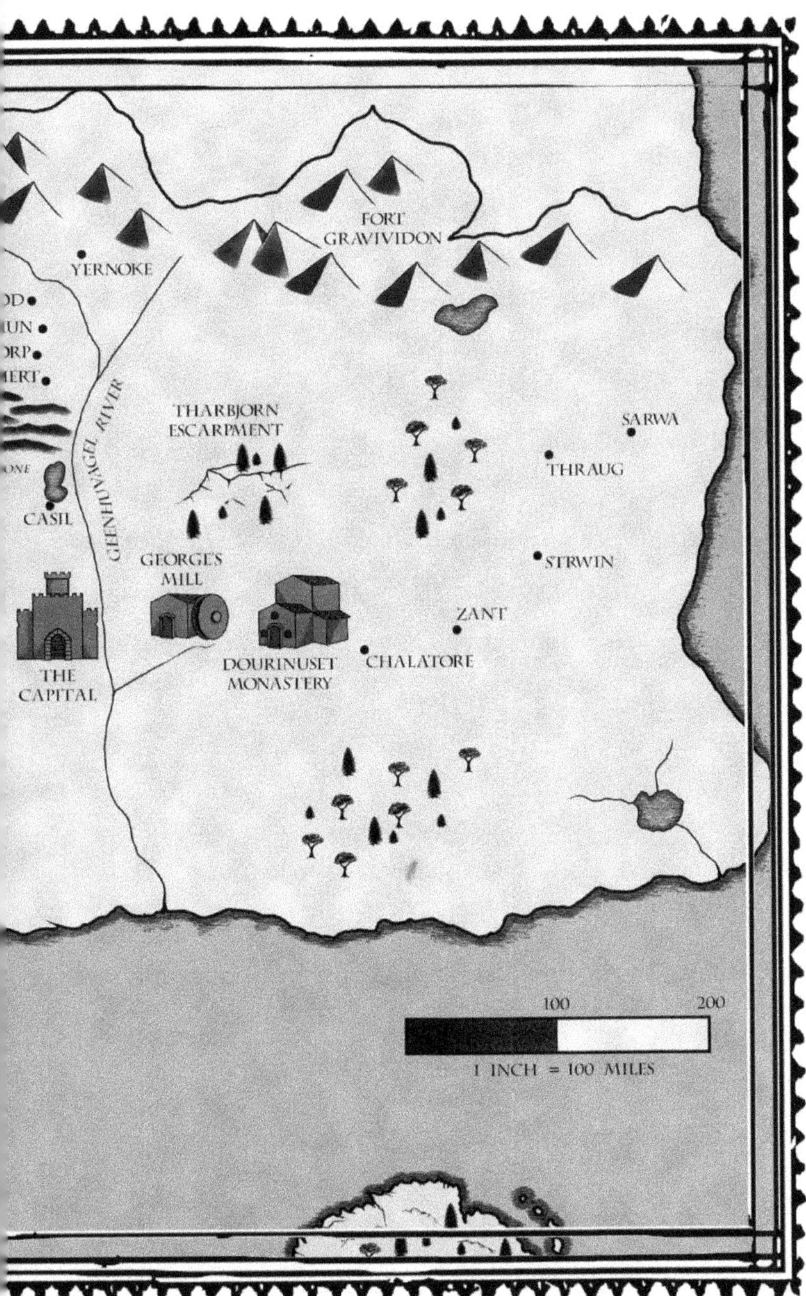

FORT GRAVIVIDON
YERNOKE
OD
UN
ORP
ERT
ONE
CASIL
GEENHUVAGEL RIVER
THARBJORN ESCARPMENT
SARWA
THRAUG
STRWIN
GEORGE'S MILL
ZANT
THE CAPITAL
DOURINUSET MONASTERY
CHALATORE
100
200
1 INCH = 100 MILES

Also by Nicholas Wudtke

—NOVELS—

Black Needle, Book One: Parabolic, Magnetic Key

Black Needle, Book Two: Blunt but Imminently Fatal Projectile

Black Needle, Book Three: Deserved, Contorted Relics

—SHORT STORIES—

The Swords, Friendships, and Winds of Far Off Places:
A Collection
~ FREE copy available at website below ~

Find out more, join our list, and purchase your next
great read at www.NicholasWudtke.com.

Black † Needle
Book One

PARABOLIC, MAGNETIC KEY

NICHOLAS WUDTKE

BLACK
NEEDLE
BOOKS

For Lifeson

PROLOGUE:

THE MOUNTAIN WAS undefeated. The mountain was powerful. It stood mightily, within grasp of the pinnacle of final victory. Doing all within its power to impede the competition, the mountain summoned every facet of obstruction it knew existed. But in the end, it couldn't establish superiority, and was unexpectedly defeated.

He finished the climb to the mountaintop, sighed, looked down below from a lofty precipice, and meditated on all elements presented during the journey. Driven, he stepped off the precipice, turned his eyes forward with purpose, and started the self-proclaimed mission to summit the next mountain. When completed, exhausted, he spent the same amount of time contemplating on that journey, as he did after the first. But this time he was able to compare the two contrasting challenges, judging which added more to his state of self-worth, contentment, and morality.

He utilized a host of factors in his comparison, including but not limited to: rarity of opportunities to repeat the feat; implementation of natural talents; difficulty of the tasks relative to energy expenditure; contribution to attributes required for other mountainous exploits; and negative effects. Upon the finalization of his deliberation, he realized he needed more information, so he set to move right into the ascension of the third towering mountain. When this new brave/foolish voyage was completed, he started the comparisons all over again, but with the equation having an additional variable representing the third mountain.

He thought with great focus, but still, answers eluded him. Bound and determined to know, he ever journeyed, searching the ultimate accomplishment. There was no rest. Persistence never left his side. The routine escalated into the fourth, fifth, and sixth mountain quests. Even these weren't enough, so he continued onward, in true understanding of perseverance. Climb. Contemplate. Climb again. The pattern went on and on, seemingly indefinitely, chained to a driving obsession.

One morning, a pair of particular adventurers came upon a formidable mountain and could see the contemplative mountaincer's footprints heading up the mountain. They scratched their chins in deliberation and decided to follow in his footsteps. And because others can learn much from what resulted, the adventurers' story must be told.

CHAPTER 1

WITHIN SIGHT OF a creek-merging, an aged and secluded log cabin rested impressively. The fact the cabin was so old and still standing wasn't what made it impressive, nor was it how year after year it remained dry, as spring thaw caused nearby creeks to rise substantially, and reach dangerously close. No, the impressive part was the great magnitude of a certain coincidence—the sheer chance that the cabin had spent more of its considerable long life being the temporary refuge for weary travelers than it had in the decades housing permanent residents. It was as if the cabin stood at the unimaginably exact intersection of every route taken by excursionists worldwide. The funny thing was there were no well-worn, main trails around it—only side trails, thin trails not much more than animal paths. For no known reason than happenstance, the cabin was a lightning rod for opportunists, and impressively represented a coincidence most remarkable.

It had been a memorable twenty-four hours.

An aforementioned duo of adventurers–both the sort who if informed their story would be passed on through the ages wouldn't object to the telling–ended night-time dreams consisting of glory, specifically, a well-earned glory that had been presented to them the day previous by the hands of an arm-wrestling tournament.

Content in having received a full night's sleep, Mick Thraiker and Dave Ghrere nimbly levered themselves out of their warm weather sleeping bags, stood, and cracked their joints—a joint-cracking performed so precisely an onlooker would've thought the two had carried out the same routine for half their lives.

Like most days, but not all, Mick and Dave woke to being surrounded by lovely Garobansurovian lands. Not everyone considered Garobansurov to be all that lovely, but an overwhelming majority certainly did.

Garobansurov was a country on the multi-climate continent of Taraosk, which was said by scholars, judging by fossil evidence, to have been inhabited by people for almost a billion years, during which time civilizations had been built and rebuilt repeatedly. Constant failure and rebirth. For those looking, many vestiges of those civilizations could be seen strewn about the countryside. The land lacked the natural resources to sustain the advancement of science enough for continued civilizational growth, a theory once presented by an unknown individual, one of many names lost in time. Towns in Garobansurov were small, technology was limited, and travel was only accomplished by one's own feet.

Greatly free from any of the nauseating verbal pollution that can sometimes be closely associated with people talking for the sake of talking, Mick and Dave planned, joked, and discussed personal observations while cooking portable breakfast foods in an abandoned cabin near a creek-merging.

Mick and Dave were thirty-one and thirty years old respectively, and of more or less average build, Dave being a little brawnier, Mick a little more aerodynamic. Both had facial features contributing to an exposition of wisdom—a display not as prominent as some, but more than most.

Neither Mick nor Dave had ever been married, both childless. Since completing their youth, they had enjoyed a life full of adventure, trail, and road; a lifestyle which made it difficult to settle into the family life. However, they've had their fair share of girlfriends along the way. Mick and Dave's attraction to beautiful women was only separated by the fact Mick preferred blondes and Dave brunettes.

After their longer than normal breakfast, Mick declared to Dave, "I think it's about the time when it would be advantageous for one of us to look out the east facing window to see if there's anything interesting sprouting, or if there's anything new with the army situation."

"You sure unpacked a lot with that sentence." Dave loosed half a chuckle. "But, yes, that sounds like time well spent. I think we should fill our canteens as well," Dave let be known, as he tapped out his canteen's last drop of water onto his left hand.

Mick yawned, then replied, "Good idea. I'm gambling with running out of water too. Do you want to look out the window to the horizon, or should I?"

"I'll look, old friend."

Dave peered out the dilapidated window, and besides a canopy of clouds, he could see the tail end of Ulfenkerki's army, an imposing mass, miles in the distance. He figured they were probably headed for Zant. After performing a few mental calculations, Dave determined the figurative flag of proceeding was what he was going to present to his partner in adventure. "So, Mick, it looks like the Black Bear's armed force is unleashed, heading towards Zant, a thrilling development to be sure."

The Black Bear was General Ulfenkerki's nickname, possibly given to him due to his enormous amount of black hair. Nobody knew the reason for certain. General Ulfenkerki's visage was rugged. Actually, he was one of the rare few whose facial features added more to a physical display of wisdom than Mick and Dave's. One look at the military leader and you'd know in a second the man had experienced much.

Mick proposed, "I think if we follow them, we will know best where General Anolski's dastardly crew is stationed."

"Yeah, probably, if we ever do decide that Anolski is a step in our plan."

"So, by your assessment then, would it be best for us to leave within the hour?"

"Definitely, my legs are starting to tighten up a bit," Dave replied, as he began stretching.

"Okay, I'll start getting articles together, and fill the canteens with water from one of the adjacent creeks. Although it's drinkable, I personally wouldn't designate it the most crystal clear of water sources, it being up to the drinker's imagination as to what it could best be categorized."

"I think I'd label it a *four* on a water-clarity scale of one to ten. It resembles the water that used to sit in the ditch in front of my childhood home," declared Dave.

Mick chuckled; he remembered.

Mick and Dave gathered their significant amount of travelling gear, which wasn't particularly easy, because they were still sore from the all-important arm-wrestling tournament the day previous. Their backpacks were heavy, probably too heavy for most to even lift off the ground, but years of practice with such loads was enabling.

They went out the door in hopes of experiencing another memorable twenty-four hours—twenty-four at the least.

Having taken a few hundred paces in the direction they wanted to go, they noticed an older gentleman walking towards them, who was obviously extremely physically fit for his age. The man was exhaustingly pulling a heavy tarpaulin-covered wagon.

Before the stranger was within earshot, Mick said to Dave, "I would've never expected to see someone else in these parts."

"Apparently this area isn't as secluded as it seems," Dave replied. "Mystical."

Having closed the gap and let go of the wagon, the stranger, adorned by a winning smile, greeted Mick and Dave. "You fellows look like you need to rest. Your bodies plainly show it. Are you headed anywhere in particular?"

At first glance, Mick could tell the stranger, Brom, was overflowing with stories. But he could also tell the man didn't have the time to share many of them. Mick replied, "I'm not sure yet to where exactly our path will lead us. We just go where the wind takes us sometimes. And as for the rest of which you speak, our bodies are uncharacteristically sore. I'm sure they'll recover shortly. Arm-wrestling tournaments tend to sap strength from the entire body, not just the arms. Yesterday, we entered the tournament in Chalatore."

In reality, Mick and Dave did know where they were generally headed, they just didn't know exactly what they were going to do when they got there. Their minds were on the war and everything about it.

"Indeed, they can do that. I too participated in a few grueling tournaments back in my day," Brom shared. "On a different note, hopefully you don't end up in Zant. I think a battle is going to commence there."

"That's quite possible. Both."

"Aaah, war, what can you do."

The three exchanged names, and without warning, Brom switched gears from pleasantries to salesmanship. He took the tarp off the cart he was pulling, and proclaimed, "What I have under this tarp is my life's work, but I have to sell it all to continue the search for the most important thing in my life: my children. Specifically, my search is for my son. He went missing a while ago, and my resources are getting too low for me to continue my search much longer."

Dave looked upon Brom with a heartfelt glance, and replied, "We will unquestionably do as much as we can to help you out."

"In my cart are three complete sets of armor that need to be sold, each one taking me ten years to complete. Thirty painstaking years of my life are in this heavier-than-it-looks cart. All three sets are constructed from the finest metals."

Mick and Dave looked into the cart, and started to examine the suits in their entirety. They surveyed all the intricate details, and studied the metals from which each piece was made. They noticed how all three suits glistened in the sun. They picked up a breastplate, and realized that it was the lightest but strongest breastplate they had ever seen. The same was also true for the greaves, gauntlets, boots, helmet, and the rest. The people across the continent of Taraosk sometimes called each item of a suit of armor a different thing, depending on where they lived; but in Garobansurov it was all pretty standard.

"These are indeed the absolute finest sets of armor in all Garobansurov, and we would certainly love to be clad in these, but I'm afraid, however, I don't think we could ever afford it," said Mick, while mentally picturing himself and Dave going into battle with such fine craftsmanship protecting them.

"I understand, I know there aren't too many people that would be able to afford one of my armor sets."

"Actually," noted Mick, "we do know of one person that may be able to help you out: an old man who lives back near our hometown of Chalatore. He may have sufficient funds to purchase one of the suits. He is a collector of all sorts of arms and armor."

Brom sadly responded, "I just came from back that way, and would hate to do that much backtracking. I'm actually trying to get to Sarwa, because I've heard there are certain people interested in this sort of thing there."

Dave jumped into the conversation, almost in interruption. "Please, please don't head to that part of the country. We've heard many murders are transpiring in that section, due to the war. I'm afraid you'd risk suffering the same fate."

"Your advice is certainly well respected by me, and I know your wisdom is just, but I have to head in that direction. I feel my son's life depends on it."

"Godspeed to you then, my friend, and may your journey have a happy ending. In the future, if we ever can help you, we will," Mick said with utmost sincerity.

"I will certainly count you among my friends, and appreciate your offer of helping me more than you know. Hopefully my journey is short, and we all come out alive. Until we meet again. Goodbye."

"Farewell, friend," said Dave and Mick simultaneously, just before Brom started to turn and walk away, pulling the cart containing arguably the three best sets of armor on the entire continent.

When Brom was out of earshot, Mick said to Dave, "Those sets of armor are too good to be worn by anyone. They should be displayed on pedestals for all to look upon, so nobody scratches and damages them while wearing them into battle."

"I don't think that will ever happen. I just hope the armor doesn't end up in the wrong hands."

"I doubt that Brom is really worrying about that, and who can blame him. He needs to do what needs to be done for the good of his family."

"That's true, hopefully next time we see him, he isn't in such dire straits."

"Yes, hopefully."

Mick and Dave started to walk again, but kept Brom on their minds for quite some time.

After a period of relaxed walking, Dave looked to Mick, and said, "Oh dang, I forgot that roll of seemingly combustible paper sitting on the table back at that house. I think it would've been a nice thing to use for starting up our next fire."

"Yeah, that would've been a good thing to have. It's too bad there aren't very many *paper birches* around," Mick returned. Paper birch bark was used as tinder frequently by many. Also, trees were capitalized in Garobansurov, due to how important they were.

Realizing that paper birches in Garobansurov were as abundant as stars, and that Mick was being sarcastic, Dave chuckled, "Classic."

Mick blurted, "Sorry for the randomness, I guess it isn't too random since he's only a handful of miles ahead of us, but I wonder if the Black Bear likes his moniker."

"I know I would, if it was my nick-name, not that I don't already have a good one. Although, it would suit me, since I'm as strong as a black bear."

Mick chuckled. "Yeah, buddy, just keep telling yourself that."

"Well, holding my umbrella of illusion is what keeps my world dry and comfortable."

Chuckles immediately turned into laughter, and as the day progressed, wisecracks turned into even more wisecracks.

At midday, clouds began accumulating and obscuring the sun. Neither Mick nor Dave paid the change much attention, being too lost in thought at the time.

Mick snapped out of his trance, because he heard clashing metal emanating from the distance. He stopped walking, and said, "Did you hear that, Dave? Sounds like a skirmish."

"Yes, I heard it, but it doesn't sound like a full battle, only a handful of sword or battle-axe fights."

Mick turned his head, so his right ear was facing where he thought the metallic sounds were coming from. He listened carefully, and communicated to Dave, "I think if we get a little closer, we'll be able to see better. Let's sneak up on them, staying within the tree shadows, especially within the dark shadows of the Hemlocks to the left."

"Sure, Mick, but keep from snapping the twigs this time, we don't want to relive what occurred at Vanderliest."

"Definitely, we don't want that again. I think that whole town doesn't want that to happen again."

The pair chuckled at the nostalgia.

They crept silently atop the gnarled root bases of the ancient, storied hemlocks, and got close enough to the action to fully understand what was going on. They saw five pairs of men sparring with each other vigorously, for a reason unbeknownst to them at the time.

Dave whispered to Mick, "So what's your input, should we just ignore them, or see what they're up to?"

Mick replied, "I think it would be best to ignore them for now, because I'm honestly not in the mood for talking, and dealing with possible repercussions."

"Sounds good to me. Besides, my mind is full at the moment, no need for additional matters for reflection," Dave replied.

"They might not even be a part of the army. Just farmers playing around."

"True."

The day wore on, and Mick and Dave realized it had just been farmers, and that the real army, Ulfenkerki's army, was headed for a stopover in the town of Zant. Ready for a little rest themselves, the pair started to make plans for the evening.

"Dave, near that rock outcropping looks just as good a place as any for the nightly campsite. I'm pretty defunct. With the army sojourning just ahead, we might as well stop too."

Wiping sweat from his forehead, Dave replied, "Okay, I too could use some down time right about now. I'll set up the tents."

"Alright and I'll gather all necessary firewood, paper birch bark, and some of those raspberries we passed on the way here for a midnight snack," said Mick, as he unloaded his gear. "I'll also perform anything else ingenuity suggests."

"Perfect."

"That abandoned shack in which we stayed last night sure had its highpoints; but sometimes nothing beats a good old-fashioned night in a homemade tent. Don't you think, Dave?"

"Definitely. One of my favorite activities in all of life," Dave declared. "Did you happen to inadvertently notice what exactly was written on that roll of paper back at the cabin?"

"No, I didn't. Did you?"

"Not really. I think it was just one of those information parchments, describing inconsequential comings and goings."

"I guess we'll learn all about the important comings and goings, when we go into Zant tomorrow."

"That we will, Mick."

When Mick finished gathering wood for the fire, and igniting it, he said, "It turns out that Brom was wrong about where the next battle was going to be, because I'm not hearing any battles over there in Zant."

"Oh yeah, that's right, Mick. I almost forgot he said that. I do hope he is getting his immaculate sets of armor sold, before having to walk the treacherous road to Sarwa."

"As do I. My heart goes with him."

Dave stirred up the pot of stew cooking over the fire, loaded to the brim with tasty ingredients. He recalled and gleefully recited to Mick the occurrence a year ago when the two of them were playing cards with unconventional thieves, a one-armed individual and an elderly lady missing half her hair, and how they had to go to drastic measures to get their stolen money back from the unusual robbers.

After the good-humored expatiation, Dave prompted Mick to sharpen his sword.

"Thanks for the reminder, Dave. I almost forgot. Without you, I would've run headfirst into battle, without the ability to slice even a delicate loaf of bread."

"Now I know you're exaggerating."

The night progressed, and more stories were told. Comradery at their campsite was as thick as the stew. Mick and Dave were no doubt as close to being blood brothers as humanly possible, without actually being so.

"Why do you think Gunther's and Haglerand's companies lost in the battle of Smirkoff against the Black Bear?" Mick asked Dave.

"It's anyone's guess, but I think it had a lot to do with the power of his notable warriors, Jason Thorncat, Sven Algar, Steve Johnson, and Ralph Engelheinz, and the fire with which they play. Those four warriors when fighting together can turn the tide of any battle, even when fighting numbers much greater."

"They say Gunther's squad alone had at least twelve-hundred men," mentioned Mick. "An impressive number."

"A single person can never be underestimated, and one day you and I will turn the tide of this war."

"Let us have a drink to that."

"Fantastic," said Dave, enthusiastically, "we shall."

Chapter 2

THE NIGHT CREPT ever steadily on, and while the two men slept soundly in their tents, one of the passes of the Baustic Mountain Range, many miles away, played host to a notable battle of archers, although technically the conflict didn't occur in the mountains, more so the weather-eroded foothills of the mountain range.

Provoked, Rayton's archers of Garobansurov fired their arrows at Bomsov's archers of Molisia at great range, continuing to do so, well into the morning. Neither had many casualties because a close-range conflict never ensued. Nevertheless, blood was spilt, and soldiers were lost. Garobansurov's war with Molisia was in full swing.

Because the Baustic foothills were so far from any other company, sending reinforcements would've been difficult.

Eventually, news of the battle reached General Ulfenkerki, the Black Bear, information which put him into a quandary at the time. He had to decide whether to continue pressing on to Anolski, or avert course and aid his countrymen: Rayton and his archers.

HAVING CRAWLED OUT of their tents, Mick and Dave once again performed their morning joint cracking. Afterwards, they looked around at their campsite, and remembered the drinking and camaraderie the night before. They gave each other a look, the kind of look that only true friends can give each other, the kind that would intimidate many people, due to the sense of unbreakable loyalty it implied.

"So, Mick, do we hope to accomplish anything this morning in Zant, other than a little reconnaissance?"

"I think that's the main plan, but if we run into some of the other warriors, it would be pleasant to talk of experiences. It would also be nice to run into Jason Thorncat and relive some old memories of our childhood."

"Yeah, hopefully that happens. I haven't seen him since that time the three of us broke into Old Man Johnson's cabin just to look at his ancient sword collection," Dave communicated, while reflecting.

"Yup, that was a good time. Too bad his parents sent him away after that. I wonder to where they dispatched him, I never knew."

"Me neither. Maybe we'll see him today, and find out."

Camp was packed up. Dave made sure the fire was out, and that no flaming embers remained. The legs got stretched, and the walk into town began. A slow trot surfaced, which increasingly got faster, as their anticipation for town activities started to set in.

They had about a mile left to go when they stopped at the side of a creek for a small break.

With a hand grasping his canteen, about to submerge it into the creek for refilling, Dave started a small conversation. "Why do you think there aren't many people going into Zant this morning? We should've seen tons of them by now."

"You would think that'd be the case, since an entire army spent the night there and all," Mick replied.

"It sure is strange. I hope there isn't anything weird going on." Dave stood up from renewing his water supply in the creek, and motioned his finger towards his canteen cap that was sitting out of reach on a rock next to Mick, an unspoken favor request from a friend to a friend.

Encapsulating efficiency, Mick complied by tossing the cap without hesitation. "Well, are we ready to move on?"

"Yup."

Westward they travelled, in possession of a lease guaranteeing a vigorous day, heading towards the medium-sized town of Zant. They knew a bridge crossing was imminent for anyone approaching Zant from its eastern side.

They arrived at said bridge crossing and cautiously proceeded over the rickety, wooden construction; both

Mick and Dave having an eye designated for danger. There was a small possibility the bridge would give out as they crossed it, but they more so clung to attentiveness because bottlenecks of bridges always seemed to be the trapping zone for thieves and bandits. Dangerous times indeed.

Having successfully crossed the bridge, Mick and Dave resumed their not-so vigilant attitudes. But they weren't so lucky the second they stepped into an Aspen thicket along the path. The reason why all the roads on that side of Zant were so empty became immediately evident to them: standing encircled around Mick and Dave were four stoic men, all clad in the most potent of armor and weaponry.

Three of the four were highly skilled in fighting discipline; but Mick and Dave could see that the fourth wasn't. They could piece together that information by noticing the fourth's lack of coordination in his walking gait. The fourth was just occupying the quartet to serve as an expendable diversion if conflict ever actually ensued.

The successful thieves had yet to draw weapons, due to their threatening disposition, having effortlessly gathered vast loot from easy to fleece people on their honest way into Zant.

With the sinister men surrounding them, Mick and Dave instinctively grabbed the hilts of their swords. They prepared for the first of the spoken words from the obviously aggressive confronters.

The leader of the bandit group, the tallest, who carried an almost four-foot broadsword was the one to speak first. For some reason, probably to be humorous, he uttered his opening line in a courteous way. "May we please have your money? My name is Paul and we are on a pilgrimage to Lake Buyanhuel to pray at the shrine of Macont, but our funds are getting extremely low—too low to continue."

Responding with a laugh of sorts, Mick reciprocated, "Our funds are also getting pretty low, for we are as well on a pilgrimage. May we please have *your* money?"

Beginning to show signs of anger, Paul riposted, "I guess we are at an impasse then."

Dave decided to add to the intriguing conversation. "So, if we just trade all our assets with each other, the stalemate will be broken, and we'll all be happy in theory. Am I right?"

After Dave's remark—a comment that could've been misconstrued as arrogance—Paul grabbed his broadsword, and with a show of fury, swung it at his nearest opponent: Mick.

Reacting accordingly, Mick ducked.

Dave, being free to move quickly, took out the expendable diversion, who was trying to flank his right side. Dave knew it would be a quick kill, which is why he decided on that as being his first course of action. It left two standing for him to fight. The combat styles of Dave's adversaries were congruent, a particular style which Dave had faced before, but he wasn't sure if he could handle them both simultaneously. He attacked with the utmost confidence, nevertheless.

Meanwhile, Mick had his hands full with their leader, who could handle his long broadsword like most could handle their own arm. After Mick and Paul exchanged a considerable number of unsuccessful lunges, thrusts, and parries, Mick looked over at Dave and noticed he was about to get overwhelmed. Mick decided he needed to take a certain drastic course of action. Guided by intuition, he dug deep into his reserve rage cistern, and waited patiently for the opportune moment. The set-up had to be perfect.

In a precise manner, Paul progressed, undercutting Mick's lower guard with his sword. Seeing this, Mick strategically sacrificed immediate gains for later ones, and allowed what he hoped wouldn't be too deep of a cut to the leg from Paul. Sustaining the excruciating hit, Mick spun around a hundred-eighty degrees in stride, and drove his sword into the neck of the closer of the two thieves battling Dave.

With Dave's impending danger neutralized, Mick now had a chance to see how deep of a cut to his leg he suffered. It bled profusely, but it wasn't life threatening. Fortunately, the broadsword hadn't punctured the vital femoral artery running through his upper leg. He sighed relief.

Wielding rage leftover from the move assisting Dave, Mick was able to slay Paul with a three-part maneuver managed with exactitude.

Motionless, Paul lay dead on the ground.

Mick now had the chance to further assist Dave, but as luck would have, he noticed Dave had just easily defeated his single combatant. So instead, Mick quickly and exaggeratedly sheathed his sword for effect. His unconscious mind summoned the type of euphoria that an individual could only experience during a moment of glory.

Dave's level of exuberance immediately grew to match Mick's. After they simultaneously relished in a few fist-pumps of triumph, they shook each other's hands, congratulating each other on the well-played battle.

There would be no more fake pilgrimages, no friendly exchanges of money.

Mick and Dave felt bad people had to die, but knew the thieves were too aggressive to prevent it.

Mick tended to his wound by temporarily wrapping basswood leaves around it to stop the bleeding, a remedy that would have to work until getting into town, where he could obtain more suitable bandages.

When Dave's victory elation dissipated enough to talk clearly, he exclaimed, "Unbelievable, Mick, that maneuver you unleashed to slay the first of my opponents was fantastic. Who would have thought they'd be so oblivious."

"I improvised. And equal in impressiveness, your ability to hold the line against the two for so long was remarkable, and of great valor, my friend."

"Thank you, thank you. Let's gather their stolen property, and head into town to bring it to the authorities."

"Lead the way."

THE TOWN OF ZANT was positioned just off-center of the country Garobansurov—the nation to which Dave and Mick owed their perpetual allegiance, to which they owed their most prized possession (their freedom), and for which they'd die. Encasing Zant at its perimeter and standing sturdily were walls twenty feet high, which were just wide enough at the top for sentries to keep a solid look-out.

Within the walls were multiple commercial and residential buildings. Only the hotel, Boyer Manor, and the steeple of one of the churches could be seen towering over the wall. The census usually revealed a population of no more than three hundred residents, but because Ulfenkerki's army had spent the night there, the current population had swelled to over a thousand.

Although the army was set to leave shortly, people from all around were still trickling in from the countryside just to lay eyes on the troops, and envelop themselves in the excitement spawning from such a spectacle. The people wouldn't soon forget all the stories told to them by older family members. Unforgettably true tales of the great battle that took place in Zant more than two hundred years ago, of when the town took stage, and became the turning point for Garobansurov.

Garobansurovians hoped these new invaders would flee back to their home country just as they did in the old stories.

The people of Zant clung onto optimism as they did the old stories.

In an adequately-sized tent flapping uncontrollably in the wind, which primarily served the purpose for holding war-councils, stood General Ulfenkerki; his second in command, Sven Algar; and notable warrior, Steve Johnson.

"I never knew that's why you don't like being called by your first name," said Steve to Ulfenkerki. "If I were you, I too would much rather be called General Ulfenkerki or the Black Bear, instead of Kermoy."

"Anyways," Ulfenkerki interrupted, "I do agree with you, Sven, on what you suggested about the next course of action. Sometimes in life you must take a chance. I would really like to go directly to aid Rayton's archers, but I would give it a sixty-five percent chance that Anolski will try to infiltrate Strwin next, instead of marching on to Thraug, where my friend, General Nighteagle, can intercept. Furthermore, I can also assume Anolski wants to meet up with Bamsov and his archers to reinforce his campaign. It is decided then. We will go directly to Strwin and hopefully meet up with Rayton there, instead of going directly to him. Send word to Archer-General Rayton of my intent right away."

"Yes, General, sir," returned Sven.

Before exiting the tent, Ulfenkerki said, "We really should find a way to keep this tent from flapping in the wind so much."

IN THE MEANTIME, on the other side of town, Mick and Dave entered the law enforcement headquarters in hopes of discussing the stolen property they confiscated and were bringing in.

After about a ten-minute conversation, Mick and Dave walked out the door with the five hundred giti—government issued trading item—reward that had been posted for the dead or alive capture of the wanted thieves.

"Slightly more ceremonious and verbose than necessary, I thought," Dave said.

"I agree. I'm just glad the thieves are going to get a proper burial, and that all the stolen money will be returned."

"Same here," Dave said to Mick. "Should we, first, seek to replenish our supplies, or try and find out what the military is up to?"

"I think we should make contact with members of the military first, because it sure seems their activity as of late has started to increase, as if they were just about to leave."

"I guess I just noticed that now too. To whom should we talk?"

Mick scanned his surroundings to gauge the situation, and replied to Dave, "Over there, those two soldiers standing against the wall look like they're in a talking mood."

They walked the forty yards to the strangers, and began a conversation.

"Hello fellow countrymen. I am Mick Thraiker, and this is my friend, Dave Ghrere."

"Nice to finally meet you, Mick and Dave," Mike, the shorter man, replied. "In this company at least, your names precede you. Our most elite warrior, Jason Thorncat, always speaks of his childhood, and how he constantly got bested by two of his friends in sword training—*you two*. But he refers to you more often by your nicknames, "Hawk" and "Leopard." He hopes someday you will join this company."

"Those were some good times," Dave emitted. "We called Jason "Fox." I don't remember why, though. Hey Mick, I think we should help resurface those names again."

"Sounds like a plan, Leopard," Mick replied, saying the last word of the sentence emphatically. "So, where is our old pal Jason at? We were actually hoping to run into him while we're here in Zant."

Making himself known, Bob, the taller man, voiced, "I don't think you'll get a chance to communicate with Jason anymore; we are all pulling stakes in haste at this very moment. We're headed to Strwin, hoping to absorb Rayton's archers and secure the town."

"I suppose that answers the question we came to you to ask," Mick voiced. "Unrelated, have you any news of the Eastern Front?"

"Nothing new as of late," Mike responded.

After a few more minutes of exchanged pleasantries, Mick said, "It was nice to have met you, Mike and Bob. Maybe we'll run into you later."

Mike and Bob shook the hands of Mick and Dave, wished them well, and took leave of their company.

The commotion of the army vacating town engulfed the senses. Travelling in Zant started to become constrictive.

"I think it would be best to sojourn here awhile. Maybe sleep, and replenish supply."

Planting himself on a bench, Dave supplied response to Mick's statement. "I'm good with that, but for now, I'm going to sit here for a spell and try to stay away from this stampeding crowd."

Mick sat on the adjacent bench. Overall, there were three benches at the rest-stop.

The three benches were surrounded by towering Oak trees, which provided sufficient amounts of shade and beauty. Ornate pots bookended the three benches, containing an assortment of flowers, which probably needed to be watered every few days or so.

"Let's play a game, Dave. It's called, *Guess which person in town is the one who actually waters these flowers.*"

"I would if I could, but I can't. My energy at the moment is drained, so I'm just going to sit here and think. I'll possibly regain my composure in due time," said Dave, while stretching and yawning.

After a while, and a few up-close visits from a myriad of bird species coming from the tree canopy above, Mick and Dave became well rested. They started to get up from their own personal perches, but both coincidentally had to sit back down, because of the notorious headrush.

"I haven't had that happen lately," said Mick. "Let's try that again, eh Leopard."

"Ok, Hawk," Dave replied, with hands on head. Dave pointed towards one of the storefronts. "There's your pot waterer right there, the woman holding the watering can. She looks like she is waiting for us to leave these benches, so she can do the watering."

Mick responded, laughing slightly, "Looks like you're the winner after all."

"Yup. That store in front of which she appeared has food to sell, let's go and grab a few accoutrements there."

"Good idea."

Mick and Dave entered the tiny store, which exhibited no more than four showcases of fruits and vegetables, a meat counter, and two or three setups of miscellaneous food stuffs. Along with the bandages for Mick's leg, they bought five pounds of potatoes, three pounds of onions, two pounds of tomatoes, some flour, a pinch of salt, and a small bag of sugar. Necessities. Enough to refill the food compartments of their packs. The rest of the food they ate was accumulated throughout their travels, such as fish, small game, and random edible plants.

As efficiently as always, Mick and Dave finished up at the food store. The lady, whom they earlier spotted intending to water the flowers, walked back into the store. Dave found the woman to be exceedingly beautiful, so he couldn't help but desire a conversation with her.

One man temporarily possessing the courage of ten, Dave walked towards the lady holding the watering can.

Mick in the interim gave Dave space in the name of teamwork.

"Sure is a wonderful day," Dave said to the lady with what he hoped was a successful attempt at a winning smile.

The lady nervously set down the watering can in hopes that it would buy her enough time to think and respond somewhat eloquently. "It sure is. It was supposed to rain today, but who listens to those weather predictors anyways? Pure mysticism, if you ask me."

"I certainly don't listen to them, they're never right. Nice to meet you, my name is Dave, and my fellow traveling companion over there looking suspiciously at the fruit is Mick."

"Nice to meet you, Dave. Nice to meet you too, Mick." She spoke the latter in a slightly raised voice so it could be heard from afar. Mick heard, and raised his hand in recognition. She continued, "My name is Serana, and this is my grandfather's store. Believe it or not, he actually turned one hundred years old last week, and still works the store once in a while. Usually, though, it's either my mom or I who tend to things here."

"It certainly is a nice store, and the goods are certainly reasonably priced. Thank you so much for keeping those pots at the wayside watered; it sure is a beautiful place to stop and rest."

"You could kind of say the nurturing of the spot runs in our family. My grandmother, rest her soul, was the one to plant those oak trees from seed when she was a child. She also designed and built the place. Ever since her death, it's my mother or I who perform the anonymous required maintenances. We also catalogue every bird species that visits. It's a bigger list than you'd think."

"I imagine." Dave took a second to ponder, and put forth, "So if your grandfather is a hundred years old, and assuming your grandmother was about the same age, the oaks will soon celebrate their centennial."

"You would be correct. We should throw a celebration in their honor."

Dave chuckled. "Good idea, you should. There's nothing more artful than an old tree, I always say," Dave spanned the impressive trees with admiring eyes.

"I agree, Dave. Just imagine how artful they'll be in another hundred years."

"Glorious to be sure. You could throw a bicentennial celebration then."

"I won't be throwing much of anything, if I've managed to live that long." The pair laughed together.

"Same here." Endeavoring to conclude the conversation with poise, Dave communicated, "Thanks again for tending to the spectacular wayside locale. It was pleasant to have met you, Serana, and maybe I'll run into you again sometime soon."

"I am glad we met also; and yes, maybe we'll encounter each other again sometime, somewhere. I'm always taking produce to neighboring towns to sell at the farmers' markets, so maybe then."

"Yeah, hopefully. May the rest of your day be as beautiful as you."

Serana blushed.

Dave and Mick took leave of the store, clutching their fresh supply of goods. Mick removed the basswood leaves around his leg, and applied the new bandages.

They continued to meander down the main thoroughfare, looking for a place to spend some of their newly acquired reward money. They spotted an arms and armor dealer, and decided it would be a great place for a visit.

Looking through the store's wares, Mick noted, "Leopard, I know you are attached to your ancient greaves you currently use for aggressive confrontations, but this is a virtually unavoidable price on this set here."

"You're right, I am attached to them," Dave replied, humorously ignoring the latter part of Mick's sentence.

Mick took the hint, chuckled a little, and continued looking around, mainly at armor. They didn't bother looking very long at the weapons; their present ones would probably never need replacing. In particular, their swords were priceless, having a storied past of their own. An interesting story that not many knew.

They purchased a set of arrows for their shared hunting bow, and left the quaint shop ten gitis lighter.

Just subsequent to exiting the shop, they were quick to notice the entire army had vacated town. All that remained were townsfolk and visitors.

"At least the roads aren't so stifling anymore. I was starting to get sick of dodging all the people who weren't watching where they were going."

"As was I, Hawk," said Dave, realizing that he was going to enjoy resurfacing the old nicknames.

AROUND THE SAME time the inattentive people of Garobansurov were being complained about, Ulfenkerki and his army were marching to their next destination. General Ulfenkerki had been talking with Jason Thorncat about the world and its many idiosyncrasies.

"I never knew you looked at it that way," said Jason, referring to a topic religious in nature.

"Yes, I always have. Changing the subject, I must say I'm thoroughly prepared for the job at hand: securing freedom for us and for all who want it," the Black Bear declared with utmost pride.

"We are behind you, sir. The company and I are grateful for your leadership, and will follow you to death if need be."

"I don't think that'll be necessary. Have you seen yourself in battle lately? You alone could defeat an entire platoon."

"No, I haven't, The enemy doesn't exactly bring mirrors into battle, in which for me to admire myself," Jason said, through laughter. "You exaggerate though,

I'm only a little better than you with a sword. There are others in this world better than me."

"Let's hope they're not from Molisia then," Ulfenkerki replied, just before striding through the lines to speak to another officer.

Molisia certainly did have great warriors of its own. Their goal may not have been extending freedom in the normal sense, but they felt their resolve was noble, and they fought for it just as fiercely.

While the Black Bear was marching his army, many miles parted, the Molisian general, Anolski, was marching his. Anolski's army was greater in number, and ready for any battle they might face while in Garobansurov.

Molisia had other armies led by other generals, located currently in different parts of Garobansurov. As did Garobansurov.

BACK IN ZANT, Hawk and Leopard were still wandering aimlessly through town, trying to spend some gitis, but it wasn't something they were particularly good at. They basically only went shopping out of necessity.

After circling the entirety of town at least six times, seeing every market and storefront multiple times, they decided to halt the procuring of goods, and call it a night.

"Hey, Leopard, why don't we stay at the inn tonight, so we don't have to carry the extra weight of the fifteen gitis it would cost to do so."

Knowing how light gitis really were, Dave chuckled. "That's just as good of a reason as any, I declare. We passed up the only inn a few moments ago. It's back that way." Dave pointed with his forefinger.

Having entered the inn known as the Zant Hotel—one of the buildings that towered over Zant's wall—Thraiker and Ghrere requested a room with two beds. The room was paid for and shown to the purchasers.

The room's two beds were made from grey spruce, which was a common tree species in Garobansurov, but not a common one from which to make a bed. The spruce was a pleasant surprise. Propped beside each bed were end tables, accentuated by oil lamps. The floor was decorated with a flamboyant rug, its colors being just as unexpected as the beds' wood. And on the walls were hung what some would call "art," probably fashioned by a local artist aiming to make a quick giti. By no means did the colors of the art coincide with those of the rug. The size of the room was adequate, and smelled like a fireplace. That part was typical.

"I can now feel my pockets being lighter. It was worth it," said Mick, just before testing the bed for comfort.

"I'm hungry; do you want to eat some of our supplies, or should we go downstairs to see if they have any food here."

"I think we'll go downstairs and try some of the inn's gourmet cuisine."

Hungrily, they went down to locate food, and found they only had potatoes and squirrel meat available.

"So much for our grandiose expectations of gourmet," said Dave, laughing.

"I'm for not wasting gitis on this, not even for a lighter load. Let's go back uptown to see what we can find."

"Okay, let's go."

Looking for a place that might prepare food per request, Mick and Dave began traversing back uptown. Along the way, they talked about the indigenous vegetation, and the time they went into a restaurant and saw a waitress working while being blind—quite the feat.

Having located a dining establishment, the pair went in, and ordered. In no time they were enjoying what had been prepared for them.

"Now this is more like it. I haven't eaten any of these tiny morsels of sea goodness in a very long time," Dave commented, shoveling shrimp into his mouth.

"I think the last time I ate seafood was at my cousin's wedding about a decade ago."

"I missed that one. I don't remember going to any weddings with seafood."

By the time they got done eating and started the walk back to their room, daylight had disappeared, along with their hunger pains.

A new pain arose: abdominal bloating. Silence befell them.

When they got back up to their room at the inn, their stomachs were once again well.

Mick and Dave felt they needed to talk about a little bit of everything before falling asleep, everything except for the indigenous vegetation and the impressive, blind waitress again.

Having fallen asleep at 11:00, the duo woke rejuvenated. They grabbed their gear and supplies, and left behind the comfort of the grey spruce beds and the eyesore of the clashing colors. Walking with a purpose and set destination, Dave and Mick headed towards Zant's egress.

"I wish some of the beasts lurking in the deep parts of forests could be tamed enough to ride from place to place," blurted Mick, rubbing out a pain in his calf muscle.

"Yes, too bad there isn't a species of animal docile enough for that. Oh well, what if."

"I know many have died while attempting to tame them. If these individuals had succeeded, and shared their craft, it sure would've made things easier for the rest of us."

"Just imagine how different warfare would be," Dave suggested. "Battles would take place way more frequently, because it'd take less time to get around."

"I guess the travelling situation is better the way it is now. I'm no warmonger."

"I agree. Plus, folks wouldn't be as physically fit. Let's just be happy we have to walk everywhere we go," Dave vocalized.

The pair spent some time thinking about all the good times they had travelling the countryside by foot, as they travelled the countryside by foot.

Eventually the avalanche of memories lost momentum, and they stopped near a foxhole to rest. While sojourning, Mick and Dave gathered all the stones required to play the time-honored game of *rocks*, an unparalleled game of strategy needing forty-six stones of varying degrees of size. Each stone represented a certain point value and coordinating trump value. The game could be played with various numbers of people, but usually Mick and Dave just played as a game for two. They thought it was fun to play, because it was tactical and easy to gather the necessary pieces.

After playing rocks for an hour, seeing baby foxes come out of the hole three times, and resting their bodies enough to continue their journey, they rose up from the cool grass, and threw on their packs. They kept the rocks, because they wanted to continue playing later in the evening, probably when the nightly camp was set-up. The additional amount of weight wasn't too bothersome for the volunteer carrier, since they only had a couple more hours of walking scheduled. Besides, they had previously lightened the load by spending gitis.

Strolling along at a reasonable pace, Mick said to Dave, "We're entering an interesting locale; so many shades of blue and green, making it hard to determine where the green ends, and the blue begins. I've heard about this particular place before, they call it the Narrows. It goes on for a couple miles when you're walking the width of it like us, but if you're walking the length of it, it stretches out for twenty miles. But you definitely don't want to walk the length, that can be quite the wet traverse. Tentatively, we'll be walking down this raised corridor through the swamp, for the duration. There'll be nothing but swamp for as far as the eye can see, or so I hear."

"That's good news; I like swamps," Dave declared. "One time, when I was a kid, I got lost in a swamp, but I had an enjoyable time. I imagine many other people would've had a terrible time of it. Getting myself out took me a few days, and I was soaked by the end, but my summer was all the better for it."

"I heard about that, it made me jealous."

"Hopefully you don't get us lost now intentionally, just so you can experience the joys of it as I had."

Mick laughed, and responded to Dave. "Normally, I would do something like that, but I know there are important things to do elsewhere."

"I have a good idea. I say we stop here, while still somewhere in the Narrows, so we can listen to all the swamp noises before falling asleep."

"That sounds fine with me. You're the one with all the swamp experience, Dave. You know what you're talking about."

As soon as the tents were ready, and the fire was blazing, they took advantage of being in the swamp, and pulled out their fishing net. It had been tucked into Dave's pack, rolled into a neat, compact cylinder.

After throwing the net into the water, Dave said, "There are a lot of small bottom-feeders in these kinds of swamps usually. I don't think we'll have much of a problem procuring ourselves a large supply of fish."

"Is that your swamp experience speaking again?" Mick asked, with a chuckle.

"Oh, you know it." Dave chuckled back, before pulling the net out of the water. "See, look at all these fish in the net. I don't think I'll even have to throw it out again. There are plenty in here."

"I think we'll cook a handful for tonight's supper, and we'll leave the rest on the fire overnight, to get smoked."

"I'm going to have two for supper, along with all the fixings," Dave said, failing to realize that his mouth was watering.

The late day meal was consumed, and as planned, the remainder of the fish was set over the fire for smoking. Not only did smoked fish taste great, but the process served as a way to preserve them. They'd have plenty of fish for future consumption.

As the sun ambled its way into its nightly position, Mick and Dave resumed playing rocks.

"What's the overall score again?" asked Dave, two hours into playing.

"Including the seven matches we played earlier today, ten wins for me and eight wins for you, Leopard."

"It doesn't look like I can catch up, if we only play one more game. Let's play two more, that way maybe I can win them both and force us into a tie-breaker."

"Sure."

The next game was won by Hawk, therefore, no additional games were needed. They played one more anyways, before calling it a night.

Knowing it would put them to sleep swiftly, Dave and Mick lied in their tents, listening to the enchanting swamp song. Frogs, crickets, loons, and other nocturnal animals played their instruments for Mick and Dave, talented creatures oblivious to the fact they had an audience.

Zealously, they rose early to continue their journey, an energetic awakening due to a deep sleep. An extravagance thanks in no small part to the night-long symphony orchestrated and performed by the swamp-dwellers.

"A thank you extended to you and all your swamp experience, Leopard. That was one wonderful night of sleep. To show you my gratitude, I'll carry an item of your choice to lighten your load for today."

"That sure is nice of you. I think I'll choose the sword. I could be mean and give you my heavy breastplate, but I'll be nice to you today."

"That's a change," Mick replied, with a cackle.

Dave also supplied a laugh, and said, "It looks like we are now leaving the Narrows."

They both turned around to get one last look at the Narrows. Mick thought about how the place would look after an extremely heavy rainfall. He assumed it would resemble nothing less than a lake. As his last thought about the locale, Dave pondered what part contained the deepest water. He laid out some mental calculations, but worked out no answers.

Taking advantage of all their energy, a brisk morning pace was set.

A couple hours went by. They closed the gap between themselves and Ulfenkerki's contingent considerably, being pretty certain they'd catch sight of them soon. The town of Strwin was also near.

Crucial moments called Thraiker and Ghrere to the mental preparations of battle, for it was possible the enemy, General Anolski and his army, also drew near Strwin. A dangerous air enveloped them. Mick and Dave grew cautious; they knew certain situations had the propensity to escalate quickly, especially battle situations.

"Hey, Dave, not that I'm trying to weasel out of my offering, but would you like your sword back now; there's a chance we might run into some hostile scouts spying on Ulfenkerki."

"Yes, good thinking, I'll take it back."

What Dave and Mick really needed was information at the time, so they decided to stop at a stranger's cabin on the outskirts of Strwin. Wishing to inquire about particulars concerning the war, they approached the door and knocked.

One of Strwin's guards, Gregg Hogarty, opened the door with his foot, while simultaneously sliding into his armor, showing great coordination.

"What can I do for you?" Gregg emitted, slightly out of breath from maneuvering quickly.

"Hello, I'm Mick, this is Dave. We stopped to see what news of the enemy."

"I see the Garobansurovian sigil on your helm," voiced Gregg, suspiciously, "but how do I know you didn't kill a Garobansurovian soldier, and take his helmet just to come here to kill me, a Strwin guard."

"Just the same may be true of you and this cabin, but since we are the ones who approached initially requesting information, we'll be the ones to prove we are Garobansurovians," articulated Thraiker.

Mick perfectly described practically half the people of Zant, amongst other things only Garobansurovians would know.

Gregg recognized most of the descriptions and realized only truths were transpiring at his cabin. He started summoning the information sought by Mick and Dave. "A messenger stopped here thirty minutes ago telling me to prepare for battle. I'm to be in town by sunset. Ulfenkerki and Rayton's joint forces are presently camped just outside of town. Continuing her mission, the messenger raced off to other outlying homes of Strwin guards."

Dave emitted, "I'm glad Rayton and his archers are still intact, and in conjunction with Ulfenkerki; they will be a powerful army combined."

"Including the guard, there are roughly fourteen hundred soldiers prepared to defend. I've been told Anolski, combined with Bamsov, has an army of twenty-five hundred fully equipped soldiers. And I imagine they're pretty hungry for blood."

Dave responded, "Strwin has its high walls in its favor. I think Anolski would be foolish to assault Strwin, facing that disadvantage."

"Makes you kind of wonder if Anolski has something hidden up his sleeve," said Gregg.

"The Black Bear is a clever tactician, I'm sure he has something up his sleeve also," Mick remarked. "It'll get interesting."

Gregg asked, "Will you two be fighting as well? We'll need all the sword hands we can get."

Dave replied, "Does a Garobansurovian winter freeze a squirrel to the ground when it pees?"

Gregg laughed. "They even do it to me half the time."

Hawk and Leopard cracked up.

Gregg finished getting ready and then proposed the three of them walk into town together. Mick and Dave agreed.

Along the way, Gregg described to Mick and Dave his fighting style, and vice versa. One doesn't train for years in weapon craft without enjoying talking about it at least a little bit.

Halfway to Strwin, and trying to remain upbeat, Gregg spoke of some of the losses sustained by Garobansurov on the Eastern Front: "The town of Sarwa was lost to Gamald and his army. Yarundlen just couldn't handle the sheer might of Gamald."

"Was Yarundlen himself killed?" asked Mick.

"He and his army weren't just killed, they were massacred."

"Sadly, that leaves only three of our Eastern Front generals left."

"Correct," said Gregg. "I've also been informed that throughout their march to Sarwa, Gamald and/or his men had slaughtered many Garobansurovian civilians with whom they crossed paths."

"So, it's true then, what they say of Gamald. He's a cold-blooded and ruthless killer," said Mick.

"Yes, I'm afraid it's true," replied Gregg, before sighing. "There is some good news though: General Nighteagle secured the town of Thraug, and is prepared to defend wholeheartedly."

His mind in turmoil at the thought of all the innocent losing their lives to the Molisian horde, Dave was tackled by anger. "What atrocity! How can someone be so unconscionable."

Mick stated, "I didn't know there were any Molisian battalions near enough Thraug to force the Nighteagle into defensive positioning."

Gregg pondered for a moment. "It's possible the Nighteagle anticipates Gamald will think his army is large enough to defend Sarwa with one hand and send soldiers to capture Thraug with the other."

Before Mick responded to Gregg, he thought upon the implications of what such a massive army being in the area meant to his and Dave's future plans. "This war I'm afraid is going to demand a massive toll of us all."

"I'm afraid so," Dave and Gregg said simultaneously.

CHAPTER 3

ULFENKERKI'S SOLDIERS, the Strwin guard, and Rayton's archers were about as nervous as could be, practically suffering heart pain. The expectation of battle was painful. Those perched in lookout spires could see Anolski and Bamsov's armies marching in columns towards Strwin, while those with heightened senses could smell adrenaline and sweat in the air.

Five minutes after entering town, Gregg had split from Mick and Dave to join up with his fellow guard, while Mick and Dave paced the main thoroughfare, anticipating some action.

Ulfenkerki was in serious discussion with Archer-General Rayton concerning upcoming battle strategies. It was a tense situation, but at least Ulfenkerki could hear himself talk; they weren't talking in the tent that flapped easily in the wind.

"The opposing force is close enough to taste," Ulfenkerki said to Rayton, looking through the battlement. He then observed something peculiar: "I wonder why they're wasting so much energy hauling those covered carts. What could possibly be in them? Why dissipate so much vital battle strength so close to a battle?"

"They do look pretty heavy."

Just as Rayton finished his sentence, Ulfenkerki rationalized out the answer to his own rhetorical questions. "Because they aren't planning an immediate assault; they have intentions of siege. Those carts are loaded with food and supply. They have enough food to last several days, I'm sure."

Rayton responded, "Bamsov must have been stockpiling in expectancy. They're taking a chance, thinking Strwin won't have enough food in reserve for our entire army to last several days or weeks. If I knew that, I could've commanded a covert raid against him back at the Baustic foothills, just to vandalize his food carts."

Five minutes after Ulfenkerki's revelation, a gathering of ten stood aghast, staring into a nearly empty granary, dreading the contingency before them.

The chief magistrate, Tom Higgultz, was the first to speak: "It looks like we have enough grain to last the army a day and a half, if you add in the entire winter supply of salted meats. The reason why it's so low is that we sent a giant food supply back with the Nighteagle's embassy. Farmers come into town daily selling food, and because we rely on this, Strwin doesn't fare well in sieges. Not that the history books tell of very many occurring here."

Ulfenkerki stated, "Go ahead, Tom, and inform the townsfolk we'll all be on food rations for a while, and I'll notify the soldiers. It looks as if we'll be experiencing hunger pains."

Ulfenkerki ended up being correct in saying there'd be a siege; the tell-tale signs were unignorable. Anolski and Bamsov had set up a huge war camp just outside of Strwin's arrow shot. The Molisians had stationed several outposts along every entrance into town, designed to stop all traffic from entering and exiting. Satisfyingly, the Molisians uncovered their wagons, revealing an enormous food supply for the whole world to see. Also, sad to say for fans of Garobansurov, the previous estimation of the size of the Molisian force at 25 hundred was low. The new estimation was 28 hundred armed soldiers, almost double that of what Strwin housed. Any coward would've shuddered at being on Garobansurov's side of the mismatch.

Morale was desperately low, so Ulfenkerki acted.

Per Ulfenkerki's request, all the villagers and soldiers were gathered together in the middle of town, which didn't take as long as you'd think. To them, the Black Bear loudly proclaimed, "Men, women of this army, townspeople, refugees hold strong, be confident, for I have a few tricks up my sleeve to unleash when the time is right. We will know victory when it chooses sides in the end." The Black Bear spoke inspirationally to the crowd for five minutes. At the conclusion of his speech, he raised his sword to the heavens, gleaming confidence, and shouted, "Garobansurov will never falter! Strwin will never lose strength! We will fight until there's no fight left to give!"

Ulfenkerki's speech drew unanimous applause from the audience of soldiers and civilians, some cheering so wildly their throats hurt the next day. Everyone immediately began feeling better about the situation. An inspirational, confident general can go a long way for morale.

All that could be done now was wait.

ALTHOUGH TENSION HAD eased, everyone remained on guard. Movement in town was minimal. In the few hours after the speech, like everyone else, Mick and Dave didn't do much of anything.

Realizing that nighttime had snuck up on him, Mick said to Dave, "I think sleep is going to elude me tonight, it seeming as sneaky as the darkness."

"I would, at the least, like to sleep for three hours at some point this evening," Dave said, through a yawn. "Maybe there's a tree or something in town for us to sleep under."

"Well, I'm sure there's at least one tree in town to sleep under, but the real question is, how much do trees charge for room rental here in Strwin?"

On the verge of a laugh, Dave smiled, and the pair started searching for the perfect tree, under which to sleep. After hunting for twenty minutes, the perfect bush was found: a thick, low-lying juniper bush on the western side of Strwin. The bush was so old and gnarly that it formed roomy cavities within, perfect places for a couple of weary travelers to sleep. They had to perform a little pruning so they didn't have to sleep on any branches, but overall they couldn't have asked for a better place under those conditions to spend the rest of the night. And because of the unorthodox circumstances in town, nobody really cared there were two strangers sleeping in a bush.

Hawk and Leopard rose the next morning, having slept longer than what they had thought they would.

"At least the battle didn't happen without us, eh Mick," Dave said, performing the usual morning routine. "Speaking of battle, I sure wouldn't mind having Brom's armor right about now."

"You can say that again," Mick declared. "I slept pretty well, but I would've slept better, had I trimmed the root underneath where my left leg spent most of its time."

Dave, sometimes exuding the mind of a naturalist, responded, "It's better now the fact you didn't. The less stress the tree succumbs, the longer it will live; the better chance it'll be here in the future for us to use again, or maybe someone else."

Mick chuckled, and said, "First, swamps, now, bushes; you are indeed the master of the wilderness."

Dave smiled. "You forget, you are technically the master of bushes and small trees."

After hearing Dave's remark, Mick pondered deeply, remembered the story to which Dave was mostly referring, and replied, "It seems we are both bushmasters."

The villagers and army were on food rations, which forced lethargy, hunger, and conservation of energy.

Mick and Dave had donated all the food they had to the war effort, a considerable stockpile, because of all the fish they had caught back at the Narrows. It practically doubled the town's fish supply.

Dave and Mick woke to nearly empty streets. The soldiers were all dug in at their designated posts, the townsfolk seemingly asleep. Time stood still. Thraiker and Ghrere rested at their juniper bush for a considerable amount of time, waiting for any further development with the Molisian army, or until town became a little livelier. Which the latter eventually did.

"It looks like the civilians are gaining their evening endorphins; the atmosphere seems more sociable," Mick commented to Dave.

"Yeah, it seems to be so. Let's mingle amongst that crowd gathered over there by that flower garden to see what's new." Dave pointed.

A small crowd had formed around one of the locals taking advantage of the situation, performing a juggling routine. More people in town meant the possibility for more spectators. Mick and Dave were impressed, so they gave her a few gitis, as did a few of the other members of the audience. Deservingly, the whole crowd applauded at the conclusion of the talented woman's performance.

Pointing at one of the sections of the hard, stone wall that surrounded the city, Leopard uttered, "Over there looks like a good spot for a bird's-eye view of the Molisian army and the unfolding siege."

The wall section to which Leopard pointed stood twenty feet high, a pretty customary height for a defensive wall of the period. It had a solid granite battlement, four-foot-high, perfect for war tactics.

Unless Mick and Dave walked all the way across town, the only way, it seemed, to get a bird's-eye view from the top of the wall was to perform some kind of impossible acrobatic leap to it from atop one of the houses.

Leopard had an ingenious plan. Having left Mick in the street, Dave knocked on the door of the house nearest the wall. To the lady that opened the door, Dave said, "Hello. You don't know me, I'm Dave, but I'm playing a joke on my friend standing there in the street, and I'd be absolutely thrilled if you could play along. You'll get a laugh, I promise."

After a bit more sweet talking, the lady agreed to take part in Dave's ruse.

Dave initiated his scheme. He pointed at himself, pointed at the rooftop, then made a motion with his hand and fingers implying that he wanted to run across the top of her house, and make the eighteen-foot leap across to the top of the wall, all the while making sure Mick saw all the hand gestures. He and the lady gave each other a quick grin, and the next phase of the prank began.

Dave waved Mick over. Unaware of what was really happening, Mick approached from the street, and greeted the woman. They all went into the house and climbed to the top of it.

Once atop, Mick said, "You're nuts, absolutely nuts. I'm not attempting this jump, and if you try, you'll end up agonizingly on the ground. Trust me, I've seen your leaping capabilities."

Dave, knowing two things that Mick didn't, offered a proposal. "You want to bet? I'll bet you a day's worth of item carrying that I make it to the top of the wall right now."

"As long as the lady here presents no ladders, it's a bet."

Dave agreed, then backstepped to the furthest from the wall corner or the rooftop. To add dramatic effect, he held up his finger in the air in an attempt to gauge wind direction and speed. He spat in his hands, and rubbed them together for more drama. He waved everyone out of the way (pretending there were dozens to move aside), and took off running with a vengeance. After running ten steps in full stride, he came to an abrupt halt at the last possible moment before the would-be jump.

What Mick apparently didn't notice, being a part of Dave's perfect plan, was the fact the sentry on the wall eyeing the far-off Molisians happened to be Gregg Hogarty.

Dave hailed Gregg, "Hello, friend, how goes it?"

Gregg turned and was surprised to see Dave and Mick where they were. "Good to see you again, what are you two doing on a house?"

"Not much, just hanging around," Dave replied, failing at being funny. The other thing Dave knew that Mick didn't was the fact there was a rope coiled up atop the wall, probably put there by the guards for easy access to the wall-top. "Say, you wouldn't mind tossing that rope down, so Mick and I can come up to inspect the Molisian army, would you?"

"No, I don't mind at all. That's why it's there."

With a smile the size of all Garobansurov, Dave turned around to look at his defeated partner, and saw

Mick shaking his head, donning a smile. But Mick's smile wasn't as large.

"You're too much." It was all Mick had to say in the face of defeat.

Thraiker and Ghrere canceled any notions of leaping to the wall from the rooftop, and left the company of the lady, who was greatly amused with it all, having received the laugh she was promised. Having gotten down off the roof, Mick and Dave exited the house, took the twenty steps to the wall, and climbed the rope Gregg had thrown down. The mission of getting a bird's eye view: officially accomplished.

"There they are, all 28 hundred of them," Mick said to Gregg, as he scanned the distant field. "Twenty-eight hundred, right?"

"Yup, that's also the number I was told. I hope they're not as menacing as they look," said Gregg. "Did you guys get a chance to sleep at all last night? The other guards and I were only able to sleep for a couple hours."

"We slept a few hours in a bush."

"That doesn't sound very pleasant."

"Actually, it's not as bad as it sounds. Our bush was rather accommodating."

Dave finished his inspection of the scene, and joined the conversation. "I wonder for how long Anolski can keep this up? I'm sure his ration supply isn't unlimited."

Gregg responded, "My guess is as good as anyone else's, but I would say they'll make us suffer for another couple days."

"Hopefully, it's only a couple more days and not weeks upon weeks," noted Mick.

"I'm thinking it'll be a short siege," Gregg said. "They don't look like a patient group out there."

Mick and Dave talked with Gregg for fifteen minutes on the looming battle, before climbing back down the rope and strolling downtown.

They ventured to the side of town containing the army barracks. All of a sudden, they heard a strangely familiar voice yelling their names. They turned and noticed the man behind the voice was on an intercept trajectory. The man they soon discovered was their much sought after childhood friend, Jason Thorncat.

"Oh my, I would never have recognized you two, if I hadn't heard from Mike and Bob that you were in the area," said Jason Thorncat, producing a countenance of excitement.

"It's about time we finally caught up to you! We almost crossed paths with you back in Zant, but the army pulled out just as we were pulling in," Mick stated, waiting patiently for Dave to finish shaking Jason's hand, so he could do the same.

Jason explained, "Yeah, at that moment, Ulfenkerki had just made his decision to meet Rayton here in Strwin, so we were all in a big hurry."

"I still can't get over this! Hawk and Leopard, after all these years, standing right in front of me, in the flesh. The last I saw you, we had just broken into a cabin to view some old swords. Ironic; here I am now, living by the sword."

"Speaking of which, what did happen to you after that innocent point of our lives? We had heard nothing. You disappeared like a fart in the wind."

Jason responded, "I guess it would seem that I was dragged away because of how much mischief we were getting into, but that wasn't the case at all. My grandparents were getting too old to tend their farm, so they asked my parents to allow me to come work it. I was there for seven years, until I joined the army."

"Have you been aligned with the Black Bear this whole time, Jason?" asked Dave.

"I've been with him for three years now, having spent the rest of my military career following orders of various other officers."

"One thing I do have to state," Mick said, "is whether it's Ulfenkerki's influence or just plain hard work, the stories of your great skill in battle have reached the farthest corners of Garobansurov. I've heard the stories from many travelers. The remarkable accounts of Jason Thorncat have even reached Chalatore. Those of our hometown love those stories."

"The answer is a little of both, hard work and Ulfenkerki's tutelage. However, the legend concerning those two items far exceeds anything I've done," Jason remarked, pointing at Mick and Dave's swords. "I would love to hear the story behind their origin sometime. I've even heard they're magical."

"I don't know about magical, that's a little far-fetched," pronounced Dave. "But yes, someday we will tell you of the sequence of events leading us to these weapons. For now, we'll save that utmost excitement until later. At least until the gathering gloom dissipates."

"I'll hold you to that. And I have faith the Molisians will be defeated," responded Jason. "I have also heard of your most righteous, current freelance work. There's nothing more in this world I would like than to fight side-by-side-by-side with you two, seeing you join this company. But I'm sure there's a reason you do things the way you do."

Dave let be known, "That is correct, our minds need room to roam and a flexible plan; but honestly, there wouldn't be any other soldiers we'd rather fight beside long term than you and General Ulfenkerki."

"I'm glad to hear that. At least for the moment, it looks like we'll be dealing out death blows together, here, at this battlefield."

"Indeed, we will."

"Before we part ways for the evening, I have to ask," Mick emitted, "why did we call you Fox back then? I forgot."

"I think it was because of my slyness and tracking prowess. You were Hawk because of your speed and ability to spot the smallest of objects at any distance. Dave was Leopard because of his strength and reflexes."

"Ah, memories–those were some pretty good times. We'll see you later, I'm sure," said Mick.

"Later it is, old friends."

Hawk and Leopard left the company of Jason, soaking in the feeling of life coming full circle.

Soon after their long-awaited coming together with Jason, the duo began to feel the effects of not eating. Resultantly, they decided to spend the rest of the day and evening back at their juniper bush. But first, they had to stop at the weapon and armor shop to pick up some shields. They normally didn't like to carry shields around on their adventures, due to their enormous weight, but with the battle approaching, shields would definitely come in handy. They spent seventy-five gitis each for the added protection, nothing fancy.

They walked past almost the whole of town, back to their juniper sanctuary, and decided to eat a small amount of what food they did keep. Dave fashioned a cooking fire with ease, close to their temporary abode. They figured a single potato and tomato for each would suffice.

"Here's some tasty tomato concoction for the top of your potato, Hawk."

"Thank you, buddy. You know, if I had a couple more of these, I'd barely notice town was under siege. They're sort of filling."

"Would you like to go double or nothing in a game of rocks?" asked Dave.

"You're just itching to lighten your load, aren't you." replied Mick. "I'll play though."

They already had all the necessary pieces for rocks—technically, only rocks—and played well into the night. In the end, despite a solid effort from Mick, Dave doubled the longevity of his item lightening, very pleased with the day's activities.

MEANWHILE, IN A secluded backroom of the army barracks, a meeting was being held. In attendance were General Kermoy Ulfenkerki; his second-in-command, Sven Algar; Jason Thorncat; Steve Johnson; Ralph Engelheinz; General Hugo Rayton; Rayton's second-in-command, George Rebine; the company's best archer, Chad Loytin; and the head of the Strwin guard, Pturet Weeler.

With so many people in one small room talking all at once, not a whole lot of what was being said was of any real importance to the group as a whole—not a paradigm entirely rare. An exception to the inconsequential rabble being Ulfenkerki speaking to Rayton and Pturet Weeler.

"You have to have the arrows timed just right. The wall-defense personnel will be spread thin. I guarantee, Anolski will press his advantage if one is given," the Black Bear insisted. "And don't forget to coincide bow arrows with crossbow ballistae."

"I'll wait for the most opportune moment to launch," asserted Rayton, fully understanding Ulfenkerki's secret stratagem. "I'll also take charge of all ballistae and triggerable traps, making sure they're mounted with superior positioning and optimum angles."

"Good. Very good." The Black Bear scratched his bearded chin, liking the state of things.

After his talk with Rayton and Weeler, Ulfenkerki changed the essence of the room, discoursing on relevancy to all, laying out the entirety of the city defense plan. The defensive blueprint mainly consisted of making sure there were enough rocks (to be hurled) and archers for the top of the wall; and ensuring all warriors were well equipped. He also filled everyone in on the scheme he had going with Rayton and Weeler—the trick up his sleeve, of which he spoke in the speech he had delivered to all of town.

Confident everyone was properly informed, Ulfenkerki adjourned the meeting, and thanked everyone for attending.

With the small room to himself, Ulfenkerki clung to perfectionism, repeatedly playing out the future battle in his mind. At the end of his thought storm, he still liked the state of things.

The effects of hunger and fatigue had set in firmly for everyone in town. Happiness was scarce. But on the plus side that night, most of the army and guard had stolen eight hours of sleep, along with Mick and Dave back in their trusty Juniper bush. A full night's rest was a soldier awaiting battle's best friend.

CHAPTER 4

B EFORE THE NIGHT was over, there had been an unlucky youth courageously attempting to help with the war effort. The brave lad gave his life, trying to sneak a cartload of food into town, meeting his demise by the hands of an attentive soldier amongst Anolski's ranks.

News of the hero filtered into town, and justifiably so, plans of honoring him and his family were set into motion by Tom Higgultz and the town council immediately. Memories of the boy were discussed by all throughout the day.

It was a rare bravery most commendable.

Just after waking, Mick and Dave heard the news of the brave boy, and were hit by a shock wave of anguish, which ran straight to their hearts.

"I can't wait till we get a chance to avenge this loss!" Dave exclaimed with vehemence.

Mick agreed with Dave, and said, "Hopefully we don't have to wait too much longer to do so. My sword-hand is starting to twitch due to inactivity. Even my sword is starting to not recognize me."

"There you go again, giving souls to inanimate objects. What's next, are you going to start talking to your sword?"

Mick laughed, thought briefly about the possibility of talking to a sword, then replied, "If my sword could talk, it would say, *Dave, make breakfast.*"

"I don't need a sword to tell me to do that, I'll do that easy task voluntarily," said Dave, just before digging in his pack, and handing an apple from the ration supply over to Mick. "See? Easy."

Mr. Thraiker, after finishing his far-from-complex breakfast, decided he was in the mood to discuss the sciences of the world, for they both enjoyed many sciences, including physics, astronomy, geology, biology, and philosophy, among others. Mick—who especially enjoyed philosophy, physics, and geology—started to discourse on the workings of the universe.

After Mick's ten-minute deliverance, Dave weighed in, "I understand the possibility of there being an infinite number of universes, which many call the Multiverse Theory. But here's where my comprehension goes hazy. It's hard to know if in all those universes the physics remain the same as in ours. Possibly, given an infinite number of permutations, the physics would be so different in at least one that the diversity would allow that universe to be perceived by another universe. So perhaps, knowing the fact that we can't see any other universes in our universe might prove that the physics are the same in each and every possible situation of the multiverse. Which, perchance, is why none of us can shoot lightning bolts out of our hands; giant bird-like creatures can't tempestuously spew fire on us all; or we can't close our eyes and open them to a different point of space when not affected by our own locomotion or an outside force."

"Among other crazy things people have dreamt of throughout time," responded Mick.

Dave thought for a second, and emitted, "But what if because there are an infinite number of universes containing infinitely numerous and distinct physics, they interweave, canceling each other out. And that's why we can't see any of them?"

"I can see your point. Who knows?"

"I guess we'll never really know the truth. Though, I definitely agree with your theory involving how the species of other universes could take different paths of evolution than the one all the species in our own universe took. Maybe in other universes there are animals on which to ride from place to place. There could even be giant birds to ride, but I postulate they could never breathe fire, because there are no known bio-elements that can withstand that amount of heat."

"None known as of now, but new things are found every day in the realm of science."

Another half an hour was satisfyingly spent discussing dizzying subjects with cosmic implications. Afterwards, Hawk and Leopard went for a late morning walk, and ran into their acquaintances (Mike and Bob) they had met back in Zant. The quartet talked for a while about the siege, the looming battle, and a little about women. At the end, they wished each other a good fight and a safe conclusion.

When walking back to their refuge they spotted Gregg Hogarty on the wall, Mick also seeing him this time. Gregg being too busy at the time to talk, they all raised their hands in salute as Mick and Dave walked past.

"I do have to say, Dave, you really did get me good yesterday," said Mick. "I will have to get you back someday."

"Someday never comes," Dave responded, followed by a light-hearted cocky laugh.

They arrived back at the bush, and just as they were about to relax, the town was up in commotion.

"Look, over there, that's too many people running at once to be considered exercise."

"I think this pandemonium can only mean one thing: the battle has begun."

"I believe you're right, Mick.

"It has definitely begun; an errant arrow just whizzed past me."

Dave and Mick threw on their battle armor frantically but efficiently; grabbed their swords, arrows, hunting bow, and new shields from out of the juniper bush; and ran to the wall to climb the same rope they climbed the other day.

In an instant, they were amongst all the soldiers and guards scattered intermittently on the wall. Everyone on the wall was a member of Ulfenkerki or Rayton's army, or a member of the Strwin guard—all except Mick, Dave, and one other civilian from town. The civilian went by the name Rod Tyrug; who, along with Mick and Dave, wanted to fight alongside the army in the name of honor. Technically, the country of Garobansurov allowed anyone to fight for it. Though, you hardly ever saw any civilians doing so, because almost all warriors at heart desired the prestige of being in the army or guard.

Mick nodded to his fellow countryman, Rod, who was already hard at work throwing the previously gathered rocks at the fast approaching enemy. The entire lot of Molisians, all 28 hundred, were approaching with fury from all sides of town. The math worked out to be a Molisian soldier for every three feet of wall surrounding town.

Dave was the more skilled of the two with their hunting bow, so he started unleashing the reasonably large supply of arrows at the nearest targets. Mick began chucking rocks with all his might over the battlement, in hopes of crushing a multitude of skulls.

As the Garobansurovians hurled rocks and loosed arrows from above, arrows were shot at them from below. Mick noticed Rayton's archers were all on the other side of town shooting their well-practiced arrows into the enemy horde.

Dave yelled out to Mick, "It doesn't look like they have many wall-climbing ladders or grappling hooks. I think judging by the fact the lead man in every column is equipped with a heavy war-hammer, they intend to break through the wall."

"I wouldn't necessarily say it's a stupid plan; these walls are extensively weathered from being so old, and may have some weak spots."

"Is that your geology expertise talking there, Rock Master?"

"Yes, it is, Swamp Master."

Mick and Dave shared a mid-battle chuckle, while ferociously continuing to defend. The ratio of soldiers being killed was about four to one in favor of Garobansurov at the onset of battle, due to their advantageous high ground.

On the other side of town from Mick and Dave, Ulfenkerki was fighting alongside Jason and Sven on the wall. They were holding their own, while holding their weapons.

Mick and Dave couldn't wait until the fight became hand-to-hand, because that was where their true skills lied. But if it never came to that, they would be happy; it meant the enemy was never able to get past the walls. It didn't seem like that was going to be the case, though.

Mick noticed all the Molisians with giant warhammers were intensively pounding on the walls, looking for a weak point, while successfully dodging rocks and arrows from above. Wall chips flying through the air were a thousand times more plentiful at the time than birds flying through the air.

Time passed and dreadful reverberation sprung, which was distressing for the Garobansurov soldiers, because it was the resonation filtering through Molisian ranks announcing they found the weak spot in the wall. All men wielding hammers were to report directly to the weak spot to finish punching through the wall.

Three more pounders arrived at the scene, and immediately began striking Strwin's wall with their hammers. Two others were killed on their way to the wall.

With the added firepower it didn't take long to expand the hole enough for entire squads to infiltrate the enclosure. At that moment, the numbers were still in favor of the Molisians: approximately 23 hundred to Garobansurov's 13 hundred-and-fifty.

Molisia's virtually unconquerable numbers advantage was about to change, due to the Black Bear's ingenious plan—or so the General hoped.

What most people didn't know was the fact that before Ulfenkerki was an army general, he was a stonemason, possessing the uncanny ability to know the structural integrity of any building made from stone. Therefore, he could inspect a wall and know exactly where the weakest site was just by looking at it. Which is exactly what he did beforehand. He knew where the wall was going to be breached, so as a result was able to plan ahead, by stockpiling and installing an enormous amount of crossbow traps and small ballistae at the locale. He also positioned Rayton's archers at the most propitious place, so on the order of Rayton, the archers could climb from the wall to said area across pre-built ladders arranged on the housetops. From the housetops, Rayton's archers would form a defensive ring above and around the unsuspecting Molisians as soon as they burst through the wall.

The invaders who were about to flow through the hole in the wall had no idea what was about to hit them.

After eight hundred unsuspecting Molisians rushed through the hole, Rayton gave the order, and his entire squadron rushed across the ladders, and got into position. The ladder trick was a necessary maneuver, because the wall defense would have been spread too thin otherwise. In which case, Anolski would've been able to get over the wall with what small amount of wall climbing gear he did have, instead of having to perform the much more arduous task of breaking open the wall with hammers.

The crossbow traps and ballistae were all released simultaneously via counterbalance mechanism controlled by Pturet Weeler. The crossbows took out a hundred and fifty soldiers, while the ballistae took out another hundred, leaving five hundred and fifty Molisians surrounded by Ulfenkerki's trap. The best archer, Chad Loytin, lead the arrow storm. They say he alone killed twenty-five men during the inceptive cascade. A torrent of bow missiles wiped out the entire first wave. However, a second wave came in through the hole directly behind the first.

Eventually the Molisians were able to get around the Black Bear's trap, and break out into town. The temporary fences strewn about did next to nothing to impede them.

When the break-out occurred, the archers were sitting ducks, so Rayton ordered them all to scurry back onto the wall, and to grab the ladders as they went.

Ulfenkerki's considerably brilliant plan was responsible for evening the odds. The Molisians were no longer viewed as unconquerable.

The numbers stood as thus: Molisia, 15 hundred; Garobansurov, having only suffered ten deaths during the first wave infiltration, 13 hundred and forty.

Ulfenkerki's Strwin operation would come to be known as The Black Bear's Slaughter Den. Military scholars would study the maneuver for years to come.

The archers resumed firing from the top of the wall, while the rest of Garobansurov's army rushed to where the break-out occurred. Half the infantry stayed on the wall to sustain high ground superiority, while the other half began ground fighting in order to ensure the safety of the villagers, and to keep houses from being burnt to the ground.

Mick and Dave chose ground fighting, having sprinted as fast as they could to encounter the melee. Almost all of the Molisian army was now inside the wall. Mick and Dave, amid the madness, were about to finally experience some hand-to-hand action. But instead, Mick snatched Dave and corralled him behind an out-of-the-way barrel.

Crouching behind the empty barrel, puzzled, Dave said, "I'm assuming you have something up your sleeve?"

"Yes." Mick pointed at a particular spot amongst the Strwin forces, and said, "Notice how at the moment our forces are trying to flank theirs." Next, Mick pointed at the enemy commander, Bamsov. "Now, notice how Bamsov is communicating vehemently with all his archers."

"I follow you so far."

Mick pointed at a small clearing in the middle of the market, saying, "I would bet a thousand gitis that commander Bamsov is telling his archers right now he wants to turn the table and be the flankers themselves. And to do that they have to be positioned in the clearing to which I'm pointing."

Dave started to smile, having figured out where Mick was headed. "Unless we're already standing over there inconspicuously, taking the advantage for ourselves."

"Right. The plan implementation has to happen fast, because once the confusion of the battle's inception is over, our plan would be useless."

"Okay, let's go. I do know I've heard the words flank and plan enough for one day," replied Dave, as he began creeping out from behind the barrel. Straight to the nearest house they headed, as was the best path to the clearing.

Mick followed directly behind Dave, as stealthily as possible, into a house through the front door. Then, out of the house through the back door. If anyone was in the building at the time, they surely would've found the event humorous.

Continuing on, Hawk and Leopard hugged the edge of another house, staying out of view. Having arrived at the back side of the market and said clearing, they snuck into the adjacent weapons shop. Conveniently while there, they quickly swapped out their shields they'd just purchased from the very same store, in exchange for a second sword each. Upcoming tactics favored them having a sword in each hand. They waited at the door for their chance to make a difference.

MEANWHILE, BACK IN the figurative creature's lair, Jason Thorncat and Kermoy Ulfenkerki were hacking and slashing with as much ferocity as they could muster. Jason had just killed a giant of a man with the second swing of his sword—the first took off an arm. General Ulfenkerki was holding his own in battle, watching patiently for chances to improve from a tactical standpoint. Further down the line, the rest of Ulfenkerki's army was trying to do what they did best: win battles. However, from an onlooker's point of view, it seemed the tide was just about to turn. Bamsov and his archers were slipping out the back in what looked like an attempt at adept strategic maneuvering.

With trepidation, Ulfenkerki said to Jason, "Watch your back; we're going to be outflanked. Bamsov is escaping to that clearing to gain position superiority."

After noticing the officers Sven Algar and Ralph Engelheinz had been afflicted by arrows in their backs, falling dead, Jason yelled out in agony. And to make matters worse, he found himself having to block an incoming foray of deadly sword thrusts, one of which almost landing true. He returned the offensive with one of his own, and eliminated that particular threat, but was starting to get seriously concerned for the outcome of the battle. Jason tried to escape the immediate turmoil and regain advantageous positioning. He wanted to work his way to Bamsov. But the fighting was too thick, an impossible endeavor.

Another negative element for Garobansurov was the fact volleys from Rayton's archers stationed on the walls weren't having enough distance to reach their mark.

The tide was indeed turned. The numbers at the moment stood thusly: Molisia, eight hundred soldiers, weapons in hand; Garobansurov, seven hundred weapon-equipped warriors.

After failing to reach Bamsov, Jason dutifully decided to fight at the rear of his leader, in an attempt to prevent Ulfenkerki from being on the receiving end of an arrow to the back.

A man with a war hammer came charging at Jason, forcing him to think fast. Simply stepping out of the way was a bad idea: too risky, Ulfenkerki might get hit in the back of the head. Taking the brunt of the charge wasn't a wise decision either. Instead, he ripped off his helmet and threw it directly at his opponent's face, praying it didn't miss. Luckily, it hit exactly at the spot Jason was aiming, and staggered the war hammer wielder just enough so the two could fight on even terms. After three sword hacks to the Molisian's face, Jason was the vanquisher. But after the vanquished dropped to the ground, Jason looked to the sea of blood and swords and noticed his countrymen were losing. Hope was fleeting.

In an instant, however, thoughts of death disappeared. He noticed the rear of Bamsov's archer formation dropping four at a time, nearly in a perfect pattern. He craned to get a better look, and was astounded to see who was accomplishing such a feat. Because of this, he regained hope and battled with renewed vigor.

MOMENTS BEFORE JASON'S rebirth, Dave and Mick were waiting at the door of the weapon shop, swords in all hands, waiting to pounce on unsuspecting victims like jungle cats in the brush waiting on prey.

When Bamsov's columns were all formed, and every one of the archers had their backs to Mick and Dave, and the duo flew out the door to wreak havoc. Wound springs unwound violently.

Starting on opposite sides, Mick and Dave in coordination jabbed both their swords into two archers each, eliminating four enemies at a time. Each puncture a perfectly placed death-blow. They were able to do this right down the line, until Bamsov himself noticed what was happening. But by then, it was too late; Mick and Dave had already eliminated half his archers.

With the flank neutralized, the rest of Ulfenkerki's squad were free to move. Pandemonium erupted. The tide was turned yet again, seeming that day to not know what in the world it wanted.

Mick and Dave were now fighting in the mob, and doing a mighty fine job of it. At one point, Mick came face-to-face with commander Bamsov; who, along with being proficient with a bow, was pretty good with a sword. Bamsov was able to keep Mick on his toes for a few minutes, before succumbing to the overwhelming skill of Mick Thraiker.

There was a moment in the battle when Dave happened on Gregg Hogarty and exchanged head nods. Dave noticed Gregg was covered in blood, but none of it seemed like it was his. Before Dave was able to appreciate the apparent wellbeing of his friend, he encountered a well-accomplished warrior.

The conflict went on for a few minutes, near the end of which Dave's opponent tried a slice to his weapon arm, but missed due to a last-second parry. Dave countered with many monstrous lunges at the chest, only dealing a nick, physically. But mentally, the lunges dealt much more. Winded and overburdened, the Molisian tried a flurry of quick, imprecise hacks in a show of desperation. Dave noticed the desperation, evaded, and waited patiently for the most opportune moment to strike. When it came, Dave summoned his favorite sword combination: a fake swing at the shoulder, initiating a 360-degree arc, culminating in a slice to the top of the head. Suffering disorientation from a huge gaping intrusion in his skull, the Molisian was administered the death blow.

Dave smiled at Gregg for two reasons. Number one, he now had a moment to appreciate his friend being alive. Number two, that friend had witnessed his finishing sword sequence, a maneuver Dave thought probably looked impressive to anyone seeing it.

Mick didn't have to defeat any more elite warriors after facing commander Bamsov, but there was a point when he was in frontal and rear combat simultaneously. Neither of Mick's adversaries were practiced swordsmen nor did they understand the value of flanking, so both were easily defeated. Had they been more experienced, they would've exhibited better teamwork. Mick slew one with his right sword, and the other with his left.

Subsequent to Mick's double slaying, Garobansurov had a 125-soldier lead over Molisia. Miraculously still alive, Anolski noticed the superiority of the enemy he now faced, and had to come up with a plan. It ended up being not the most inventive of plans, but it did end up saving the rest of his army and himself. He simply ordered a retreat.

All of Anolski's remaining 335 warriors ran as fast as they could back through the hole from which they came. Twenty-five were chopped down on the run, but Anolski and the remaining 310 were able to escape. Outside the wall, Anolski ordered them all to split up to help prevent any kind of organized chase. He also informed them all where to reconvene. All told, between his original army and the addition of Bamsov's archers, Anolski lost approximately 2,500 soldiers—a substantial loss.

Anolski lost his teammate, Bamsov, and the newly appointed officer whose extreme night attentiveness had put a stop to the brave lad's previous supply reinforcement attempt. The youth's death was now avenged.

"Victory," was shouted within the walls of Strwin with tremendous enthusiasm. Even though Ulfenkerki lost slightly over half his army, he still enjoyed the celebration, and by the end of the day, he was able to thank personally every single soldier who fought.

Cheer erupted, matching that of the initial victory cheer, when Tom Higgultz rolled out the mead barrels. The barrels were hidden away for just such an occasion. The very young, the very old, and everyone in-between came out of hiding to partake in the festivities.

Hawk and Leopard were also in the mood for spirits, gladly putting a mug in their hands filled to the brim of the finest mead the Strwin countryside had to offer. Unlike swords during the latter part of the battle, they only wielded one mug each. They toasted to victory, as a loving couple danced in the street beside them, and slammed half their mugs' contents.

"I guess I was thirsty," Mick declared, displaying a beard half full of froth.

Dave remarked, "I guess I too needed to quench a great thirst." He thought back to the battle. "After all these years, it's evident we were right in giving you the nickname Hawk. You sure can see anything at any distance."

"You probably could've worked out that plan too—it just would've taken you longer." Mick chuckled.

"One thing I can see before you is the fact you're spilling your mead all over yourself when you drink," Dave replied, and joined his friend in laughter—the best kind of laughter: the kind exuding great comradery.

Having a good time with his long-time friend, Mick looked up and saw General Ulfenkerki approaching. "General Ulfenkerki, my pleasure to meet you," Mick voiced above the clamor of the crowd.

Dave followed suit.

"I'm also at great pleasure in meeting Mick Thraiker and Dave Ghrere: for two reasons. The first is to give you a thousand thanks for your incredible plan I witnessed involving Bamsov's archers—how you were able to do that is beyond me. The second and most important reason is that I finally get to meet the childhood friends of a person for whom I have great respect: Jason Thorncat. He speaks very highly of you. Due to the unfortunate death of Sven Algar, I'm naming Jason as my first lieutenant."

"We're glad to hear of the good news for Jason, but also full of sorrow in the loss of Sven. We didn't know him personally, but we're acquainted with the great things he accomplished in his lifetime," said Mick.

With humorous timing, Dave answered Ulfenkerki's previous rhetorical question. "Mick here had a brilliant plan, he dragged me behind a barrel, and we put it into action. The plan was put into action, not the barrel." Laughter ensued all around.

"The plan would've failed miserably if it hadn't been for Dave's fighting skills. I'm almost certain he wiped out a few more of Rayton's archers than I did," revealed Mick, full of pride in his friend.

"But you achieved victory over Bamsov on the field, killing him with impeccable sword work," Dave added.

"Just in the right spot at the right time. Enough about us, we would've all had grimmer destinies, General, if you hadn't conceived your clever trapping arrangement."

"You can thank my dad for that. He's the one who employed me in the mason business for many years, before my military career. I didn't particularly enjoy it, but I sure learned a lot about the dynamics of wall strength."

After a few more minutes talking about the war, Ulfenkerki presented an offer to Mick and Dave: "Jason had informed me of the fact you guys are freelance freedom fighters. If you ever decide you want to sway from that path, there'll always be a spot in my army for you. I'd even make you officers on the spot, due to the heroics you presented here. I would sleep far better knowing Hawk and Leopard were covering my back."

Mick turned to look at Dave, and the pair exchanged all-telling facial expressions. Mick responded to Ulfenkerki, "Your back will always be covered by Leopard and I whenever we can. As for your extremely generous offer, we must decline, for we will always be searching for that which can only be obtained from within. Participation in your army could indeed add much to our mountainous task of satisfying our mission to solve the equation of life. But I'm afraid questing for answers unencumbered will always be a part of our math."

Ulfenkerki rubbed his jaw, then replied, "I understand what you say, and am truly satisfied in knowing you're on our side, and have my back. But there is one other thing: Jason and I both, among others, are really looking forward to the telling of the tale of your legendary swords. We hope hearing the story soon is within the realm of possibility."

Dave smiled, and said, "The story is long, but the night is young, so it just might be summoned."

The Black Bear left Mick and Dave's company. All three were content in now knowing each other.

The revelry at Strwin hit a zenith. Debris started to pile up everywhere, inconsequential things got broken. Such ramifications were expected. Nobody worried.

Mick and Dave, while leaning up against the side of a shop surrounded by festivity, were joined by Gregg Hogarty.

"Pleased to see you, Gregg. Are you enjoying the merriment?" Dave asked.

"Oh, you know it, my friend."

"Near the end there," Dave said, "you really must've been doing some fine killing. There was a point when I had to give your direction a second look to make sure the blood in which you were encased was not your own. I concluded quickly that if you had lost that much blood, you wouldn't have been showing as much kick as you were."

"Yeah, I remember seeing you doing that, and asking myself, either I look near death, or I look rather impressive. I had finished an adversary with a carve to the neck. The wound bled like a waterfall, spilling all over me."

"That it did; and, yes, you did look rather impressive."

"I didn't see you in the battle," commented Mick, "but even as we're standing here now, your appearance looks pretty intense. So, what now? What does a member of the impressive Strwin guard do after such a great victory?"

"Actually, my Strwin guard term is up in a couple days, so instead of reenlisting, I decided I'm going to join Ulfenkerki's army. There is a lot to get done in Garobansurov as a whole. Sarwa needs to be retaken for one thing. For another, Thraug is vulnerable and in need of reinforcements."

"And who only knows how the Molisians are getting into our country? There must be a weak link on the border somewhere," said Mick.

"I'm not sure; all I know is we can worry about the future later," declared Gregg. "As for now, we can rejoice in our victory here. Maybe the upcoming winter will keep all battles grounded for the time being."

"We can only hope. Have you gotten a chance yet to talk with Ulfenkerki about your enlistment into his army?" inquired Dave.

"Yes, he was thrilled," replied Gregg. "He told me he had a lot more recruiting to do, before he could assemble any more war demonstrations. He wasn't sure exactly where he was going to do that recruiting, but he knew it was going to start as soon as possible."

"I don't think it'll take long for him to regain the power he had before this battle," announced Mick. "I'm sure the news of this victory will spread far and wide, and potential soldiers will search him out."

"No doubt," agreed Gregg. "On a different note, I heard about your part in our win. Well done. I'm glad I hesitated before roughing you up for trespassing a few days ago."

"We're glad you did too." The three laughed.

"I'll talk to you later, Mick, Dave. I have to go ask that gentlemen something, before he disappears into the crowd." Gregg pointed.

"Hope you get your answers, Gregg," said Dave.

Gregg walked away, leaving Hawk and Leopard to lean against the storefront by themselves again. They were enjoying their lives; no doubt starting to feel the euphoric effects of a good, strong mead.

Within the next hour, Mick and Dave entertained a plethora of guests coming and going from their spot in the shade. Among the guests: Mike, Bob, Steve Johnson, and the lady who allowed Dave passage on her housetop for the trick on Mick. She told them it was one of the best gags she'd ever seen, and that she couldn't remember a time when she laughed so hard.

At a point in twilight, Dave walked away from Mick without saying a word, which left Mick a little perplexed. But his bewilderment was short lived; he quickly noticed whom it was that Dave saw in the crowd. Mick smiled at the discovery.

Dave approached the familiar face, and bade greetings. "Hello, Serana, nice to see you again."

"Well that's a pleasant surprise, if ever I did see one. Nice to see you again too, Dave. It certainly is a small world."

"It sure is. What brings you to Strwin, other than this fine victory celebration?"

Serana put her arm around the woman standing at her side, and said, "My cousin, Valerie, and I brought a load of provisions for the troops and the rest of town. We heard about the siege, and started the journey here a few days back. For safety, we waited in the forest until the coast was clear. We saw the retreat, heard the celebration, and knew that was our cue."

"I'm certainly glad you waited, instead of attempting something brave. There was an incident involving a young lad attempting to sneak into town with supplies during the siege, but he met his untimely death in the act. All of town, including me, was grief stricken that day."

"Oh, that's horrible. So incredibly sad," said Serana. "No, we're usually not that brave."

"I heard his death was avenged at least," Dave stated.

"That's good," said Valerie.

Dave extended his hand towards Valerie for an introductory handshake. "Nice to meet you, Valerie." She returned the pleasantry, then, Dave all of a sudden remembered he utterly abandoned Mick. "Why don't we all venture over there," Dave said, pointing in Mick's vicinity. "I'm sure my good buddy, Mick, is wondering what happened to me. I kind of just came over here without saying a word to him."

"No problem."

The party of three zig-zagged through the crowd towards Mick, who was all smiles when the three made contact.

Dave said, "I don't think you met Mick officially, Serana, when we were back in Zant. Serana and Valerie this is Mick, and Mick, this is Serana and Valerie."

Greetings were exchanged by Mick, Serana and Valerie.

Dave quickly explained to Mick what had brought the ladies into town, then digressed. Addressing everyone, Dave said, "As I'm sure you can gauge by context clues, Serana and Valerie, Mick and I are here because we partook in the battle. We were honored to meet and fight alongside some of the best soldiers this continent has to offer. General Ulfenkerki is as brilliant as they say, no doubt."

"So, you were here during the siege then too?" voiced Serana. "Good thing you bought all those supplies at our store in Zant."

"Yes, we were. And, yes, the accoutrements really helped out the cause. We also donated a ton of the fish we netted in the Narrows the other day," replied Mick.

"Remember when we were kids, Serana, and we use to fish there too," Valerie said, engulfed in nostalgia.

"How could I forget, those were some of the best memories of my life. So carefree."

Obvious was Dave's attraction to Serana. Obvious as the sun was hot. Mick and Valerie also gravitated towards each other. The paradigm of discussion became more one-on-one.

"Valerie, what do you do for a living?" asked Mick.

"I live just outside of Zant, farming the land, raising pigs and chickens for food. For extra gitis, I spend hours upon hours sifting through the nearby creeks for gold, and anonymous gems of value."

Mick responded, "Do you do all this by yourself?"

"Ever since my father died eleven years ago."

Mick declared, "Your independence is admirable, Valerie."

"Thank you. I guess self-reliance is in my blood."

Valerie continued her conversation with Mick, while Dave discussed current events, personal matters and the weather with Serana. They all talked well past the twilight hours, and into the blackness of night.

Chapter 5

THE ONSET OF night didn't hinder the town's celebration at all, for good spirits still enveloped all. If anything, there were more people in Strwin during the night hours, than there were during the day. Thraiker, Ghrere, Serana and Valerie, between the four of them, were up to thirty mugs of mead in total, and feeling pretty good.

Having been preoccupied during most of the celebration, due to his newly appointed office, Jason Thorncat was now finally able to join the rest of the warriors and townsfolk in the fun. The first thing he wanted to do was search out Mick and Dave. He found them by the storefront still talking with Serana and Valerie.

"There they are," Jason exclaimed. "I saw what you did during the battle. I was losing all hope, but then, I looked up and saw you taking out the flankers from behind. Now that was a force spent creatively. I was proud beyond measure."

Dave proclaimed, "I'm sure I also speak for Mick when I say this, but we wouldn't be the warriors we are today, Jason, if it weren't for your hard work ethic when we were young lads. It was no less than inspirational."

"I wouldn't go that far; but, yeah, I do remember a few days having to get you two out of bed, so we could practice with our wooden swords."

"Wouldn't trade those days for anything," said Dave. "Have you ever met the astonishing Wapertery cousins from Zant? This is Serana and Valerie."

"No, I haven't. Nice to meet you ladies."

Valerie and Serana returned the greeting, and Mick spoke. "Ulfenkerki told us of your appointment as his next in command officer. We are certainly glad for you."

"I am very happy with the appointment as well, however, I would've been more pleased to hear Sven survived the battle. Such is fate, though, and I will perform my duty with all the pride and honor of the station."

Mick stated, "The Black Bear, I'm sure, is aware of that resolve, and that's why he chose you. Sven would be proud too. Isn't that right, General Ulfenkerki?" Unbeknownst to him, Ulfenkerki had approached Jason from his blindside.

"That's right. Hello everyone."

All returned the General's salutation, and the six of them talked about Garobansurov in generality. But the conversation about the nation was relatively short lived; for Mick, speaking with great enthusiasm, digressed. "I'm in the mood for a story, how about you all? General, where are the rest of your soldiers? I would like all who desire to hear this have the opportunity."

"Most of them are at the Mead Hall, the rest are in the barracks. If this is for what I'm hoping, I'm very excited," uttered Ulfenkerki. "I will inform the men in the barracks, and meet you back at the Mead Hall."

Wasting no time, the General separated from the group, and headed for the barracks, while Mick, Dave, Jason, Serana, and Valerie made way for the Mead Hall.

They arrived at the tavern, and saw see a large number of soldiers, some bruised and bloodied. The Strwin post-battle party had passed climax, the numbers in town having dwindled, but the tavern was still pretty full and untamed, definitely looking the part of a celebration. There were empty mugs strewn everywhere. The tavern was enriched by bards still playing, but showing signs of lethargy. A small amount of men and women were dancing to the bard's music, but most patrons were scattered at the bar or utilizing the many wooden tables. The soldiers were mainly standing together in a handful of groups, except for the few attempting to ensure a sleepover with the local women.

Because the tavern was saturated in dimness, hardly anyone noticed the party of five walking in. Jason led Mick, Dave, Serana, and Valerie to the soldiers, and proclaimed loudly, "Pour a round for my friends and I, for we are all in for a treat. This is Mick Thraiker and Dave Ghrere, and apparently Mick is going to finally elaborate upon the story of how he and Dave discovered their famed swords."

The soldiers, including notable warrior Steve Johnson, were all excited to be a part of the moment. Most of them had heard about the swords and remembered Mick and Dave's part in the battle. While waiting for the General, the soldiers complimented them on their well-conceived plan.

Uncharacteristically, the Black Bear entered the tavern enthusiastically (the man was usually stoic as stone), bringing with ten more soldiers. He yelled out to the crowd, "Gather 'round everyone; we're about to hear a story I've been waiting many years to hear."

The crowd gathered, the bards stopped playing, all were silent, and the story of the swords as told by Mick Thraiker began:

Almost a decade ago, as you know, times were different. War hadn't yet begun to seep into the country. And for some reason, it seemed the weather was better—that could've been my imagination though. Dave and I spent half our time tending to fields for extra money, and the other half chasing through the countryside, trying to satisfy our young hearts' ambitions to make something of ourselves.

One day in particular, a few weeks before crop planting, while the frost was still in the ground, Dave and I decided to take a trip to a geological anomaly twenty miles north of our hometown of Chalatore, called the Tharbjorn Escarpment. We both enjoy the science of geology, and try to get out as much as possible, attempting to experience firsthand the ancient forces of nature at work.

We departed Chalatore with all our traveling gear and enough food to last a week and a half. Since this is a story about obtaining our current swords, we'd carried our old swords with on the trip, and no, Jason, not our childhood wooden swords. At the time, we wielded inexpensive specimens we had bought from a traveling merchant.

The first day we covered eight miles, and made camp on a picturesque knoll, surrounded by morass, if I remember correctly.

The next morning, before we started off again, Dave crawled out of his tent, and said, "If we can cover the same amount of ground today as we did yesterday, we should arrive by midday the day after today."

"You mean tomorrow?"

"Yes, the day after today." Dave exuded a quizzical face.

"Tomorrow," I repeated.

Dave continued to be puzzled.

I couldn't help but carry on the charade. I began to laugh.

Dave finally realized I was being a pest, and replied, trying to hold in his smile, "Oh just finish packing your gear and let's go."

So, we started on the day's walk, and kicked off many miles by nightfall. We camped again, and by that time, we were really starting to enjoy the trip.

I recall that night, while staring endlessly at the stars, Dave talking about a girl he used to like, a real brown-haired stunner according to him.

The next day, we arrived at Tharbjorn Escarpment, and constructed our campsite right away. We were planning on staying for five days and nights.

The Tharbjorn itself was an ancient place, encompassing approximately ten square miles. The whole locale was a densely forested, dark landscape, containing boulders from a prehistoric formation; immovable masses scattered onto almost every spot a boulder could be put. In many places, the actual formation itself reared its awesome facade high above the ground, and especially in some places it seemed to almost kiss the sky. The main escarpment was a huge hundred and fifty-foot-high cliff face running down the middle of the entire area, like a spine. There was also a river that tore through the locale, and rare, fascinating plant species strewn about, which were indigenous to that setting alone. None of the rare plants, however, had any real value; none known of anyways by anyone at the time. There were also remnants of old ruins leftover from some primitive civilization that had settled in the area many thousands of years ago. Very interesting stuff.

But the main fascination with the Tharbjorn wasn't the boulders everywhere, stacked on top of each other almost infinitely. It wasn't the darkest forest you could possibly imagine, or the huge drop-

off seen from the top of the cliff. Nor was it the massive rock formations, or rare native plant species. It wasn't the interesting stone ruins of a town built long ago by ancient inhabitants. The real fascination was the fact that millions of years ago an ancient river flowed through the Tharbjorn, fifteen times bigger than the current river, in the opposite direction than it does today.

And because that river was so big and powerful, a person could walk around and find the smoothing of rocks caused by the rushing water. The formation was an extremely hard, igneous rock, so the only force strong enough to smooth it out was the torrent from a tremendous amount of water. Where the prehistoric river flowed over the escarpment itself, a person could really see the vestiges of the river and its powerful force. The exact locations of the smoothing on the escarpment is how one knows the river flowed in the opposite direction long ago.

That's where Dave and I spent most of our time, both on top and bottom of the cliff, imagining the powerful forces that once engaged the vicinity. Our campsite was also near that area.

The first thing we did though, before we were able to do any exploring, was go to the existing river and procure our supply of fish for the five days planned. That took us longer than what we wanted, so as soon as we got back to our campsite that night, we collapsed and relaxed.

"Why do you think we had such a hard time catching fish today, Mick?"

"I couldn't tell you, but it might have something to do with the abundance of beavers and muskrats down by the river. Speaking of furry creatures, look over there, a coyote. It's pacing in circles for some reason," I said.

"That's funny. I think I'm going to bed, maybe it'll still be doing it in the morning."

"Perhaps."

We didn't wake to further coyotes strangely walking in circles. Since we were disappointed we never got the chance the day before, the first thing we did that morning, after breakfast, was to head to the cliff, bringing with our most studious selves.

Having perused awe-inspiring features at the cliff for an hour, I voiced, "Come over here, Dave, look at this fantastic specimen."

Dave walked over by me, and inspected the smooth surface. He pondered for a while, looked up, and said while pointing to where he was looking, "I'm almost certain this was caused by rushing water compressed by those two giant pillars of stone up there."

"I wonder if there's smoothing on the insides of those stone pillars too."

"Yeah, we'll have to look next time we're up on top of the cliff," Dave replied.

We continued inspecting the rocks for a while; then, I came to a conclusion of sorts, and shared it with Dave. "After studying this site for a while, I think I can safely say that the only river in the entire country that would've had enough size to accomplish so much weathering is the Geenhuvagal River. At one point in its lifecycle, I believe a much larger Geenhuvagal flowed through this point producing the smoothing we're currently finding."

"The same river that flows past the capital? But that's many miles away from here." However, a few moments after Dave said that, he realized how my theory was plausible. As I did, he put into play the magnificent power of the glaciers that once engulfed the area, and how easily they could change the course of a river. "You're probably right, Mick, now that I think about it. This sure is quite the tremendous place of mystery."

After a while, we ventured to the top of the cliff, and saw the smoothness of the two giant stone pillars. The smoothing wasn't as significant as it was down below, but that was to be expected; plunge pools being violent places.

We inspected the area virtually in its entirety, especially where the ancient river flowed over the escarpment. Imagining the tremendous size and beauty of the waterfall that once towered, we couldn't help but gasp. Afterwards, we walked around, and looked inside some of the natural grottos carved into the cliff-face. We didn't really know what we were looking for in the grottos, but I do recall thinking some of them were big enough in which to sleep. I also thought maybe at one time a person from long ago slept in one, and left something behind. But in the end, we never found any tangible clues in the grottos of ancient occupation.

Our minds drifting to ancient cultures, we decided we wanted to explore the village ruins thereat. Spending a generous amount of time, we intended to really look at the details, since we had three and a half more days to range over everything.

We accomplished the forty-five-minute walk from the escarpment to within sight of our destination of the ruins. In all reality, the ruins weren't that far away, but the walk took us awhile because of nearly impenetrable terrain owing to dead trees lying everywhere. The walk back was quicker, since we'd cleared a path.

We weren't positive, but before we got to the building vestiges, we noticed something that may have also been of ancient construct. There were rock piles scattered across a morass, and what made them seem out of place was how they were all in line and equidistant from each other. A geometric anomaly leading Dave and I to believe the piles were the bases of a man-made bridge spanning the marshy area. The wooden part of the bridge's walkway had long since deteriorated. It was too bad the bridge wasn't still whole; it would've prevented our feet from getting wet.

At the predominant ruins, we split up. Dave started his probe from the west side, and I from the east, intending to meet back up in the middle. There weren't too many of the stone structures left intact, but with what was still there, you could imagine a pretty vivid picture of what the buildings use to look like in their former glory.

One of the buildings I remember surveying contained within, what resembled, stone benches, and an altar of some sort. Don't ask me for what they used the altar, but it did exhibit an ominous, red hue in certain places. One couldn't help but envision dark rituals.

After about fifty minutes of looking around, Dave and I met back up, and scrutinized one of the last ruins left for inspection. It was pretty empty, except for a tree growing alongside one of the walls. It looked like a natural place for a tree to grow, so I never gave it a second thought. But Dave started to fiddle around on the backside of the tree, and noticed some well-worn hieroglyphics on the wall behind the tree. There were about eight different pictures. Half of them were too worn to tell what they were. But of the other half, Dave and I could make out: a forest scene; a river; a group of people holding wooden weapons; and a cave containing a water reservoir, with lines radiating out from little dots on the inside of the cave.

"These all seem pretty self-explanatory," Dave said. "The glyph with the cave seems pretty odd though. We've yet to come across any cave-like structures, let alone a cave with a water reservoir in it."

"Maybe we will yet, our time here is young," I replied.

"Seems like we're done here at the ruins. I'm for heading back to the campsite," said my exhausted friend.

"Ok, let's start the walk back."

We walked back slowly, admiring all the points of interest along the way. We arrived at our campsite, and let our legs give out underneath. Our muscles were pretty drained of vigor; it had been a long day of discovery. We relaxed, and discussed everything we saw that day—quite the variety. We fell asleep, eager to continue the exploration the next day.

Early the next morning, I woke to the smell of Dave cooking breakfast. I tumbled out of the tent and joined him around the fire.

"What do you want to do first today, Mick?"

"I think I want to go the central ridge and poke around there awhile."

"That sounds good to me."

As planned, we began our day exploring the central ridge. We ended up finding something interesting on the ridge: a weird looking flower that looked like it could jump out and eat you at any moment. It never did, obviously, but it sure would've been fascinating to see it try.

After exploring the large, central ridge, we headed to the main escarpment to look for more rock smoothing, along the way exploring all the smaller ridges. Unfortunately, the smaller ridges contained nothing interesting enough to share with you now.

When we arrived at the colossal hundred- and fifty-foot escarpment, we began working our way through some of the stone rubble piled up everywhere, hoping to uncover something captivating hidden through the eons. Subsequent to coming up empty-handed—and blister-handed—in that endeavor, we once again made the steep ascent to the top of the escarpment.

Dave started to look inside the upper grotto again, and I paced back and forth on one of the flat parts of the ledge, looking at the ravine far below. In my awe inspired trance, I meditated on geological theories involving the ancient riverbed.

In the middle of trying to decide how long I thought the current river was where it was, IT happened. I could feel a small tremble radiating from the rocks around me, accompanied by a low bass hum. I could see Dave a hundred yards away, trying to find something sturdy to clasp, in an attempt to steady himself. I didn't know what was going on. I searched frantically for something to hold onto, but found nothing. Then, unexpectedly, out of the grotto near me, I heard the sound of an enormous rock cracking. Following the thunderous eruption, a relentless torrent of water poured out of the rock wall, heading directly at me. The water revealed a force so great it knocked me right off the top of the escarpment. I would've plummeted to my death, crashing onto the rocks a hundred and fifty feet below, if it hadn't been for a small tree growing out of the side of the cliff, of which at the last second, I was able to grab a hold.

As I hung, the water continued to pour over the cliff. The surge of water lasted thirty seconds after my point of fall, then, it stopped as abruptly as it started. I held onto that branch with dear might, until Dave was able to run over to where I was and help me climb back onto the ledge.

"I can't believe that just happened," Dave roared, both our hearts racing.

I was compelled to collapse to the ground, the exhaustion of holding myself out on the limb for so long taking its toll. Parallel to the ground, and with what I assumed a funny looking grin, I responded to Dave, "At least we found the water reservoir shown in the hieroglyphs back at the ruins."

Dave laughed, and waited patiently for me to regain my composure. "The ancients must've known it was there by peering into a hole in the rock, an opening since hidden by piles of rocky debris."

"Or maybe it'd erupted before. Also plausible, maybe there are other reservoirs inside the escarpment elsewhere."

"Possibly."

"They could be build-ups from groundwater seepage," I suggested.

"And over time," Dave said, continuing my line of thought, "the water pressure became too much for the rock encasement, and it broke. Coincidentally, it had to happen at the same moment you were standing precariously on the ledge."

"Only one way to find out; let's go inspect the point of impact."

Upon investigation of the spot where the deluge funneled out of the rock, we realized the hole was gaping enough for us to climb inside. So, we constructed makeshift torches, and headed into the bowels of the planet.

We climbed on our hands and knees through a narrow tunnel, until we reached the actual hollowed out reservoir itself. I can't say that crawl was exactly pleasant. It didn't take long to distinguish which rock it was that broke, effectively coercing the onslaught of water to come crashing down on me.

We were both at awe, imagining the amount of water pressure needed to bust such a rock.

We continued on into the dark, damp cavern, looking for who knew what else. When we reached the other side of the hollow, an audible screeching erupted. The situation resembling the feeling at the inception of battle, we instinctively drew our swords and waited for what was to come. We had no idea what was causing the sound.

Bats were what came. They were so numerous Dave and I had to swat them away with our swords. It was just bats, though, so our nerves calmed.

Swatting aggressively and precisely at the bats, Dave hollered, "I'm getting most of them, but occasionally one manages to collide with my face."

"Yeah, I've gotten hit in my face at least three times now," I hollered back, as I swung my sword back and forth like a pendulum as fast as I could. "We now also know what the lines were radiating from the dots, depicted on the glyph on the ruin. They represent the nightly paths of these bats leaving the cave and going out into the forest to *hunt. I'm sure the bats were here thousands of years ago too."*

"That's definitely convincing."

When the assault of bats dwindled, I took a deep breath, and said, "That sure was exhilarating. I just couldn't swing my sword fast enough to alter all of the bats' courses away from my face. It's not that I couldn't swing any faster, but it always seemed I lost my grip on the sword, the faster I swung it. It's too bad our sword handles—and all of our allies'—couldn't be made with better grips to counteract centrifugal force."

Just then, I turned to look at Dave to see what he was going to say in response. But instead of seeing the countenance I expected, I noticed a jaw so tense it looked like it was about to fall off, and an upper lip curled to surge adrenalin—an effective tool for thinking clearly. Dave was in meditation so deep it seemed as if he was in another world. In fact, he looked like he was about to come to a great epiphany. Not just any epiphany, but one as important as solving the meaning of life or something.

He didn't solve the meaning of life at that time, but what he did solve was almost as important to us.

"What did you just say, Mick?" Dave asked.

"That sure was exhilarating," I replied, wondering where his mind was going.

"No, after that," Dave stated, exuding passion, "the part about sword handles."

"Too bad they aren't made with better grips to counteract centrifugal force."

"Yes, that's it," Dave erupted. "Let's mentally rewind time for a moment, to when you fell off the escarpment, nearly hurdling to your untimely death. Didn't you think it was odd the amount of strength that little tree onto which you held was sufficient enough to hold your entire body weight?"

"Now that I think of it, yes, it was an abnormally strong tree."

"More importantly, did you notice the fact that you were even able to grip it? You were falling pretty fast by the time you grabbed it. But this is the part that's really baffling me: I didn't make conscious note of it at the time, but thinking back on it now, I recollect the tree was just sitting there, growing on the side of a cliff so smooth it resembled a pond surface on a windless day. A cliff surface with no cracks or divots, in which for the roots to plant themselves."

"So, what you're trying to suggest is that the roots of the tree could grip so well it held up my body weight by using only its own grip strength to anchor itself down?" I asked. "Using none of the mechanical advantage plants require for stability? Don't answer; I understand at what you're getting. We must, in all haste, get out of the underworld, and back to that tree."

Dave snapped out of his epiphany caused trance, and we hurried as fast as we could through the old water reservoir and the narrow tunnel, bumping our heads a few times along the way. We edged our way through the cave's small entrance/exit, back into the brightness.

We raced to where I had tumbled off the cliff.

Out of breath, we stood, staring at the tree below us, noticing a strange concoction of dust and moisture had accumulated on the tree.

I got down on my stomach, so I could get a better look, and said, "You were definitely right, Dave, the tree is anchoring itself on the tiniest of rock lips, and has no feeder roots penetrating the cliff anywhere."

Dave responded, "Just imagine how powerful of swords we could craft, using that wood as handles. One of a kind weapons with mysterious properties."

"They would have no equal. The unbelievable strength and grip capability of that tree down there is quite the enigma. I have never before seen nor heard of a tree being able to do what it's doing. There's just one problem: the tree is pretty gnarly; there might not be any wood on the tree sufficient enough in size to be the hilt of a sword, let alone enough usable wood for two swords—one for each of us."

"I'll lower you down, that way you can get a better look at it."

Dave lowered me down, and the first thing I did was shake all the dust and water droplets off. But while doing it, nothing was to prepare me for the shock of what was revealed. "Dave, can you see this? This tree just keeps getting stranger and stranger, for never before has it been written of a pine tree having black needles."

"I can't really tell from up here; the greenish tint of the rock surrounding it manifests the illusion of the needles also appearing green."

"That's probably why it has never been noticed by passersby before. I'm rubbing my hands over the trunk, and I'll confirm not only the roots exhibit superior gripping properties—the whole tree does. It's like this wood was designed specifically to be sword handles. It's almost too good to be true."

"Unbelievable."

I finished clearing the tree of every ounce of debris, and completed my survey; and then, was able to report the good news back to Dave. "We're definitely lucky today, my friend, for there is just enough wood for the hilts of two swords. And under my impression, collecting the branches won't stress the tree to near fatal levels, so it should survive."

Dave yelled out with such extreme elation that all flora and fauna of the surrounding area heard. Subsequently, he uttered to me, unveiling a noticeable nervous stutter, "I'll bring you back up, and we'll search for a suitable rock for the sawing of those branches."

I was dragged up, and when I stood on the ledge again, I loosed a huge roar, mainly for the purpose of letting the world know I thought it was great to be alive. For up until now, that was the point in my life when I felt the most alive and free.

With much effort, we found a suitable rock with serrated edges, and between that and our swords, we started the attempt of harvesting our wood.

Because the wood was so hard, we were only able to acquire the first piece of wood that day, and would have to come back the next for the other. We didn't sleep well that night, because we both had dreams of someone else stumbling on our find, and taking the second suitable branch for themselves—or, greedily, the entire tree.

We were relieved when we arrived back at the tree, discovering our paranoia was just getting the best of us. It took us well into the afternoon to finish harvesting the second section of wood from the black-needle pine. We both came to a mutual agreement at that time, as to which future grips belonged to whom. They were both unique in their own way underneath the bark. Mine has a swirl like a fingerprint, and his has a pattern resembling waves of the ocean. You can see those patterns on the swords to this day.

I kept some of the black needles, but—like all pine needles eventually do—they turned red from lack of moisture in half a year. I still kept them anyways.

Just holding the wood in our hands, we could feel the superior grip-ability, rigidness and desirable density. We took a few swings at the air while holding the future sword handles.

Dave proclaimed, "These swords will be powerful."

"That they will," I agreed wholeheartedly.

We were also glad further water eruptions were kept at bay, while we were still positioned on the ledge.

For the rest of the day, up until nightfall, we searched the immediate area for more black-needle pines, but just our luck, there weren't any more around.

We ended up searching throughout the entire Tharbjorn for others, doing so the entirety of the remaining two days scheduled. When we came up empty handed at the end of the very last day, we started to hypothesize as to why the parents of the tree were non-existent. But only summoned crude theories.

We returned back to the Tharbjorn five years after the incident, and could only continue speculating. At least thankfully the tree survived the branch harvest. We've made it one of our life's missions to discover more information concerning the elusive black-needle pine. We've been searching ever since for another specimen, finding none.

Upon comparing the five-year difference in the tree, we realized the tree was way older than what we previously thought. By gauging the five-year growth, we estimated the tree was thousands of years old, and would take another thousand years to grow enough wood for another sword hilt. We assume we'll never see that day. It's probable the parents of our tree have long since departed the planet, an inevitability for us all.

Nevertheless, we gave up our search for the parent trees, loaded up our gear, and headed back to Chalatore. Our time was up. Dave and I needed to get back for crop planting.

On our journey back, we discussed our treasures' futures. "Maybe by saving for a couple years, it'll be possible to have enough to head to The capital to hire a swordsmith to construct our swords."

"I hope so. If we have to wait any longer than that, I will grow sick with anticipation," Dave replied. "I have only been to Myothraces, the capital, once before, and don't for my part know any swordsmiths we can trust for such an undertaking."

"We'll have to ask around. Maybe we'll get lucky."

Since ours and Jason's innocent childhood break in at Old Man Johnson's, we've actually become good friends with Johnson, spending many hours talking about swords and sword craft. I bring him up, because Old Man Johnson ended up being our savior. He told us of the greatest swordsmith he knew: a man that went by the name of Tim Warmane. To our benefit, he told us Tim owed him a favor. Old Man Johnson said he'd personally write a note for us, and that if we presented it to Tim, he'd probably construct the swords for a reasonable price, with no questions asked.

So, after two whole years of saving our money, we had amassed twenty-five hundred gitis—enough to make two swords from scratch, hopefully.

With our giti cache and Old Man Johnson's note, we started our journey to Myothraces at the end of fall; having not forgotten our traveling gear, and our pieces of the black-needle pine.

After two weeks of traveling, almost to the capital, we stopped on the picturesque bridge over the Geenhuvagal River. We marveled at the possibility of the enormous river flowing through the Tharbjorn, and imagined the thunderous sound it would've made, tumbling over the escarpment. We spent ten minutes on the bridge, thinking grand geological thoughts.

We arrived at the capital and immediately began the search for Tim Warmane, who was by no means hard to find, because of how well known he was for his craft. I actually wouldn't be surprised to see many of you possessing Warmane brand weapons as I speak.

We offered introductions to Tim, who was respectable in kind. Dave and I arranged to meet the busy man later that evening to discuss our endeavor in detail.

We killed some time, and met Tim at a lovely park, a central location of the capital near to where Tim had spent his day.

"Here is the note from Old Man Johnson, to which I referred earlier," Dave said, handing the brownish-white slip to Tim.

Tim studied the note, scratched his chin, nodded his head in understanding, and commented, "Yes, yes, I'm ecstatic to hear the Old Dog hasn't kicked the bucket yet. I definitely owe him a favor, and would be more than pleased to fashion your swords from scratch for the twenty-five hundred gitis. A price three times cheaper than what I would charge the usual clientele for weapons of the highest grade. That will also cover the cost of your blades consisting of the finest steel Garobansurov has to offer."

"Tremendous," I said.

"The lengthy process will probably take the rest of fall and winter. Since the twenty-five hundred is all you have, leaving you no currency for the purchasing of accommodations, you're welcome to sleep in my shop for the duration. It's well ventilated on the eastern side."

Dave and I considered his offer, weighing the advantages and disadvantages of sleeping in the shop as opposed to sleeping in our tents the entire period.

We came to our decision, and I replied to Tim, "I think what we'll do is sleep in our tents in the woods outside of town while the weather is still pleasant, but when the chill of winter sets in we'll take you up on your offer, and sleep in your shop."

"Very well. You also mentioned you have custom hilts for the swords?"

"That is accurate," I confirmed. "You could say the hilts are the very reason we're doing this."

"It shouldn't be a problem. Very precisely, we'll have to bore through the cores, so the blade

can be properly anchored. Stop by tomorrow morning; we'll start right away."

"Okay, see you then."

We couldn't have been more pleased. Top notch professionalism if ever there was.

We arrived at Tim's well-organized shop early in the morning, and he showed us ingots of various metals, ingredients of the finest steel he knew to exist. Post the ingot tour, we discussed which sword shape we wanted. The first thing Dave and I told Tim is that we wanted swords a little heavier than optimum for us at that point, in view of us growing into their weights, as our strength increased through time.

I must say, as I stand here now, the swords are the perfect weight for us; good thing too, seeing as the war has just begun. When the swords were finished many years ago, a perfect weight would've been basically futile.

We also told Tim that Dave wanted his sword slightly heavier than mine, him being slightly stronger. Similarly, I wanted mine thinner, because I was faster, preferring a sharp, fine edge, required for all my slashing techniques. Tim showed us examples of his previous works in both categories we desired. We agreed on the blueprints. He asked us what we wanted for inlays on the blade; both of us wanted pine trees, not identical though. We would have requested black-needle pine trees, but the inlays could only be one color. Maybe someday we'll have the technology to have multi-colored inlays. The lengths of the two swords were to be about the same, but slightly longer than the average sword. He told us we could decide on the hand guard at a later day. Having pretty much all he needed to know to get started, we shook hands and he began.

Every day of those first couple months were routine. We spent nights in the woods, camping; and days in the shop, helping whenever we could, and conversing with Tim—having become quite good friends by the time the swords were finished. We watched him for endless hours manipulating the metal to perfect specifications. We never really realized how much work actually went into making a blade as strong as possible. The countless folds and endless hammering were mind staggering. Watching Tim perform all the necessary repetitions was pleasantly hypnotic. We never grew tired of the song of steel; even listening at night as we dreamt.

One day, Tim started to talk about what it was Old Man Johnson did for him. "Did the Old Dog ever tell you what it was he did for me long ago?"

"No, he never did. We never got around to inquiring about it."

"I'll tell you." Tim began. "Many years ago, there was a weapons' auction a few towns over for serious sword collectors and fashioners. I was bringing one of my swords to the auction to sell, one on which I spent a reasonable amount of time, and needed to get a good price. For I had a few overdue bills requiring quick payment.

Unluckily on the road, I ran into a couple of thieves waiting for perfect occasion, who knew *pickings were ripe in light of the upcoming auction. I wasn't looking forward to battling them, because I didn't think I was good enough to defeat both simultaneously. But all good stories have a hero. Out of nowhere, Old Man Johnson came running to help. With both of us fighting together, we were able to force the thieves into submission. We told them their lives would be spared, but if we ever saw them breaking laws again, we wouldn't be so nice. We never saw them again.*

After the battle, Old Man Johnson and I walked to the auction together as the best of friends. He was looking to add to his arms and armor collection at the auction I remember.

Subsequent the auction—and getting the money I needed, having sold my sword—we parted; me itching one day to be able to repay him for his heroism. And now finally, here I am, constructing in his name the two best swords I probably will ever make, for the mere cost of material. I just hope when I'm done you'll be pleased with my work."

"Judging by the painstaking workmanship you've already shown to us here in the shop, I'm more than confident the finished product will be to our utmost satisfaction," I replied.

Needless to say, after hearing Tim's story, my respect for Old Man Johnson only grew exponentially.

Weeks and even months went by quickly, and when the snow at our temporary home in the woods was too deep for efficient travel, we transitioned to spending nights at Tim's shop.

Tim continued to sing the song of metal. He also kept quiet about the project, because the last thing we needed was one of the many burglars of The Capital to hear about the swords, and attempt a heist. Tim worked tirelessly day and night, but once in a while took a break to play cards or rocks with us. Occasionally, some of his other friends would join us too.

Dave and I slept well every night, knowing our swords would soon be finished. We were anxious to swing our weapons for the first time. It all seemed too good to be true. Though, it felt as if ownership of such mystifying weapons was predestined.

The winter months flew by just as fast as the fall, and upon spring melt, Tim was ready for the all-important pounding of the blades by hammer. He suggested we watch, because that was something we probably would remember the rest of our lives. We looked on with great enthusiasm.

Two days later, the swords were finished with the cooling procedure, entailing quite the extensive process in itself. The brilliant crosspieces were attached, next, he inserted the decorative pine tree in-lays. The applications of black-needle hilts to blades were now ready: the most important aspect.

Performing the necessary actions to affix the black-needle pine stocks to the blades weren't as easy as a person would think. We watched on as Tim defined precision, our eyes glued open, forgetting to blink half the time.

When Tim finished the first sword, he tossed it to Dave for the first swing, who's heart I'm sure was racing in the wait. Dave is a class act, deciding to wait until mine was finished, so we could swing them for the first time together.

Not much time after the first sword was completed, Tim tossed over my sword. The unmistakable swirl pattern on the hilt immediately caught my eye. Together, we swung our masterpieces for the first time in our lives. The swords were everything we imagined they would be. The grip stuck to our hands so tightly that we immediately noticed we could swing faster without worrying about the swords flying from our hands. We estimated a minimum thirty percent increase in speed. As we swung, the swords stuck to our hands like ice to a Garobansurovian lake in winter. Completing an arc with the new weapons felt absolutely incredible.

Tim's turn was next. Experiencing the product of his hard work, he executed a few swings of the swords, performed quite gracefully I should add. After his swings, Tim proclaimed it was indeed the best work he had ever done. He was also so bold as to say we now owned the best two swords on which he had ever laid eyes. Dave and I don't quite agree with Tim, in that they're the most powerful swords made by any person or deity ever, but we do believe they're pretty close.

The next day, we bade farewell to Tim, and extended him a heartfelt appreciation for everything he did. The swords weren't the only things of value forged in those months: a great friendship emerged from the fires that we wouldn't soon forget. He told us the shop door would always be open for us, and that he would look forward to hearing of our adventures from afar.

We started the journey back to our hometown, swords firmly grasped, and eyes ever searching for another black-needle pine.

UPON CONCLUSION OF his story, Mick noticed the sun was beginning to rise, and that every single person that had started listening was still standing there at maximum attention.

Jason Thorncat was the next to speak: "Well Mick, there is one thing I know; and that is, had I known Old Man Johnson was that outstanding of a man, I would've never brought up the idea of the three of us breaking into his cabin just to look at his sword collection."

"He probably would've just shown us his collection on the asking," remarked Dave.

General Ulfenkerki looked at his sword, and said, "My sword I know is a Warmane brand weapon. I bought it at an auction a while ago. I actually wouldn't be surprised if it's the very same sword you spoke of in the story—the one Tim was bringing to the auction when he got ambushed. I remember paying a lofty sum, and the auction from which I got it was also a couple towns over from the capital. And of the same time period. Best money I ever spent.

Mick looked closely at Ulfenkerki's sword, and stated, "Next time I'm back home, I'll have to ask Old Man Johnson what Tim's sword had looked like at the time."

"And I'll ask Tim about it, now that I know the story," noted the General. "It would be interesting to know a little more of my sword's history."

Conversation on Mick's story at the Mead Hall went on for another half hour. Everyone had questions about the story and the swords. Mick and Dave supplied honest answers to them all.

After all questions were exhausted, everyone parted ways to try to get some sleep. Mick and Dave also parted with Serana and Valerie, and told them they might meet back up with them later.

Venturing back to their trusty juniper bush, Mick and Dave endeavored to sleep as long as they could, even though daylight surrounded them. Luckily, for the sake of Mick and Dave's rejuvenation, the victory revelry around the bush had dissipated.

Chapter 6

THE INHABITANTS DIDN'T like waking in the morning, staring at the flag of Molisia waving in the wind atop the city's tallest flagpole. But they knew there was nothing they could do about it for the time being. Conquered and downtrodden, the Garobansurovian people felt miserable.

Beside the loftiest flagpole and its attached Molisian flag, the largest building of Sarwa, Garobansurov resided. The building could hold roughly two hundred people, and was usually used as a dance hall. But now, the usurper, General Hyraugh Gamald, was utilizing it as headquarters, tending to all the governing of town matters.

Before Sarwa was overrun by Gamald and his army, a trial was scheduled for a certain accused criminal, and since Gamald was now in charge, and there were no signs of that power changing, the Molisian general took matters into his own hands.

At his headquarters, doubling as a makeshift courthouse, Gamald said to the accused criminal, "Do I understand correctly? You plead guilty to the accusation of stolen property?"

"No, I never said that," shouted the accused criminal.

Gamald responded, "Don't you ever shout at me again. So, you're calling me a liar then? I heard you say you were guilty"

"I'm not calling you a liar, but I never once said I was guilty," pleaded the poor man, who had a heart of gold in reality.

"That means you're calling me a liar, because I distinctly heard you say you committed the crime," proclaimed Gamald.

"I beg you, please, sir, you are unfairly trapping me."

"Now you're accusing me of trapping you! I've heard enough. Take off his hands."

Heartbroken, the man, who in all actuality was innocent, was led away for punishment. More times than not, one didn't survive the process of getting both hands chopped off, blood loss was too excessive. Many of those hailing from Garobansurov looking on were saddened by the injustice. But there was nothing they could do about it.

The General sat back down in his chair, and waited for the next activity to take place at his newly-acquired center of operations. "These pathetic townspeople need to learn their place, or they'll all be uprooted from my town."

"They will learn," snidely replied Gamald's first lieutenant and next in command, Leedle.

"I certainly hope so."

Leedle waited patiently for the right time to inform Gamald the bad news concerning the city's food shortage. He dreaded the action so much he eventually decided to let Gamald find out for himself the town they'd just conquered didn't have enough food for all the soldiers to last the upcoming winter. And it definitely didn't have enough for the civilians.

MICK AND DAVE had slept a couple hours in the bush, before commotion in town enveloped them, a ruckus impossible through which to sleep. They would've liked more restful hours, but that's the price you pay to have fun, apparently.

"I don't think I mentioned this to you last night, but listening to you elaborate our sword story summoned shivers up and down my spine," raised Dave.

"Same here. The telling was nothing short of emotional."

"It was the first time either of us had shared the sword's details with anyone, so I expected a little warmth would wash over me," Dave noted.

Mick and Dave digressed, and started to discuss future plans. They mutually agreed on flexibility, and to continue heading north-northeast, maybe to Garobansurov's northeast border. A flexible plan supplied the best fuel for a flexible mind.

They packed up all their battle and traveling gear, which had been scattered around and within their juniper refuge. While doing so, they couldn't help but notice they'd miss their woody seclusion. It was home for many nights. "The best of bushes."

Next on the list, Mick and Dave visited the arms/armor dealer to return the swords previously swapped for shields mid-battle. They explained the situation that had transpired to the merchant, who understood completely and said everything was fine. Mick and Dave told the dealer the swords were excellent quality, and well worth the price on them. They also sold back their shields to lighten their loads.

Subsequent exiting the arms/armor shop, Thraiker and Ghrere went to the army barracks. Farewells were in order. They approached General Ulfenkerki and his new first lieutenant: Jason Thorncat.

"It looks like you two are all packed, and ready for departure," said Thorncat.

"Yup, we're heading north-northeast, in search of the next figurative mountain to climb," replied Dave.

"I still wish you'd stay and be a part of rank replenishment, but I do understand free spirits need to be fed appropriate experiences and hardships," Ulfenkerki remarked.

"I'm sure news of this victory will travel far, and recruits will pile up at the door. You won't need us to bolster your army. It'll be as mighty as it was before the battle in no time," Dave unfurled.

"Having you two sure would help in that," said Ulfenkerki.

"Until the next time we see each other," said Jason, shaking Mick's hand. Next, he shook Dave's.

"Hopefully, the next time we see you, you'll have another enchanting story to tell us," commented Ulfenkerki, about to take his turn shaking hands.

"It's very well possible," Mick said, which were his last words to Jason and Ulfenkerki for a time.

Dave's last were, "Goodbye, my friends."

Mick and Dave then searched out Gregg Hogarty to bid him farewell. And after that, they went to do the same with Serana and Valerie.

"Well, beautiful ladies of Zant, we're about to exit Strwin, so we'll be seeing you," voiced Dave, donning a huge smile.

Serana responded, "We're leaving now too. We have to walk to the small village of Noblice, just north of here, to gather a few things to bring back to Zant. We also intend to stop and pray at the Shrine of Kaeletosh."

"Actually, that's the way we're headed," remarked Dave. "If you don't mind, we could accompany you to Noblice?"

"I really like that idea. It would make our journey much safer," said Serana. "Among other reasons, of course."

"Good, it's settled then. We'll trip to Noblice together," emitted a high-spirited Mick Thraiker.

Finally, after almost an entire week spent in Strwin, Mick and Dave left the recently secured city, striving to find what else they could accomplish in the world. They knew there was much battle to come, freedom still being in jeopardy. They envisioned fighting until the end. A fight they had to do on their own terms.

Together, the foursome began the trek, hoping for safety but a little unexpectedness too.

"Here you go, Mick, day number one of you satisfying the terms of the bet lost to me," said Dave, handing Serana's pack over to him. "And for day number two, tomorrow, you'll get to carry Valerie's pack."

"I was hoping you'd forget about that, but I'm glad it worked out the way it did. I very well may've carried the ladies' packs anyways."

"But now I receive the credit." Dave chuckled.

"What happened, in order to bring that about?" asked Valerie.

"Oh, just a little prank I played on Mick."

"Little!" Mick exclaimed. "You had us climbing on rooftops, for crying out loud."

"I guess you're right. The prank really was quite extravagant," Dave erupted. "Then later that evening, we went double-or-nothing in *rocks*, and he lost."

"I'm certainly glad for it. I can't argue with the importance of a lighter load," remarked Valerie, beaming her gorgeous smile.

Mick digressed. "What did you end up doing with that cart you hauled all the way to Strwin?"

"We just sold it; it wasn't worth lugging the heavy thing back."

"Makes sense, Serana. It was quite the monstrosity."

"Sure was. It performed its purpose. Now it can do the same for someone else."

The quartet walked and talked for the rest of the day, and near the end of it, made their nightly camp on the edge of a field. Serana and Valerie set up their adequately large double tent, while Mick and Dave constructed their individual tents. Supper and a campfire were made, around which they sat for a couple hours before going to bed.

The next morning, after breakfast, they continued the pleasant walk to Noblice. It was one of those walks so pleasant, it skipped time ahead.

"I think we'll arrive at town the day after tomorrow," said Serana, midstride.

"Mick and I have never been there before, in all honesty."

"Not many people have," voiced Valerie. "It's the epitome of miniscule, sometimes not even on a map."

"Sounds quaint. It'll be a welcomed change of pace from Strwin."

After another full day of walking, they set up tents again, and spent one more night sleeping along the trail from Strwin to Noblice.

When ensconced around the fire, Serana asked Dave, "Do you ever ponder settling down and having children?"

"Someday maybe, but for now, Mick and my main concern is protecting freedom, becoming acquainted with morality, figuring out who we truly are, and maintaining serenity while doing it all."

Serana took in what Dave said, and responded, "I think I understand. But what I don't understand, I guess, is how you've gotten so proficient at sword fighting in the first place. We haven't had a war in a while, so why did you train so hard?"

"Understanding that can get a little tricky. We've practiced our whole lives, but why? I feel with near certainty I know the answer. My answer, anyways. Everyone is different. It has nothing to do with gaining any kind of satisfaction from hurting a fellow man, or to a more extreme extent killing him. It has to do with the way my mind perceives a fight. It analyzes every move, every weapon swing, every aspect of the battle. And in the process, my brain will come to appreciate what it had analyzed as an art form, recognizing the true beauty of the fight itself. It's that beauty compelling the continuation of training. The more you've trained, the more you've analyzed, the more satisfaction gotten. Hard work, mental and physical, releases endorphins. So, in finality, when someone looks at a baby, a painting, a freshly-planted field, a significant other, and perceives grand inspiration, somewhere in the world someone else is looking at a fight and grasping the grandness of that."

After thinking upon Dave's discourse for a while, Serana started to understand the logic behind his answer. "Even though I understand what you're saying, I must confess I can't relate to it."

"Well, that's kind of the point. We each have different chemical makeups in our brains, and yearn to experience different forms of art. Though, things change, and what you crave one day isn't necessarily what you crave the next."

"I can appreciate that bit of wisdom," put forth Serana. "One thing I know is that I've never seen much beauty in the clashing of swords."

"Well, I'm sure there are many more variables in the equation. And there's probably many things in this world some consider momentous, whereas I consider them dull. For example, some enjoy gossip, while I personally do not."

"Yeah, some do, don't they," Serana said.

The pair thought on the discussion, and went to sleep, knowing better one another.

They arrived safely in town the next day. Noblice was one of Garobansurov's least populated villages, lacking in anything complicated. It was open to the countryside, no high walls protecting the interior, no soldiers standing guard. The townsfolk hadn't much to fear from the outside world, because they hadn't much to offer it.

"Do you need any help acquiring your goods?" Dave asked the girls.

Serana flirtatiously responded, "We don't need any help doing that, but we would like it if you came and had dinner with us one last time before you left."

"It would be our pleasure."

The quartet partook of their meal, sitting on a large, red blanket, under one of Noblice's only trees. It was more than likely the first time the tree had seen anyone eating dinner under its branches, which was unfortunate, because the shade underneath was rather comfortable.

After their huge dinner, Mick and Dave embraced Valerie and Serana, respectively; kissed them romantically; told them how wonderful it was traveling with such beautiful ladies; and promised to come and see them again back in Zant.

After their stopover, Mick and Dave continued voyaging north-northeast, Noblice but a memory. They decided on traveling through the woods, because progressing the monotonous main trail was getting old. Surrounded by an enormous number of trees was the way to go. They also liked searching for black needle pines along the way, however the forest where they were was predominantly cedar. Cedars and pines didn't typically share soil and light requirements, so they didn't expect to run into many pines, let alone a black needle one, although they did expect to run into a few unfriendly animals—and a few friendly ones.

Much of their journey through the cedar forest was cedar swamp unfortunately, so they spent considerable time hopping from root base to root base, trying to avoid water.

Mick blurted, "Nothing worse than having wet feet, as Dave Ghrere would say."

Good luck ran out, for they finally encountered unfriendly animals—mosquito swarms so thick they resembled stars in a clear night's sky. But that was just one of many expected obstacles in the swamp, all of which Dave and Mick planned to deal with in stride. It wasn't their first cedar swamp crossing, and they had no intentions of it being their last.

After four hours of strenuous root hopping, they emerged from the swamp, and all its irksome mosquitos. Though, there was no denying the mosquitos knew how to choose a beautiful home. The cedars gave way to the high ground of an oak/maple forest, beautiful trees, but not as old and mystical as the cedars.

They stopped for a breather on an old building foundation perfect for sitting. The building itself was no longer there, but a few signs of past human habitation were visibly strewn about. An old debris pile consisting mainly of metal fragments existed on a hillside behind the foundation. Two towering trees, which seemed planted for shade long ago, stood in front of the foundation. Obviously extremely old, the pair of eye catchers were still alive and robust.

"Hey, Dave, remember the time in our youth when you climbed that tree behind your house, and got stuck, because you were afraid to climb back down past the bees' nest?"

"I remember that all too well. I probably would've just spent the night in it, if my mom had let me."

"I'm surprised we never slept in a tree canopy back then."

"We should've."

Dave strolled around the foundation, afterwards, he said, "You can still kind of see where each separate room in the house was."

"You can also perceive where the front and back doors were," Mick replied, tugging at his sock. "I think in the near future, I'm going to have to procure more socks. I ruined too many pairs in the swamp."

"I could use some more as well. Why don't we just start making some right now with the bark from that paper birch over there?"

Mick chuckled, and responded, "I'm not so sure paper socks would be very effective."

Dave laughed back, and sat back down on the foundation. "I think we should rest here for the rest of the day, giving our legs ample recovery time."

"Sounds good to me. After that last leg of the journey, our legs sure could use it."

"Nice double usage of the word leg there," Dave declared.

"Caught that, eh."

"Yup. We could even set up our tents on the inside of the foundation."

Mick sat kitty-corner Dave on the foundation, stretched his arms and legs, and said, "Sounds good. The weather sure is fabulous today. I love these cool autumn days."

"Enjoy them now, winter will soon be here."

Following the stretching of arms and legs, the relaxed gentlemen pitched camp and made a fire. They also set up a clothesline spanning two trees, fashioned from plant stems braided together, so they could try to dry all their clothing articles that had gotten wet in the swamp.

They stared at the fire, and talked, initial discussion being of Serana and Valerie.

Dave commented, "I definitely have a lot of respect for Serana and Valerie. They exude a memorable intelligence."

"Yes, I agree. Plus, they're both kind and honest."

"I don't think we'll get to see them again for a while, however, I'm afraid."

"Lamentably true."

"Hopefully, the next time we see them, they're not already married, and off the market," Dave remarked.

"I doubt we'd be so lucky."

After the Wapertery cousin's topic ran its course, Hawk mentioned, "I think I'm hungry for a squirrel or any kind of furry, tasty mammal. I'm going to set traps, and try to snag ourselves a morning meal."

"Have at it, my friend," Dave voiced. "I've seen many four-legged blurs on the distant hills, so I think your odds of a tasty morning meal are better than the Wapertery cousins being single the next time we see them." The pair chuckled.

Mick searched out the ideal rock for a trap, which had to be flat and heavy. He found a suitable rock sitting next to a bigger rock, no doubt the one off from which it broke, maybe millions of years in the past. He propped it up with a conglomeration of balancing sticks, and a trip mechanism baited with the last of the smoked fish left-over from the Narrows. He was satisfied the trap was triggerable, and the bait was in optimum position, right below the rock. For Mick, this particular style of trap had a three out of ten success rate. Mick hoped it would be one of those three times, waking to rock-flattened breakfast. He knew he could double his odds of success by making a second trap, but wasn't in the mood momentarily to search out another flat rock. Skinny, flat rocks were relatively rare.

After the trap's completion, for the fun of it, Mick and Dave began searching the metal pile for anything interesting.

"Whoever lived here sure could've buried their refuse a little better."

"If they did, we wouldn't have anything through which to curiously rummage, now would we?" emitted Dave.

"I guess that's true. I wonder what's in here," said Mick, as he pulled out a little metal box from the pile.

"Only one way to find out."

Mick enthusiastically opened the small container, but was disappointed when nothing but air, rust, and dirt was revealed. "That's too bad. At the least, I was hoping to discover something disclosing a little about the people who used to live here."

"Yeah, that would've been interesting. I wonder how long ago the house that used to sit here was abandoned, and for how long was it occupied."

"I don't think we'll ever know for certain. There aren't enough clues around for us to determine exactly. But one thing we do know is that it's been abandoned for at least fifty years already."

"How do you know that, Mick?"

"Because of the dead tree lying on the ground inside the foundation. It obviously grew in there, as shown evident by that stump. And judging by the rings on the stump the tree was fifty years old when it died. The tree wouldn't have been growing there if the house was still intact."

"Oh yeah, clever observation," said Dave, before picking up a sturdy branch from the ground. "I've always wondered which one of us is better at throwing a spear."

"Yeah, I wonder too. I know you're better with a bow, Dave. I also know one couldn't find a more evenly matched pair of sword wielding combatants than the two of us."

Dave replied, "I may be better with the bow, but you are definitely superiorly astute in battle strategy."

"That's probably true. Alongside throwing a spear, it would also be nice to know who's more proficient at fighting with one."

"Along with other weapons," Dave added, "like battleaxes, war hammers, daggers, and so on."

Mick shook his head, thought for a while, then commented, "You know, it would be plausible to determine today who's better at throwing a spear, and possibly, if we're feeling a little adventurous, we could distinguish the better spear fighter. But one thing I know is it wouldn't be wise, in my opinion, to fight each other with weapons huskier than spear-simulating sticks. I doubt we'll ever ascertain who's better with battleaxes, war hammers, or anything of the sort. Too dangerous."

"I agree," noted Dave. "Let's have at it then. We'll start with throwing spears, and maybe progress to stick fighting."

"I'll search for a spear for throwing purposes for myself, and you can utilize the one you're holding, or go look for a more suitable one."

"This branch is too brittle. I'll forage the woods for one better." While Dave was looking for a better throwing spear, he yelled to Mick, "So, if we decide to spear fight after spear throwing, do we have to use the same spears used during the spear throwing contest, under the Mick Thraiker brand spear-tournament restrictions?"

Mick rolled out a slight chuckle, and replied, "It's up to you, Mr. Leopard. You can decide the rules pertaining to that particular aspect."

"Okay then, I decide that if we progress onto spear fighting, you can either use the same spear or pick a different one."

"Very well. Now that that is decided, I'll go and look for a target at which to throw," replied Mick, confident he'd just found the perfect spear suitable for throwing.

Mick had a harder time searching for a target than what he wanted. He could've used the time to search for the rock for a second animal trap. Eventually, he found an old wagon wheel suitable. Conveniently, spokes in the wheel were minimal. Points would be scored with successful throws through the center.

They proceeded to set up the target, not far from their tents situated inside the foundation. Using a rope made from twisted willow branches, they suspended the wagon wheel from a branch of one of the old shade trees in front of the foundation.

Next, they discussed a sufficient point system.

"I think we should make a throw going all the way through the tire worth three points; a throw where the spear goes into the tire but not all the way through worth two points; and a throw where the spear bounces off the tire completely only worth one point."

"That sounds like a sound plan, my friend, Hawk."

"I propose also having different stages of competition, where distances and angles are variably changed," voiced Mick.

"I don't think we'll have to change angles, because all that would do is make the target smaller for the both of us, which, relatively speaking, wouldn't change the competition much."

"True. I think three, symmetrically different distances would be optimal. The first distance from the target being thirty feet, the second being sixty feet, and the third being ninety feet."

Dave responded, "Maybe we should make further distances worth more points than closer ones, because of the increasing improbability of success."

"Maybe for you, but I plan on hitting target with all my throws from all distances evenly," Mick said comically, disguised as an uncharacteristic attempt at pompousness.

"So, I'm to understand that for all these years I've known you, during all the countless dangerous incursions we've encountered, standing at my side was the greatest spear thrower in the known universe? Predicaments that could've easily been remedied by just a simple twitch from your spear-throwing arm?"

Mick stared at Dave sheepishly for a moment, trying to think of a comeback. In the end, he used the hesitation to heighten comedic interplay, and erupted in laughter. Almost an entire minute of shared laughter resulted. Mick finally responded, "Apparently, my pre-competition provocation psychology isn't going to present any advantages for me this time."

Dave wiped away tears of laughter. "On the contrary, I think your pre-competition psychology might give you a small advantage, in light of the fact my focus practically went away."

"I'll take whatever advantage I can get. I think we'll leave the points the same, but throw at the further targets more times."

"So, then we're looking at three throws each from the closest distance, six throws from the middle distance, and nine throws from the furthest distance of ninety feet."

"That'll require more walking to retrieve our spears from the target, but I think that's the best way to go about it."

"Alright then, shall we begin? You can go ahead and throw first, Mick. We'll start from the closest distance and work our way back."

"Okay, here I go."

They both successfully launched their spears through the wheel on their first attempt, then walked to get their spears, got back into position, and performed their second throws. Mick hit the tire that time around, but Dave missed completely. For the third and final throw of the beginning round, Dave hit the tire, while Mick missed, effectively keeping the score even at first round's completion.

When the duo's six throws each for the second round were delivered, Dave clung to a two-point lead over Mick. Dave kept the two-point lead right up until the final heaves of the last round.

"Alright, Mick, the only way you can win is if I miss completely, and you sail your spear through the middle," Dave stated. The points leader unleashed his spear, and hit the willow rope holding the wheel in suspension, missing target completely. Dave's spear stuck in the rope, but eventually gravity did what it did best, and pulled the loosely embedded spear to the ground, a plummeting action not unlike Dave's spirits. "It looks like you have a chance to win now."

Mick saved his most aggressive channeling of focus for his final throw, switching wholeheartedly to *eye of the hawk*. Dave's spine a' tingle watching on, Mick released his spear.

Dave shrunk in agony, having witnessed the spear go exactly where Mick intended. After an audible groan, Dave declared, "I guess you're the better spear thrower, but things will be different with the second phase of our competition."

"So, I take it you're in the mood for your second loss of the day, because I'm feeling extra mighty after that victory. I don't think you stand a chance." Mick beamed with confidence and exhilaration. Both he and Dave loved the comradery forged by friendly competition.

"We'll just see about that. I'm going to search out a better spear with which to fight than this lousy thing that cost me my win."

"I need to exchange mine as well. I'm afraid my throwing spear here wouldn't last two well-executed blows. I need to find some ironwood or something."

WHILE MICK AND Dave were spending excessive time and energy finding perfect fighting spears, a man on whom nobody in Strwin had ever laid eyes was seen pulling a tarp covered cart into town.

Also occurring in Strwin, and at the same time as Mick and Dave's spear search, General Ulfenkerki discussed new recruit potentials with his second in command, Jason Thorncat.

"From what I've heard, the latest five are the strongest group among the recent arrivals," commented Jason.

"Excellent. I've been impressed with what I've seen hitherto."

"The five are due here any moment to report to you for assessment."

"Very well," remarked Ulfenkerki.

Ten minutes passed, and the new recruits presented themselves to Ulfenkerki. Eyeing them up, Ulfenkerki said, "I'll watch you each battle with the practice swords, and make my decision on whether or not to accept your enlistment."

"Yes, sir," all five shouted in respectful unison.

Each of them fought a different highly skilled member of the army. They all fought reasonably well, one of them even winning, though the winning hopeful was not the one who drew Gregg Hogarty.

Gregg reported to Ulfenkerki, "My guy fought hard, and has a good understanding of battle patience. He has a few things to learn, but not things that couldn't be taught. I strongly recommend him for enlistment."

General Ulfenkerki thanked Gregg for his personal assessment, then, listened to the other fight evaluations. After deliberations, the Black Bear put forth, addressing all involved, "I appreciate you all for coming, especially you newcomers. Since I've gotten nothing but positive feedback regarding your battle skills and eagerness to learn, it's my responsibility and privilege to inform you five that if you're ready to fight and possibly die for Garobansurov, I'd be honored to accept your enlistment." Hearing the unanimous response of dutiful acceptance, Ulfenkerki continued, "We'll find places for you all immediately."

All five were ecstatic, thanked the General, told him how they'd never let him down, and followed Gregg to the army barracks to get acquainted with everyone and everything. Ulfenkerki and Jason stayed behind.

"It's looking good so far, even better than expected," emitted Jason, facing Ulfenkerki. "I think we'll be back to substantial numbers soon. Probably before having to commit to another major deployment."

"I wish I could see the future, and know when and against whom that deployment will be. Whether it be a regrouped Anolski, a new threat, or possibly against General Gamald over in Sarwa."

"That'd be nice, sir. Have you any news from The Nighteagle, regarding enemy moves and positions?"

Ulfenkerki replied, "Just the fact Anolski and his diminished army haven't been spotted in the countryside yet, and Gamald's presence is creating an intolerable atmosphere for all inhabitants of Sarwa. I can only hope the rest of the country isn't currently worse off than all of us here in our corner of the world."

"Let's hope," said Jason. "So, news from the capital and the other provinces is still minimal?"

"Correct, unfortunately."

"Do you think the rumors of Gamald's ruthlessness are as bad as what they're saying?" asked Jason.

"I certainly hope not, for the sake of us all. Whether it's Gamald or his soldiers acting unrestrictedly, I haven't heard of such cruelty in a very long time," answered the Black Bear.

"I don't think I've ever heard such diabolical acts in all my life. There've been reports of many farmers and their families within the vicinity of Sarwa getting murdered for their crops. I don't understand why the crops weren't just taken by force, with the civilians still being allowed to live."

"I've heard the atrocious reports as well, and make no sense of the Molisian's actions either."

As Ulfenkerki tailed off his statement, Gregg Hogarty unexpectedly returned from showing the new recruits their bunks and responsibilities. "General, sir, there's a man back at the barracks wanting to speak with you. I think he wishes to sell articles to the army."

"Alright, I'll see what he has to sell. Bring him to me."

Gregg walked back to the barracks and told Brom Quintaga to follow him to the General. Brom grabbed the handle of his cart eagerly, and dragged his armor suits to where the General and Jason were standing.

Brom released his grip on the cart, and began. "First of all, I had heard of the great victory here, General, and would like to personally extend gratitude to you and your command. My name's Brom."

"I appreciate your thanks. You've met Gregg. The other man standing beside me is Jason. What can we do for you?"

"I'm on a mission to locate my lost son, but assistance in finding him isn't exactly why I stand before you. I've run out of funds to continue my journey, and need to sell my life's labor. For the bulk of thirty years,

I've been constructing the three finest sets of armor in all of Garobansurov—at least many have told me they are. Each set has taken ten years to forge, and all contain cuirass with shoulder protection, helmet, gauntlets, greaves, and boots. I made them using the best metals available, and they're lighter and stronger than any other armor sets in existence. Initially, I formed them for my two sons and I, but since one has gone missing, and the other has also been searching, I've decided to sell in order to continue, for I've no idea how long the search will go on."

The Black Bear and Jason thoroughly inspected the armor, picking up and examining every piece. The focused duo surveyed for quality as best they knew how. Knowing entirely what they were doing, having many years' expertise between them, they came to their conclusions post five-minute inspection.

Ulfenkerki emitted, "I don't know of whom you speak, those boldly telling you that you had crafted the greatest sets of armor in all the land, but I must confess I concur with them. I thought I'd seen some pretty remarkable suits of armor in my day, but these are definitely the best I've ever viewed."

It took a while for Jason to speak of his opinion on the armor, for he was simply mesmerized by what was laid before him. He always dreamed of one day donning such metallic perfection, fighting for Garobansurov with an advantage other than one achieved through tireless training. Finally managing to snap out of his trance, he put forth, "If only one day I could accouter myself in a set as magnificent as this. Only then would I feel like an invincible warrior. They are the best on the continent, bar none."

Brom was happy to hear appraisal from such honorable and knowledgeable men. "I hope what I'm about to say doesn't influence you to think any less of me. But if I don't sell the armor, I'll have to continue on to Sarwa to offer it to the nobles therein, or anyone else interested in purchasing. I'm prepared to do anything to possibly save my son's life. I'll offer each set to you, Ulfenkerki, for half of what I'll offer anyone in Sarwa because I owe my and my family's freedom to you and your company. That would be five thousand gitis per set for you, ten thousand for the people of Sarwa and everyone else."

Ulfenkerki touched the armor one last time, and summoned, "First off, I'll tell you I'd do the same thing you're doing. Family comes first in situations such as these."

Before Kermoy Ulfenkerki continued, Jason blurted, "I agree, sir."

Ulfenkerki resumed, "Secondly, even though your price is more than fair, there is no way we could ever afford such an expenditure at this time. The toll of battle has far exceeded any of our imaginations, the expense of food particularly. And thirdly, you offering it to us at half the price does mean a lot to me."

Brom responded, "I thank you for your understanding of my situation, your compassion, and your time. I am truly heart-stricken at this pitfall, but I will persevere. Once I reach Sarwa, I'm hoping to sell the suits to Garobansurov loyalists."

"As for that," the Black Bear asserted, "even though you're doing what you think is best, I strongly feel you're risking your life going into the lion's den the way you are.

There are nothing but dangerous roads lying ahead in the direction of Sarwa."

"If my life is forfeit, then it's forfeit. I'm prepared to do anything," declared Brom.

Before a downcast Brom walked away, Ulfenkerki said one final thing to him: "May your road be free of peril, and your mission satisfied." Deep in his heart, Ulfenkerki knew Brom would run into trouble.

Jason popped back into his trance, depressed by the fact he couldn't afford the armor he yearned for all his life. He kept the memory of the sight of Brom's armor in his head for a long time.

As Brom walked despairingly away, lugging his cartful of treasures, he once again thought of how wonderful it would've been to fight alongside his sons. All three clad in the armor fashioned with his own two hands.

CHAPTER 7

HAVING ALREADY SPENT way too much time searching, Mick and Dave decided to be satisfied with what fighting sticks they found. Mick found a sturdy length of oak, while Dave located a firm piece of maple. Dave's was longer, but not as stout. They both spent a fair amount of time carving points at the end, not wanting the points too defined for safety purposes. They weren't technically trying to hurt each other. Just a friendly competition.

"Which rules shall we implement, Mick?"

"I think first and foremost there should be no eye lunges."

"Right; we wouldn't want to lose our eyes over a recreational spear fight," responded Dave. "I think a rule banning swings to the groin would be beneficial to all parties involved."

"I agree. Furthermore, a winner is declared when someone can no longer sustain the beating, and cries out the phrase, 'I'm no match for you in spear fighting.' We do have to make the punishment somewhat humbling."

"Definitely. I can't add further to fight protocol, so I'm ready if you are."

"Let's begin."

They both grabbed their spears, and initiated distance-check swings. Obviously, Dave reaped the advantage with distance, due to his longer spear, so immediately Mick aimed to counter this disadvantage by keeping the fight at close range. At the onset, they avoided any unnecessary spear-on-spear swings, because neither wanted to take any chances with their spears snapping—only being tree branches and all, not metal rods. For of that reason, Dave couldn't use his intrinsic strength much to his advantage, so Mick's elevated speed was a key factor in the fight. Dave countered the disadvantage by trying to keep at a distance, but it wasn't the easiest thing to perform, since Mick's objective was keeping the fight close range.

After roughly five minutes of the contest, both Mick and Dave had successfully landed countless blunt offenses and minor stab wounds. Even though they were equally battered, Mick was gaining the upper hand, due to Dave's constant struggle to stay out of Mick's sweet spot. Mick's speed advantage was too much for Dave to handle, and he couldn't keep up. Dave wasn't too distressed over the impending loss, because he knew he couldn't utilize his strength with tree branches.

Dave decided to capitulate from exhaustion, and started to vocalize the predetermined phrase, but had a hard time following through—he just couldn't stop laughing. "Oh, come on, is it imperative I say it?"

Mick replied, "Remember when we had our rock throwing contest? No matter how many times I asked not to, I still had to openly declare you the ultimate rock throwing champion. And that was in front of an audience."

"I remember. Yeah, that was a good day. Touché`. Alright I'll say it."

Dave focused on stopping his laughter to call out the submission phrase, but failed to see the hole in the ground gaping enough to ensnare a foot. He lost his balance and tripped to the ground. "I haven't done that in a while," Dave said, staring into the sky. "The bad news is I think I sprained my ankle."

"Do you think you can walk on it?"

After failing his attempt to walk further than fifty feet, Dave replied, "Nope. Not very far anyways."

"In an obliging world, your ankle will heal after a good night's sleep, and we can continue our journey in the morning. We've a lot of walking ahead of us."

"Yeah, hopefully."

Mick and Dave went back to their tents in the foundation, and went to bed early, in the hopes a longer sleep would help Dave's healing process. But to Dave's surprise, the ankle was worse in the morning.

Having witnessed Dave suffer an arduous exiting of the tent, Mick emitted, "I guess it seems we're going to be here a while yet."

"We could've been stranded in a much worse place than this," Dave communicated, while gazing admiringly at the surroundings.

"That's true. It won't be so bad to spend another night or two in this old foundation. I really hope it won't be any longer than that."

"Maybe If I sleep better tonight, the sprain will heal."

"Let's hope."

Mick made breakfast for the both of them, and sharpened swords. Since their swords were made from superb steel, they didn't require often sharpening, but because of the battle of Strwin's intensity, the swords needed a good honing.

The rest of the morning was spent playing rocks.

By afternoon, Mick's legs were getting a little restless, so he decided on a nature hike. "Don't get eaten by any wild animals, while I'm gone."

Dave chuckled. "I imagine in my immobilized state, I do look pretty vulnerable."

"If I was a wild animal, I'd eat you."

Mick chose the route offering the best scenery. For a time, he followed a ridge harboring mostly hardwoods, with an occasional balsam fir that Mother Nature decided to throw in for dramatic effect.

When Mick went hiking, he always liked to find the oldest tree in the area—a quirky habit he'd enjoyed since childhood. The winner of that particular walk was an oak he determined exceeded two hundred years. He touched it for whimsy.

Subsequent thirty minutes of walking, the ridge ended, so to prevent from getting lost, Hawk needed to find another landmark to follow through the wilderness, one that didn't lead him right back to the tents. After a scan, he located a creek at the bottom of the ridge he could follow.

He approached the creek, and noticed a small twelve-by-twelve cabin, camouflaged seamlessly against the surrounding flora. Mick noticed whoever lived there, or used to live there, was very proficient at living off the land. There was a small watermill situated at one of the creek's depth drop-offs, probably used for anonymous grinding purposes, grain perhaps. One of the deeper holes of the creek had a net-rigging suspended over it, just waiting to be put into action for the catching of trout. There were also small farming plots.

Upon further inspection, Mick concluded someone was definitely still living there, in light of the fact some of the farming plots were half-way harvested. Mick was in one of his more curious moods, so he decided to walk down to the cabin and knock on the door to meet this ingenious recluse.

An older, bearded man answered the door, holding the thickest book Mick had ever seen. Mick said, "I'm sorry to bother you, but my name is Mick Thraiker, and during my nature hike, I couldn't help but see your very interesting way of life. My curiosity got the best of me, and I was driven to meet you."

"I'm glad your curiosity got the best of you, because when I get visitors it's almost always a pleasant experience. It's mostly folks like you, interesting people bested by inquisitiveness. Not that there's been many."

Having been led into the cabin by the elderly, intriguing gentleman, Mick said, "Thank you so much for your hospitality, sir."

"People usually just call me the Hermit. I like to forget my past, and the name that went with it."

"I can respect that." Mick nodded in veneration. "I can't help but notice the novel in your hands, and its enormity. I've never before seen a book of that size."

"Nobody has. I wrote it, and could never acquire enough funds for its mass production."

"What's its premise?"

"It would take too long to give it justice, but you're welcome to sit here and read it."

"I certainly don't have the time for that, but your offer is more than generous. Maybe someday I'll come back and read the whole thing." Mick looked around at all the cabin's curiosities. He was drawn to the vast library, the books of which the Hermit had collected throughout time—company during lonely nights. "Your library is almost as impressive as the size of your book."

"I wish I had more. I've read each one at least three times now."

"How long have you lived here in God's country?"

"Come next spring, I've lived here fifteen years."

"The definition of solitude indeed. Do you have a copy of my favorite book, *Dom Quixoke?*"

"I sure do. Third one ever made is propped over there on that shelf," replied the Hermit, pointing at a shelf next to the fireplace.

Mick walked to the shelf, and as he looked at the book, he asked, "I'm guessing I probably don't have to ask, but do you have a copy of my second favorite book, *Davud Copperfeal?*"

"Yup—It's over there on the shelf with the rest of the sizable Chirles Deckons canon."

"I like it here," declared Mick. "Unfortunately, I can't walk back to my injured friend, and carry him here, so he can enjoy seeing this library while mending."

"How badly was he hurt?"

"Not too bad, he just sprained his ankle. He tripped in a hole while we were sparring."

"As soon as your legs are rested, I will follow you back to your friend, and see if I can help out medically. A person doesn't live alone out here in the wilderness without picking up at least a small amount of medical knowledge. Strolling down seclusion's path does have its advantages."

"That would be greatly appreciated, furthermore, I'm sure my friend, Dave, would love to meet you. We'll leave shortly—I'll finish ogling your extravagant library here, peruse a bit of your fat book, and I'll be ready."

"Take your time. If inanimate objects had souls, then certainly, my books would enjoy the attention."

Mick loosed a slight laugh, and asked, "Do you plan on living here for a long time yet?"

"I hope so, unless something drastic happens to me, an unforeseen occasion where I can no longer perform all the labor necessary to sustain myself."

"I imagine there to be a good amount of that." Mick finished his perusal, and said, "I'm ready when you are. I could stay and look at your library for the rest of the day, but I'm sure if I did, Dave would think something happened to me, and create a lone search party, limping his way through the forest to find me."

"A good friend indeed. I'm ready."

Mick and the Hermit left the cabin, and followed the ridge back towards Dave, but not before Mick asked if he could see the fishing net and watermill in action. The Hermit gladly complied, showing them both to Mick. Mick didn't notice it at first, but the net wasn't stationary. The Hermit could move it whenever and wherever he wanted. The Hermit deployed the net and actually caught three fish on the first try. As well, the watermill was no less than extraordinary to Mick, who was thoroughly impressed with all the Hermit's machinations.

After the thirty-minute walk, and the foundation and tents propped therein were within sight, Mick yelled out to Dave, signaling his return. Dave heard the announcement, and hollered back for the fun of it.

Mick led the Hermit to Dave for introductions. Mick told Dave everything about his encounter with the Hermit. He also informed Dave of the Hermit's intentions to help with the ankle.

Dave was pleased to meet the interesting fellow. Conversation began immediately. "With you living in the area for fifteen years, have you ever seen the people who used to live within this foundation when it was a more complete house, or heard any stories concerning them?" asked Dave.

"The house was long gone when I built my cabin, nor have I come across them or any new home they may have built. I did utilize some of the nails I found scattered in the rubble here, to supplement my own building supply. As for stories concerning this site, the only ones I've ever heard were they used to farm the surrounding area, and when they got old, the married couple still tended to the farm right up until the day they died. As you can see, most of the old farm fields are now covered in trees."

Mick returned, "So judging by my estimation of the trees' ages growing in the old farm fields, and the age of the one in the foundation, I put the downfall of the farm at minimally fifty years ago."

They continued their conversation for a long time, of which a chunk comprised Mick explaining to Dave the impressiveness of the Hermit's library. Dave grew envious of Mick for being able to see it, and declared that when he could walk, they'd walk past the cabin on their way north to see the library. He didn't have to convince Mick very much on that point, Mick was already thinking it.

The Hermit had inspected Dave's ankle halfway through the long conversation. He knew what he wanted to do about the ankle.

When twilight came the Hermit told Mick to follow.

After ten minutes of following, Mick found himself in a marsh where the Hermit began searching for a specific plant.

When the Hermit found what he was looking for, he hand flourished for Mick to come by him. "See this plant here? It's always found in low-lying wetlands and recognizable by its fishlike odor, especially when the stem is snapped."

Mick noticed the smell of the plant and generally how it looked. It didn't really have any recognizable features other than the smell, but Mick was pretty certain he could find the plant again if needed. Mick commented, "I would've never thought there was a plant with such a noticeably pungent smell."

"Indeed, there is." The Hermit harvested a couple of the plants and said, "I got for what we have come. We can walk back to Dave now."

Upon arriving back by Dave, the Hermit worked the plants into a pulp by using two rocks to grind them down. Then, he mixed the powder into a cup of water. "What this concoction will do, when drinking before falling asleep tonight, is help your ankle heal better by putting you into a deeper sleep than normal. It's pretty much a well-known fact your body is a superior healer when you sleep better. If you drink it way before you intend to fall asleep, it'll probably put you asleep anyways."

"Sounds good, I'll do that," voiced Dave.

Mick and Dave both thanked the Hermit for his medical help. After a few more minutes of conversation, the Hermit started the not overly long walk back to his cabin, confident Dave's ankle would mend, and he'd see the pair at his cabin in the morning.

When night came and he was ready to fall asleep, Dave grabbed the cup of brew, and chugged. "Hopefully this works. I'm sick of being immobile."

AT THE CRACK of dawn, eight hours after Dave had slammed his sedative concoction, First Lieutenant Leedle rushed into headquarters (once a dance hall) and announced to General Hyraugh Gamald his presence was needed at Sarwa's main gate.

Gamald stood up, and angrily said, "This better be important, I haven't even eaten breakfast yet."

On his way to the gate, Gamald proceeded past one of the housekeepers, and elbowed her in the face, showing no remorse. He wasn't sure if it was an accident or not. He didn't entirely care. Gamald hated being inconvenienced by being asked to report somewhere so early in the morning.

The woman ended up with a broken nose, and no apology.

When arriving at Sarwa's main gate, Gamald was surprised by what he saw. Throughout the night, all of General Anolski's army who'd survived the battle at Strwin had filtered into town. They were reporting at Sarwa's main gate, because that was the point where Anolski had told them in the confusion of battle's end to meet up.

General Gamald approached a battle-bruised General Anolski, and said, "I was aware you endured, General, but unaware so many of your soldiers did too. Apparently, I wrongfully assumed the bulk of your force got wiped out at Strwin."

Anolski responded, "I wish more had lived, but this is what's left of my army."

"I'm glad to see you. We need all the soldiers we can get for future undertakings."

"Which undertakings are those?"

"I couldn't tell you yet, but I can guarantee they'll be a force spent creatively—certainly an endeavor in the realm of Molisian-style warfare," responded Gamald. He projected an unholy smile, accentuated by the showing of only a few of his bottom teeth, the kind of smile that scared children and small animals.

Anolski reveled in Gamald's intentions. "Excellent. I hope my soldiers and I won't be too much of a bother regarding available food rations and sleeping arrangements."

"No, no, don't you go and worry about that. There are plenty of beds and food for us. It's the townsfolk who'll go tired and hungry."

"I like your thinking," Anolski remarked. "It's too bad we lost Bamsov and almost all his archers. They would've been helpful in these future undertakings of yours."

"Don't go and worry about that either. I already have a plan in motion that'll secure a new contingent of archers."

Anolski was satisfied with the state of affairs and the rendezvous at Sarwa. He parted with Gamald and headed for the nearest tavern.

Immediately, Gamald went to instruct the cooks to prepare more food at future mealtimes. Also, the General spread the word that beds needed to be made available for the new soldiers, which meant more civilians would lose theirs. Content in the size increase in his battle-ready army, Gamald joined Anolski at the tavern.

MICK WOKE AND crawled out of his tent, anxious to see if the Hermit's remedy had worked for Dave. At first, he was surprised not to see Dave out and about right away in the morning, but after a while, he was glad Dave was sleeping in. It was a good sign.

Dave finally woke and, to Mick's satisfaction, gracefully exited his tent. He walked around with renewed vigor. Clearly, his ankle had mended. "I slept so well last night I must've had at least seventy-five dreams."

"That and seventy-five times of waking me with your snoring."

"Never-mind that right now. We've got things to do."

"Good subject avoidance there."

Dave chuckled. "It's good to be good at something."

Mick and Dave took down camp, and resumed their self-chosen mission. But first, they stopped at the Hermit's shack to offer thanks, and so Dave could experience everything within.

"It's good to see you were able to walk here, Dave. The plant must've worked," emitted the Hermit, after opening his front and only door.

Dave responded, "I don't think I've ever experienced a deeper sleep in my life."

"Good, that's what was intended. Try and keep the plant's identity somewhat secret. If everyone was aware of its properties, the plant would surely become endangered."

"Makes sense. Will do."

"What's your favorite book, Dave? And I'll tell you if I have it."

"I've always been partial to *War, And Then Some More War*."

"Not including my own masterwork, it's the fattest book of the library. It's sitting over there." The Hermit pointed to the mammoth sitting invitingly in the upper-right corner of his largest bookcase.

Dave paged through the novel nostalgically, and said, "I sure do love these characters." Dave carefully placed the fragile book back onto the shelf. "What do you usually grind with your mill by the creek?"

"Sometimes wheat and oats, but I mainly grind field corn. It's the crop that grows the most consistently and efficiently here. I have many stands of it strewn about in forest clearings within a mile radius of here. I use the cornmeal to create my fabulous cornbread. Do you want to try some?"

"I sure would."

"Would you like some as well, Mick?" asked the Hermit.

"Definitely, thank you."

"It's a delicacy for me here, certainly. I eat it pretty much every day."

The Hermit went into the cabin to fetch the cornbread, and handed it out. He waited to see whether or not it tasted as delicious to Mick and Dave as it did to him. Both Dave and Mick ended up telling him the cornbread was a real treat. The pair received a bundle of it to bring along for the journey.

Dave and Mick took one last look at the library and its multitude of interesting books, most of which they'd never before read. Given the time, they'd love to sit and read them all. So many captivating stories.

When the titles of every book were read at least twice by the duo, they decided it was time to part ways with the fascination of a bearded man.

"Thank you so much for stopping by my little corner of the world. I do hope you stop back some time. Maybe spend a few days reading the book I wrote."

Mick responded, "We will someday. It may take a while, but we'll make a commitment to return. I do think it'll take more than a few days to read your monster of a book though, probably closer to a week."

Dave added, "Thank you so much for the help with my ankle. Speaking of ankles, you wouldn't happen to have extra pairs of socks lying around, would you? We both ruined practically all of ours in the last swamp we traversed."

"They would be yours, if I had some, but as you can see, I don't wear them myself."

"You know," Dave said, "I didn't even notice that at all. It's not too often you really get a good look at someone's feet."

Just before Dave and Mick turned to depart from the architecturally simple, yet astronomically cozy and feature-laden home of their new friend, the Hermit supplied parting words. "Always remember to sometimes switch into coast mode, because the point of the journey is not just to reach your destination."

Mick smiled in agreement, and said, "Very true. A great aspect of life is indeed found in the sum of all your experiences."

The Hermit returned the smile, waved goodbye, and enjoyed the rest of his day.

MILITARILY EDUCATING AS best he knew how, Jason shouted to one of the new recruits: "Along with your arm swing, don't forget to utilize some momentum from using your head as a sort of pendulum to gain extra ground during your sword lunges." Training was in full bore.

General Ulfenkerki heard Jason's teaching words, walking into the training grounds, and added some words of instruction of his own. "Along with what Jason said, remember don't just aim for the heart when performing lunges. Aim for the entire heart, lung, neck area. Hitting the heart is a pretty hard feat to accomplish, especially on a moving target. So, by aiming for a bigger, also vital, target, you greatly increase the chance of success."

In unison, all the new recruits shouted, "Yes, sir."

Training continued, while Jason met up with the General in an out-of-the-way locale to discuss military matters.

"You're doing extremely well with your new duty, Jason, but that comes as no surprise. Unrelated, I'm undoubtedly pleased in how close our headcount is to where it was before the battle at Strwin. I'm sure it won't be much longer than a few weeks to be battle-ready again. The new recruits will be a little raw for future operations, but they seem adequate. They'll only get better under your tutelage, Lieutenant."

"Thank you, sir. I must admit, I'm a little worried about the new archers filtering through the ranks. Wouldn't it be more advantageous for Rayton to take on new archers."

"True, but I guess he has his reasons for not taking any of them on."

"Though, the thought is nice of having archers under our command."

"Agreed," said the Black Bear. "I'm sure we won't have any problems optimizing the situation. Come with me to the gate. I'm expecting an emissary from the Nighteagle."

Jason dismissed training session for the time being, and accompanied the General in meeting with the emissary.

The three convened near the front gate, and proceeded to Ulfenkerki's office, exchanging small talk along the way.

Upon arrival inside the office, the emissary started on important matters, those instructed by the Nighteagle to discuss. "Nobody knows exactly what Gamald is going to do next, but the Nighteagle expects the Molisian general will organize a battalion, and attempt to add Thraug to his list of conquered cities. General Nighteagle isn't very confident he can hold Thraug against what forces Gamald is capable of sending."

Ulfenkerki politely interrupted the emissary before he continued. "I know what you're going to say next, but let it be known you didn't even have to say it. Our army will be up and running very shortly, and will unquestionably assist the Nighteagle in defending the Garobansurovian town of Thraug. I'd hate to see anything unfortunate happen to that grizzled, up in years general of yours. Tell him I said that last part too."

"I will definitely relay that verbatim, emphasizing the honor reflected in your words," put forth the emissary. "I'll relay the good-humored jab too."

With his information, the liaison exited the office in hurrying fashion, and headed back to Thraug.

"I like it when these meetings are short," Ulfenkerki said to Jason, as the wind from the closing door wafted past.

"Me too." Jason inquired, "If he does, when do you think Gamald will march?"

"Hopefully not for a few weeks yet. Our army isn't quite ready. Nevertheless, we will assist the Nighteagle no matter how ready we are."

After five minutes talking about inconsequential matters, Jason left Ulfenkerki's office, and returned to training grounds to resume the training session. The General remained and thought heavily on consequential matters.

MICK AND DAVE had covered a couple miles to the north since parting ways with the Hermit. Dave was still in amazement at how quickly his ankle healed during the night. He gave the old injury a shake every once in a while, just to see if the mending was indeed real, and not a figment of his imagination. Astonishingly, it was still real. Plus, judging by how efficiently he was walking, Dave determined his ankle was supporting his body weight well enough for battle if need be.

They approached a site nestled serenely on a lakeside, constituting a handful of sturdy, semi-permanent tents. There was evidence of recent activity. But the inhabitants were nowhere around.

Mick and Dave didn't dawdle at the site, they didn't want the residents to return with hasty judgement involving whether or not thievery was transpiring. They took one last look around to admire the homeliness of the place and continued on.

They weren't but ten paces away from the campsite when Mick and Dave saw the population of the tent community returning to their homes from what looked like a day of fishing out on the lake. Mutual hand waves in the name of friendliness were extended. Mick and Dave gave thought to going back to the site to view the day's catch and exchange banter, but decided against it. They returned to walking northward.

"It'd sure be agreeable, if we were strong enough to carry around tents similar to those on that lakeside," commented Mick. "The tents were a husky lot. We'd be sojourning in style."

"I concur, but if we were that strong, we wouldn't even need tents. Forces of nature would be so afraid of us they'd simply redirect their paths around us."

Mick stared at Dave with his jaw dropped. A smile eventually crept over, and he erupted into an all-out laugh.

The morning laughs echoed right up until lunch. They, of course, had to eat cornbread for the midday meal, since having received so much from the Hermit. The sweet, yellow treat had to be finished off before getting wastefully moldy. A task they by no means minded.

CARRIE NOSTALGICALLY ROLLED the jeweled adornment across her palm with her thumb. Her new husband, Loyd, had given her the necklace as a birthday present when she was younger. It was one of the happiest days of her life, it being the day she knew she wanted to spend the rest of her life with Loyd, a decision she's been ecstatic with ever since.

"I know the degree of turmoil going through your mind right now, for I'm burdened by the same," offered Loyd sympathetically. "It took me a year and a half of hard house-building labor to earn enough money to pay for that necklace. I truly wish there was another way, but we need the money now, and I don't see any other ways of acquiring it."

"I know. It's just that it's so hard to do. Other than my engagement ring and your love, it's the greatest thing you've ever given me. I suppose I could look at it in more positive terms—at least we're not to a point where I have to sell the engagement ring. So, it could be worse."

"That's the spirit, honey, let's hurry or we won't catch up to the caravan," said Loyd.

Carrie quickly put the necklace back on. "Alright."

Starting to run, Carrie and Loyd tried to catch up to the traveling merchant caravan that'd passed them by previously. They had high hopes of selling the necklace for a handsome price.

The caravan had certainly seen its share of the road, and consisted of multiple personalities, none overly virtuous. Had Loyd and Carrie been gifted with hindsight, knowing the merchants to be of an unscrupulous nature, they would've never approached them. There was no way of knowing—traveling merchants didn't typically air such ruthlessness.

But sometimes things happen the way they're supposed to.

With Carrie's right hand in Loyd's left, the duo finally caught up to the wagons. Loyd attempted to get the attention of one of the stoic guards walking in the rear, but failed. They hurried to get around to the front end of one of the wagons to try and get a better response. "Excuse me, excuse me," shouted Loyd.

"Speak quickly, we're very busy," responded Urt, a merchant.

"I see you deal in various goods and merchandise. Do you also happen to buy certain items of value?" Loyd blurted.

"From time to time we'll buy an item or two, if it grabs our attention," said Urt, before slowing the caravan to a halt. "What is it you have to offer?"

While still holding Carrie's hand, Loyd kissed her on the cheek. He let go of her hand, removed the necklace from her neck, and whispered in her ear, "It'll be okay." Loyd felt the necklace in his hands for what he assumed the last time, and handed it to Urt. "It's solid gold and the jewel in the pendant is a ruby."

Knowledgeable in the realm of jewelry, Urt began examining the necklace. He looked at the jewel with a magnifying glass he'd pulled out of his pocket. "This is quite valuable. You must've spent a pile of gitis on it."

"Certainly, sir. I had saved for a year and a half to pay for it. I'm not expecting to sell it for what I paid, but if can get half, I'd be happy, which will give you plenty of wiggle room to make a profit."

Urt tightened his hold on the necklace, and uttered, "I'm sure I'll have even more wiggle room, if I don't pay anything at all." Urt slid the necklace into his right pocket, gave a particular sort of nod to the hired guards, and hid behind the wagon.

On the command, four hired guards surrounded Loyd, tackled him, and pinned him to the ground before he was able to unsheathe his sword. Carrie couldn't run away, because she couldn't bear the thought of her husband getting hurt. Full of rage, she tried her best to rescue Loyd, but two guards grabbed her, and stole everything else she possessed—including her engagement/wedding ring. Still pinned to the ground, Loyd was stripped of his weapons, and his dignity. The holler Loyd loosed was heard for miles.

The guards tied the couple to a tree and the caravan sped off south, Urt menacingly clutching what was now his.

"Are you alright, my love?" Loyd asked Carrie, his back to a tree.

"I'm okay, but they stole everything, including the ring," replied Carrie.

"We will get it back. We will get everything back, I promise. Luckily these ropes aren't tied very tight. I think I can struggle free."

After a slight struggle, Loyd freed himself from his bondage. Carrie was also free in no time. His excitement from the freedom was short-lived, however, for a thought crept into his mind that was so terrifying he nearly froze. He didn't want to share the thought with his beloved, it was too heinous. Post-haste, Loyd sent the terrible visualization of his wife being raped as far away as possible.

The pair started up the hill to the south in pursuit of the caravan, looking for weapons of any kind along the way.

Chapter 8

Hawk and Leopard had just finished their cornbread when they heard a holler emanating in the distance.

"I don't know who or what is making that holler, but I can guarantee the agony behind it is genuine."

"It sure sounds that way."

Mick and Dave returned to their own journey northward. After traveling for not much more than twenty minutes, they spotted a caravan from a high vantage point, moving briskly towards them. The caravan was a half a mile in the distance, and closing the gap quickly. But when the caravan managed to close half the gap, they abruptly turned to the left, down a barely discernible, far less travelled road.

"Something weird is going on. See how they stopped to cover their tracks. They're probably being followed, and don't want to get caught," said Mick. "I don't think they saw the two of us."

"I think we should post up at the point where they veered off, and wait patiently to see what happens. If the plot thickens, we'll act on the course of action seems most honorable."

"Very good plan."

Mick and Dave hid behind fat oak trees, and waited quietly for whomever or whatever was pursuing the caravan.

Five minutes went by, and Mick and Dave spotted the likely pursuers in the distance running towards them. They surmised the two were the pursuers, because it wasn't too often folks were seen performing their morning exercises so far from civilization.

When the man and woman were close enough to see clearly, Mick and Dave could tell they both were pretty battered.

Mick and Dave removed themselves from behind their oak trees, unintentionally spooking Loyd and Carrie.

"Oh, what new hell is this?" erupted Loyd, in shock.

Mick calmly put his hands in the air, fearing irrationalities from the stranger, and said, "We mean you no harm. We've been witnessing a scene unfold before our eyes for a while now, and wish to understand the truth of it all."

"We're in pursuit of a caravan. Have you seen it at all?"

"Now that depends," emitted Dave.

"On what?" asked Loyd, trying to calm himself.

"Supplying the information you seek depends on whether or not relaying it to you would be the right thing to do. We will hear your story; and then, make our judgement as to the course of action applied forthwith," responded Mick.

Loyd and Carrie understood the logic behind what was being presented to them, and explained everything that had transpired as quickly as possible.

After hearing Loyd's narration, Mick and Dave looked at each other and nodded. In many circumstances, because they knew each other so well, Thraiker and Ghrere knew the other was thinking on the same page without saying a word. This was one of those occasions.

They both deduced Loyd wasn't making his story up, due to the fact they knew it was astronomically rare in Garobansurov for a person with obvious sword fighting skills to be running around in hostile wilderness wielding just a pointed stick as a weapon. Loyd being an adept swordfighter stuck out like a sore thumb to other swordfighters.

Mick pointed at Loyd's stick, and said, "That's one of the reasons we believe your story beyond the shadow of a doubt. You weren't the aggressors, in light of the fact nobody commits a violent crime with a brittle tree limb. They're good for friendly competitions, but not violence."

"Even if it's the best stick in their immediate woods," commented Loyd, trying to alleviate some tension.

Both Mick and Dave smiled, reassured Loyd and Carrie things weren't as bad as they seemed, and said they'd do their best to help.

Dave walked to exactly where the caravan turned, and said, "Right here is where the caravan veered off, and covered their tracks. It wasn't too long ago, so I think we could probably catch up to them, before they reach the next town or settlement."

Loyd clapped his hands together in vigorous enthusiasm, and emitted, "Okay then, I'm ready, let's go."

Mick grabbed the trusty stick from Loyd's hand, and threw it back into the woods. He reached into his greave to pull out the dagger, and handed the freshly sharpened weapon to Loyd.

Loyd looked over the dagger. "I suppose this will work better than the best stick in the woods."

Dave gave his dagger to Carrie.

Turning back not an option, the quartet started their feverish pursuit. They caught up to the caravan after only an hour of running. With the wagons in sight, they paused to discuss their plan of action.

"Nightfall will arrive shortly, so I think we should wait until then to initiate our ambush."

Loyd, Carrie and Mick considered Dave's words, and Loyd responded, "Good idea, but why not wait until they fall asleep? That way their defenses are limited."

Mick answered, "Normally that'd be best, but in this situation it's possible they won't sleep, and if we spend time waiting, it may decrease our advantage. We don't know if more allies intend to join them while we're waiting for them to sleep."

"Sound logic," Loyd said.

Dave remarked, "Also remember we're just here to retrieve stolen goods, this isn't a deadly mission of revenge. Aim to wound, not kill, unless absolutely necessary."

Loyd and Carrie shook their heads in agreement, and the strategy meeting was adjourned.

The four of them continued to follow the criminals from a distance, far enough away to avoid being spotted, but close enough as to not lose their quarry. When nightfall was almost upon them, they finalized their operation's blueprint.

"Carrie, my beautiful wife, I'm sure you're just as full of rage as I am, but I would be far more comfortable if you stayed out of the fight, waiting at a safe distance."

"I will, but I can't promise if I see you getting badly hurt, I won't come rushing in."

"I guess there wouldn't be anything I could do, if you decided to do that." Loyd was proud beyond measure his wife exuded admirable courage.

Mick asked Carrie and Loyd, "Did you happen to see inside what kind of apparatus they put your jewelry?"

"All I know is last I saw the necklace it was going inside the man called Urt's pocket. The ring and other smaller items, I've no idea where they were stowed," Carrie responded.

"I guess we'll have to operate on the fly for the most part when we make contact."

Dave weighed in, "There's six of them, upon my investigation—four guards, two merchants."

"That seems correct," Loyd noted. "Urt is the smaller-statured merchant, and may still have the necklace in his right pocket. I don't think either merchant is very skilled in combat, since they supplied nothing physically to the robbery. Now on the other hand, the guards certainly knew what they were doing."

Mick thought a bit. "With it generally being our three against their four, the three of us claiming the element of surprise, I don't think it'll come to anyone having to die tonight, our side or theirs."

"That should stand true," said Dave.

"The moment of attack should be initiated when one—optimally two—of the guards is isolated from the others. That way we can better our odds before they even know what's going on," said Mick, while inspecting his *Black Needle* sword for dirt.

Dave, Carrie and Loyd agreed, and due to the power of unconscious suggestion, they all started inspecting their weapons for debris as well. When all were satisfied in their weapons' appearances, they resumed the hunt.

They trailed patiently, until the caravan finally stopped for the night. In moonless darkness, with eyes on the enemy, the quartet hid behind a boulder balancing three gigantic logs. They patiently waited for when the time was right.

When one of the guards stood by a tree to alleviate himself, the trio struck. The three snuck quietly up to the isolated guard, and before he knew what hit him, he was tied to the same tree he was poisoning with urination. The guard's surprisingly dull sword was stripped, and discarded deep into the woods. Literally, the caravan was caught with their pants down.

However, after the success, Mick, Dave and Loyd lost their element of surprise. The remaining three villainous guards charged. The merchants, thinking they were sneaky, tried to hide themselves and their carts in the thicker part of the woods. Carrie watched it all unfurl from a safe distance, hoping it would be over quickly.

Judging by numbers alone, the battle was evenly matched—one opposer for each. Although in reality, the matchup was pretty one-sided. Mick and Dave were far superior to their opponents in swordsmanship, but because Mick and Dave didn't want to simply stab the guards in the vitals, they had to resort to less dramatic maneuvers. Ending the fight proved to be difficult.

Loyd was having a harder time than Mick and Dave in holding back the urge of killing his opposing guard. So far so good. Loyd also had to deal with the fact that his opponent kept trying to work the fight over to where his ally was tied to the tree. Loyd cycled through a mental litany to help abstain from killing—*Don't kill; they have a family; they're just hired guards; grab the ring, necklace and go.*

It took five minutes for Hawk and Leopard to force their respective opponents into a state of exhaustion, enough so Dave alone could handle the two guards, while Mick searched for jewelry.

Mick easily located the feebly hidden carts, and began searching for the items, simultaneously repelling the two merchants. The weak merchants were no longer of any age to threaten someone as skillful as Mick, or even significantly hinder his job at hand.

The necklace was no longer in Urt's pocket, so Mick searched for it elsewhere. He started by going through the wooden boxes in the front of the biggest cart, but came up empty-handed. He proceeded to the back of the cart to look for any possible places one might've stored a cache, but found nothing there as well. One more wagon to search.

Meanwhile, Dave was doing his best to keep the guards at bay, same with Loyd. Dave's technique involved executing repeated slices at the legs, while keeping his adversaries off-balance. Loyd continued to go through his litany, while repeatedly knocking his opponent in the head with the butt of the dagger Mick gave to him. Dave and Loyd were trying to stall long enough so Mick could do his thing, unimpeded.

There was a point when Dave started to be a little preoccupied by a noise coming from the bottom of Loyd's boot—a weird clicking noise. Dave couldn't understand what on a pair of boots could possibly make that kind of noise. He kept thinking about it during his fight. Eventually he gave up his mind's pursuit, and put more focus into his task at hand. But he knew it was going to bother him until he found out what the sound was.

Everything was going exceptionally smooth, until bad luck struck. The guard with whom Loyd was clashing managed a lucky sword swing, and nicked the ropes keeping the fourth guard from joining the fray. The fourth guard had been waiting patiently while tied to the tree, gathering vigor. With fresh muscles, the guard unleashed a torrent of sword swings so mighty they changed the entire dynamics of the fight. Loyd was overwhelmed.

Dave did his best to help, but options were running out. They either had to start killing, or Mick had to find for what he was looking, so they could all run off into the night.

Dave found just enough time to let out shouts. "Mick, the fourth is loose. We're having a hard time keeping them away from you. I hope you're almost done. We can't hold much longer."

Immediately after Mick heard Dave's shouts, he nervously located a locked wooden box amongst the merchandise in the small cart. Hoping he'd found for what he was looking, he took a massive swing at the box's lock with his sword. Luckily, the lock popped open. When he swung open the lid, he was both excited and heart-stricken. He'd found a supply of jewelry and anonymous gemstones, but there was no way he'd be able to locate the right ones in a reasonable amount of time. Just then, he heard another holler from Dave. "Hurry, Mick, it's almost to the point of our lives or theirs."

Mick thought quickly and with great focus. He rationalized instead of witnessing any deaths, he'd rush to help, taking the whole box with, and hope the ring and necklace were amongst its clutter. He clutched the box, pushed Urt to the ground one last time, and ran towards Dave and Loyd.

Having reached the skirmish with box in hand, Mick executed a few sword swings aimed at the guards to slow them down.

Mick, Dave and Loyd, defining the phrase all of a sudden, took off running as fast as they could. Loyd yelled out to Carrie, informing her to start running, but she was attentive and already doing so. The four guards, Urt, and the other merchant started to chase after them, but failed to catch up, due to fatigue from the fight.

The thieves were out of Loyd and Carrie's lives forever.

The quartet reached a point far enough away to feel they could stop running. Coincidentally, it was right back to where Mick and Dave had stashed their gear before getting involved in the predicament.

"Well, hopefully this was all a great success, and what you lost is in this box somewhere," said Mick, handing the box to Loyd and Carrie.

Carrie opened the box, and as luck would have it, located her stolen items rather quickly. She spotted them fast because she was well acquainted with their exact appearances, due to having worn them half her life. Every contour, every facet a staple of her memory.

She put on her treasures, and ran over to Loyd for an unforgettable embrace. She would've held him for an hour, but realized she hadn't yet thanked Mick and Dave. "Our new friends, I've never met a more noble pair in all my life. What you did today, in our most vulnerable hour, we couldn't possibly ever repay. Hopefully, someday, we can try." Carrie dished out hugs to Mick and Dave.

Loyd added, "Where did you guys learn to fight like that? You fight as if you were born with swords already attached to your hands. More importantly, I must say I'll always be on your side, whatever you do. Such genuineness is rarely seen, but when it is seen a person is sure to remember."

Mick and Dave smiled huge. Mick responded, "I see the same respectable character in the both of you. It really has been an honor to fight alongside you both."

Dave joined in. "I really hope the two of you live a long, blissful life, never having to go through with something like this again. Though, there's one thing I just have to know. Loyd, what in tarnation makes that odd clicking noise on the bottom of your boots? I heard it in the fight, and just couldn't take my mind off it."

Loyd smiled, removed his boot, handed it to Dave, and said, "A few years back, I bought this really nice pair of boots, but for some reason, compared to the left, the right boot received much wear at the heel, so much wear a hole was forming. Because I had paid so much for them, I couldn't just throw them away and buy new ones. Instead, I had a cobbler insert a durable, metal plate over the hole in the boot. Now, every time I step on a stone, twig, or basically anything hard, the plate does this sort of bending at the hinge action, producing the clicking sound you hear."

Dave examined the plate on the boot, and pressed on it to create the sound. "I do have to say this is definitely the first time I've seen such a thing. It's not too often metal is used to repair boots. Ingenious. Thanks for showing me. I probably would've lost sleep trying to figure out the sound on my own."

"My pleasure."

Loyd and Carrie both hugged their new friends, and said their goodbyes. They started to walk away, but before they got too far, Carrie abruptly turned around and ran back to Mick and Dave. "I almost forgot, here you go," said Carrie, as she handed back the box of jewelry swiped from the caravan.

"I'm afraid not, that box belongs to you now for everything you had to go through. You might need it in the future," Mick said.

"Are you sure? You don't need any of it for traveling expenses or anything?"

"We're sufficiently covered in that department. Thank you for the thought. Please, take it," Dave implored.

Carrie unexpectedly carried the box back to Loyd. One more time, the both of them shouted, "Goodbye!"

"I'm glad to have met those two. Their heroism is indelibly implanted in my mind," Carrie said to Loyd, as they resumed their journey.

"Hopefully we'll see them again someday," Loyd proclaimed, before turning to glimpse Mick and Dave silhouetted against the distant light.

GREGG HOGARTY WAS proving more and more every day how valuable he was as a new enlistee of General Ulfenkerki's army. His skill in and knowledge of battle was top-notch. He was charged with assisting Jason Thorncat in transforming green recruits into battle-ready status.

"I think in a week or two the General will have us heading to Thraug to help out the Nighteagle in his defensive quest," said Jason to Gregg, as the two walked down the avenue.

"By then, I'm sure almost all of the trainees will be ready. There are a few progressing too slowly, who'll be left behind, but that number isn't very high."

"They'll understand. There'll be plenty of battles to come for them."

Completely changing the subject, Gregg commented, "When you were a kid, had you ever thought about living the freelance lifestyle with Mick and Dave? Did they at the time express their interests in such pursuits, or converse on it from a philosophical standpoint?"

"They occasionally openly discussed their theories," said Jason, "and showed signs they wanted to experience the world untethered, while still risking their lives for honor. I can't deny I've thought of immersing myself in such a world, but I 've always been the kind needing to express my combat skills alongside many people—the more the better."

"I'm the same way. I wouldn't be here if I wasn't. I doubt I could handle Mick and Dave's relative solitude. I'm happy to be friends with such unique individuals."

"As am I. Honestly, I wouldn't be surprised to see the return of Hawk and Leopard at some point during this war, in some unorthodox fashion," replied Jason.

"You know them better than I. But let's hope they do."

Gregg and Jason spent a moment of their walk pondering what possible adventures Mick and Dave were currently experiencing.

The two soldiers arrived at the training square for the appointed battle exercise, and got right to work on the recruits. Jason instructed the students to begin morning stretches, while Gregg watched on for chances to impart his experience.

Occasionally, during training sessions, the General would present himself—the new recruits always enjoyed being in his presence. Many of the enlistees had joined the army strictly because of things they'd heard of his merit. Ulfenkerki's legend had spread far and wide.

However, that day, the Black Bear was busy in the armory, cataloguing inventory, and making sure everything was in prime working order. The new cadets were never granted the chance that day to show off for the General.

After initial calisthenics were completed, the students sparred with each other at half strength for a few hours.

The morning training session was concluded with a thirty-minute discourse by Jason on fight theory, with occasional additions from Gregg.

After session was dismissed, Jason and Gregg decided to partake in an hour's worth of small game hunting in the nearby woods, an enjoyable activity to escape the drudgeries of a busy schedule. Plus, it didn't hurt to gain a little meat for winter freezing.

Ready for action, the pair walked out Strwin's front gate and towards the woods to the east. Along their way to the nearby conifer forest, Gregg and Jason walked past Rayton holding archery training. From a distance, they could see Chad Loytin's perfect cluster of target arrows embedded deeply and centrally.

When the pair drew closer to Chad, Jason commented, "Shooting well this morning, I see."

"I shoot well every morning," Chad replied with a cocky smirk.

"No doubt, no doubt," returned Jason. He and Gregg walked away from Chad, and over to Rayton for what they hoped would be a better greeting.

"Sure is a fine day for the whistling of swift arrows," Jason said to Archer-General Rayton.

Rayton looked at Jason as if being disturbed, and remarked, "That it is. What brings you out here this morning?"

Jason ignored Rayton's unaffable expression, thinking bad days happen to us all. "Gregg and I are heading to the east forest for a little hunting between sessions."

"Good luck with that. Things are busy here." Rayton glanced at Jason and Gregg, and inched away, presenting no chance for further discussion.

Rayton resumed his participation in the archery assembly, while Gregg and Jason went on to flash two squirrels and a rabbit away from their cozy, forested existences. It wasn't enough meat to impact winter freezing, but the kills were enough for the pair to feel their aim that day was true.

RAIN CAME DOWN pretty heavily when Hawk and Leopard reached a point many miles from where they'd parted with Loyd and Carrie—a cold and very unpleasant sort of rain.

"I wouldn't be surprised if this was the last rain of the year. I'm sure it'll switch to snow soon."

"You're probably right, Dave, dreadfully. It's been a while since we've had any excitement in the snow. Hopefully our toleration level of the colorless disarray of frozen ice crystals hasn't decreased in degree."

"We are getting older," Dave replied.

The duo took refuge in a throng of balsam firs to wait out the rain—an inevitable exercise in patience.

After an hour's halt, the rain cloud dissipated, and Mick and Dave persisted on.

Smooth terrain was under foot for a couple hours, and eventually they came upon a slow moving, highly eutrophicated river. They couldn't remember the name of the river, but they knew it was on a map somewhere.

"This sure is a hindrance. I know we have to cross this swamp hole somehow to get to the northern border. Who knows where the nearest bridge is?"

"I hope we find one, Mick. Swimming across ole' weedy here would greatly ruin my day," declared Dave.

Post an hour search of the river line, they triumphantly located a bridge, but the triumph was short-lived, for they were ten years too late. The bridge was in utter ruin, and seemed to have been for a long time.

"If I have to swim through these leech-infested weeds, I'm going to scream. How in the world does anyone get across this thing?" said Dave, in a raised voice.

"We usually just swim," a stranger said unexpectedly.

Mick and Dave walked towards the stranger, a youth accompanied by an apparent friend or relative. The carefree children had been playfully catching frogs on the opposite side of the river from where they lived.

"We always swim across to this side to catch frogs, because it seems there's always more over here," commented Tyler.

Tyler and Timmy—both blonde haired, blue eyed— clearly looked as if they'd swam across a weed infested river, covered in mud and weeds. Boys will be boys.

Mick and Dave were not in the mood to look the same. Mick asked, "Are there any other places to cross near here?"

Timmy replied, "Not if you don't want to backtrack twenty miles. There aren't enough people living around here looking to cross the river to repair the bridge."

Just after Mick and Dave's hearts sank, Tyler quickly added, "You know, we've always been meaning to fix this bridge ourselves, using wood from a nearby house. The long-abandoned dwelling collapsed a few years ago. It's not too far from here. With your help, I'm sure we could get it done in a few hours."

Dave didn't hesitate a second to respond to the offer. "Wonderful. I like that idea way better than to what we would've had to resort."

The children led the way to the wood supply, and the four began gathering as much as they could carry. The wood showed signs of decay, but for the most part it hadn't rotted enough to prevent it from being used as a bridge, and supporting the weight of whoever wanted to cross it.

When the quartet finished bringing their first armloads of wood back to the river, they decided to repeat the trip three more times. On the last trip, one of the boys procured a sufficient collection of nails from the site.

"I think this'll be enough wood, guys," said Dave, wiping sweat off his brow.

"Timmy and I know where there's a pile of rocks. We'll go grab a couple to use as hammers."

"Splendid."

As Tyler and Timmy left to find hammers, Thraiker and Ghrere started to mentally visualize the best possible layout of the bridge construction. Lines and curves filled their brains. It was a good thing the stone pylons used to hold the old bridge up were still standing, otherwise it wouldn't have been possible to fix the bridge. *At least fix it in a reasonable amount of time, anyways.*

They agreed on the blueprints and began sorting out the lumber. By the time the children returned with the rock hammers, the hammers were already needed.

At the latter side of an hour's worth of work, the bridge was already taking shape.

"Our stone and wooden creation looks pretty dependable so far. I think it'll only take us another hour and a half for completion," commented Mick, while carrying a board.

"You guys are pretty hard workers. I would let you build my house any day," Dave said to the kids.

Timmy responded, "Actually, my father is a carpenter. We work with him all the time. We both plan on doing it when we grow up, just like him."

"Are you guys brothers? I never thought to ask."

"We're not actual brothers, but close enough. My parents died a few years ago, and my friend Timmy's parents were kind enough to take in their only child's orphaned best friend. I'm extremely grateful because of it, and couldn't ask for a better family other than my own. I wish my real parents had survived the fire."

Mick replied, "I'm sorry to hear about your birth parents. But I would bet my life, Tyler, your adopted parents also feel the same way about you, and are extremely proud to call you their son. I'm sure they appreciate how intelligent and how hard of a worker you are."

"Thank you so much."

"You're welcome," returned Dave. "Hopefully we finish our bridge before it starts to rain again."

LIKE ALWAYS, GRUNT and Roar were the final two left standing. Gamald was a strong believer in holding gruesome battle tournaments in lieu of more orthodox battle-training styles. On paper his tournaments weren't supposed to be to the death, but more often than not bloody fatalities occurred. The heroic deaths only heightened Gamald's preference for tournament training.

Grunt and Roar had been given more eloquent names by their parents. Although, sadly, the names and their parents had been long forgotten. Since Grunt and Roar didn't talk much, names were given to them at some point in time by the sounds they most frequently used. Their lack of customary names was more than compensated, however, by their absolute superiory over all challengers in battle. They possessed proclivities for killing. Most southern Molisians who knew anything about swinging a weapon would state there were no other warriors even close to Grunt and Roar. It was no surprise Grunt and Roar were always the winners of Gamald's tournaments.

Gamald was no fool, he never pitted the two against each other. There was no reason to risk losing either one. Absolute chaos would ensue in a fight between the two. It's not that either held any grudges against the other, but both were very prideful, and would do anything to win.

Grunt fought with a giant, forty-five-pound war-hammer, which was said could easily crush the skull of any man or beast. Roar wielded a massive battle axe. Stories proclaim that with his battle axe he once felled a tree with only a dozen swings. But this was no ordinary tree. It was so immense only its lumber was used to build the town church. It was information elders of Grunt and Roar's hometown told travelers. Many thought it was an exaggeration, but nobody since has had the guts to dispute it.

Grunt and Roar were congratulated by Gamald and celebrated their tournament victory.

Later that night, Gamald held war council in his chambers. The five in attendance were Lieutenant Leedle, General Anolski, Grunt, Roar, and Gamald.

"The contingent that'll be sent to capture Thraug will be sufficient enough in number to defeat the Nighteagle's forces, while leaving the bulk of our army here in Sarwa for future campaigns. If what you say is true, General Anolski, I'm not worried at all in the amount of reinforcements that could be sent by Ulfenkerki in the Nighteagle's aid."

Confidently, Anolski responded to Gamald, "His losses at Strwin were indeed considerable, as were mine. I'm certain Ulfenkerki will pose no threat to your body of soldiers."

"I'm undetermined about the timeframe concerning when we're going to attack, though," emitted Gamald. "I'm just playing that part by ear, mainly relying on my spy network, and watching the weather for that decision. Hopefully, we can march on Thraug before the snow flies."

"I hope that too," said Anolski, pondering how miserable it was the last time he mobilized troops in the snow.

"What percent of our available soldiers do you plan on sending to Thraug, general?" asked Leedle.

"With Anolski's numbers now added to our own, we possess roughly 53 hundred soldiers. I'm leaning towards mobilizing thirty-three percent of that, giving us a raiding party of almost 18 hundred—more than enough in my opinion to capture Thraug, a town that doesn't have walls as high as Strwin's. So, we wouldn't need such overwhelming numbers. The Nighteagle commands only a thousand, I hear from the scouts."

"I'm guessing, due to their lower walls, we intend to use ladder technique to get past?"

"Yes, mainly that, and as you know I also have a few catapults to deploy. Optimistically speaking, to go along with the ladders, we'll punch a few holes in the walls for easier access."

"Sound plans, General," said Anolski.

"I'm done here, unless any of you have anything else to add." Gamald looked at the other four to see if there were any objections to adjourning the meeting. He saw none, so he stood up and started for the door. "Now I say we all head down to the tavern and get ourselves a few beers, and a few women."

"Good plan."

"Here, here."

"Grrrrrrr."

"Roaaar."

CHAPTER 9

❧

"I DON'T THINK even the King's carpenters in their youths revealed as much promise as you both," said Dave, after surveying the finished bridge.

"Now, all that's left to do is try it out," put forth Timmy.

The four of them walked out onto the bridge, and stood safely at the center, admiring the view.

"I have to admit I'm not at all going to miss swimming across this slop hole," commented Tyler.

"Especially when it's as cold as it is now."

"I hope this bridge serves you and your family for many years to come, but now we must continue onward." Mick pointed north.

Tyler said, "If you're ever back in the area, feel free to stop by at our house. It's the only one in the area, other than those of the limestone miners. There's a big group of them, living at the compound over that way. They're always working, so we hardly ever see them. They're really nice, though. I think it's three families."

"We'll do that," said Mick, "if we're ever back in the area."

After thanking the boys for their help, Mick and Dave grabbed their gear and walked across the river atop the new, sturdy construction. They resumed the mission, but had to go out of the way a bit, parallel the river, to take the best possible route northward. They looked back after walking a hundred feet and smiled at seeing the kids galivanting back and forth on their new bridge.

About a quarter mile from where they crossed the river, before heading deep into the northeast corridor, Dave said, "I think we should stop and catch another supply of fish, before our path strays from the riverbank. We might not gain another opportunity to stockpile meat for a while."

"I'm good with that. I do love moving water's aroma, even if is highly eutrophicated. Go ahead and break out the net. I think I'm going to fish for a little bit the old-fashioned way: tying one end of a string to a pole and the other end to a baited hook."

"Sounds fun. I'm pretty sure we have a few of our proven-true hooks left."

Mick fashioned his fishing pole, and gathered a supply of earthworms he found from lifting up head-sized rocks in the area. "I don't think we'll have any difficulties bringing in an abundant load. I saw all kinds of fish outlines from the bridge."

"I saw a bunch as well. The river may seem a giant mud hole, but in all reality, I think the water itself is fairly sterile. The enormous number of weeds alter the appearance—a delusion."

"You could probably drink this water for a few years before getting sick. The weeds are so copious due to the fact it's in one of the final stages of its life cycle. I'm sure if we were to come back in a thousand years, it'll be nothing but swamp for as far as the eye can see, with barely a stream's trickle."

"I once heard there's no such thing as a truly motionless swamp. Is that true to your knowledge?" Dave inquired.

"You heard that from me a long time ago. And yes, all the water contained within all the swamps on this planet flow from one end to the other, though some of the water evaporates or filters into an aquifer first," responded Mick, attaching an unlucky worm to his hook. As gracefully as he could, Mick tossed the baited hook out into the water.

"So, if you know something about swamps that I don't, does that mean I have to relinquish my title of 'The Swamp Master' to you?"

"Nope, it's still all yours, unless I know two more things about swamps that you don't."

Dave laughed, tossing the small portable net into the river. "Let's hope that doesn't happen."

It only took ten minutes for Dave to pull in his first load of fish with the net. Mick, meanwhile, was catching a less than impressive number with his pole. "I'm going to amble over there, and try to stand on that precarious contraption to get myself further out into the water," said Mick, pointing to a barely standing dock-like structure about fifty yards away.

Having walked up to the dilapidation, Mick studied it and figured it had a forty percent chance of holding his weight, a risky undertaking to be sure. He was feeling particularity gutsy at the moment, so he decided to try it despite the risk. "No guts, no glory." He made it out onto the end without falling into the river, but not without stepping onto the first board and having it snap, forcing yet another wet foot.

He stood on the old-as-time dock with his wet foot for twenty minutes, catching a few more fish, one being decently-sized in the ten-pound range. When Mick cautiously walked back off the dock, he peered through the thicket, and noticed a few cabins and sheds. He realized they were probably structures of the mining compound, of which the kids spoke upon parting ways.

"Look at the size of this monster," blurted Mick, having met back up with Dave. He proudly held up his ten-pound trophy for Dave and the world to see, as fishermen tend to do.

"That may be the biggest, but I certainly have the most. We have enough fish now to probably last us a month."

"When I walked off the dock, I did notice the compound nestled in the woods Tyler and Timmy mentioned."

"I see you have another wet foot to enjoy too."

"Actually, that's one of the reasons I mentioned seeing the housing complex. I'm so fed up with not having any extra socks I think I'm going to go over there and see if they've any superfluous pairs to sell to me. I figured since there were three families, there ought to be at least one person with a sock surplus."

"I'll accompany you, Hawk. I need more socks as well. We'll just leave the fish right here, and come back to preserve them later."

"Hopefully not too many opportunistic carnivores find them."

"I'll cast a magical ward over them."

After a good, hearty laugh, Leopard and Hawk threw a bunch of concealing ferns over their fish to help prevent flies from defecating on their bounty. They proceeded towards the compound.

When they got to the other side of the thicket hiding the houses from the river, they were amazed at the drastic change in geology compared to what they were seeing. For the last few miles of their journey, it'd been nothing but typical, rounded granite boulders. The new landscape consisted of a dichotomy of rock formations. Half were littered in limestone—the object of desire for the miners of the compound, for it was readily used in masonry countrywide. The other half consisted of a form of rhyolite—the same metamorphic rock encompassing most of the Tharbjorn Escarpment. The latter rock type was of particular interest to Mick and Dave, it had the appearance of being very ancient. Technically, it *was* very ancient—over a billion years old. The rhyolite showed defined edges and angular corners, as opposed to the general roundness of the more widespread granite and other similar rock varieties. It also reminded them of the mystical terrain from where the *black needle pine tree* came. They didn't expect to find another black needle pine, but it didn't hurt to look while they were there.

It was a gradual upslope to where the main housing was located, roughly a hundred and fifty yards from the river. The landscape was peppered with all kinds and sizes of trees, but not too thick as to inhibit someone from walking from A to B efficiently. One might've thought because the property was so close to the stagnant, weedy river the whole place would reek of the pungent odor of decay. On the contrary, the inescapable smell of the river was easy to get used to, though Mick and Dave were surprised not to smell the burning of wood, a customary scent in places such as this.

"It sure is odd we haven't seen anyone, or signs of anyone, so far."

"That is strange. It seems like at least twenty people would live here. On the surface, there are no signs of action anywhere."

The pair finished the uphill walk from the river to the two main houses—log cabins, more than likely constructed by the inhabitants. Intrinsically tense, they knocked on the front door of the first homely cabin, and waited patiently. The silence compelled them to stare at each other awkwardly. Both tried but failed to come up with something stupidly funny to say during the awkwardness.

When no one answered the door, they proceeded onto the next cabin, and performed the same system.

"I don't know about you, Leopard, but I certainly didn't expect for this to happen. I think the sock gods just don't want to endow us with any of their gifts."

"That seems to be the case. I'm definitely getting a bad feeling about this place. I feel something has drastically gone wrong here."

"Maybe we should scrutinize the whole area, trying to come up with some clues as to the whereabouts of everyone. We should definitely check their small operation mine. I doubt they would all coincidentally be inside the mine at once, but it's worth checking."

The small operation mine was dug into one of the cliffsides on the southern side of the compound. They noticed it had a large main chamber, which was reasonably well lit for a mine, due to the enormity of the main entrance. Unfortunately, no one greeted Mick and Dave. On either side of the main chamber were two smaller, dimmer antechambers. There was just enough available light without spelunking far for someone to see both antechambers and main chamber were devoid of people.

"They've certainly pulled a lot of limestone from this cavern. I wonder how much a ton of limestone is worth these days?"

Dave replied, "I'm not sure, but I'm positive it was rather profitable at some point. However, they're losing money now without it in operation."

"There were other places I saw we could check for them, but I'm starting to lose hope these people are safe," said Mick. "It's highly unlikely every single one of them completely abandoned their mine. There's plenty of limestone left in here."

"Those were some pretty nice homes to abandon as well. In addition, I'm sure they didn't all go on vacation together without leaving someone behind to safeguard from theft. Not even including the limestone itself, there are plenty of valuables scattered around, on which any thief would love to get their hands. Even though we've already spent too much time dawdling, I don't think we can just leave now, knowing something may've gone drastically wrong here."

"I agree. Let's go and check everywhere else in the immediate area for signs of life."

The pair peered inside every hiding place, every nook, every cranny, but came up empty.

They knocked on the door of an unobtrusive third house they found, built up against the side of a cliff. Mick and Dave both thought even though this third house was small, it seemed a superlative place to live, due to its cozy appeal. It supplied the illusion the cliff and home were the same structure—an elegant duo of house and rock. Nobody answered the door, so they peeked into the windows, but to no avail.

They peeked into all of the windows of the other houses again, and saw no one.

"It wouldn't be so bad, if there were signs resembling the fact they went on a trip or something and didn't care if everything got stolen. But all the evidence points to them disappearing suddenly."

"I think we'll have to spend some time solving this problem. Our trip north to the border is going to have to be temporarily postponed, yet again," suggested Hawk.

"I agree. We'll make it to the border soon enough, we're not too far away now. I think one of us should walk back by Tyler and Timmy and talk to them or their parents, enquiring a little more about this matter. Maybe they've heard something about it."

"Okay, I'll go do that, while you start a fire, and preserve our fish. Someone has to do it, before a raccoon decides to search and consume."

Dave agreed. "I think I'm just going to bring the fish over here and take advantage of their pre-existing fire pit."

"Okay, good thinking. I'll see you later then," said Mick, before starting back down the hill towards the bridge they'd just finished making not long ago. To Mick it seemed the bridge project had taken place much longer ago than it did in reality, a few days perhaps. Life was like that sometimes.

Since it was along the way to his destination, Mick stopped to check on the pile of fish. He sighed relief, after noticing the future food supply hadn't been disturbed. Mick angled himself in a straight line towards the bridge and resumed.

The only point of significance for Mick's short walk back to the bridge occurred at a semi-dead bush containing six orange-winged blackbirds. Mick pondered if they were the exact same six birds perched in the tree he'd seen the first time through. He made note of them the first time, because he thought it was funny how all six chose to rest in the same bush, instead of perching on their own. The area certainly wasn't deprived of bushes for them. He chuckled for the heck of it and moseyed on. *Silly blackbirds.*

Upon the bridge's arrival, Mick noticed the lads were still present and screwing around. Twilight hours had already accosted, so he was surprised they hadn't gone back to their house for supper yet.

"I didn't think to find you guys still here at this late hour. I was going to head to your house to enquire about something."

"We just got done eating our supper of frogs' legs," noted Tyler. "Sometimes we just cook and eat them here, instead of dragging them back to the house. If we lugged the frogs to the house all the time, we sure'd have a lot of frog guts in our yard. It's good to see you again. Where's Dave?"

"He's at the compound of which you spoke earlier, preserving the fish we caught. Which is what brings me back here to talk to you about—not Dave preserving fish, but the compound itself, or its inhabitants rather."

Tyler and Timmy smiled at the humor of a situation involving Mick coming back for the reason of discussing something having to do with Dave preserving fish. The sense of humor of a child can be a different animal altogether. Erasing his smile, Tyler remarked, "Why, what's going on with them?"

"We got there, and for the purpose of bartering for socks, we approached the houses, but couldn't find a trace of the inhabitants anywhere. We searched high and low, and found nothing but signs of a sudden departure. We started to get worried about the people, and resolved to spend some more time trying to solve the problem of their disappearances. I guess you could say lately solving problems is what we do. Have you heard anything concerning where they might've gone, or what may've happened to them? Or do you think anyone in your family heard?"

Timmy replied, "We haven't heard anything from them lately either. Just the other day, Dad mentioned he thought it was weird he hadn't seen them in a while. On occasion they'd stop by to talk for the fun of it, but that hasn't happened in quite some time. And I'm sure they didn't go on vacation, they never do."

"I don't like the sound of this," said Mick. "Alright boys, thanks again for your help. Dave and I hope to get to the bottom of all this. Like I said before, lately coming to aid is what we do."

"Good Luck," said Timmy.

Mick walked away from the boys and the bridge for the second time that day, and arrived back by Dave in the black of night. Dave wasn't quite done preserving the fish, but only had one more batch left to go.

"Thank you for setting the tents up, Dave. I was hoping to make it back by dark, but failed apparently."

"No problem. What did you find out?"

"I reached Tyler and Timmy at the bridge, before they went home, and they told me they hadn't heard anything, that the compound dwellers never take vacations. Even their dad was worried about it. Apparently on occasion a few of the miners would stop by to converse, but they haven't done so for quite some time now."

After pacing around the tents a few times, Dave responded, "Another thing that's really bizarre is the fact there aren't any signs of them stepping off this property. We'll do a more thorough inspection of that tomorrow, I suggest. It's almost as if they vanished somewhere on the property itself."

"That's pretty hard to fathom. But, yeah, we'll look into it tomorrow," said Mick, grabbing a fish off the fire. "I have to see if your cuisine here turned out well."

Ten minutes elapsed and satisfied stomachs manifested. *Dave sure had the ability to sufficiently cook a fine tasting fish*, or so Mick said.

The pair decided to aimlessly wander in the dark for a while, not really to see if they could find any clues to the miners' disappearances, there wasn't enough moonlight for efficient searching. Their wandering was mainly for the viewing of a full panorama of stars. A beautiful cosmic display mesmerized.

Staring up into the night sky in awe, both Hawk and Leopard could feel danger brewing somewhere, but because of the peril they also felt more alive. No matter how many times they faced uncertainty, risking their lives for a cause, they wouldn't have changed a thing about how they approached life.

After their necks got sore from craning to stargaze, but before becoming disoriented in the vastness of thought, they went into the tents for slumber. Peacefully, they slept in their cold weather sleeping bags, handwoven masterpieces of cloth that could keep a person warm in the coldest of climates. Good thing for such excellent handiwork, for the really cold stuff was sure to come.

"I'M IMPRESSED. I really didn't think it would happen so fast, but I'm glad it did," said the Black Bear, looking at his new and improved army. He felt proud he now commanded as many soldiers as he did at the battle of Strwin. Garobansurovians really knew how to come together.

Jason Thorncat also felt pride in the army, for he worked hard training them, getting them up to a level needed for battle. He replied, "I've no doubt the men we selected to march to Thraug tomorrow morning are ready for the task at hand. And no doubt the soldiers we plan to leave behind will be enough in number to protect this town, along with its already proven city guard, in case of an attack."

"Indeed," said the Black Bear. "I think we'll do one more battle drill, before ordering them to bed. I want to start mobilization at the crack of dawn."

"Yes, sir. On which drill should we close out the evening?"

Ulfenkerki closed his eyes in contemplation, and rubbed his nose. Opening his eyes back up, he answered Jason's question, "I think the best drill to do now is rock practice. I know we're going to need it."

Jason agreed with the General, but he wouldn't have put up a stink with *any* drill selected. It wasn't exactly easy to debate a man so knowledgeable in battle, and with such pronounced wisdom lines (or so some called them) decorating his face. "Okay, I'll get them started on it right away, sir."

"Don't forget to get some sleep tonight yourself, Jason."

"Oh, I will, sir, same to you. It's common knowledge you stay awake for nights on end in pre-battle situations, thinking of further strategies."

"That's true, but I foresee Gamald won't start his march on Thraug for another week or so, so I've plenty of time yet to think."

Jason smiled and walked within earshot of the lower ranking officers, and told them what final drill Ulfenkerki wanted. The soldiers formed up and the drill was put into motion.

First, about a hundred stakes were pounded into the ground, evenly spaced with ten feet between each one, and all of them thirty-five feet from the bottom of the wall. Each stake represented a singular member of an invading army.

Next, all easily available rocks (hence the drill's name) were gathered and brought to the training grounds. Upon the completion of the gathering, a signal was given notifying participants to race to grab a rock for each hand. Those who succeeded in getting two, carried their rocks to the top of the wall, and threw one at the stakes positioned below. If a stake was hit, you got to throw again. If you missed, you had to climb back down to the bottom and grab two more rocks, leaving one behind. The one left behind was for adept throwers who could hit successive targets. The amount of available rocks at the top of the wall always seemed enough. Rocks running out at the top had yet to happen in all the years Ulfenkerki implemented the drill. It also never happened where so few stakes were hit there were hardly any rocks to gather and carry up.

Not carrying rocks would've defeated the purpose of the drill's aerobic aspect. The possibility could've arisen where the partakers realized the exercise could be performed at a slow, less taxing pace. That way they wouldn't have had to carry many heavy, exhaustive rocks. But that also never happened, because the drill was fun and competitive. Besides, there weren't too many people in the world who didn't like throwing heavy objects from heights, while simultaneously getting in shape. Everything always seemed to work out in the end of Ulfenkerki's drills.

Satisfied all the soldiers received a good workout, Jason ended the drill and dismissed everyone from the day's training. They all had plenty of time to go to the barracks, wind down, and fall asleep.

Early the next morning, the army prepared for their departure to Thraug, which caused the civilians of Strwin to wake up early as well. People of Strwin enjoyed exuding patriotism and liked to drink, the mobilization of an army just cause for both.

A thousand battle-ready soldiers handpicked by Ulfenkerki and Jason for being the most suitable for the mission got into formation. The remaining three hundred stayed behind for two reasons: they weren't quite ready for battle, and for the unforeseen chance Strwin got attacked by an unknown force upon Ulfenkerki's exodus.

Tom Higgultz and the Black Bear discussed a few last second details. "Please wish the mayor of Thraug the best of luck for me. I know from firsthand experience his town will be in good hands."

"Thank you, Mayor, for all your support and generosities. I'm not sure whether or not it's in the cards for us to soon return. Battle plans can be chaotic, changing at any time for any reason."

"I understand. Remember, whenever it may be, your return will be welcomed by every man, woman, and child of Strwin. And especially by me."

The army was ready and led out of town by the General and his First Lieutenant. "What a town, General, sir. It sure makes me proud to secure the freedom for such outstanding people."

"As it does for me, Jason, as it does for me."

CHAPTER 10

AT ABOUT THE same time Ulfenkerki's army began their march, Mick Thraiker and Dave Ghrere woke from yet another magnificent sleep in their cozy tents. "I'm really not in the mood this morning to eat fish for breakfast."

"For what are you in the mood?"

Dave stretched thoroughly, cracked his joints, and replied, "Eggs and toast."

"We've a little cornbread leftover, and a few remaining embers which you can use to restart the fire for bread toasting. But I'm afraid you're out of luck with the eggs, unless you spotted some wild birds running around willing to part with their offspring."

Dave chuckled. He loved a good morning hilarity. "I guess toast will just have to do."

In a matter of moments, Dave had restarted the previous evening's fire, and rigged a crude toaster for the morning's meal. Mick also partook in the toasting.

"Do you want to start searching on the north side or the south for clues this morning?" raised Dave.

"I suppose I'll cover the ground on the south side. You can have the north."

Methodically, Mick searched the compound's southern half for clues regarding the enigma of the missing people, while Dave meticulously searched the north side. First, Mick inspected the mine again, but found nothing new there. He combed small groves of trees scattered amongst the ancient rhyolite rocks. The area was beautiful, but he got no further along in accomplishing anything. The only thing gained in the experience were sore eye muscles from straining to look at all the mesmerizing sights. He eventually walked to the river for further scrutiny. The only signs of life he found there were old hooks discarded by past fishermen—too rusty to keep for himself.

Dave, meanwhile, was executing his part when he noticed it was beginning to snow for the first time of the year. He observed the light fluffing a few seconds earlier than Mick, because he was positioned on the high ground. Thankfully, it was melting as soon as it hit the ground, but nevertheless, it was still winter's grand entrance.

Leopard searched around the houses, half tempted to open the doors and inspect from the inside. He figured he would wait to decide on breaking and entering until he could discuss it further with Hawk. Together the two could come to a mutual verdict.

Just like Mick, Dave wasn't finding anything usable either—that is until he looked at a certain tamarack tree growing close to the door of one of the cabins. He gasped when he saw one of the tree's lower branches and some of its trunk covered in what was unmistakably dried blood. It was as if someone badly wounded was being dragged away, and tried to grab onto the branch to prevent themselves from being dragged away any further. Dave visualized the ghastly occurrence and grimaced, and as a result his resolve was only strengthened.

Dave also noticed something about the third cabin, the one built abutting the cliff—neither he nor Mick had noticed before. He concluded the cabin was actually built into a fissure of the cliff, so in essence, the part of the cabin that could be seen was more or less a facade. On top of the cliff was where Dave found his evidence. He could see faulting in the cliff, leading right up to the house, and could tell the cabin was built around the crack, effectively using the gap as living space. It was all rather intriguing.

Dave realized his decision on entering the cabins for inspection would be tainted by his own curiosity to see the inside of the cliffside cabin, so he vowed to let Mick make the final decision on the breaking and entering. Mick wouldn't let curiosity infect his decision as much, because he didn't know the information Dave sluiced out about the cliff cabin.

Mick was naturally drawn to a certain rock in the area, maybe because it was the biggest, or maybe because it just looked storybook-like. It was another keen-edged, angular slab of rhyolite. It, to all intents and purposes, resembled a big cube. The monstrosity was eight feet long, eight feet wide, seven feet high, and was really suspicious due to the abnormal amount of foot travel that seemed to have occurred around it. There were mini trails and footprints all over. That much traffic around one seemingly unimportant spot was out of the ordinary.

Mick endeavored to get to the top to examine it from that point of view. However, he couldn't quite pull himself to the top, so he searched the area for a log with which he could use to climb. After searching for many minutes, he finally found one suitable sitting next to a fat, hollowed out black spruce tree, a weird tree that looked dead at first glance, but surprisingly still very much alive.

He collected the log and propped it beside the rhyolite cube-rock. Mick didn't expect to see what he saw when reaching the top, for on top was a smattering of dried blood. It didn't make any sense to Mick. *Why would there be blood up here?* he thought. It was a slightly bumpy surface, but by no means capable of cutting someone climbing to the top.

He climbed back down, more puzzled than before.

Hawk left the log beside the rock, knowing Dave would probably want to see the mysterious discovery, and continued searching the area for more clues.

Around supper time, the light snow was no longer melting as it hit the ground, and started to— depressingly—accumulate. Mick met back up with Dave at the campfire to discuss the day's findings, and eat.

"You'll never guess what I found today on the top of a giant, cube-shaped rock."

"I bet you a day's carrying that I could guess," Dave proposed.

"I'm not falling for that again. You might as well tell me what you know," replied Mick, trying not to turn his smile into a laugh.

"Judging by what I found, I would say you probably found some dried blood."

"I did. Well done. I'd guess it's somewhere between a week and three weeks old."

"That would be my guess too. I found some on a tree just outside the front door of one of the main cabins. To me, it looks as if a struggle had transpired at the locale. It appears the victim was dragged away from their home, and in the process tried to grab anything firmly planted for leverage. Outcome? *Bloody tree trunk and branches.*"

The pair proceeded to investigate each other's findings, and came to a definitive conclusion of the blood having something to do with the missing personnel. They were certain the two bloody investigation sites related to each other somehow.

Dave spoke: "I was wondering what you thought about the option of us continuing our task to the insides of the three cabins. Maybe something important waits for us that could lead us to solving this mystery."

"That does bring up an interesting moral dilemma, but I think the gravity of the situation implores us to breach privacy and enter the homes."

Glad at himself for handling the situation the way he did, Dave replied, "Very well. With which house shall we begin?"

"We'll start at the main two, then go to the third by the cliff."

There was about an inch of snow on the ground when Mick and Dave pried open the first door. They opened their eyes widely, and began the search of the first house.

They performed the initial investigation more hastily than they would've wanted—they wanted to get to all three before running out of daylight. They spotted lamps, but they doubted they'd find fuel for them.

The first cabin they searched was the one with the bloody tree just outside. Its interior smelt pleasantly of smoke, and was pretty tidy. There was one big bedroom containing three beds, and a wood stove next to the doorway. As expected, there was blood on the inside of the cabin, but no evidence of what had caused it to be spilt.

"It seems the incident occurred while the injured party was sitting at the kitchen table eating a meal," Mick observed. "The degree of food decay on this loaf of bread on the table coincides with our previous hypothesis the transgression happened between a week and three weeks ago."

"And it seems the bedroom has no further clues, nor does the bathroom," added Dave. "Everything looks used, but not recently used."

Before moving on to the second cabin, they inspected all the drawers and cupboards in the kitchen, not finding anything of suspicion therein. They also made note there weren't any valuables anywhere. Mick and Dave surmised the valuables were more than likely stolen.

Unlike the first, the second cabin had two stories and a red complexion. It had two small bedrooms, and also exuded the musty but satisfying smell of chimney smoke. The upper level didn't seem to be used much, probably getting too hot in the summer for any sort of practical living. Apparently, it was just used for storage.

Hawk and Leopard scoured every niche and found only one noteworthy item. Mick found an empty scabbard in the corner of a closet of interest. The sword that belonged inside the scabbard had been stolen. But Mick and Dave knew something whoever stole the sword and all the other valuables on the premise didn't. A while back, Mick and Dave were in a weapons shop, where the proprietor showed them an identical scabbard, one with a hidden compartment near the bottom, a convenient chamber for concealing a plethora of different things. This scabbard also had the compartment.

Mick shook the scabbard, and said, "A person would probably think the rattling noise is made by all the loose straps and appendages clanging around, but I'd bet there are coins stowed away in the hidden compartment."

"Okay, I'll take that bet," Dave replied with confidence. "The usual bet, a day of item carrying? Or maybe something different for the winner's purse?"

"I'll wager a day's worth of item carrying this occasion. I know you can't be a step ahead of me this time. You entered this room for the first time as I did."

"I did indeed," Dave said. "The bet is on."

"Before we discover what's in the compartment, first, I want to know what makes you confident enough to make this bet?"

"Simple logic. Odds are against there being a specific thing in the chamber, because of the possibility that it could be so many other things. If you do end up winning, it's sheer luck."

"I guess it's my lucky day then," said Mick with a silly grin, after opening the scabbard's secret compartment, and pouring gold coins out onto his hand.

"At least your luck has given us a clue. I think it's beyond safe to say these miners by no means left their home willingly. Nobody would leave this much money behind. There has to be at least eight hundred gitis worth of gold here."

Mick put the gold back in the compartment, slid the scabbard back into its resting place, and replied, "I agree. I couldn't fathom someone voluntarily leaving that kind of treasure behind. I really think beyond the shadow of a doubt an abduction of some sort occurred here. And before you even think of it, since we're more than likely still going to be here tomorrow, my bet winnings will be implemented on our next day of travel."

Dave laughed, and responded, "I wouldn't have it any other way."

"Oh please. Plus, I still plan to get you back even better for your rooftop stunt back at Strwin."

"That too, I wouldn't have any other way."

The duo completed the search of the second cabin, and stepped outside onto two inches of snow. "I think this'll all melt tomorrow."

"I hope so, Dave. I'm not ready for white landscapes yet."

There was one house remaining to search, and they had one hour's worth of daylight left in which to do it. Dave knew going inside the third house would be an eye-opening experience, because he'd never before entered a house anything like it.

Dave opened the door of the home built into a cliff, and the pair went inside.

Mick was surprised. He expected the house to be homely, but never expected it to be as extraordinary as it was. Dave was correct, about two-thirds of the house's walls were rock, advantageously utilizing the fissure. All the angles and contours of the rock supplied perfect harmony, a satisfying balance of disarray and organization. Plus, the interior woodwork seemed to coexist with the rock seamlessly. There was one bedroom nestled in the limestone, which contained one bed, two buttress poles for stability, and a bookcase with twenty books and an assortment of odds and ends.

Throughout the house there were furs for the floors and various nooks and crannies, which Mick and Dave thought looked pleasant. And last but not least, because most of the home was basically inside a cliff, the ambient temperature was a comfortable forty-five degrees, compared to a much colder twenty-five degrees currently outside. It wouldn't take much of a fire to warm the home to what most considered room temperature.

"I'm guessing this limestone is a different grade than what they mine," said Mick conversationally.

"More than likely," replied Dave.

"This is the neatest house I've ever seen."

"I have to be honest with you, I knew it would be, due to my previous clue gatherings. I couldn't tell you because I felt the decision to trespass into the houses would be tainted, if we both were curious as to what the interior of this particular house looked like."

"Good point. I suppose we can halt our gawking now, and perform our search."

"Indeed."

Mick and Dave searched until they ran out of daylight, but didn't find anything new to add to their stockpile of clues.

"You could say we've been only semi-productive this evening. We've virtually concluded the compound residents were abducted, but we've yet to determine how, why, and to where."

Dave proposed, "I think we'll give one more entire day to the answering of those questions, but if they still remain unanswered by then, we should move on."

Mick nodded his head in agreement, and replied, "I think we should take a night off from being so noble, and commandeer this beautiful cabin for the hours of darkness, as opposed to sleeping in our much colder and snow-covered tents. I'm sure they wouldn't mind, seeing as though we're only here to help."

"I couldn't agree more. Sometimes you can really come up with some good ideas, Mick. I'll go grab our sleeping bags, so that way we can still keep some of that nobility, refraining from sleeping on their beds and soiling their blankets."

"Good thinking."

In no time, Dave returned with armloads of sleeping apparel. The pair continued to pace around the innards of the cabin, admiring.

When legs no longer felt energized, Mick and Dave switched into relaxation mode. Eating some of their fish preserved the previous night, they sat in good moods on the couches, talking of days long since passed. They took in the moment, because they both doubted they'd ever spend a night in a cabin quite like it again.

MORNING CAME QUICKLY. The pair was jolted awake by a sudden but natural cracking of the wall. Dave commented, "That was intense."

"I concur," said Mick. "I don't even remember falling asleep."

"Unusual. I hope we solve the disappearance riddle today, because the people of this homestead sure seem to be the sort giving a good name to civilization."

"That they do. They appear to be efficient at both mining and enjoying life."

Aiming to leave the house, Mick and Dave grabbed their sleeping bags and fish refuse. The bags were thrown into the tents, and the fish bones into the firepit.

They began the day's sleuthing at the big, cube-shaped rhyolite stone, the locale they thought to be the most curious.

HE'D TRAVELED THROUGH the night, due to apprehension of being stopped and harassed, a predicament that would've occurred on a few occasions, if not for Brom's craftiness. He'd successfully hidden himself and his cart amongst dark, forested backdrops every time trouble arose, he being no rookie in the art of camouflage.

Brom Quintaga had finally made it to Sarwa and what he hoped, his salvation.

He'd waited at the gate for what seemed an eternity, having earlier spoken to the guards about his admittance. He'd explained to the sentries what was under the tarp, and what he wanted to do with it once inside town. Details shared were minimal concerning the suits of armor, but Brom did let it be known to the guards they were of considerable value.

After two hours of sitting and standing by his cart in the scorching sun, the gate finally creaked open. Brom did eventually wise up, and sit underneath his cart in the shade at one point. Someone on the inside had turned the wheel attached to the gate by a simple system of ropes and gears—the only way the gate opened.

Allowed to drag his cart straight to a designated spot, Brom sat for another hour, waiting for what he hoped was a host of dignitaries and rich noblemen. A category of folks he hoped would come and listen to his sales pitch—an eloquence practiced repeatedly on the road from Strwin.

Instead, all who finally greeted him was a lone Lieutenant Leedle.

"I've been commanded to come and inspect your goods, before they're presented to anyone important," Leedle emitted. "We wouldn't want to squander key peoples' times by presenting inferior wares now would we?"

"True." Brom began the opening section of his sales pitch, as Leedle examined.

Leedle didn't have to spend much time scrutinizing the armor, for he, like all the others before him, concluded the armor was exquisite.

Leedle halted the sales pitch, and asked, "I see three, five-piece suits, am I correct?"

"Yes, sir, you are correct."

"Out of my own curiosity, how long has it taken you to construct these pieces?"

"Thirty years of my life lie before you."

"I guess that's probably why I've never heard of you or your work. You've been spending all your time constructing these."

"Yes. The person who supported me the most throughout the endeavor is the very reason I have to sell. For he went missing a while ago, and I need the funds to continue searching for him, *my son*. Maybe you've seen or heard of him, his birth name is..."

But before Brom could finish his sentence, Lieutenant Leedle barked, "I don't have time to listen to any more squabble on personal matters, we must get a move on. Grab your cart and follow me."

Quintaga and Leedle met up with Gamald near soldier quarters and began discussion. General Gamald wasn't exactly the sort of person for whom Brom had been hoping.

Gamald spoke first in the exchange. "I understand you want to try and sell these three suits of armor, or perhaps auction them to the wealthy. But I must inform you all sales of war commodities first need to go through me. Furthermore, all sales of war commodities go *only* through me, effectively making me your only hope for a successful transaction today in Sarwa."

"Very well, I understand, General," responded an extremely disheartened man.

Brom slipped the tarp off his cart, once again, and began his well-rehearsed sales pitch, once again.

An avaricious Gamald listened on as Brom unleashed his best effort, spewing almost every adjective in his vocabulary to describe the intricateness of his armor. On at least one point in the speech, every single item in the cart was picked up, shown, and the value explained. Brom could sense the captivation of his audience, but Gamald by all means was not an easy man to sway with a sales pitch.

Brom was correct in assessing Gamald's level of captivation, for at the conclusion of the pitch, Gamald expressed his intrigue. "I am actually interested in these items. How much did you say you wanted for them?"

"I'm asking ten thousand gitis a piece. You'll find no better value on all of Taraosk."

Gamald took a few minutes, privately conversing with Leedle. The two looked rather animated as they talked, Brom thought.

Mustering his most personable smile, Gamald addressed Brom after concluding his talk with Leedle. "There are a few tests that must be performed, and we'd like to try the suits on for size, before this whole thing can be taken any further, but we may be able to procure a deal."

"Sounds fair." Brom's spirits suddenly picked up.

"We'll perform the experiments and negotiations tomorrow morning. I've a busy schedule the rest of today," Gamald stated. "Early in the morning is when would work the best for me. Is that doable for you?"

"That sounds splendid."

"You can sleep in the army quarters tonight, if you'd like. Lodging in this town can be rather expensive, plus nobody likes to sleep in the dirt."

"Thank you, sir, I will take you up on that."

The trio parted ways, Brom's happy mood magnified. *Maybe, just maybe, I'm finally going to be able to sell my life's work, and save my son.*

Brom spent the rest of the day in solitude, thinking of further ways to express the high quality of his armor at the morning meeting. When his mind grew tired of thought, he ceased mental preparations, and went to sleep alongside the Molisian army—*the enemy.*

FAR AWAY, BUT not entirely out of walking distance from where Brom performed his thinking, the Thraiker/Ghrere collaboration did some thinking of their own. Thinking and searching. They combed the whole area of the compound twice, an unfruitful endeavor, and ended up back at the cubed rock, basically their secondary basecamp.

They were running out of time, but they were still determined. It would be their last day of searching before continuing on north/north-eastward.

Dave sat atop the cube, while Mick contemplatively and repeatedly swung his sword near the hollow spruce tree—the same tree from where the log used to bound to the top of the cubed rock had been found.

From his heights, Dave projected loud enough so his voice would travel to Mick, "Have you ever looked into the knothole of that spruce for anything interesting?"

"Actually, yes. I peered inside between noticing the log next to it would be perfect for my desired purpose, and inevitably grabbing it. It's a curious but bare knothole."

Dave climbed down from his perch, walked over by Mick and sat down next to the knothole in the hollow spruce tree. Mick continued to swing his sword back and forth for the heck of it.

While swinging, Mick voiced, "I'm surprised all this snow hasn't melted yet. It must be colder than I think it is." Mick stopped swinging momentarily to glance at the snow-covered ground.

Twisting his body so he could rest his ear on the tree, Dave said, "Do that again."

"Do what again?"

"Swing your sword close to this tree, without hitting it, but close enough that it almost touches it. I heard something."

Mick complied.

Dave's suspicions were confirmed. "When you do that, there's a clanging sound resonating inside this tree. Here, you listen, while I do the swinging."

The roles being reversed, Mick also heard the mysterious sound. "I think there's more to this knothole than meets the eye. Let me try and listen with my ear almost inside the tree. My head is too big to put it entirely inside."

Dave chuckled, and loosed another swing. "A big head, eh."

Mick heard the sound more distinctly. He extended his arm into the hole to probe around thoroughly for whatever was causing the clanging, and pulled out an interesting looking apparatus. "Here's the culprit. It was hugging the inside of the tree, resting on some nails. I bet this gadget is a tremendous magnet, which would explain why it was affected by the swing. Every time the sword passed nearby, the magnet followed and clanged against the tree."

Dave examined it, and added, "It's parabolic shape is why it was concealed so well in the tree, and why when resting on the nails it made the clanging noise. If it was a perfect semi-circle, it would've fit more snugly and made less or no noise."

"Right. I'm guessing it's no mere coincidence this magnet was resting by the only thing in the area that could be used to climb to the top of the cube-rock."

"It's also probably no coincidence the blood on the cube-rock coincides with a mysterious, hidden object," Dave said, while placing his sword over the newly found device to confirm it was indeed a magnet. "Instant attraction. This is definitely the largest lodestone I've ever seen, or even heard anyone possessing. It certainly has the weirdest shape."

Mick replied, "I concur. Let's go see what the connection between this magnet and the big rhyolite stone really is."

The pair methodically moved the parabolic lodestone around the cube-rock's lower sections to see if anything happened. Then, they worked the upper sections of the rock's sides. Nothing transpired. But they were pretty certain that because the blood was on the top of the rock, if there were answers to be found, on top would be where they'd be.

Hawk and Leopard both climbed to the top, and began the search for who knows what. The magnet was maneuvered all around. After a few minutes of seeking enigma's answer at heights, they stumbled upon a single point that attracted the magnet, the slightest bit of pull.

"Perhaps there's a system of metallic parts inside the rock, some sort of elaborate latch, and the magnet is used to move a lever in and out of a locking position," Mick rationalized, fidgeting with the magnet.

Dave returned, "Who knows if it's even in the lock position now? We can only assume. We'll try moving the hypothetical lever in every direction and pulling up on the hypothetical hatch. When one direction fails, we'll return the latch back to the neutral position, and try another. Can you feel or hear anything move on the inside when you move the magnet?"

"I can't really hear anything, but I can tell something is there, and that it does slightly move with the magnet."

First, Mick tried pulling the lever north, while Dave grabbed a hold of a few of the bumps on the rhyolite and pulled. The point on the stone where Dave grabbed to pull was basically guesswork—a person really couldn't tell where it would open, if it did. There were no obvious seams. Many cracks zig-zagged across the whole of the surface disguising an entranceway—if it was indeed an entrance to something. The first try was a failed attempt. No beginner's luck greeted them that day.

The second attempt, trying to move the lever east, felt different for Mick. There was a more solid connection. He knew it would work. Dave pulled a slab of rock right off its resting place, revealing a deep, dark passageway.

One look down into the tunnel, and Mick confessed, "I don't think we'll be leaving the compound in the morning."

"I don't think we will be either. There could be anything down there." Looking at the dried blood, Dave said, "One thing we can surmise is whoever, or whatever, caused this blood to be on this lid is down there, lurking somewhere."

"Now we need to decide if we're spelunking tonight in the exotic dark, hoping there's some sort of light down there, or do we wait until morning, when there's more available light?"

Dave thought for a second, then, replied, "I think we'll make that decision upon my return. I'm going to lower myself into the bowels. Once I'm down there, I can assemble a better assessment of the light situation."

"Are you sure you want to do that?"

Dave didn't respond to Mick; he was already halfway down the tube.

Having lowered himself about twenty feet to the ground (or what was hopefully the ground) Dave brushed the dust from his face. There was still a small amount of daylight left poking down the shaft, so Dave could look around a little bit once his eyes adjusted.

He evaluated the situation in the near darkness, and climbed back to the top to give his report. "For starters, it sure is no tropical paradise down there. I think it's another mine. I couldn't see much with what light I did have. We'd be better off starting tomorrow. Other than rock, I didn't see much of anything else."

"Okay then, in morning's first light, with small torches, we'll journey the underworld."

Mick and Dave walked back to their tents, and further discussed the day's activities and what was to come.

"THIS WILL BE the first time I set foot in Thraug," said Jason Thorncat, as Ulfenkerki's army was about to reach their destination in the dark.

"I've been here before, but only a few times—twice for Strwin guard purposes, and once for a family vacation."

"You never told me you had a family, Gregg?"

"Everybody has a family," responded Gregg Hogarty, with a chuckle. "I went as a kid with my parents, I only remember it vaguely. The town is smaller than Strwin, but seems to have more places of interest."

Jason's curiosity was piqued. "What kind of interests?"

"There are more shopping establishments, but unfortunately fewer taverns. There's an informative history museum near the center of town, one in which I once spent an entire day, reading every single thing with words available. I never knew it, but the famous artist, Lucinda Vonal, was born and raised in Thraug. Last I saw, there was an entire half-wing showcasing her magnificent paintings."

"I've heard of her, but have never seen any of her work."

"There's a church I think was built over a hundred and fifty years ago, and countless other old, interesting buildings. I also remember the giant oak tree in the middle of the town square is an estimated three hundred and fifty years old. It is said being in its presence has occasionally cured blindness, among other things."

"It only does it occasionally?"

"That's what they say. There have been two or three dozen accounts of the miracle worker in action throughout history."

Jason commented, "Well, I guess I'll have to go over by the inexplicable tree, and ask it to magically manifest for me some new armor. I sure could use some. I'm more fragile than I used to be."

Gregg laughed, and responded, "I don't think it has ever spontaneously generated articles of warcraft."

Jason returned the laugh, and began to prepare the army to enter town. It wasn't something usually requiring much preparation, but the gate was small, so the army had to form an organized single file line to get inside efficiently.

After twenty minutes, the whole of Ulfenkerki's army, minus those left behind at Strwin, was inside Thraug and assembled, all one thousand of them.

Off to one side of the mass, Commander Rayton and Chad Loytin held a meeting with the archers, while on the other side of the mass, Jason held a conference of his own.

Immediately, the Black Bear searched out the Nighteagle to hold discussion. It'd been a while since the old friends had talked face-to-face. Bears and eagles commingling didn't happen often.

The Nighteagle's real name was Bob Smith, but due to the commonness of the name, it was decided long ago—not by Bob himself, or any members of his army—only the *Nighteagle* would be used, a proclamation that's stood the duration of his command.

"Good to see you again, sir. I expect your travels were free from adversity?" the Nighteagle asked, exuberant at the sight of his old friend and ally.

Matching the Nighteagle's animation, Ulfenkerki extended an arm to shake hands, and replied, "Totally free from misfortune, except for the random spasms of my sword hand. It does that sometimes when it yearns to be used."

"I'm sure that can be remedied soon."

"I'm sure it can. Do you have any estimations as to the arrival of the ominous Gamald party? At what kind of timeframe are we looking?"

"My trusty scouts haven't reported any movement yet, but I'm sure it won't be long now. You have no idea how pleased I am to see you and your soldiers here right now. I am genuinely happy to see your far from beautiful mug."

"I knew someday you'd grow to appreciate that." Ulfenkerki and the Nighteagle churned out the brand of laughs only old friends share. "I'm glad to be here, and delighted to help, knowing how hard my soldiers have been training and preparing."

"Sir, you are the epitome of honor, always were. The pride I feel in seeing you standing here at my side without the slightest hesitation, or without me even having to ask is overwhelming. I will never forget this, neither will the people of this town."

"Your words are humbling," Ulfenkerki returned. If ever there was a time the Black Bear grew red in the face, that moment would've been closest to it. "Enough pleasantries. Let's go and do something fun, like arms and armor cataloguing, or even better yet, let's go have a drink. I haven't had a drink with you in ages."

"We'll do both."

"I like your thinking."

Before going mobile, the Nighteagle asked, "How did you replenish your ranks so quickly since the battle of Strwin?

"I'll share those secrets as soon as we have drinks in our hands."

"I like your thinking too, general."

The two of them sat in the Nighteagle's office, discussing a myriad of topics, with face-sized mugs in their hands, never empty.

Closer to the end of the day, the Nighteagle eagerly refilled Ulfenkerki's beer mug for the umpteenth time, overflowing it with froth. Pipe smoke crept through gaps between the office door and its doorframe, as the pair finally began seriously discussing strategy for the looming battle. "One thing I do know," communicated the Nighteagle, "is I think we've a pretty good advantage in the likelihood Gamald underestimates your soldier increase since the battle at Strwin. I sense he'll send a proportionally small raiding army here to Thraug, while leaving behind an excess amount of his military personnel at Sarwa. He'll do this because he knows it's inevitable for Garobansurov to eventually try and forcefully reclaim what is hers."

"We can only hope that'll be the case. My influx of soldiers has surprised even me. In the future, Sarwa will be a challenge though."

"Indeed. Adding your thousand to my thousand gives us a pretty formidable city-defense. I'm confident. Gamald knows my numbers, and hopefully he assumes your numbers are fewer than five hundred and corresponds by sending an assault party of only seventeen or eighteen hundred. He'll definitely still want the advantage in numbers, due to our defensive benefit. If our walls were higher, I'm sure he'd send double."

The Black Bear thought about all the information, his mind housing a plan gaining momentum. "I've a scheme brewing. When I have it entirely worked out, I'll present it to you, and we'll make a co-decision as to whether or not it'll be implemented."

The Nighteagle responded, "That's the Ulfenkerki I know and love, thinking of battle plans at every possible moment."

"Not every moment. I took a relaxing, absent-minded piss this morning."

They both laughed, and spent half an hour longer discussing strategy. The next and last half hour they reserved for talking of the past.

While the generals conversed, Jason Thorncat continued spearheading the in-settling of the army.

The soldiers were nervous. Battle was near. They could all sense it.

CHAPTER 11

JUST LIKE FOR the Garobansurov army at Thraug, a hurdle was near for Mick and Dave, one which only they could clear. Only they were near enough to intercede. Triumph or failure was ultimately up to them.

Poised, Thraiker and Ghrere woke up an hour before sunrise so they could have everything ready to enter the cavern system at first light. They suited themselves up with their entire arsenal of armor and weapons. Meticulously, they emptied their packs of everything not useful for the moment, and filled them with an assortment of organic materials, so they had a ready-supply of fuel for their torches and light, a necessity for eyes in dark places.

"I don't know what it is about caves, but they make me more nervous than they should."

Mick replied to Dave, "It's only natural. I didn't think I'd be this apprehensive either. There could be anything down there."

"Very true."

At first sight of sun, the duo walked down to the cube-shaped rhyolite stone, opened it with the parabolic magnetic key, and climbed down the shaft to the mystifying underworld.

"I think maybe we should've waited another ten to twenty minutes to climb downward. It's still pretty dark down here," voiced Dave, barely able to see to whom he was talking.

"We can just sit here, and listen for abnormalities, until it gets a little lighter."

Dave half-chuckled, "Alright."

Time elapsed, and all they heard waiting for daylight were the sounds of water trickling through the limestone and occasional fluttering of insect wings.

When they could see at least five feet in front of their faces, they started walking deeper into the cave system. They stepped lightly, as to not alarm anyone or anything that could've been lurking inconspicuously.

In most of the tunnels they encountered there was plenty of room to walk, but in some they barely squeezed through. "That last constriction point was tighter than a sailor's knot."

"If it gets any tighter, we might have to take some of our gear off."

"True," said Dave. "Ambient light is minimal. Good thing our torches are holding up nicely."

Every thirty or forty feet they ran across a new water dribble. "Thousands of years of water erosion at work here, forming these caves," said Mick, running his hands through one of the cascading water streams."

"I'm surprised we haven't seen any stalactites or stalagmites yet."

"I'm sure we eventually will."

At a particular point along the way, they slowed to examine fossils in the tunnel walls. The walls were ancient compositions comprised strictly of sedimentary rock. Fossil species were abundant. Corals, crinoids, and shelled sea creatures were the primary fossil categories, but an occasional trilobite or miscellaneous invertebrate was seen.

"Too bad we're stuck in the middle of a pressing issue. I sure would like to examine these fossils for a longer span of time," voiced Mick.

"Without the pressing issue we wouldn't have come down here in the first place."

"Very true."

The fossiliferous layer eventually gave way to a darker shade of sedimentary stone containing far fewer fossils. Mick and Dave stopped fossil hunting and picked up the pace.

"This new rock zone may be shale infused. There isn't enough light to tell for sure," said Dave.

"Some mysteries are meant to be unanswered."

Finally, they reached a point in the tunnel system revealing a slightly open atmosphere, which eventually transitioned into a vast chamber. The new environment was devoid of light shafts, so other than torchlight it was completely dark. Their fuel supply for the torches was holding up well.

"I sure hope we don't miss out on locating any sudden drop-offs," said Dave. "You never know when it comes to places like this."

"Danger follows us everywhere."

While progressing forward, they continuously wrapped new bark and plants around the torches to keep them lit, a procedure in which they were experienced.

Suddenly, Mick relinquished most of his torch's flame into a pile of dirt. Dave instinctively did the same.

Mick halted, put one hand on Dave's shoulder, used the other hand to point, and whispered, "Look over there, in that direction, about a hundred yards away."

Dave looked to where Mick was pointing, and could discern the glow from a fire. It seemed to be a small fire in a small firepit. "It seems as if we found our quarry. Hopefully they can't see our faint torchlight."

"It seems they haven't noticed us, but they may just be playing dumb in order to spring a trap. There's no way of knowing for sure."

"I think the only thing we can do is play *no guts, no glory* and sneak up on them, assuming we have the element of surprise on our side. And if it was a trap, then we'll just rely on our good looks to save us."

Staring frankly, Mick scrutinized Dave and replied, "Don't you mean rely on *my* good looks?"

"Nope."

The duo muffled their laughs, and walked slowly and quietly to the firepit. They got close enough to ascertain if there was anyone tending to the fire. They spotted a pair of silhouettes—human silhouettes. Upon creeping a little closer, they realized the two people were staring at the fire mindlessly and not gazing out into the abyss watchfully as if expecting someone to be approaching.

Dave whispered in Mick's ear, "Their empty-headed demeanor too could be a trap, a brilliance sprung when we make our move on the decoys, unleashing an armed horde filtering out from hidden posts."

Mick whispered back, "Well, that's when my good looks will save us."

Dave just shook his head, rolled his eyes, and inaudibly chuckled.

Carefully, they snuck within fifty feet of their target and took one last look at whom they were facing, sizing them up. Using darkness as their ally, Thraiker and Ghrere attempted to sneak up behind the two staring at the fire.

Mick and Dave were lucky, for they were never spotted in their approach, also lucky a trap was never set. And better yet, Mick and Dave were helped by the fact one had his feet propped up tranquilly on a rock-stool. They were able to sneak all the way up to the cave inhabitants and with minimal resistance simultaneously grab their necks from behind, rendering them subdued for interrogation.

Before questioning began, Mick noticed their opposers hailed from Molisian, an observation made by spotting the insignia on their shields, which along with their weapons were thankfully far from grasp. Forfeiting, the Molisians submissively slumped, prepared to speak.

"We see you're foreigners, adversaries in war, no less," Mick noted, initiating semi-affable interrogation. "Though, I'm not concerned with that now. What we really need to know is where are the residents of the surface housing complex harboring the hidden entrance to this cave?"

The Molisian spoke, with an arm still wrapped around his neck and his foot still on a rock-stool. "I'm actually impressed you found that. We never thought anyone would ever discover that contraption. How did you know where it was?"

"First, you answer my question, and then, maybe I'll answer yours. And be honest with me."

The Molisian unexpectedly spouted, "Honesty—I never really understood that concept. What reason does anyone ever have to be honest with each other? I always say a person accomplishes the most when they only look out for themselves, doing everything in their power to make sure they're the one coming out ahead. And if you have to lie to do it, that's all part of the game. The whole world does it, and we're all better off because of it. People only say lying is immoral to hold back the strong."

With a quick, confident grin, Mick responded, "To yourself, it might appear you're correct in your gathering of wisdom, but I'm afraid your naiveté will be your undoing in this particular logical debate. On the surface, it may seem once you've successfully lied your way to the top, you are actually at the top, having everything you've ever wanted. But in all reality, you're not at the top. How is it possible to build the superior structure atop a shaky foundation? A society only relaying truths is the one that can progress most efficiently.

"False information and distortion can only *hinder* advancement. Obviously, if you have only lies on which to build, you're only going to waste time trying to solve riddles that weren't worth solving to begin with. Both society as a whole and the individual can more effectively generate a better structure over a solid base of truth. If we all only relayed truths, who knows what greatness could be accomplished.

"Maybe right now, as I speak, we wouldn't have to be walking everywhere we need to go or defecating in holes in the ground, or maybe we could see what's on the moons. Or perhaps, we could go beyond that, the mind reaching heights no one has ever even imagined possible. Lying is a path to the top, but it's a false pinnacle. So please, accept my veracity, and I ask you kindly to answer my initial question."

The Molisian pretended to pay attention until the end of Mick's discourse, and replied, "That sure was a really nice speech, but I still don't know anything about any housing complex residents."

"At least tell us what it is you're doing down here."

"We are enjoying the rocky landscape, camping."

Dave smirked, and hurled back, "You clearly hail from a foreign country, one with which we just happen to be at war. And you expect us to believe you're this far from your home enjoying the scenery, camping in a cave system half a mile below the surface, a mysterious place that can only be infiltrated through a secret entrance, an entrance that can only be unlocked by the most powerful magnet in the known universe. The thing is practically magic. You've got to be kidding me."

The Molisian responded, "I guess that would be pretty farfetched, but that's all you're getting out of us."

"Very well, have it your way. Dave, let's start tying 'em up."

"Let's make sure we bind these two better than the last guy we tied up. We don't need these two eventually getting loose, similarly making things rather difficult for us."

"In all fairness, we hastily tied the last guy in the heat of battle."

"True."

As securely as possible, Mick and Dave bound the probable accomplices to the kidnapping. It wasn't easy finding something stable to which to tether the Molisians, but after some effort they found something. "Don't worry, we won't leave you here forever. We'll come back to untie you later, after we get what we came for."

Before treading down the only tunnel, other than the one from whence they came, Mick and Dave grabbed the Molisian's weapons lying on the ground and hid them.

The light from the Molisians' fire was bright enough to illuminate their path for some time, so they didn't have to add much fuel to their torches for fifty or sixty yards. Eventually, the passageway grew uncomfortably narrow again.

Post the incident by the fire, the exploration remained uneventful until Dave, who was walking point, put his hand up signaling Mick to stop. "Do you hear that?"

Mick listened carefully, and replied, "Yes, I hear voices. Let's get a little closer, and maybe we can make out what they're saying."

"I agree."

Hawk and Leopard slithered around the tunnel's next bend, and came upon a split. The passage to the left was quiet, the one to the right was not. The duo stood by the juncture, and listened to the conversations being held. Nothing really caught their ear, until a new voice came into the picture.

"Okay you three lousy excuses, it's time to start pounding again," said the new voice. "Life will no longer be as comfortable as it was in your cozy house built into the side of the cliff. You're ours now, and you have to pull your weight."

The piercing sound of hammering began to reverberate, completely halting further deciphering of the dialogue.

"Well, Dave, that's all I needed to hear to take action. There are at least three or four Molisian impeders, so I don't think we'll be able to sneak up on them like the last time."

"We'll get close enough to see what we're up against and then, more than likely we'll trigger a charge."

They proceeded cautiously down the right-sided tunnel.

"It seems as if," Dave whispered, "the mineral consistency of the surrounding walls completely changed. Something I didn't expect along the way. The limestone is becoming fused with sections of the rhyolite formation. It's like back up on the surface, where the two stratums lie side by side."

"I bet there are precious gems within this new rock presentation, and the Molisians are using the compound dwellers as slaves to mine out the valuables."

"That would be my guess too, Mick."

Dave and Mick got as close as they could to the scene, without risking being noticed, and observed. Upon a single glance of the slave's obviously tortured appearance, they formed their resolve, and silently launched their irrevocable battle charge. The aggressive forward rush was initiated by a non-verbal look—a look that was practiced, a look that was perfected, and a look that was used similarly in the past.

There were four adversaries in all—three sitting by a fire talking, and one tending to the slaves, commanding.

The struggle began. One of the Molisians sitting by the fire was too slow to react to the new danger and lost an arm right away but still continued to fight, basically ineffectively. After Mick Thraiker sliced off the arm, he worked his way to the slaves, because he knew if he could just undo their shackles, three allies would be gained. He wasted no time, moving as quick as someone's mood having just realized they got their arm chopped off.

Mick skillfully knocked the slave-tender off balance, and sliced open one of the compound dweller's bondages with one mighty, metal-splitting blow from Black-Needle. Mick looked into the freed man's eyes, and swiftly pointed to a sturdy, grapefruit-sized rock lying on the ground, signaling to the new ally. The ally knew right away what was meant by the point.

Mick continued to sword fight with his single opponent, the slave tender. He parried just long enough to witness his opponent getting snuck up on from behind, and getting lethally knocked in the head with a grapefruit-sized rock.

While Mick released the remaining two prisoners from their chains, Dave was multitasking, simultaneously battling three Molisians. One was missing an arm, so not really a threat; another, also not posing much danger, having fallen victim to Dave's sneak charge, limited by a huge hole in his body, a gaping cavity caused by a sword being shoved through his leg and twisted. Dave's third opponent, even though mediocre with his sword, wasn't too hazardous. Dave barely suffered noticeable expenditure of energy in the exchange.

When Mick returned to Dave's side wielding three new allies, Dave already controlled the upper hand. The rest of the battle was over almost as fast as it began.

The three surviving Molisians were all tied down, two who were unconscious, all diminished by huge, gaping wounds. They weren't necessarily left to die, but were certainly left at a near-death state, until the mission was completely concluded.

"How many more of your companions have been kidnapped?" Mick asked the liberated.

The oldest of the unfettered replied, "There are fifteen more of us—men, women and children. I'm pretty sure most of them, if not all, are in the next chamber over."

"Is that the chamber that'd be reached by going down the other tunnel, the left-sided one at the fork in the road, to the right, if looking at it from this vantage point?"

"I think so. Everything is so disorientating down here."

"It is." Dave emitted, "We stumbled on your dilemma by chance. We'll talk more about that later, but for now we must hurry if we're to save the rest. There are six people in total tied down, and if any escape, we lose our element of surprise."

"We're ready," voiced a free man, fire in his eyes.

Silently, the group crept back down the corridor to the intersection, and went down the only path Mick and Dave had not yet taken. They all squeezed through the tight corridor, until a vast mining chamber was in sight.

Dave peered into the ominous cavity, and muttered, "I see maybe between twenty and twenty-five would-be opposers, and I have counted up to thirteen of your family members. Is it possible one of you three can spy where the others are? I hate to say it, but you know the area better."

One of the freed miners came forward and looked. "Our other two family members are probably just around that corner, either lying down in the hay or going to the bathroom in the area our captors barbarically designated."

"Do you know if there are any other tunnels leading into or out of this hollow?"

"I think there is one other. I'm pretty sure it is the other way down here. They hardly ever use it though."

Thinking of a plan, Mick buried his chin into his chest, closed his eyes, and squeezed the skin atop his skull into folds with his fingertips. Dave's plan-thinking paradigm for the moment was a bit different.

When finally coming face-to-face with the optimum stratagem, Mick emitted, "First off, we should try and minimize the numbers we'll have to face head on. It would be nice to halve the force, but I can't think of a plan that good. I think maybe we can eliminate a huge chunk of them, Dave, by using the *trap method*."

"One of my favorite methods," Dave released excitedly but quietly.

Mick and Dave explained to the others what was going to be done. No failure to understand arose.

The next task needing performing was locating a fairly large amount of gravel and rocks. For such a load, they had to backtrack all the way to the other mining chamber.

When Mick and Dave arrived at the other chamber, relief washed over them. Thankfully, the Molisians they tied up previously were still tied up. As premeditated, they used a few of the helmets lying on the ground as buckets to scoop up what gravel they needed, while the prisoners wondered what the heck was transpiring before them.

Having hurried back to the crossroads where the rest waited, Dave and Mick voiced their success. Mick and Dave parted from the compound dwellers again, and walked out into the open cavern, hid, and listened for any further dialogue that would help. Nothing came.

The plan's main part was activated.

For the initiating step, Dave and Mick used the gathered rocks and gravel to simulate a small cave-in. They threw their helmet-loads toward the Molisians, so the mock cave-in was sure to be heard, and heard it was, for almost half of the Molisians came rushing.

Mick bravely stood his ground in preparation to simulate another cave-in. Dave backed up about fifty paces back into the tunnel and waited patiently. While the Molisians stood around looking dumbfounded, Mick tossed the remaining loads into the tunnel.

To investigate, ten Molisians with their weapons of choice at their sides ran to where they thought the second cave-in occurred. Mick and Dave's gambit was paying off.

Dave knew the disadvantages of facing greater numbers, but paid it no attention, since this was where the plan would come into full effect. Dave reaped the benefit of knowing he could only be attacked by opponents in a single file line, owing to the narrowness of the tunnel.

On his end, Mick stood firm and confident and with sword firmly grasped.

When the ten Molisians went down the tunnel expecting signs of a cave-in, they got something completely different—*Dave*. The ten got sight of just one contender standing before them, and did exactly what Mick and Dave wanted them to do—attack aggressively, without hesitation, and without returning back to the mining chamber to warn the others.

The lead man was dropped instantly, before the remaining nine even knew what'd happened. The next in line wasn't such a pushover, who was able to execute a few sword blocks, enough to prevent an immediate impalement by Dave's Black-Needle. Dave's second opponent lasted longer than his first, but in terms of sword-fighting time was put to death reasonably fast.

Suddenly, aided by the element of surprise, Mick came rushing down the tunnel, full force. The trap was sprung.

Barely enough room to swing his axe, the Molisian furthest from Dave spun around and came at Mick. Unlike Mick and Dave's first two rivals, the axe-wielder was able to get off a few offensive maneuvers, before having to shield himself from death. With his opponent winded, Hawk countered and successfully chopped off his axe hand. Having shoved the butt of his sword into the enemy's head with a backswing, Mick effectively knocked the one-handed man out cold.

Mick's next contender, having witnessed the quickness of the three deaths before him, was hesitant in attack, but knew his compatriots would brand him a coward if he retreated, so he forged ahead, and reluctantly faced the whirling onslaught of Thraiker. Without tremendous effort, Mick caused the man a neck contusion, and slew the poor fellow who should've heeded his instincts and thrown down arms.

The two-man flank was working splendidly, however, the *trap method* was now at its pivotal moment. Along with fighting opponents, Mick and Dave had to fight slight exhaustion. Facing multiple opponents in succession wasn't easy, though Mick and Dave had a trick up their sleeves, an old trick. They pretended to be more worn out than they actually were. The tried-and-true bait-and-switch maneuver hardly ever failed.

The next in line unsuccessfully threw a rock at Mick's head, while aggressively advancing, sword extended, yelling many profanities. Mick dodged the rock, the charge, and the profanities.

Mick performed a decoy swing at the Molisian's head, and pulled out a dagger from its resting place at his side. He rotated the knife to the ready position, and swung it in a full arc, having gained a small amount of momentum by dropping to the ground to a crouch. He had swung true, driving the knife all the way to the cave floor, through the boot, and the foot to which it was attached, staking the man to the ground, effectively rendering immobilization. More kicking and flailing ensued than Mick had ever seen in his life. Before the Molisian was able to do anything about being tethered to the ground, his lights went out forever. Even the Molisians in the tunnel who were still alive thought Mick's maneuver was a masterful piece of artwork.

Mick and Dave continued to work with a seemingly inexhaustible supply of vigor. The realization of imminent doom was starting to set in for the remaining Molisian combatants.

Dave battled the next in line, while the remaining two Molisians realized they'd unquestionably been duped. The two tried to get past Mick and back to the chamber where the rest of their friends were idly sitting clueless as to what was transpiring. One of the escaping two was slow due to wearing too much armor, and the other was just slow inherently. Mick was able to hunt them both down before they reached their compatriots.

At the trap method's conclusion, almost half the threat was purged, leaving the now accomplishable task of freeing the rest of the prisoners. Chalk another success to the trap method. The remaining warriors would definitely be harder to defeat, due to the loss of the neutralizing tunnel, but Mick and Dave were confident they could win.

The three freed prisoners joined back up with Hawk and Leopard, and they all rested minimally before resuming.

Mick said to the three, "Unless any of you have significant fighting experience, I suggest when the battle begins, you focus your efforts into trying to release the rest of your companions. That way our numbers are enhanced, allowing us a better chance for survival. The shackles are weak at the wall mounts and can be destroyed with a well-placed blow."

"We will do our best."

Dave commented to Mick, "Things are going pretty smoothly so far, now to go finish them off."

"Sounds fine to me, my old friend."

The rest of the Molisians eventually had a clue as to what was going on, so when Hawk and Leopard made their charge into the hollow, there wasn't anyone caught off guard. Immediately, Mick and Dave, upon reaching the horde, were surrounded by fierce challengers. But on the positive side, the three previously liberated prisoners went seemingly unnoticed on the onset, so they were free to attempt their rescue. They snuck in behind, about thirty seconds after Mick and Dave entered the hollow, and inconspicuously made their way to the rest of the prisoners.

When Dave and Mick ran into the chamber, they picked out the best possible place to make their stand and headed towards it. It was a spot in the middle of the cave, where two giant monoliths rose impressively, mighty stalagmite pillars forged from dripping water long ago. They used the towers to defend their backs, so when the pair stood side-by-side, they only had to face enemies coming at them from the front and sides. And that is exactly what the remaining Molisians did, except for the leader, who patiently waited in concealment to study his opponents before rushing into battle. Plus, it was wise by the Molisian leader to refrain from letting the intruders get an inkling as to who was in charge.

Facing five at a time between the two of them, Hawk and Leopard were up to the challenge, but wouldn't have been afraid to admit they thought initially this time perhaps they'd bitten off more than they could chew. But they shrugged it off, knowing the test would bring new mental opportunities.

Sword tips and edges came at Mick and Dave from every angle, but only slightly wounded them. The pair's offense was far outweighing their opponent's defense, Mick and Dave's cluster of enemies shrinking in stature parallel the passage of time. The Black-Needles were performing magnificently against the reddish/gray rocky backdrop.

The underground contingent's leader, biding his time studying, was almost ready to join the fray. In his mind, he uncovered a weakness. But one thinking he was a step ahead of someone who was already thinking two steps ahead, was bound to spend his force wastefully. Mick noticed the leader—who wasn't as adept at hiding as he thought—standing in the back scrutinizing. Mick worked out yet another one of his masterful schemes.

Mick perceived the twelve-pound splitting maul the leader wielded was his primary weapon, and knew the advantages someone who fought with such a weapon reaped. All a person needed was one good solid connection to an opponent's head, and the battle was over. As soon as Mick noticed he and Dave were being watched, he implemented all his full-extension sword moves to supply the illusion he had a larger range of motion than what he really had, a deception which, when the time came, Mick could use in his favor.

At that instant, Dave had only two left to fight, while Mick solely focused on the leader, employing his gambit. Technically, the only reason Mick pretended to have a large range of motion was to prevent the leader from getting lucky, and connecting with one of the deadly maul swings. It was a stall tactic. The reason Mick did this was because he had a strong feeling about something.

Heading for his face, Mick successfully dodged a tremendous amount of momentum generated from a kinetic twelve-pound piece of metal. After the hairs-on - end moment, Mick's erstwhile strong feeling became true—the leader was fatally stabbed from behind by one of the freed prisoners. Dave's last enemy followed, having received the same demise, and just like that, the battle was over. Hawk and Leopard were surrounded by eighteen of the happiest people in Garobansurov.

No time was spent doing any extravagant celebrating at that moment. They first had to get out of the cave system, before any of the tied-up/severely injured Molisians regrouped. However, a small amount of time was spent by all to fill their pockets with the Molisians' gems. Even Mick and Dave couldn't resist snatching a few. They weren't the highest quality gems, but valuable enough to justify the time spent.

Treasures successfully gathered, they all walked through the tunnel, past the fork, and through to the first dimly-lit chamber Mick and Dave encountered. Thankfully, the first two exposed to Thraiker and Ghrere's wrath were still tied-up. Dave told the two that soon they'd be released, and that then they could unfetter their compatriots in bondage elsewhere in the cave. Dave also told them if they did anything stupid after that, they'd suffer even further humiliation.

Once the group was far enough away, Mick and Dave went back, made sure no weapons were available, and undid the enemy's ropes. The pair was surprised Mick and Dave actually returned to set them free, thinking the whole while their sands of time were almost fully depleted. The two Molisians did what they were previously told. They and the rest of the surviving members of the underground Molisian appendage never returned.

The party reformed and headed straight for the exit. Relief washed over them all when they caught sight of light from the surface seeping in. Mick and Dave were glad they'd successfully led their party past every precarious ledge the subterranean decided to present.

Everyone climbed out, single file, and erupted euphorically once the cold air hit their faces. All were surprised to jump off the cube-shaped rhyolite stone into a foot of snow, even Mick and Dave.

As those around them rejoiced, Mick and Dave knew they'd been immersed into a rather interesting concoction of people.

CHAPTER 12

AT AROUND THE time Mick and Dave's rescue mission reached its triumphant conclusion, Brom Quintaga found himself experiencing feelings he hadn't felt in a long time, but before that's explained more extensively, the events leading up to those feelings should first be made known.

The testing process for Brom's armor didn't happen as early as anticipated, for more urgent matters had kept Gamald's attention. The matters involved the layer of snow on the ground making the army at Sarwa grow restless. The soldiers knew they were going to attack Thraug, but didn't particularly yearn to march there in further accumulations of snow. Who would?

While Brom waited in the bustling courtyard for someone to tell him what was going on, he watched and listened to all the activity going on around him. The scuttling about and small talk of the townspeople weren't exactly entertaining, but having something on which to focus was more agreeable than passing time through the friction of nervous boredom.

As Brom waited, General Gamald, Lieutenant Leedle, General Anolski, Grunt, and Roar were holding conference in a secluded, locked room of the army barracks. It was so isolated the bulk of the soldiers weren't even aware of this backroom. The dark rectangular space contained a desk and chair; a couple fake, six-foot trees in pots; and a painting of a bridge suspended over water—purple for some reason. Since the room was hardly ever used, four folding chairs had to be brought in so everyone could sit, except Gamald, who sat in the already provided chair.

Tapping his fingers on the desk, and staring at the weird picture—specifically the purple river—Gamald noted, "At least we only received a foot of snow in the storm. I've seen relentless blizzards which didn't stop discharging until it supplied five feet of fresh snow."

Anolski remarked, "I think I remember that storm. It happened about ten years ago in the Grenakon Vale."

"Yes, I was there with a squadron. We were snowbound for a week, before we could shovel ourselves out," responded Gamald.

"Where I was located during it, we only got two feet, but I was supposed to be in the Vale that day, but got hung up. I'm sure glad I got hung up that day. I'm not a big fan of copious shoveling."

Finally releasing his judgmental stare at the room's only picture, Gamald said, "I wanted to wait for the return of the latest detachment of scouts, before I made my decision on when to send the army to claim Thraug. But due to everyone's relentless complaining about the snow, I'm ordering the army to leave today, before it gets any deeper."

Glad at the decision, the four in attendance responded in unison, "Yes, sir."

"I'll be sending eighteen hundred troops, assuming only fourteen or fifteen hundred Garobansurovian soldiers will be waiting. The walls are low, so I don't think they'll last long with all six of our catapults aimed at one spot."

Anolski vocalized, "I agree. I'm sure we can punch a hole through the wall relatively quickly, way before they're able to destroy any of them with return fire."

"I'm glad you agree Anolski, since I will not be accompanying. You'll be in charge of the Thraug offensive."

"Affirmative, sir. Thank you."

"I want the rest of you, Leedle, Grunt, Roar, to stay in Sarwa. I'm sure Anolski can handle it at Thraug."

"Yes, sir," said the three.

General Anolski shuffled himself into a different position on his folding chair and said, "With everyone already wanting to leave, I'm sure departure preparations will be speedy. By midday, we'll be ready to march."

"Good to hear," returned Gamald. "Do what you want with the Nighteagle and Ulfenkerki. It's your decision whether to keep them alive or not. I don't care one way or the other."

"Yes, sir."

"Once you have the town secured, wait for word from me on your next assignment. I'll more than likely leave you be for a while to defend."

"Yes, sir. Good, sir."

"That's enough 'yes, sirs' for one sitting." Gamald stood up from his chair, took the piece of artwork with the purple river off the wall—a quaint picture most would enjoy, despite the off-kilter river—smashed it on the floor, and dismissed everyone in the room.

The two biggest were the first to leave and the happiest to leave.

"Grrrrrrr," said the biggest.

"Roaaaar," said the second biggest.

Having sat on a stone in front of a wooden edifice for hours, Brom noticed a slew of soldiers starting to line up in preparation to go somewhere—it smelled like a battle. He was starting to think he was forgotten.

But eventually, amongst the chaos, he was approached by Leedle, and was informed the tests were to begin. The two of them walked to a sector of town where army training occasionally occurred, and met up with Gamald along with an assortment of other military personnel.

General Gamald spoke to Brom: "I trust you slept well in the company of my soldiers?"

"I did. Thank you, sir, for the accommodations."

"And I'm sure you caught sight of the assemblage of manpower, preparing to conquer another one of your country's cities."

"Aaah, war, what can you do?" said Brom for the second time in a month.

"Right. Okay then, let's see your armor in action."

Brom pulled the three sets out from the cart, and organized them, propping each piece neatly alongside its respective counterparts. The suits weren't all the same size, but it was hard to tell by looking at them they weren't. The cosmetic designs of each suit were all the same, though. "The suits are ready. What's first?" asked Brom.

Everyone in attendance observed up close and personal all the pieces, picking them off the ground, inspecting and touching all the facets. Afterwards, everyone stepped back and huddled together at a distance—everyone except for Brom, Gamald, Leedle, and three others unfamiliar to Brom.

Gamald instructed the three unfamiliars to put on the suits. Brom watched on, hoping they weren't going to be too rough and scratch the metal. There was nothing he could do about it now. In his mind, it was now or never.

Three other soldiers came out of the woodwork at Gamald's command, wearing customary armor. Brom thought the new three were probably joining in to serve as benchmarks in the suit comparisons. He was right.

The first test was initiated, which was nothing more than a running race. The six had lined up and raced around the yard's circumference. In the end, all three of the soldiers wearing Brom's armor had beaten the three benchmarks, except for one.

Leedle addressed Gamald at seeing the result: "The outcome would've been the other way around, had they raced in normal dress. This first assessment is a testament to the superiority of his suits, at least in the department of speed."

"Very well. What's next?"

The second experiment made Brom a little more nervous, but he didn't let it affect him. *There's no going back now*, he said to himself. Each suit bearer was given a wooden sword or hammer, and matched up in pairs. They did their best to pit individuals possessing equal skills.

On the word *go*, they all began fighting each other, wildly, trying to force their respective opponent into submission. They bludgeoned each other with their weapons—the swords were blunt and the hammers light—numerous times, surely feeling the pains of being struck violently.

Ten minutes went by, and they were all ordered to stop. The six were all exhausted beyond measure but none had given up. None wanted their commander seeing them as a coward, so they all fought as if their lives were on the line. On paper, the test wasn't specifically designed to force combatants into submission as much as it was designed to compare the effects on the suits when the fight was over.

Upon Gamald's inspection of all six suits, he commented, "Well, well, well, Mr. Brom Quintaga, my degree of positive impression of your suits just keeps increasing. Come look. Barely a scratch on your suits, compared with the battered appearance of our army's stock suits. Things are looking pretty good for you. Only one test remains."

Brom was heartbroken, seeing even minimal damage to his suits, but he remained upbeat.

The third and final test shocked Brom, for it was a test that was definitely unorthodox in situations such as those. He almost protested, but bit his lip. He knew if he objected, the deal would've been off, there being no way of resuming the task of finding his son if he did. He would try his best at looking in the opposite direction of the surmounting terror.

An inconsequential individual came out of the woodwork, carrying six swords. Each soldier donning armor was given one. These were no wooden, blunt weapons. These were six of some of the finest swords the Molisian army had to offer, and were definitely made for killing. The already fatigued men were now ordered to fight again and, like before, didn't want to show any signs of weakness. They complied with only minimal hesitation. Brom was starting to think Gamald handpicked the six, due to their bravery.

They all started off aggressively, but it didn't take them much time to become virtually stagnant. Onward they persisted, even though their swords felt ten times heavier than they really were.

The fifteen-minute mark went by, and still they weren't ordered to stop. Brom couldn't look away any longer, so he peeked. To him, it seemed as if the soldiers expected this, and accepted the fact they were fighting to the death. Grinding his teeth and cringing, Brom resumed looking away.

Brom could tell right away when the first kill was made, due to the fact the clashing sounds of two of the swords ceased. Curious to know who was victorious, Brom hoped it was a bearer of one of his suits, though his eyes still wanted no part. He continued to stare at the sparrows flying back and forth through his field of vision.

He tried to determine whether they were landing on the ground in-between flight paths, or just continually circling. It was impossible to know for sure—the city wall was in the way. It was as good a distraction as any.

When only three soldiers remained, the tests were finally over. Brom finally looked and saw three honorable men (honorable for all he knew) lay bloody and defeated on the ground, face down, all wearing the stock armor. Even Brom himself wouldn't have been able to foresee the superiority of his suits shown. The results were unprecedented.

Gamald slapped Brom on the back, and said, "Your armor is as good as sold. Now all that's left are negotiations, which I'm sure will be short and sweet. If I remember correctly, you were asking a price of ten thousand gitis a piece?"

"That was correct, sir."

"Good, good. I'll submit a counteroffer of seventy-five hundred a piece, which I can promise is more than just."

"You're right, General Gamald, sir, it is surely just. But If I could be so bold as to re-counter, requesting nine thousand a piece, I would be much happier."

"I'm sure you would. We're all happier with more money. But in these tough times I can only afford eight thousand a piece."

Brom was now content at the price and gladly remarked, "Then, that will be the price—eight thousand gitis a piece. You were right, negotiations were short and sweet."

Gamald, also happy with the outcome, proclaimed, "Wonderful, let us celebrate. Tonight, we will throw a luxurious celebration in your honor, a gay occasion where the transaction will be made. Your money will be given to you in Garobansurovian currency, we'll all feast, and we'll all more than likely get drunk."

"I like the sound of that," Brom emitted. "I'll try to procure something fancy to wear and see you then."

For the time being, Brom left the company of Molisian military personnel. In reality, he didn't really want to wait around for any celebration. He just wanted to be paid, and to be on his way. But he seemed to not have a choice in the matter, so he tried his best to look forward to the feast. Eventually, he came around to thinking he was going to have a good time that evening.

Brom and his cart spent the majority of the waiting time in a garden that had seen better days, which wasn't far from where the celebration was to take place. He'd already waited for two hours and figured he only had one more hour left to wait. He was starting to get nervous—the upcoming evening was an important one.

Mr. Quintaga spent the final hour of waiting peering at his masterworks, and remembering all the hard work put into their crafting. He also pondered the good memories they represented, of all his family members who watched on as he made them, giving him their full support. Not many people would've undertook such an enormously ambitious venture, but his family, especially the son for whom he was searching, was always there for him, as he toiled away for those thirty years. It was a happy thirty years.

When Brom's emotions were climaxing, it was time for him to head towards the grand hall for the festivity.

He walked slowly, wearing his best shirt, not really wanting to give up his armor, but knew it had to be done.

He finally reached the entrance, and a pair of finely dressed greeters assisted him in bringing his cart into the building. There were fewer people present than what he'd anticipated, and almost all were part of the Molisian army. Before Brom had a chance to decide where to sit, Lieutenant Leedle directed him to his assigned seat. "The man of the hour needs to sit in a place of importance, obviously," said Leedle.

Brom was positioned at the head table, and a waiter immediately poured him a glass of wine. Over the dull roar, an eight-piece orchestra was playing in the southeastern corner of the main room. The whole place was decorated, but to Brom it seemed hastily decorated. The extravagant building at least had noticeably pleasing acoustics. Scattered all over the main room were big, blue flowers, a species Brom had never before seen. They appeared out of season, but he didn't really know much about flowers to know if they were. He liked them, nevertheless. They were the highlight of the decorations.

General Gamald arrived ten minutes after Brom, and sat at the same table. "This is your night Brom, enjoy. Don't think you have to go easy on the wine, there's plenty to go around."

"Thank you," replied the anxious man. "What's on the dinner menu?"

"I'm not exactly sure, but it's more than likely going to be chicken and potatoes. It seems that's always what they make at these kinds of things."

Brom laughed at the remark, and sat back in his chair a little less uneasy. He was really hungry, and didn't care what the servers brought out. Chicken sounded splendid to him.

The evening progressed, and it turned out Gamald was right about the chicken. No surprise. Brom ate his share, and had two glasses of wine, opposed to everyone else at the table having at least ten each.

Throughout the night, a scattering of anonymous people approached Brom to initiate short conversations. It was almost always about his armor, and they were almost always as drunk as a sailor on shore leave.

When it seemed the orchestra had finished playing for the night, Gamald stood up and toasted Brom. "I want to thank everyone for coming to this event, especially Mr. Brom Quintaga, for whom this night was dedicated. His skills in armorcraft are matched by no one. I'm ecstatic the army is gaining such workmanship. The night is now over, and we must pay Mr. Quintaga the money he's been promised."

About half the crowd dispersed after Gamald's toast, some of them leaving through the front door, and some exiting through some of the other doors, to where Brom had no idea where they led. The other half just stayed in their chairs and continued drinking. They seemed the type normally oblivious to their surroundings. Brom thought they'd probably keep drinking until the sun's return.

Gamald thanked Brom one last time and said goodbye, as Leedle approached from their backside.

Leedle put his hand on Brom's shoulder, and said, "Come with me. I will get you your twenty-four thousand gitis. Hopefully you feel extra strong tonight, the bag is going to be heavy."

Brom smiled, and followed Leedle to one of the doors in the back. Just before going through the door, he turned around to glance one final time at his armor. He took a deep breath, ignored the sorrow, and walked through the door.

On the other side of the door was a lip and a spiraling staircase leading downward. At the bottom of the staircase, he noticed another one of the big, blue flowers was tied to the railing. The flower was attached by a purple ribbon tied in a bow. Brom was normally a man's man, tough-as-nails kind of a guy. But for some reason that evening, probably because of the significance of what was happening to him, he truly noticed the aesthetic beauty of the flower. It brought a sincere smile to his face.

Along with the flower, a narrow corridor met them at the bottom of the staircase, down which they proceeded. When they reached a point thirty feet past the spiraling staircase, Leedle stopped in-between two closed doors, one on either side of the hallway. He said, "Wait right here, your money is in the safe. I'll be right back with it."

As Leedle opened the door, Brom remained where he was, but stole a quick look into the room Leedle was about to enter. He didn't see the safe in plain view, before Leedle entered the room and closed the door, but Brom didn't think anything of it.

Brom waited patiently, staring at the door through which Leedle had just passed. He noticed he was standing equidistant between the staircase he had just descended, and another one that led even further down. He also noticed there were only two doors in the narrow hallway, one in front of him, and one behind him. The one in front was through where Leedle had just proceeded; the one behind was locked. He had checked for the heck of it while he waited. The passageway was lit by a pair of weak lamps on either side of the hall, which kept the corridor just bright enough to see ten feet in front of him.

He'd been waiting in the hall three minutes—*an eternity*—when he heard the sound of someone in heavy armor walking up the stairs at the other end of the corridor. When the armor-clad entity reached the top of the stairs, Brom noticed it was a pair of soldiers, and that they were now starting to walk briskly directly at him. His survival instincts kicked into gear.

He turned to run back up the stairs leading to the main hall, but another pair of soldiers sprang forth. They had been ominously waiting in the dark cavity behind the spiraling staircase the whole while. They cut Brom off before he could make it to the first step. Brom couldn't believe he hadn't seen four eyes staring at him through the gaps between the steps, despite the poorly lit hall. The soldiers were sitting there the entire time, waiting for the ambush. They jumped into action the exact moment their counterparts came into view—a perfect plan, really.

Brom tried to elude the soldiers, but deep in his heart he knew he couldn't escape.

Just before the four soldiers corralled Brom, they pounded the walls. On that cue, the locked door suddenly opened. Before Brom could react in the slightest, a huge man waiting behind the door with a sack almost as huge performed his part of the plan with precision. He slipped the sack over the whole of Brom's body with ease. The last thing Brom saw before he was sacked and beaten into unconsciousness was the beautiful, blue flower tied to the staircase with a purple bow.

And at that sight, his eyes glossed over, and he thought about how all the beauty in the world was being stripped away, and what Leedle had said—*a heavy bag indeed.*

THE COMPOUND DWELLERS made it known they surely didn't mind the fact Mick and Dave had entered their houses to look for clues to their disappearances.

Hawk and Leopard enjoyed a few beers and shared in the story of the rescuing. Mick asked, "Do any of you happen to know where the other entrance to the cave is?"

The father of the Dearn family answered, "We have no idea, but I know the path to that entrance/exit was longer than the path to the one here, because I always heard profuse complaining when one of them had to use it."

Along with Dearn, the other two families' last names residing at the mine compound were Tyson and Burg.

The three families, Mick, and Dave spent an enormous amount of time jovially conversing upon everything that occurred, including the very reason Dave and Mick stopped at the compound in the first place—socks.

Down came a barely noticeable sprinkling of snowflakes, and up came the topic of the cliff house. Mick and Dave learned it was constructed by the Burg family. Dave explained how one night they got lazy and slept in the warm cliff house, as opposed to their tents.

The Burg mother responded to the statement. "That's fine with us. You are heroes, whom we owe our lives. I would've done the same thing in your situation.

You're welcome to do it again tonight, if you want, before you again set forth on your journey."

"That probably will be determined on how many more beers we have," Dave said, jokingly. "Too many and our legs won't want to take us anywhere."

Mick and Dave listened attentively to the miners, as they described from their points of view how the kidnapping transpired. Poignant stories to be sure. Subsequently, conversations moved to the topic of war, and everything that happened heretofore. The Battle of Strwin was conversed, along with how Sarwa got captured, and what battles they all thought might happen in the future.

The conversations eventually lightened up. Mick and Dave were asked to play ball by the younger generation. They accepted the invitation with enthusiasm and spent an hour running, throwing, and tackling. A good time was had by all who played, while the older generation watched and cheered.

At the game's completion, Dave said, "That was exhilarating. I sure wish we received chances to do that more often."

Mick agreed wholeheartedly.

Many expressed hunger, so the next activity was a meal. As you'd assume, folks living on a fish-abundant river would possess abundant fish, and you'd assume they'd serve that fish when a lot of food is needed to be served.

The cooking of much fish is exactly what materialized.

During the meal, because Mick and Dave never stopped drinking beer, they decided they'd spend one last night at the homestead, before their departure. Not entirely imposing on the Burg woman's offer, Mick and Dave aimed to just slept in their tents.

It ended up being a great day. Not excluding a soul, everyone had fashioned their own lasting memories. Mick and Dave proudly fell asleep in their tents, knowing they'd just pieced together A-games. The world would've been a far worse place if the people they'd just met were caged forever. They were fantastic humans, and would've attempted the same thing for a stranger Dave and Mick had.

Mick and Dave slept really well, and woke up the next morning fully rejuvenated. They took down their tents, and packed up all their gear, weapons, and armor. They went to say goodbye to the miners, and weren't surprised to see all of them already gathered together to offer as warm a farewell as possible.

The father Dearn produced heartfelt words. "We owe you our lives. Speaking for all of us, yesterday turned out to be the greatest day imaginable. Not only because of you rescuing us, but for the great fun we all had at our celebration of sorts. Has anyone ever told you how much fun you guys are at a party?"

Mick and Dave chuckled. Dave responded, "Nope, I can't say either of us have heard that before from anyone."

The Burg woman suddenly remembered something: "Please don't leave before I get back! I have something for you. I'll be quick."

She ran to her house, went inside, grabbed to what she was referring, and returned before Mick and Dave could even finish their thoughts on what it could be she was getting. She said, "I just remembered what you told us yesterday, about what actually started this whole chain of events." She smiled and handed Dave and Mick both a heaping pile of socks. "If not for all your socks becoming uselessly wet and tattered, you wouldn't have felt the need to stop here inquiring about new ones, and we never would've been saved."

"That's so true," Dave returned.

"We owe our lives to your wet, useless socks."

Everyone laughed heartily at her comment.

Individual *thank-you's* were expressed one last time to Mick and Dave, not a single one failing to touch the heroes' hearts. Some were poetic thank-you's, some were short and sweet, but each and every emotionalism was given much thought.

Mick and Dave wished them all the best. Mick voiced the third-to-last sentiment. "You folks truly are a great bunch of people. I hope you don't mind, but we'd like to keep this magnetic key we found. I have a feeling it might be useful for us again in the future. Plus, its parabolic nature allows us to squeeze it into our packs quite easily without wasting much room."

"Go ahead and keep it, granting you that is the least we can do." The eldest emitted the penultimate showing of heart. "I truly mean this: Someday, somehow, we'll return the favor, and help you."

In response, producing the final sentimentality, Dave said, "We have no doubt you will. Farewell, lovely people."

Pleasant departure accomplished, Thraiker and Ghrere continued their journey north/north-eastward. They resumed their original plan of trying to aid the war effort at the border. But now they had a fresh supply of socks.

THE NIGHTEAGLE WASN'T surprised when his veteran scout, Sea-Sand, informed him Gamald's force was on the move, separated by only a two day's march. The Nighteagle knew bloodshed was inevitable. After hearing the scout's data, he went directly to Ulfenkerki to tell him the news.

"Far from astonished," returned the Black Bear, upon hearing the intelligence. "I'm sure the prospect of deeper snow weighed heavily on Gamald's mind."

"I know we couldn't be any more prepared, and I've utmost confidence we will succeed here at Thraug."

"I share your view entirely. Do you have any idea as to the size of their force?"

The Nighteagle responded, "Just like we hoped, only eighteen hundred. They're bringing six mobile catapults. Fortunately, six is exactly what past reconnaissance revealed they could muster. We're well fortified and ready."

"Very well. I'm going to go inform my soldiers of this information, starting with the officers."

Without much effort in his search, Ulfenkerki located Jason in the barracks playing cards with Gregg. They were in a room with an angled corner, presenting the illusion the room was tiny. "It smells like card counting in here."

Jason replied to his commanding officer, "If I was an owner of that talent, I'd boast a lot fancier armor than I do now."

The General single-breath chuckled, then relayed the Nighteagle's data.

Jason Thorncat remarked, "Do you want the soldiers to train harder, or should I lighten the load, so they can rest up efficiently?"

"I've been told they're two days away, so perform today's drills at normal pace. Tomorrow, have them run through a few hours' worth of some of the less physical drills, so that way they're good and fresh for when the fight is upon us."

"Yes, sir."

Setting his sights on notifying everyone else of the news, Ulfenkerki left Gregg and Jason to their tiny room and honest game.

Gregg asked, "Which are the less physical drills?"

"For him, it just means lighter rocks to lug."

Jason and Gregg laughed, and continued their game, playing until the aroma of dinner overwhelmed that of the apparent card counting.

CHAPTER 13

MICK AND DAVE had been navigating a fairly wide trail for an hour when they noticed they could still see the river and parts of the compound behind them. Dave said, "They weren't kidding when they said Northern Garobansurov is higher than most of Garobansurov's other parts."

"They sure weren't, Dave. I'm glad there's a fairly frequently traveled trail here, preventing us from having to break snow along the way."

"Yeah, it seems at least three or four people have done that for us already today. God bless 'em."

"It also seems warm today. I bet by noon, it'll get above freezing, persuading a large chunk of this snow to melt," Mick noted, kicking an intruding, irregular snow hump.

"Hope so."

Ghrere and Thraiker trotted along all day, and by 2:00 p.m. in the afternoon they hardly noticed they were walking in snow. Along with the broken trail, a lot of it did eventually melt, but only about half.

Having reached a locale comparatively thick with vegetation, Mick stopped for a second and asked, "Do you hear that?"

Dave stopped, listened and responded, "I hear it. Sounds like a decent-sized waterfall. Not much water, but a really high drop off."

"Now, how in creation can you tell it's not a low drop off with a lot of water?"

"I figured I'd take the fifty-fifty chance, and try to get one past you. Being called the Waterfall Master, along with Swamp Master, has a nice ring to it."

Mick laughed. "I was unaware you harbored such life aspirations."

"There are so many sides to Dave Ghrere."

"Don't I know it."

The duo inched closer to the falls, as the sound of the cascade grew increasingly louder. The terrain was pretty rugged, almost impassable. To get to the not-yet-visible waterfall, they had to walk off-trail, through arduous landscape. They trailblazed farther than what they'd thought they needed, or wanted to. The sound traveled well through the thick timber, sound waves traveling better through a solid than a gas, making it seem the waterfall was closer. Eventually the thick brush gave way to a small clearing, where the waterfall called home.

"Looks like you were right Waterfall Master. That is one tall, skinny plume of water."

"Thank you, Bushmaster."

Despite the rough trail coming in, the pair felt rather lively, so they climbed down the steep embankment to get to the plummet pool's domain. After a bit of inspection, they observed the pool wasn't very large or very deep—not deep enough to not see the bottom, but not shallow enough that it didn't strike wonder upon its gazer. They noticed how much the scene seemed like its own ecosystem. Everything seemed to be happening free from the rest of the world—the plants, the crustaceans, the fish, even the inorganic elements, they all lived in their own little niche, never wanting to expand their boundaries. It was their territory and no one else's.

Mick and Dave, beyond doubt, were captivated by the beauty they were witnessing.

"You know, Mick, right now, I'm looking at a gold nugget sitting in the creek, and I'm not even going to pick it up to keep. I don't want to disrupt the perfect balance. Upsetting the equilibrium might interrupt something beyond our immediate perception or understanding."

"Wise decision. I would do the same."

Suspended not far from the nugget, they both glanced at the biggest trout they'd ever seen. Dave escaped to a thought pertaining to how wonderful it would be to have a fish like that mounted above his fireplace. "Too bad that fish isn't swimming around in one of our streams back home. Now, that's a trophy."

Of course, as was their tendency, they studied the geology of the area for a short while. They concluded the ravine had existed for millions of years, and a force other than cascading water formed it. Natural faulting as the cause was their hypothesis. Along with final glances, they both took final deep breaths, allowing the fresh, undisturbed air to flow through their systems, hoping the moment would seep into their permanent memories.

Almost on their hands and knees, they climbed out of the gorge and made their way through the rough terrain back to the wide trail.

"Now that was a good experience," said Dave.

Mick added, "Yes, I'm glad we had to know whether you were right or wrong about the fall's identity."

"We probably still would've made the trip if I hadn't said anything."

"I'm sure we would've. It's too fun not to."

The pair continued their journey along the wide trail north-northeastward with enthusiasm, electrified by the pulses of enchantment received at the plunge pool, the kind of electrification that can only be caused by nature. They did, however, perspire a lot by the exertion, and had to change their sweaty clothes, so they didn't get too cold by sunset. One of the only things worse than facing a cold night in the tent was facing one when having been already cold for hours.

Further up the trail, they noticed a few more footprints in the snow. "We're probably getting close to something or many somethings man-made," said Mick. "Numerous paths seem to be diverging, a tell-tale sign of nearing civilization."

"Or something resembling it. Hopefully there's food. I'm in the mood for something other than anything we have."

"Really, you don't want fish again?"

Dave cackled, spun around, and upon noticing his friend was also about to laugh, lengthened his own.

They walked for another mile, and saw where it was that everyone was heading. In the distance, they could see a conglomerate: one bigger building in the center, surrounded by many smaller buildings, all underneath a copse of trees. It didn't resemble a permanent town, but it did look like a lot of people lived there. When they got closer, they could see a medium-sized lake adjoining the community of buildings, which was probably why there was so much of a gathering at this one spot. For that point in time, the fishing in the lake was probably supreme.

They couldn't quite confirm what all the buildings were exactly until they were almost on top of them. The big building in the middle was a saloon, and all smaller buildings were dwellings—not the prettiest of dwellings, but dwellings, nevertheless. It was a small, temporary fishing village, not on the maps.

There were a few fishermen in boats out on the lake, braving the cold, and a few more fishing from shore. Many of the village's inhabitants were more than likely in the saloon.

Mick eyed the relatively large, centralized building and said, "I suppose if we don't go in, we'll never know if they have only fish to eat here too."

"Let's hope not."

Hawk and Leopard walked through the front entrance and were taken aback by how so many people could fit into one building. Men, women, and children were everywhere.

"The good news at first glimpse is I see a few people eating some kind of sausage."

Dave looked at Mick. "Don't get too excited. It's possible they're all out of sausage now."

Mick let out an indelicate chortle, and looked at Dave with a funny expression. "We better hurry and order then."

Supplying a fair share of tavern ambiance, the popular establishment seemed just as big on the inside as it looked from the outside. There were about twenty five tables for eating, and a long bar for drinking. It was somewhat dark, as most bars were. In a few of the sections it looked as if a little remodeling was transpiring, but not with much intensity judging by the gathering of dust on some of the tools and materials. The ceiling was high, and the floor was dirty, probably only swept once a day. In that particular saloon, the smoke filling the atmosphere was more pipe smoke than fireplace smoke, which was a little annoying, but it wasn't so much that it drove anyone away, including Mick and Dave.

They walked up to the bar, and once the barkeeper got to them, Dave said, "We'll have a couple glasses of mead, and a couple orders of sausage."

Anticipation followed the ordering, but the bartender's response was positive. Mick and Dave were relieved. "Coming up," said the bartender. "Your meals will be done in about ten minutes."

"Wonderful."

Flagons of mead were delivered promptly and tasted excellent.

While they waited for the meal, they turned to see what else was going on in the saloon within their proximity. They noticed about half the patronage were families, and the other half were a rowdy group of men in the corner, drinking and telling stories. The rowdy ignored the families, and vice versa. The smell of the establishment was slightly egregious, but you'll have that at a fishing village.

A short, attractive waitress approached Dave and Mick, and delicately voiced, "You gentlemen can sit at a table to eat if you'd like."

Dave answered, "We'll do just that." Dave and Mick got up off their stools and followed the lady to a table.

Upon Mick and Dave's sitting, the waitress said with an even more delicate voice than before, "Your food will be ready in just a bit."

Since they hadn't had a chance in a while—there not being too many beautiful women roaming the wilderness and all—Mick and Dave both stole a glance at her backside, as she walked away. A few minutes later, she returned with plates of sausage and sauerkraut, and gave them both a very pleasant, shy smile, a lovely, bashful beam that could've been read as she somehow knew her backside had been viewed.

As the waitress walked back to the kitchen, Mick declared, "Only at a tavern."

While they ate, heat from the bar's multiple fireplaces turned their faces red, a common phenomenon that happened often in the colder climates of places in northern Garobansurov. Besides the sausage being mouthwatering, probably why everyone ordered them, the accompanying sauerkraut seemed to taste better than it normally did elsewhere. Perhaps, though, Thraiker and Ghrere just *thought* it did. Their fish diets had been a little disproportionate.

The waitress and her wonderful smile returned twice while they were eating; the first time to ask if everything tasted satisfactory and if they needed anything else, the second time to bring the bill.

After they settled the bill at the bar, Dave and Mick ordered a couple more locally-brewed meads. This time, when they went to the bar, they strategically found an opening closer to the crowd of men telling stories, so they could listen to what was happening in the area. It didn't take too much listening for Mick and Dave to hear news of interest. After five minutes of talking about the weather, the group seemed to resume a conversational thread previously begun. It concerned a fort thirty miles to the north.

"If only we would've been able to hold Fort Gravividon, the war may not have even escalated," said a burly man.

"I agree. It's practically the only spot the Molisians can funnel into our country, due to it being the only bridge spanning the border river from the sea to the Baustic Mountains," returned a rather impressively dressed man, donning an even more impressive beard.

"I'm sure it won't be long for even more of their seemingly young soldiers to cross over," said a third.

The impressive beard vocalized, "They say Thraug will be attacked soon, and I'm sure the Molisians will want more troops to hold Sarwa. The battle to recapture Sarwa looms, and in my opinion will be the battle for the ages. The Molisians will certainly need to reinforce their ranks after marching a chunk of their army to Thraug. Crossing the river at Gravividon is the best way for them to accomplish it."

"If only we had an army in the area to retake that fort to prevent any more border crossings. Now that would really turn the tide," proclaimed the burly man, looking as if he wanted to slam a fist of resolve on the table.

Hearing the burly man's determination sent a shiver up and down Mick and Dave's spine. They both looked at each other, as they had before, knowing exactly what the other was thinking and what they had to do.

Mick smiled, and said, "Well, that's that then. Our search is over, our destination set."

Painting a mental picture of things to come, Dave smiled back with a poised grin, and nodded. "That fort will be retaken, you can count on that."

Dave experienced feelings of patriotism at that moment greater than he'd ever before felt. His oldest and truest friend followed suit, already machinating fort-capturing strategies.

Mick and Dave gulped the rest of their beverages and then—nearly hard enough to gather attention—slammed the flagons onto the bar. They walked out of the saloon with a renewed and powerful sense of urgency.

Upon stepping out the door, their ideas of running halfway to Fort Gravividon were put to a halt, due to the surprising fact it was already dark. So instead, they cancelled their unspoken plans of traveling at speed, and decided to find a nice place to pitch their tents on the outskirts of the village.

They found a place next to the lake, far enough away as to not bother anyone. Surrounded by thick alder bushes, their point of seclusion nestled on a slightly sloped embankment, where they could enjoy a decent view of the lake. They didn't fall asleep right away. It took a while for their nearly uncontrollable, adrenaline-driven states of mind to pacify. Sometimes, when the Thraiker-Ghrere tandem had their minds set on something, their inner tempests raged on for far too long.

It was unfortunate they fell asleep when they did, though, because if they would've stayed awake just a little longer, they would've witnessed a huge meteor shower. Only once in a great while was the sky graced by such a grand, stellar performance. The blackness of night was torched by massive fluorescent bands flowing from one end of the horizon to the other. It was too bad they didn't see it.

LOYD AND CARRIE had covered a great distance, since the peril, and were now only a day's walk away from their destination of meeting up with a family member. They had asked many travelers to where their grandfather was headed, and the ones that knew all replied the same.

"I can carry that for a while, my dear."

Loyd handed the box of jewels to his wife, scratched an itch on a hard-to-reach spot of his back, and said, "Thank you, Carrie. Good thing you're strong. I don't know if I would've had the muscular endurance to carry the box everywhere if you hadn't been relieving me. These breaks go a long way."

"You're welcome."

Loyd and Carrie left the side trail behind, stepping onto the main trail leading to Sarwa. They noticed how the main trail seemed much more utilized than a normal trail headed to a town the size of Sarwa, judging by the uncanny amount of prints in the snow. "I'm guessing we just missed the Molisian invasion army, the one we've heard so much about."

"Good thing we missed it. I wouldn't have wanted to get tangled up in that mess."

The thought of the town they were headed to being controlled by the Molisians scared Loyd for a moment, but he shook it off. He realized at least he and his wife probably wouldn't have a problem getting inside the gates—an easy entrance, due to the fact he had a friend living in Sarwa, who could vouch for their visit.

"Good thing Al lives in Sarwa, otherwise I don't think we'd ever get in."

"Hopefully he still lives there," said Carrie.

"Yes, hopefully."

"When we get there, don't tell anyone what's in the box. I don't think that'd produce good result for us. Better yet, it's best we keep it completely out of sight."

Loyd responded, "Good plan, lovely."

Carrie eventually handed the valuable box back to Loyd, and they continued setting a respectable pace to their desired destination.

WITH HIS ENTIRE body covered in colorful bruises and deep cuts, Brom woke up in an overly constrictive jail cell. Worse than that, he'd been infused by an inner lens of anguish changing his entire world dark. It took him awhile to remember exactly what had happened, but when he did, his legs gave out, and he crashed back onto the tiny bed in despair—a feeling he hadn't felt in a long time.

After a few hours, he gathered the strength to stand back up again, and peered out the openings in the bars to see if he could catch a glimpse of anything of interest. He noticed there were no fires blazing for heat, and that he was in an underground cell. Nothing but walls of solid rock made up the foreground. As for the background, he couldn't distinguish anything. His eyes were still blurry from the beating. His cell was a mud and limestone conglomerate, more than likely iron-reinforced. To make matters worse, there wasn't even a place for a person to sit and take a comfortable crap. The only thing available was a small hole in the ground. In reality, the cell was hundreds of years old, and hadn't been used by the former regimes of Sarwa in almost that long.

Hardly with the ability to move them, he lifted up his arms in an attempt to get the blood of his extremities to circulate better. He also tried a few stretches, but failed. Brom wondered if he was ever going to be fed, or given water. *Is this where I'll meet death?*

Eventually someone did bring him food and water, however the food was moldy, and the water was dirty and half frozen. The inexpressive guard didn't allow him much time to eat, so he quickly removed the mold from the bread and cheese of his cheese sandwich. He hastily scarfed the sandwich down, hoping it wouldn't make him sick. The highlight of the meal was the apple, which only had minimal rotting. He drank what water he could, and removed the ice chunk from his cup and set it on the bed, so he could suck on it later.

His stomach only halfway full, Brom sat and thought. At least he was lucky in that his cell was underground, below the frostline, reaping the benefit of the relatively warm soil. An exposed, above-ground cell would've been intolerably cold, since the Molisians surely wouldn't have heated it.

He stood up and paced in circles. When he grew sick of that he pivoted on the ball of his foot in a figure-eight pattern, hands resting at his sides. And when that got old, he went back to pacing in circles, an endless rotation to which he grew accustomed.

His thoughts raced, revolving mainly around his momentous failure, but he didn't give up, spending the rest of the day thinking of ways to break out.

HAWK AND LEOPARD rose with the sun and quickly took down camp after breakfast. "Maybe it'd be best for us to ease up a little," said Mick. "I highly doubt when we get there, we'll be able to charge the fort, relying on nothing but our battle skills and charismata. I'm sure our onslaught will take some time to plan and carry out."

"You're right," said Dave. "We're undeniably being a little urgent. For crying out loud, we'd intended to *run* half the way. It doesn't pay to wear ourselves out before we get there."

"Yes, sensible."

The dual adventurers changed their mindsets, now intending to only run occasionally to Gravividon. Before leaving the fishing community, they dropped by the tavern one more time to purchase an uncooked supply of their delectable sausages for the road, the unhealthy links were too delicious not to. They also secured a huge assortment of other foods, for what was sure to be a long time in the wilderness.

On the way out the door, Mick uttered, "We should've eaten some sausages for breakfast too."

"Shoulda, coulda, woulda."

The traveling was easygoing for the first few miles, but got progressively more arduous the further they got from the settlement, a state of affairs due to next-to-no snow on the trail being compacted by other trekkers. They knew they wouldn't cover the thirty miles to their destination in a day, so they shot for covering half the distance the first day, and the remaining the second day. They also aimed to not neglect the enjoyment only a long, contemplative walk could provide.

The first leg of the journey was fairly uneventful. Noteworthy natural landmarks were few and far-between. They passed the time of the first leg by talking about hunting. Neither of them hunted abundantly—usually only when food was needed—but once in a while they were compelled to compare big kills, and brag correspondingly.

"You may have brought down the bigger wild boar, but the turkey I slew when I was young was probably twice as big as any you've seen in your lifetime," boasted Dave Ghrere.

"I'll give you that. That turkey was an outright freak of nature. It seemed like it was born with double the growth hormones. It probably could've kicked my ass."

The pair began to laugh. Through the laugh, Dave responded, "I'm surprised it didn't rip out the arrow from its chest, snap it in half over its knee, and tempestuously charge after me."

"Yearning to draw your blood in revenge."

After the laughter died down, they resumed their conversation about hunting, and things associated with it.

By the time half the day's mileage was covered, all hunting topics and sub-topics were exhausted. Next, they talked of weather and storms. They carried that conversational thread for many hours, as they hiked towards the imaginary line separating earth from sky.

Eventually, Dave and Mick did come across an interesting landform. Just a few paces off the trail began an endless, almost desert-like mass of sand dunes. It was especially attention-grabbing at the moment, because the relatively hot sand was the only place in the area devoid of snow cover. Not wandering too far out of the way, they spent a short time walking around the dunes, looking for anything engaging. Easily recognizable animal tracks ended up being a point of interest. More than twenty five different animal species were identified without much effort.

"It's weird that the only human prints are ours," vocalized Dave in wonderment.

"I guess we're the only ones interested in this particular spot in the universe, at least since the last rain substantial enough to wipe out tracks."

"True. Guess what? There's only one tree within a hundred yards of us right now, and I just happen to bang my elbow on it."

Mick chuckled. "Better you than me."

When they'd received their fills of track recognition, and the pleasant sensations of sand beneath their feet,

they concluded the sojourn, and resumed the straighter
motion of heading towards a destination.

272

Chapter 14

❧

HE FELT THE calming winds from the four corners of the land in his face, currents emanating from the far stretches of the world. Quite often, Ulfenkerki liked to get away and think things over. He felt the isolation and free-flowing air sometimes supplied a more focused form of thought. The secondary reason for standing on that rock, a red granite beast decorated by a few scraggly crabapple trees, was to get a look at the approaching army. He knew the Molisian horde was due to appear in the valley at any moment. From his lookout, he could see for many miles, though he wouldn't be the first to see the Molisian army approaching. That station was held by the advanced scouts. Thraug and all nearby settlements had already been warned—Ulfenkerki just wanted to see them for the novelty of it.

On his rock, the Black Bear finished up final deliberations concerning battle details. He knew exactly what he wanted his soldiers to do during the battle and when to do it. The general had confidence in his plan, and felt it would be as effective as the one he spearheaded at Strwin. But only time would tell for sure.

Finally, Ulfenkerki spotted the oncoming commotion. Gamald's army was two miles away from the red granite rock, and coming over the distant ridge. They were impressive, Ulfenkerki thought, but not devastatingly so. He could see the six catapult silhouettes which the scouts reported to be in tow, and the 1,800 soldiers taking turns dragging them. Given the numbers, he extrapolated the success rate of his battle approach and was moderately content. It could've been much worse.

Since he was finished with his study of the enemy and his pre-battle strategizing, feeling the tranquil wind in his face, Ulfenkerki decided to head back. Having grabbed a bitter, late-season apple from one of the crabapple trees surrounding his rocky precipice, the Black Bear began the walk back to Thraug. He finished the entirety of his barely edible apple before arriving back to town, and discarded the core into a knothole.

On the west side of Thraug, a huge group of Ulfenkerki's soldiers hung around store fronts, for which there was no apparent reason other than killing time. Among the accumulation were Jason and Gregg sitting on a stone wall. Jason and Gregg discussed the wall and why they thought it had been built, but came to no real conclusions. What they didn't know was that it was built long ago to help deter geese and rabbits, animals that liked to leave droppings everywhere. They transitioned into talking about their homes—their non-wartime homes.

"I never got around to buying a house—not that I couldn't afford to, or didn't have the time to—mainly because I sleep better when I know I'm going to wake up somewhere different once in a while," explained Jason. "Inn rates can be a little steep, but for me, it's a small price to pay for my comfort."

"I can understand that," responded Gregg Hogarty. "To each their own."

"I've probably stayed at more than fifty different inns since joining the army. One in particular, though, I've stayed at the most."

Gregg laughed, and replied, "I imagine that decision was influenced by a woman."

"None other. She was something else, alright," returned Jason. "More than likely, I'll end up buying a house someday, but for now, given I survive the upcoming battle, I'll continue blowing my funds on nightly and weekly inn rates."

"My funds mostly go to the bank," said Gregg to Jason. "The loan I took out for the wood for my house wasn't bad, but the one I took out for the land was astronomical. I'm a sucker for a vast property. If I hadn't built the house myself, I would've never been able to afford it."

"Yeah, that's one thing about our country—no shortage of wood. Our forests are first-rate, in my judgment, second in stature to no other country." Jason cracked his knuckles, thought he heard something, dismissed it, then said, "Good thing you bought the land when you did. I'm sure because of the war effort right now, land is even more expensive."

"True. Last time I checked, an acre had a price tag seventy-five percent higher than what I paid. It was all worth it for me, nonetheless. Even though it's usually just me alone at my cabin, I really enjoy being able to do with it what I please."

"Nice." Jason heard the noise again he had heard previously. He turned around to decipher what it was and realized it was a squirrel trying to get out of a trap, a device probably placed in the brush by someone the night before. "I dare you to go and put your fingers in that trap," he said.

But before Gregg could let it be known whether or not he would comply with Jason's dare, a great uproar began. Close-range scouts had returned, heralding the Molisian army was upon them.

Gregg and Jason halted their conversations about homes and squirrels, and reported to where they thought General Ulfenkerki would be—his desk.

The Black Bear ended up not being at his desk, so Jason went to search out the Nighteagle or Rayton for information, while Gregg went to talk with some of the other soldiers.

Jason finally caught up with Ulfenkerki, the Nighteagle, Rayton, and the other officers, who were already in discussion. Jason paid due diligence to everything being said about the war strategies to be exercised. Ulfenkerki's plan utilized an advantage they'd receive by keeping it a secret they were superior in number. All thought the stratagem was brilliant, professing no reservations about putting it into action.

At the conclusion of the discussion, the generals went to inform the soldiers of their respective companies the plan. They didn't know exactly when, but they knew the battle would soon be upon them, probably within the next twenty-four hours. The exact time depended on whether or not the Molisian army—again, led by Anolski—planned to rest before they fought.

WITH THE BATTLE of Thraug soon to begin many miles away, Dave and Mick kept moving, having covered a few miles since rendezvousing with the sand dunes. They too had to be on the lookout for Molisians, since they were starting to get somewhat close to the border. The two of them kept their minds in the ready, hazardous conditions could've taken shape at any moment. Night was soon to be upon them, so they started to put a little slack in their energy consumption—and Mick and Dave slept a little better when they could wind down at the end of the day.

"I'm pleased with the expanse we traversed today," said Dave. "I don't think we'll have a problem reaching the fort tomorrow."

Mick responded, "If it doesn't snow."

"Hopefully it doesn't," said Dave, "but I'm sure it won't be long before the snow really starts accumulating."

"Who knows? Maybe a good layer of snow will give us some kind of advantage in our retaking of the fort."

"Or disadvantage."

Mick jerked his hand forward with a flick of the wrist, symbolizing *relax*. "*Aacchh*. It'll be fine."

Being in good spirits, the pair successfully set up camp, again. It hadn't been officially recorded how many times up to that point they'd set up camp since leaving Chalatore. But if a person was really interested, they could determine the number on their own with relative ease. A much harder task would be determining how many times they'd set up camp since their childhood, and how many times they had in their lifetime. Perhaps numbers didn't go that high.

It was a frigid night, so the cold-weather sleeping bags were deployed. When this was done, the warm-weather bags were used as mattresses. Snow was always removed from underneath the tents. If they didn't, their body heat would melt the snow, causing a sloppy mess inside the tent. This time there wasn't much snow, so they didn't have to spend much time on snow removal. Instead, they spent the rest of the night sharpening weapons and inspecting armor. The armor could've been in better shape, but as always, it would suffice. They spent a couple hours honing the black-needles and daggers into unprecedented sharpness.

Convinced their arsenal was prepared for what was to come, they wedged themselves into their thick sleeping bags, and slept off their sore legs.

Having slept well enough to mend their legs' muscle tissue, they were ready for another full day of walking. They intended to cover a distance equal in caliber to the day previous. They designed a big breakfast, a pre-planned measure to limit meal stops, and packed all their paraphernalia.

The sausages (excellent walking fuel bought the day before) simmered on the fire, the smell of which forced debilitating hunger chemicals through Mick and Dave, making them uncharacteristically unproductive. As a result, taking camp down was a slow process. Uncontrollably compelled by the aroma, they grew impatient and ate a few of the sausages half-raw. Large breakfasts were their own reward and their own punishment.

They finally got camp taken down and their gear packed up, having done most of it on extraordinarily full stomachs, and resumed heading north-northeast.

Post a thousand leg turnovers, and with the sun being at approximately quarter mast, Dave stole a good look at his beautiful surroundings. He interlaced his fingers, cracked them with a sudden snap, and trying to be poetic, spouted, "Just as we become degrees faster and stronger with practice, each overlapping layer of the surrounding hills and mountains gain in their magnificence with every level."

"True," Mick agreed. "I can't remember ever seeing so many layers in the topography. The Baustics are definitely a sight to behold."

"They perhaps look more breathtaking from the top."

"Perhaps."

Another thousand leg-turnovers later, Hawk and Leopard sensed they were at the periphery of something big—something really big. The stones were getting immense, so much so that it couldn't just be random. The wind was eerily picking up, but that part was more than likely random. One of the stones was so immense, the edges couldn't be discerned—the rock ran right into the earth, like a formation would, but the stone still had the qualities of a boulder.

Since they were making good time, they decided to climb the huge rock for shits and giggles.

Mick led. When they got to the top, they realized it wasn't really the top at all, for the stone just kept going. They eventually registered that the mountainous stone went on for as far as the eye could see. Since their curiosity overruled their better judgment, they just kept climbing, as if driven by some outside might. The wonder was exhilarating.

After many dozens of minutes of climbing, the top was finally reached.

Mick announced, "Alas, the mystical summit has been conquered."

Dave pinnacled soon after, and emitted, "That endeavor sure was interesting. I'm glad we delved into this one."

Blasted by extreme curiosity, both looked all around on swiveling hips. Mick said, "It would take us many a day to study this freak of nature thoroughly, determining exactly how big it really is, and how it was formed."

"That it would. We'll just add it to our already long list of things needing a return visit."

"Already added it halfway up."

Dave returned Mick's words with a chuckle, and joined his friend in one last scanning of the scenery before starting the descent.

On their way down, they tried to walk a different path, so if they had missed anything interesting the first time, maybe they'd see it the second.

And see something new they did.

About a third of the way back down, before the gradient turned less sharp, Hawk and Leopard found stone ruins they thought maybe had been built by the ancient people of the Atrudagar. The Atrudagar were a culture from a long time in the past, long gone like so many others. The ruins weren't very expansive on the surface, but that was more than likely a front to something that was, something inside the stone mountain.

They decided to not spend too much time at the relic, however. They had places to go and people to see. Furthermore, it more than likely had already been explored by countless archaeologists and adventurers. But they did find an entrance to the inside of the ruin, and they did go inside for a bit, just to see what it looked like. It was impressive, but they had much more travelling to do that day, so they only spent ten minutes admiring the stonework and mysticism, before exiting the ancient underground labyrinth.

Just before the two of them started to make their way back down the stone mountain, back to their path heading north to Fort Gravividon, Mick noticed something imperative: a stone arch with emblazoned petroglyphs. It included words of primordial Atrudagar dialect. The words were bookended by hieroglyphs of a sword and an axe.

Mick yelled, "Hey Dave, come over here, and take a look at this. These are definitely Atrudagar ruins." As soon as Dave was standing next to Mick and gazing at the arch, Mick read the imprinted words out loud. Both Mick and Dave had studied the Atrudagar for a time, and possessed the ability to translate their text. "It takes a stone to know a stone."

"What do you suppose that means?" asked Dave.

"It could mean many things, I imagine. It sure is an interesting discovery."

"I'm surprised the arch has stood this long," commented Dave.

Thraiker and Ghrere put the words—which were obviously important to the Atrudagar—into their memory banks, and finished the descent, seeing nothing more of importance along the way.

"We lost an hour and a half of our time, but the ends definitely justified the means."

Mick replied, "For sure. I doubt we'll have a problem finishing off this leg of the trip before running out of daylight anyways."

"I doubt it too. Onward."

The pair walked efficiently for the rest of the day, and didn't stop again for anything other than a quick bite to eat; a filling of the canteens in a cool, clear mountain stream; and reaching their destination.

THE LINE WAS thin, ten yards long, and imaginary. For the last hour, Ulfenkerki had paced back and forth on it, trying to stave off nervous anticipation. He already made sure everyone was well-informed of his plan, in the proper position to perform it, and poised for battle. Any minute now, Anolski was expected to advance. The enemy could be seen in the distance organizing formations and mobilizing catapults.

Being all paced out, the Black Bear went to rendezvous with the Nighteagle.

"I really hope this battle is short and sweet, for one thing I do know is that when we try to recapture Sarwa, bloodshed will be untold. Gamald seems to be prioritizing Sarwa, thinking it's the most valuable city in the region. I draw this conclusion due to the fact it looks as if Gamald didn't even tag along on this campaign," noted Ulfenkerki to the Nighteagle.

"I'm afraid that might be true. I haven't spotted him, either. I don't know when the battle for Sarwa will happen, but when it does, lives will surely be lost aplenty. Promise me one thing, though, old friend."

"What's that?"

"You don't go and get yourself killed in this battle or the next. Your strategic mind will definitely be needed in the war to come. But more importantly, I look up to no man more than I look up to you. I care not to see you die."

Throughout Ulfenkerki's life, he'd faced many hardships and adversities, leaving a certain hardening, a certain rejection of outward emotion,. But upon hearing the Nighteagle's words, for a rare, brief moment, Ulfenkerki's rough exterior softened and projected a ray of true happiness. He responded, "I do believe you've never dispersed such sentiment before."

"You're right. Only two things bring out what someone really feels—being confronted by death, and an overly hard bout of drinking."

"We must be facing death, then, because I see you're pretty sober. I know I haven't drunk that hard since the victory at Strwin."

The Nighteagle gave Ulfenkerki a slap on the back, smiled, and before walking away to the armory to finish gearing up, he said, "I'll take that as a yes."

"Yes, I promise to not die. I'm not going to let you have all the fun defeating that ruthless, black-hearted Gamald."

The short walls of Thraug were manned with soldiers. Rayton and his archers were stationed on the east side, including Chad Loytin, who was starting to get a reputation of arrogance. But he was still known by almost all as the best archer in Garobansurov. Loytin thought the supply of arrows wasn't quite up to par, but good enough. Ulfenkerki commanded the ground troops while Jason Thorncat commanded those positioned on the southern wall. The Nighteagle's troops were arranged on the northern and western walls, whom he commanded alone. Some would've said if he broke down his command in subsets, he'd reap a greater capacity for a stronger war-machine in city defenses, but just as many would've said the opposite.

Stoically, Gregg Hogarty waited on the south side for orders from his friend and leader, Jason, who coincidentally was heading towards Gregg's grouping at that moment to do just that. Gregg and all in his party nodded their heads and saluted Jason, in recognition of their senior officer.

Jason said, "As you all know, our primary objective is to follow the plan General Ulfenkerki laid out, so until that is in full swing, stay alive and kill as many enemies as possible. Go ahead and bunch up on the western wall if our own side gets ignored, but wait until my command to do so." Jason started to walk to the next grouping, but stopped, and walked back. "Oh yeah, one more thing:

Stay away from whatever those catapults shoot at us. That could get ugly."

Most produced a half-smile; all responded, "Yes, sir."

Everyone fighting for Garobansurov was positioned and ready. The brave inched closer to the enemy, the not-so brave inched further away.

The Battle of Thraug began.

The Molisian catapults immediately began firing at maximum amplitude, while Anolski ordered all his archers and soldiers possessing a bow to surround the city. They attempted to peck off soldiers on the wall, wishing to keep the defense honest. Anolski didn't plan on infiltrating the walls until one was breached by catapult fire. Anolski was confident he was superior in numbers, so in his mind he could afford to be patient. What he didn't know was that he wasn't superior in numbers at all, with his 1,800 to Ulfenkerki/the Nighteagle's 2,000. He still thought he was only up against 1,500. Unforeseen by Anolski, Ulfenkerki lied in concealment with a secret force, waiting until the time to strike was at hand.

On the battlefield, Anolski stood amidst the pandemonium of the six furious catapults, each firing loads at two shots per minute. He pointed at a spot in the wall, and said to the nearby catapult operators, "Right there, focus at that point. That's where the best hole is forming." He walked to the outlying catapults and told those handling them the same thing. In no time, all of their projectiles were aimed at a hub. Soon, the hole would be big enough for the Molisian infantry to enter town.

Occasionally, one of the Garobansurovian wall-soldiers would get lucky and score a fatal arrow-hit. But because the Molisians weren't trying to get over the wall at the time, those hits were extremely limited.

The Black Bear, upon seeing where the catapult operators were focusing their fire, smiled. Anolski was playing right into his hands. Ulfenkerki instructed his 500 concealed ground troops—obedient as ants—to gravitate to where the hole in the wall was forming, and be prepared for his cue.

All part of the plan, Jason ordered half his contingent to sneak down off the wall to join Ulfenkerki, his charge, and his secret stash below. The stash was an unorthodox arsenal to say the least—massive piles of rocks. A hundred-pound rock was designated for each of Ulfenkerki's hidden ground soldiers and the members of Jason's battalion who came down off the wall. Rock practice was about to pay off.

A direct hit blasted material in every direction. Anolski, satisfied with the hole he created, yelled, "charge!" His warriors rushed into the hole as fast as they could, trying not to get hit with arrows flying at them from above.

Due to Anolski's tutelage, the Molisians weren't stupid like some tended to be when amongst a crowd trying to squeeze through a small opening. They abstained from going through the bottleneck slowly and stopping/slowing once through. Anolski knew navigating slowly at any point in the procedure would create a dam, holding back soldiers and efficiency. They went through intelligently, and in no time a third of the Molisian army was inside the city, weapons drawn, ready to slaughter.

But even more intelligently than Anolski performed his wall infiltration, Ulfenkerki prompted his battle-plan through perfect timing. All at once, 750 troops—Ulfenkerki's original 500 plus the 250 who snuck over from Thorncat's regime—charged out of concealment, carrying huge rocks. They quickly ran to the hole in the wall and threw their rocks into the opening, attempting to plug the entrance. That way the 600 Molisians who got in would be cut-off from the rest of their force, rendering them more susceptible to flank maneuvers.

A few of the Garobansurovian soldiers got killed on their way to the hole by alert enemies, but most were able to dump their load into the opening. Many of them were also able to scoop up some of the scattered debris of the wall itself to use to plug the breach. Some of the soldiers standing on the wall in that area had rocks to throw down as well. All in all, 1,500 boulder stones were virtually instantaneously added to the hole in the wall. The pile that formed was enormous, but more impressively, it happened fast. It didn't quite reach the top of the original wall, but any soldier who tried to climb over the pile was easily shot down by the archers in the area, one of them being Chad Loytin, who never missed.

As previously premeditated, when the trap occurred a force of soldiers risked broken ankles, and jumped off the top of the wall to reinforce the ground troops. Only one came close to breaking his ankles in the leap. Apparently, he'd been absent the day they taught grace. But another showed up and stayed late, for she'd impressively tucked into a barrel roll, immediately followed by a sword unsheathing.

The flanking set-up was gapless. In the matter of mere moments, a thousand Garobansurovians had encircled 600 Molisians. Ulfenkerki knew the ensuing battle would be relatively short due to the number advantage and perimeter positioning.

Garobansurov's initial thrust of manpower was overwhelming. Arrows flew everywhere.

The Black Bear got himself entangled in an intense man-to-man struggle with an opponent half his age. Ulfenkerki's first move was a running lunge with his sword tip extended, but the young Molisian was powerful, and was able to deflect the maneuvers. Most of those in the Molisian frontline facing the encirclement weren't as skilled as this particular young man. After the lunge was blocked, the Molisian countered with a flurry of sword jabs, but failed in his intention of knocking Ulfenkerki off balance.

With his opponent now winded, the Black Bear summoned an offensive consisting of multiple sword swings aimed at his opponent's sword hand. He connected on one of them, rendering the hand useless, forcing his adversary to switch his weapon into the other hand. Ulfenkerki capitalized on this advantage. After his challenger tried to get lucky with quite the showing of fanciful but desperate sword-work, Ulfenkerki sliced the face, and finished with a solid plunge of his weapon into the chest.

Upon defeating his rival, Ulfenkerki looked around, and noticed that that particular battle-within-the-battle was pretty much over. Only a few were left fighting. Adrenalized, he yelled out to his troops, "Excellent job everyone! Now we wait and see where they blast through the wall next with their catapults, and we keep them from getting in. It shouldn't be a problem at all for such a first-rate group of warriors. We now outnumber them almost two-to-one." As he respectfully pointed at them,

Ulfenkerki proclaimed, "No matter what the odds, there isn't anyone able to get past my soldiers."

Having heard the boosting words from their general, the battalion burst into unified military-style grunts. They prepared themselves for the next duty, adamant they were going to be victorious.

Instead of retreating, knowing he was now outnumbered greatly, and especially not wanting to cower back to Gamald explaining his defeat, Anolski voiced his next war command. "Punch through the wall again, and don't stop until the city is taken."

The soldiers did as they were told for the time being. They loaded the catapults and fired repeatedly. Eventually another sizable hole in the wall was formed. But instead of forfeiting their lives so easily, half of the Molisians chose treason, and snuck away before even attempting to enter the city. The other half bravely faced their doom. They met their demise by either an arrow on their way through the new hole, or by one of Ulfenkerki's soldiers as soon as they emerged into Thraug from the hole.

From afar, Anolski saw the carnage—his army obliterated, he chose treason as well. With the remaining hundred soldiers, his new personal guard, he abandoned the campaign and ventured off into the wilderness. He thought an unpatriotic exodus better than having to face Gamald and his wrath. However, he didn't escape unnoticed. The Nighteagle spotted the withdrawal.

The last few Molisians left in the city, when they learning Anolski had ditched, dropped their weapons in acceptance of prisoner-of-war status. Garobansurovians were different than Molisians in respect to the fact they treated their POWs better. These Molisian grunts knew this.

The battle had been won. Having jumped down from the wall, the Nighteagle sped off to share his valuable information with Ulfenkerki. The Nighteagle found Ulfenkerki and while out of breath, barely said, "Anolski took off into the forest with a hundred soldiers, heading in the opposite direction."

"I guess he wasn't in the mood to go back and face Gamald, informing him how badly the campaign went."

The Nighteagle chuckled, and responded, "He surely would've lost his head by choosing that path."

"Yup, that's a good way to shorten one's longevity. All joking aside, I do have to say he's too dangerous to be left out of check, and in my opinion, needs to be hunted. And I have just the man to lead such an operation."

The Nighteagle replied, "I'm pretty sure I know to whom you're referring. I have heard of his tracking prowess. I think I know where he is. And by the way, I'm glad to see you complied with the first half of my wish."

Meanwhile, victory excitement was splattered everywhere. Sitting alongside Gregg Hogarty, Jason Thorncat euphorically drank from a mug the size of a watermelon. Noticing Gregg's mug wasn't as big, Jason commented, "You know what they say about a man and the size of his mug."

Gregg laughed, and said, "Nope, I've never heard. You tell me." Jason joined in on the laugh, and realized how much he enjoyed the feeling of victory and being alive. They were just about to start talking about their own independent parts of the battle, when they were approached by both the Nighteagle and Ulfenkerki.

Ulfenkerki spoke. "Well done gentlemen. We have won, but there's more." Jason was about to take another drink from the mother of all beer mugs, when the Black Bear blurted, "Jason, hold off on your upcoming drink from that barrel with a handle. There is important business to which to attend. As you know, we're all well aware you're the best tracker in the known universe—or at the least, under my command."

Jason set his mug down, and reverently intensified his demeanor. "Go on, sir."

"I don't think you know this, but Anolski wasn't killed."

"You're right. I didn't know that."

"He and about a hundred men—whom he made his own personal guards, we think—tucked tail and ran, just as the battle was over, escaping into the opposing woods. This is where you come in. We need you to leave at once, with as many soldiers as you feel necessary, and capture him dead or alive. Alive hopefully, we're not barbarians. Most of us aren't anyways." The latter statement was a humorous jab given to a friend from a friend, the kind the Nighteagle and Ulfenkerki shared all the time.

Jason poured out the beer from his mug, as did Gregg to show he wanted to join Jason's mission. Jason responded to Ulfenkerki, "It will be done, sir. Since he wields a hundred soldiers, maybe I should bring a hundred and fifty?"

"If that's what you want Jason. You're in command of this operation. Pick whomever you want to accompany you." Ulfenkerki looked at Gregg, "Seems like you have your first willing participant already."

Jason slapped Gregg on the back, and emitted, "Sure does."

"Try and hurry though. I don't know when yet, but I'm sure the Nighteagle and I will choose a time to retake Sarwa, and I do hope you're back by then."

"Yes, sir."

"Good luck, Jason. You as well, Gregg."

Jason and Gregg both returned thank you's.

Jason started the task of choosing the soldiers of his party. It wasn't hard to do, because as soon as word of the undertaking spread, volunteers showed up at Jason's side immediately. Nearly as fast as the volunteers showed up, Jason and his crew left the city, fully armored, to pursue their quarry.

Watching Jason and his team disappear into the forest, the Nighteagle said to Ulfenkerki, "How much do you want to bet I get more new recruits than you, due to this victory?"

"You're dreaming, Log Rot. I'll bet you a hundred gitis my number of new recruits will outnumber yours by the time we march to Sarwa."

"You're on, Barn Smell," the Nighteagle responded, while the two shook hands. The Nighteagle pretty much assumed he was going to lose the bet. He knew the news would spread like wildfire of Ulfenkerki's Thraug brilliance, the soon-to-be famous plan making the battle an easy one.

The Nighteagle couldn't have been happier.

CHAPTER 15

A S SOON AS the silhouette of Fort Gravividon was distinguishable in the distance, Mick and Dave took to cover, aiming to remain under cover for the rest of the way. They didn't want anyone to see them heading towards the fort. For many miles in both directions, Fort Gravividon was the only crossing over the exceptionally deep, wide, and predominantly cliff-wall-edged Empanakaturill River, which made it of great importance for both sides. The fort was loaded with countless catapults and ballistae of many sizes, which made it almost impervious to conventional assault. It was so strategically placed that it prevented the Molisians an opportunity to build a fort of their own on the opposing side of the river.

For many decades, Molisian forces had tried to capture the fort, only to ultimately fail. That is, until a few months ago when a throng of skillful night raiders successfully captured it, greatly fortifying Molisia's stance in their war with Garobansurov.

Leopard and Hawk crept close enough to the stone and wooden defensive structure to see it clearly. But not too close. They had no intentions of recklessly storming the fort at that moment, needing time to plan the assault.

After a glance by each, they slipped back into the deeper cover, and started to locate the preferable locale to set up their base of operations, one far enough away as to avoid being seen by any guards making rounds, and one not too far away making the distance too great to efficiently travel back and forth for reconnaissance.

They distanced themselves tremendously from the fort. For hours, they searched out the perfect spot, both on high and low ground, but mainly wanting to stick to the mountains.

Dave reached a clearing in the Baustic talus, and yelled downhill, just loud enough for Mick and only Mick to hear. "Over here, Mick, this is perfect."

Mick climbed up the stretch of south face slope separating him from Dave, and responded, "Ah yes, I do believe this is it. The perfect distance away from the fort, about a mile."

Dave said, "A flat surface suitable for living for a period of time, surrounded by extremely rough terrain suggesting to the most intrepid of stragglers to avoid the area. Nobody particularly enjoys traversing through difficult topography, especially when a huge supply of winter snow looms."

Mick added, "Also, the mammoth boulders lying on the edges keep anyone from a view of our area from below and above. The many cliff dwelling evergreen trees provide cover as well."

"Once in a while," said Dave, "one of us will have to travel further away to cook a supply of food. I do believe this spot is too close to the fort for campfires. The smoke would be too recognizable."

"True," Mick agreed.

Hawk and Leopard spent a few moments kicking the small layer of snow in their new temporary home down the slope. They pitched their tents in-between a couple bigger boulders lying underneath tree cover. The boulders and trees would make their sleeping locale a much less windy one, and therefore warmer. Eventually, the winter camping would get rough, so any natural benefits reaped would greatly enhance the experience. They also planned on piling up a bunch of snow when it comes in-between the nearby boulders, creating even more concealment and wind resistance.

To finish off the initial long-stay preparations, they each constructed a simple, makeshift table to set beside their tents. So that way they had somewhere to set some of the things they'd use every day. Bending over repeatedly to grab a dish, for example, can get tedious. They also planned on assembling tables for the insides of their tents, but those were going to wait until the future, along with other things. For now, they were exhausted from having covered so many miles and ascended so much altitude. They went to sleep a little early that night, but not before making sure all their tracks were eliminated.

They woke to the thickest layer of tent-ice yet since leaving Chalatore the day of the armwrestling tournament. Tent-ice was the encasement of ice caused by the freezing of breath-moisture formed on the surface of a tent. It was convenient because it was insulating. They noticed deep snow still eluded them.

Dave called to Mick, "Go ahead and throw me a bowl of that—what one would call breakfast."

Mick tossed over the bowl of two-day old eggs, and said, "Good day for spying, eh?"

"That it is," said Dave.

Mick replied, "Since there's not much snow on the ground today, maybe we'll both go down together to gather data. But when the snow does come it'll probably be best to go individually, making track covering a little easier."

"Sounds like a plan, Stan."

"Okay, May."

The pair finished their cold, not-so fresh, breakfast, and started to make their way down the embankment towards Fort Gravividon to spy, towing their swords and a supply of drinking water. Armor got left behind.

THERE WERE MANY in Sarwa suffering. Most doing so due to the starvation starting to take hold, which, obviously, owed to the shortage in the food supply. But two in particular suffering were General Gamald and Brom Quintaga. Gamald was suffering, because he'd just heard of the loss at Thraug, and of Anolski's treacherous retreat. Brom was suffering because he, along with every other Garobansurovian in town, was barely getting fed, and was having a hard time keeping sane. There wasn't much else to do for Brom but stare at walls.

Gamald wouldn't actually have known anything, yet, about what'd transpired at the battle of Thraug, hadn't a few soldiers risked their lives returning to Sarwa, which in its own right was a treasonous act—abandoning the battle of Thraug. They thought maybe they'd be spared punishment, due to the fact they had valuable information concerning Anolski. They thought wrong, almost being killed immediately. They were sent to the wilderness to fend for themselves. Gamald was furious. He didn't know how to respond other than setting an example of the informers.

At first, the general wanted to command a thousand soldiers to retrieve Anolski, but he came to his senses soon enough, and realized he'd need all the bodies he could get to keep Sarwa his own when the war inevitably came to his doorstep. He anticipated it was going to be the biggest battle of the war thus far, and was going to do everything in his power to win.

Leedle was starting to get a little more liberal about telling Gamald about the food shortage and the number of deaths sustained because of it. He gave Gamald the report of the day, which he wisely followed by transitioning into one of the only topics he knew would calm the general—drinking. Its discussion gave way to its action.

IN THE UNDERGROUND cell, virtually out of sight and mind, and not shown any regard for reverence by any jailer in the slightest, Brom was losing weight and hope. Forlorn, Brom was sinking deeper and deeper into an inescapable misery. His wellbeing had all but been washed away by the tides of time.

Brom wished he'd at least get fed properly, that way he could focus his mind. But there certainly were no plans of that in the near future. The only thing he could do in his cell to keep his mind sharp was scratch a daily journal in the dirt lying on the cell-floor with a stick. Which wasn't exactly dirt, as much as it was dust accumulated throughout the years. Even that had to be erased every day, so he had room to write the new day's entry. Along with the autobiographical writings, he tried to exercise daily, but failed routinely, due to his body's lack of energy.

One day, however, for no apparent reason, his mind was abnormally sharp, so he was able to try and determine who among everyone he knew had at least a slim chance of rescuing him. Initial thoughts brought him to his two sons and daughter. One son, the one for whom he'd been searching, was eliminated from the list right away. The second son was also searching for his brother, teamed up with his own offspring, but he was searching on the other side of the country, and would have no idea what happened at Sarwa. So Brom categorized him as a longshot. His daughter was even more of a longshot, due to health issues rendering her immobile. There was virtually no chance for a rescue by his immediate family.

Thoughts expanded and shot straight to his granddaughter—the daughter of his daughter. He grew nostalgic and thought of all the good memories he had of her, and of how brilliant she was. He especially remembered the time when she unleashed un-expectations, using something that normally wasn't used for the purpose in which she used it. He recalled the entire story.

BROM AND HIS granddaughter were traveling together, bringing a bunch of pigs to the next town over to sell at market. It would be a four-day journey—two days there, two days back—so they brought along a tent and jovial spirits.

After traveling that first day, having benefited from the pigs' full cooperation, they stopped at the leg's midpoint, and set up camp for the night.

Inside the tent, about to fall asleep, Brom blurted to his granddaughter, "Oh no, I forgot to take the precautionary measures preventing anyone from coming and stealing the pigs in the middle of the night."

She replied, "Don't worry about it. I tied them all together, and to a tree."

"But what if someone comes and just simply unties the ropes, and then steals them?"

"I wouldn't worry about that either."

"Why not?"

"You'll see, if the time comes," she responded, with a chuckle.

He replied, "Alright then, I'll go to sleep."

They both fell asleep and slept soundly, but halfway through the night, they were woken by the ungodly sound of a pig squealing as if it was dying. Brom crawled out of the tent, weapon in hand, and scanned the scene. The first thing he saw was a squealing pig hanging in a tree by its feet; secondly, he saw a couple of would-be thieves running away at the sight of a man with a fancy sword.

He chased the thieves long enough to make sure they wouldn't come back. When he returned back to camp, he saw his granddaughter bringing the panicky pig down from the tree. Brom declared, "I do have to say that's the most unusual alarm apparatus I've ever witnessed."

"Sure is, grandpa."

"How did you do it?"

"I bent a tree down to the ground, and rigged a trip mechanism, so that when the knot keeping the pigs tied to the decoy tree was untied, the bent tree would trip, and send the squealing alarm pig into the air."

"That's ingenious. You certainly were right about telling me to not worry about it—an understatement."

The pair laughed heartily, who wouldn't? It's not that often one sees a pig hanging upside down in a tree, squealing for dear life. They re-rigged the system, and fell back asleep.

Having woke the next morning after no further incident, they brought the pigs to market, and sold them for a good price. They continued having a wonderful time throughout the rest of their unforgettable trip.

BROM SNAPPED OUT of the fantastic memory, and continued his thoughts about chances of escape. At least now he could see a ray of hope, his granddaughter the reason. She possessed the wherewithal, the sense of adventure, and the taste to be anywhere at any moment to rescue him. Now, he had a motive to keep fighting and surviving. Now, he was confident there was a chance. He said to himself, *There is someone out there with the physical capacity and mental resources to get me out.*

But what he didn't know was that she was already in Sarwa, with her husband, after having a few wild adventures of her own along the way.

MICK AND DAVE trekked the mile from their hideout to the fort, successfully keeping out of sight of anyone unfriendly. They found a dense, virgin part of the forest surrounding the fort to post up and gather intel. Their camp was closer to the east side of the fort, but they started to watch on the west side, the best side, or so they thought.

For the first part of the day, absolutely nothing happened, no movement, no gathered qualitative or quantitative data at all. There was a point in the boredom when their minds no doubt wandered. Because of the lack of action in his field of view, Dave thought of a riddle concerning that lack.

He walked silently over to Mick, and whispered into his ear, "If you can answer this riddle, I'll carry an item of yours for a day. Here goes. I am the one and only thing that can be definitively seen from anywhere, by someone able to see. I'm always moving whenever you look at me. What precisely am I?"

Mick thought on it for a good five minutes, but finally responded, "I have no idea. You got me. I won't be getting an item carried this time. The only things I came up with were the wind and dust, but I know there are places where those things can't be seen."

"That is correct. Last chance, do you really give up?"

"Yes, I give up."

"Okay then, the answer is . . . eye floaters."

Mick smiled upon hearing the answer, and replied, "Good one, Leopard. At least your mind wandering has been productive. All I've been thinking about is that squirrel in the tree over there, and wondering how many places he actually has nuts stored."

Dave doubled the smiles, and silently crept back to his watching post to stare endlessly.

Their side of the fort consisted mainly of stone, but claimed a few timber augmentations. The other side seemed more intricate at a glance. Their side had a few windows, and a few huge doors. The top contained a walkway for guards, and battle turrets, along with standard fort battlements, catapults, and crossbow ballistae. From where they were standing, they could see the other side of the fort had a long precipice, the walkway on top of the fort being extended majestically out into the void, greatly overhanging the bridge across the river, creating a battle advantage in defending attacks from the river side.

They continued to watch the west side of the fort patiently for the next couple hours, seeing nothing but the occasional arm or head of one of the topside sentries until finally, action. One of the massive doors opened, and a couple guards emerged. At first, they just stood outside the door and talked for a few moments, occasionally looking around. Eventually they made their outside rounds, staying within the glade adjacent the fort. They steered clear of the forest, barely looking into it. Mick and Dave were never even close to being in danger of being spotted.

The guards stood by the door and talked for a few more moments, then went back into the fort, totally unaware they were being watched the whole time.

"Well, at least the whole day hasn't been wasted. We learned they do make rounds, seemingly pathetic ones," declared Mick, as he and Dave walked back to their hideout, having called it a day as far as reconnaissance was concerned.

"I believe we'll learn more when we watch the east side. I'm thinking they use that side more."

"Maybe. Did you think of any more mind-boggling riddles during the second half of our isolation?"

"Nope. I'm happy to just stump you once a day," responded Dave, trying but failing to hold back a smile as he wiped away an unavoidable track made in the snow.

"I bet you are," said Mick.

Upon return, their campsite looked the same way it did when they left, except for some fallen branches scattered sporadically. Evidently, the wind had picked up since leaving that morning.

"Hopefully," said Mick, "all this wind isn't a sign of a front moving in, bringing with it a large amount of snow."

"Hopefully."

"After we eat the upcoming supper, we'll probably have enough pre-cooked food for another day or two. But after that, one of us will have to venture somewhere in the distance to do a bunch of cooking."

Dave replied, "One of us might have to go right now. I'm so hungry I could eat all we have available, myself."

"As am I," said Mick.

A huge supper was eaten, but their pre-meal discussion had been an exaggeration, for there was still enough left over for another day or two. Between the feast and sleep, the men paced in circles for a few hours, back and forth across their own thirty-by-forty-foot natural terrace with an unbeatable view.

They also searched the immediate area for black-needle pine trees. Maybe they'd get lucky and find the enigma species this time.

As it turned out, luck wasn't on their side for the search. However, they did both pick out their own favorite trees of the area. Mick's was the oldest and most massive tree near the tents. He always seemed partial to trees in that category. His selection was an approximate two-hundred-year-old pine tree, an unparalleled might. Dave was most inspired by another tree, a photosynthesis machine also massive for the area, but not overwhelmingly so, like Mick's pine, it being a species which almost got wiped out of existence a hundred years previous. A voracious tree-eating bug had run rampant, making even medium-sized ones not a common sight. So, Dave's tamarack tree was extremely rare, rarer than a two-hundred-year-old pine. Their selections established, proverbially written in stone, they went to bed.

Since snow still eluded them, they decided again to do fort investigation together, leaving right away at first light. They ate breakfast along the way. It was the east side of Fort Gravividon's turn to be stared at, so they picked a hidden nook, and started the day's mission. The new spot wasn't quite as veiled as the day before's, but it sure was more comfortable. They each had an old log on which to sit, as opposed to yesterday's ground sitting, for a log can sometimes supply what a cold ground cannot. Mick and Dave were pleased.

The east side of the fort, like previously assessed, was far more extravagant. It was the larger side, having more windows and doors proportionately. A firepit was placed in an out-of-the-way area just outside the fort, probably used for guards to stay somewhat warm while on watch when facing the elements. It wasn't being used at the moment, however. Near the firepit, the fort itself had a smaller part, an appendage, which seemed like it wasn't part of the inner labyrinth of the main fort. But it was still constructed to go with the cosmetic grain of the main fort, using the same materials. It was more than likely used to store wood for the firepit. The reasoning used by Mick and Dave to come to that conclusion was the fact there was no wood for the pit within view. *What good is a firepit with no split wood easily available?*

Unlike the day before, there was action right away. Guards came out the doors to patrol once every hour to an hour and a half. Dave and Mick had no early postulations concerning the increase in activity.

By mid-afternoon, Mick and Dave assumed they were right in their assessment of the adjoining shed-like structure of the fort. Nobody had entered or exited the appendage's door, somewhat proving it and the main part of the fort weren't conjoined on the inside. The Molisians hadn't made a fire, so it couldn't yet be determined if they correctly analyzed it being just used for wood storage.

In Mick and Dave's eavesdropping, bits and pieces of conversations were heard. The only thing disclosed of importance was the fact the Molisians had prisoners within the fort. Up came the topic, because a particular pair of boisterous Molisians didn't like prisoner duty, preferring rounds and topside watch. Mick and Dave wished, however, they'd also heard how many prisoners were within, and if they were healthy or not.

By the time Hawk and Leopard decided to go back to their camp, they counted approximately fifteen different Molisian guards, coming in all shapes and sizes.

Walking back to their home on the hill, Mick said to Dave, "I presume you heard the part about there being prisoners."

"Who didn't?" said Dave. "The guards sure nagged about them."

"Did you hear or see anything else of importance from your end?"

"Can't say that I did," replied Dave, while scratching away dirt from his eye.

Arrival at camp was appreciated, for yet again they were hungrier than hungry thanks to only eating a snack at midday and breakfast before they left.

They ate much, and cleaned the mess consequently created.

There was an hour left of daylight, so the pair decided to gather materials from the surrounding area to construct their tables for the tent interiors. They also gathered materials for a few box traps to help replenish the meat supply. They were in no real danger of meat running out, but it never hurt to have a surplus. Of course, they could set up a couple free-standing rock traps along the periphery. Rock traps were far easier to fashion, but only if you could find the proper rocks. Dave and Mick decided on box traps, mainly because they were easier to hide. Debris was easier set atop box traps than rock traps. The materials weren't hard to find, so they began construction right away.

It started to snow lightly when they were halfway finished with the tables, but it started to snow profusely by the time they began work on the traps. Being more complicated devices than the tables, the traps were more arduous to assemble. Without a doubt, the traps would take more time to shape than the simple tables.

Because of the heavy snow, they decided to work on the traps inside a tent, together. They moved the finished tables inside Dave's tent to set their trap materials atop. By no means was sleep near, so they had plenty of time to finish the traps. They tinkered away as snow piled up outside.

When darkness appeared, they lit a few candles. They didn't have many candles, just enough to use sparingly. A person would think travelers intending to frequently sleep in the woods would bring loads of candles. But since the accumulated weight of numerous candles added up quickly, and their pack loads were already heavy, Mick and Dave limited their candle supply to what they felt absolutely necessary.

"Dave, this has got to be the first time we've ever sat in a tent, during an unceasing blizzard, sculpting box traps by candlelight."

"I think it is," said Dave, "but I do recall one time us sitting underneath a rock ledge in the rain forming fishing nets."

"Oh yeah, I remember that. That was the time we went to the Hovanaskoiler Wood to study the geysers therein. If I've committed it to memory properly, I do believe I out-fished you that day."

"I can't say that I remember that at all."

Mick laughed, "I bet you wouldn't."

The night wore on. Wind beat relentlessly against their tents—stout, well-constructed equipment that'd weathered strong winds before, and in essence would endure again. Snow levels were now well over a foot deep, and the storm showed no signs of tapering off.

Mick and Dave were about a third of the way complete with the traps, when Mick opened the tent door and stepped out to look around. He really took in the beauty of the landscape, especially the orangish hue of the night-sky. Mick said, "It sure is snowing hard, but I tell you what, my friend, this is quite the experience, sitting in a tent, in the snow, keeping busy, only we and God knowing where in the heck we are."

Dave stood up, went to take a look outside, and replied, "I wouldn't trade it for the world."

Just then, as they were still outside the tent, a pair of rocks tumbled off a ledge overhead, a plummeting probably caused by snow jostling around. One of the two rocks crashed onto a rock lying on the ground, making a thud sound. The other rock hit Dave on the back, making a thud sound as well.

Seeing Dave wasn't hurt, Mick smiled. He thought for a moment, and said, "I just figured out what the Atrudagar meant by the 'it takes a stone to know a stone' inscription we saw at the ruins on the stone mountain."

Dave nodded, and replied, "Yup, me too, now that you say that. If one truly wants to be in tune with their natural surroundings, and enjoy everything it has to offer, then one has to completely be immersed in it, live in the same world, and suffer the same adversities as nature itself does."

Mick and Dave contemplated shortly on their realization, then, started pondering things happening further away.

"I hope Jason, Gregg, the Black Bear, and the rest are doing well."

"Yeah, hopefully they are all alive," said Dave. "I wonder if another battle has occurred yet."

"I wonder as well. I'm sure we'll eventually hear what's been going on with our compatriots from the mouths of the Molisians at the fort."

"We probably will. Hopefully the effects of what we're about to do here will reach them quickly enough to help significantly."

"Hopefully we haven't been paying homage to the word hopefully too much, but hopefully the effects of the things we're about to do here don't cause us to bleed to death."

The duo laughed at Mick's play on words. If having a sense of humor was a sport in Garobansurov, Mick and Dave's mantelshelves would be brimming with trophies.

Coincidentally, they were simultaneously accosted by thoughts of the Battle of Strwin's post-battle revelry. They also thought about the priceless looks on all their friends' faces, as Mick told the story of the black needle pine to them.

After the outdoor nostalgia, the pair kicked out all the snow that had accumulated in the tent while it was open, and zipped it back up. They sat back down, and continued to work on box traps.

The traps were now halfway completed. Out of sheer randomness, an almost perfect equilateral triangle had formed by the discarded pieces of wood thrown onto the middle of the tent's floor. Mick noticed the anomaly, and started to throw the rest of his refuse into the center of the triangle. At first, he didn't entirely put much effort into trying to score a direct hit. Eventually, Dave caught on to what Mick was doing, and started to throw his waste into the triangle as well. Sooner than later, the activity turned into an all-out competition. They began keeping score, with each made shot being worth a point. Mick kept track of the score, and for the rest of the time spent making the traps, they competed semi-vigorously, talked riotously, and enjoyed the storm around them.

ORDINARILY, AL WOULD leave the thick wooden door of his rustic cabin slightly ajar, because he liked a cool breeze, the fresh, breathable air. The air inside a cabin with a fire blazing constantly could get awfully stuffy. But upon entering his cabin this particular evening, he closed the door behind him all the way, due to both the tremendous blizzard occurring, and the fact he had company staying with him. His company had been there for a couple days now, and thought he was being a great host, especially since Al was only working with one hand. It got chopped off a while ago, for an incident that should've never happened, an incident forced by the cruelty and injustice of the new, tyrannical ruler of Sarwa—Gamald.

Al took off his snow-laden, ice-encrusted fur coat, hung it on the designated hook, and threw a few more logs onto the already-crackling fire.

Unaware their friend Al had already returned home from his important business, Al's guests, Loyd and Carrie, held discussion in a bedroom. "I sure hope he's back soon. My apprehension is unbearable," uttered Carrie, as she paced.

"I have a strong feeling Al will be successful this time in finding out from his connections where your grandfather is located."

"I hope you're right. I'm really starting to worry myself sick. The last few days have been brutal."

"Your grandfather shares the Quintaga name with you, your maiden name, and the one thing I know for sure is that the Quintagas are resourceful, always finding a way out of adversity. It's in your blood."

"That's true. Speaking of resourceful, I remember a time when Brom and I got accused of cheating in a game of poker at some saloon somewhere. Truth be told, we actually were cheating. Throughout the years, we've mastered quite the system of facial signals, giving us a rather substantial advantage in poker. To this day, I have no idea how he did it, but a while ago there was an occurrence where at the exact same time we were being accused of cheating, a huge bar fight unraveled, during which, we snuck out the back door with our illegitimate earnings. Good times. He would never tell me how he started a bar fight, while sitting innocently at the card table, but he did promise me when the time was right, he'd explain how it all transpired."

By the time Carrie finished her narrative, Al was finished with the fire, and standing at the doorway, having heard most of her story. Al said, "I wish I would've had a good relationship with my grandfather, but he died when I was young, and I've never known any of my other grandparents."

Loyd and Carrie looked over at Al. Carrie replied sincerely, "He's a wonderful man, and I miss him dearly. I wish you would've been afforded the opportunity to experience such a relationship, Al."

Inspired by his friend's heart, Al grew serious and emotional, "Then let us save him! My rendezvous this evening was fruitful. The good news is I learned where your grandfather is, but the bad news is he's being held captive in an underground cell. I have a score to settle with these people, these usurpers, and by my word, we'll free him." Eyes of fury, Al dramatically held up his handless arm.

Both Carrie and Loyd's jaws dropped to the floor at hearing the news. Deep down inside, however, confidence swelled.

Carrie emitted, "Thank you so much, Al, for everything you're doing for us. We probably wouldn't have even made it through the front gate, if it hadn't been for you."

"Anything for friends." Observing the shock and dismay in his friends at hearing his news, Al felt sad, but he also felt proud to be a part of the rescue mission. Al went on, telling them everything he'd learned. "From a friend of a friend of a rather large man, I've learned that Brom was trying to sell some suits of armor here in Sarwa."

"Yes, the three he's been shaping for the last thirty years of his life," erupted Carrie.

Al continued, "The armor was put through a series of tests, and passed with such exclamation that General Gamald just had to have them. He devised a plan, in which a fake ceremony was staged. At the end of the ceremony, Brom was told to walk down a flight of stairs to receive his payment. There, he was ambushed, and immediately locked into an underground jail cell, his three suits of armor stolen. My friend said his friend was friends with one of the ambushers, the rather large man. Confusing perhaps, but all true."

"So maybe, since the large man is already talking about it, he'll talk about it a little more with us."

"Good thinking, Carrie. Then, as soon as this storm dissolves, we'll see what we can do," said Al, determinedly cracking his knuckles.

Loyd stared at his wife, admiring her resolve and passion, falling deeper in love with her.

COMPLETELY UNAWARE THE wheels of his rescue had just been put into motion, Brom was aware a huge blizzard was occurring outside. He could see snow getting into the corridors just outside his cell. He was evermore starved, but still had hope. However, he'd lost all hope he'd ever see his armor again. Even if he did get out of the cell, he wouldn't even have the funds to continue the search for his son.

Brom crashed down onto his bed in despair for probably the hundred and fiftieth time since being locked up. Lying idle, he closed his eyes.

He opened them an hour later, and took another look down the corridors. The snow getting in, probably when a guard would step outside, was starting to form a little pile within his view. *It must really be snowing out there*, he thought. *It must be miserable out there. What I wouldn't give to be out there.*

A plate was brought to him, piled low with food, but piled high with snow accumulated during transportation. The person who brought it was someone new. She actually spouted more than two words to Brom, unlike the usual guards, who'd just grunt when asked a question. "We have almost two feet of snow out there already, and more to come, I'm sure."

Brom replied, "It must be beautiful."

The lady definitely didn't think so, she preferred warmer weather, but responded pleasantly before walking away, "I imagine it is."

Brom thought for a few moments on how wonderful it was to hear a complete sentence, but didn't dwell on it. He assumed his food would continue to be delivered by the same taciturn guards in the future.

It was wise he hadn't gotten his hopes up about a revisit from the pleasant woman. She almost certainly would never return. She only brought the food this time because she was performing a favor for someone, optimally killing two birds with one stone. Along with bringing Brom his food, she sized up some curtains in the guard's chamber, being under employment to replace them.

Ironically, for the first time, Brom wondered if there were any other prisoners in the underground prison. Up to that point, he unconsciously assumed there weren't any, because he never heard any sounds from other would-be captives. He momentarily thought maybe there are some and they're just being voluntarily inaudible. He shook off the thought rapidly, realizing it was ludicrous.

Later in the evening, Brom decided to kill some time by punching walls. He rationalized it as being productive, because it helped in giving him strong knuckles. Strong knuckles meant better security in theory. And it also didn't hurt once in a while to play no guts no glory, and try to bust through the walls.

Eventually, he punched himself tired, went to bed, and slept through the rest of the snowstorm. He had failed at busting himself out of the cell with his fists. In case you're wondering, only twice in the history of Taraosk had someone busted out of a jail cell by way of their fists.

CHAPTER 16

PARTNERED WITH THE challenging duty of tracking Anolski, Jason Thorncat and his crew had to deal with the blizzard, as did everyone else in that part of Garobansurov. As opposed to Mick and Dave's travel tents, Jason and company were blessed with sizeable army tents, which were pulled in a wagon by multiple soldiers. Oriented circularly, the tents were set up with a roaring fire in the middle. The snow that had been in the middle was shoveled out so all the soldiers had a comfortable place to move around for the evening. Jason was on the right track in his pursuit of Anolski, but a great distance had gotten between him and his quarry during the turmoil of the end of the battle. It wasn't going to be an easy mission.

Most of Jason's regiment of 150 soldiers were in tents, playing cards and smoking pipes. Jason and Gregg

Hogarty were standing by the bonfire at center, talking in a way one would think they'd been friends for many years. In reality, they had just met a relatively short while ago, but because they looked at life on the same plane, and knew the other was trustworthy, they formed a friendship that was strong.

A burning log fell out of the fire, which Gregg kicked back in, successful in not soiling his boots in the process. "Can you tell how far ahead of us Anolski got?"

"I'd say about three or four miles," Jason said. "I'll probably scout ahead tomorrow to see if I can determine exactly."

"Good thinking. These snowflakes, the size of fists, won't make that easy."

"At least if our path is hard going, then so is Anolski's, in which case the deep snow will make tracking him a heck of a lot easier."

"Good," said Gregg. When swiveling his neck to crack it, Gregg noticed an intruder sneaking through the tent perimeter. "It looks like the raccoons around here sure are daring."

"I think she's wasting her time looking for food here," said Jason. "This crew scarfed every last bit prepared. But then on the other hand, she may find a little something, somewhere."

"May luck be on your side, my furry friend."

Ultimately, the energy of Gregg and Jason's fire dissipated, losing all traces of the color orange. Only smoke remained. Tired, wet, and bored with watching the raccoon's unsuccessful attempt at scrounging, Jason and Gregg, before going to bed, threw more wood onto the fire to keep it burning through the night. All the tents were completely covered in snow, but that only added insulation to them, effectively keeping them warmer.

Just after the last army tent was closed for the night, the raccoon finally found enough food to call a meal, and was content.

RARELY CAME AN evening when Mick Thraiker and Dave Ghrere decided to stay up late. But driven by euphoria, the likes of which usually only caused by the excitement of severe weather, they defied statistics, and stayed awake into the wee hours of the morning. They also managed to finish up their box traps. Both their traps were in fine working order, and were placed in ready positions, just outside the tents for the evening. They knew nothing would be caught so close to their tents, but they couldn't resist the primitive urge.

Standing outside by his trap as the snowstorm dwindled in magnitude, Dave said, "I suppose we can go to sleep now."

"I suppose we shall. Hopefully my tent survived the storm. I haven't checked it at all, not since the heavy snow began."

Mick grabbed his recently made table out from Dave's tent, entered his own, and felt much relief seeing all was well within his tent. He placed his table in the perfect position, set a few handy items on it, took a huge drink of water, and went to bed.

Dave tossed the triangle game's aftermath out of his tent, and like Mick, set a few things on his new table, before going to sleep.

The morning came like a lamb, but was a complete alien world compared to all other mornings of their journey. Snow was everywhere, not yielding any color other than white and slightly off-white. The snow was so abundant virtually nothing else could be seen, foreground and background.

"I'm guessing, Dave, at least two and a half, maybe three feet of snow fell altogether."

"That looks to be the case."

Mick looked off to his right. "No surprise, there's nothing in my trap."

"Nothing in mine either, just more snow."

"I suppose the first thing we can do amongst this icy madness is clear snow from our little lawn here, so we can at least move around freely."

"It would make things easier for the future." They proceeded with snow removal by using primarily their feet. "What I wouldn't give for a shovel right now."

Mick responded, "You could've brought one with, you know. I know I sure wasn't going to carry the extra five pounds."

"I'm as well, beyond any doubt, at my pack's weight limit. I should say the pack itself could support more weight—it's *me* who doesn't want to do any more supporting."

Mick expelled a chuckle. "Same here."

After an hour, the snow removal task was finished, the snow having been mostly kicked down the cliff.

"There, now we can eat breakfast."

The morning meal was large, yet again, and consumed quickly. Things to do, people to see.

Spending a moment letting all the food settle in their stomachs, the duo paced around in circles on their snow-free lawn, thinking of their game plan.

They inspected the area, looking for something specific. They needed already-made animal paths, so their own paths in the snow, when overlapped with the animal paths, would be much more inconspicuous. With that added advantage, plus a little extra work on the snow, they could walk to their destination undetected. Nobody, barring a superiorly-trained eye, would notice their trails. They looked for a long time, but came up short of what they wanted to find.

"I don't think either of us are going to make it to the fort today."

"I'm not thinking so either. But I do think one of us should follow the bigger trail leading away, and cook up a new supply of food."

"And the other can stay behind to work on the trail to the fort, hopefully completing that for tomorrow," responded Mick.

"Okay, sounds good. I guess I'll go cook the food, and you can work on the trail."

"Fine by me. Our plan for the day is settled."

Dave ventured off far enough away to cook food without risking the smoke from his fire being noticed by anyone at the fort. He toted a load of sausages, fish, a few vegetables, and a supply of wheat and corn flour for bread making. Considering how far away from civilization they were, Dave thought they were blessed with a cornucopia of food. He also brought both traps, so that way he could set them in satellite locations, conveniently not having to double-work the trails.

Following the animal path, Dave reached a point a mile away from the tents, two miles from the fort. Along the way, he made sure to brush snow into his footprints for extra concealment. He chose a small dale as the locale for carrying out his task.

Before gathering firewood and initiating the fire, he made absolutely sure no one was around. All clear. Tinder had been spotted and grabbed along the way—paper birch bark and dead balsam branches. Paper birch worked well, because it was easy to light, and balsam branches worked well, because they burned hot, efficiently drying out any wet wood around it.

Tinder was placed at the center of a crudely constructed fire ring. He found a good supply of wood from a dead, but still standing, maple tree, which was kicked down and broken apart by the power of Dave's foot. He lit the tinder, slowly added the maple, and started to cook.

Meanwhile, back at camp, Mick began the arduous task of establishing a decent trail to Fort Gravividon. Since there weren't any primary animal trails in sight, he faked a trail down the side of the hill, hoping to get lucky and connect with one in due course. If he didn't find a suitable animal trail, his mission would become much more arduous. Fortunately, though, by midday, he came across a game trail heading the right way. Cosmic forces had cooperated.

It took him almost the entire day to do it, but his trail finally reached close to the facade of Fort Gravividon. He left the last insignificant fifty-foot stretch for the next day. Strategically speaking, he didn't want his trailhead too close to the fort that day. Later on would be fine, since trails seemed more natural, the older they got.

Dave had already returned to the tents, when Mick arrived back. "How long have you been here?"

"Only about an hour," Dave answered.

"I take it you didn't run into any problems then?"

"Nope, no problems. I got the traps set up too."

"Excellent. For how many days do you think we've enough food now?"

"I'd say about four or five. Did everything turn out well for you?"

"All's well, but it wasn't easy," replied Mick.

"I imagine."

"Hopefully it doesn't snow like that again. I'd hate to have to do it all over again."

Hawk and Leopard ate supper, and unlike the night before, went to bed early.

The next day, they followed Mick's trail, finished the last segment, and went to the area overlooking the fort's east side again. They concluded they'd more than likely scout the east side primarily, because of its constant activity. Having successfully located their priceless sitting logs, they brushed off the snow, and sat.

The spying during the morning was pretty triumphant. They learned all about the battle of Thraug and the Garobansurovian victory. They also lapped up the key cause of the Molisian defeat: Ulfenkerki's plan involving the suspended animation of the rock wielding soldiers. It didn't surprise Mick and Dave in the least.

They were well aware of Ulfenkerki's skill in war tactics. There was always something up that man's sleeve.

THE STREETS OF Sarwa were still covered in the snow from the big snowstorm two nights previous. Hungry people were unambitious people, never in the mood to shovel snow. Gamald knew sooner or later he'd have to force someone to do it, so the army could move around freely.

Al, Carrie, Loyd, and Al's friend, Brian, navigated the snow-laden streets, nevertheless. Brian was the guy who knew the guy, who knew the guy present during Brom's capture. Brian was doing a favor for his friend, Al, by arranging a meeting. They were all making an important visit with Brian's friend at his house—the next necessary link in the chain of rescue.

Upon arrival, they were all greeted pleasantly, and led into Brian's friend's house, whose name was Chaltask. Chaltask was about the same age as Brian and Al, but a little more muscular. Not that his physique mattered in the overall scheme of things.

Chaltask emitted, "I'd been given a summary on your situation, Carrie, Loyd, but I'm not aware of any of the specific facets."

Carrie explained everything to Chaltask in detail, beginning with her and Loyd's story up to that point. She detailed everything she'd heard that'd happened to Brom. Carrie finished with a powerful speech, describing how vital it was to receive as much help as possible, and how important her grandfather was to her.

Chaltask had listened to Carrie with open ears. Afterwards, he asked his guests if they wanted anything to drink. They all requested water.

He walked into the kitchen to get the waters, using the time to think about the situation, about how much he wanted to help the strangers. He was moved by Carrie's speech, and imagined what it'd feel like to be in her shoes. He also spent time thinking about how much trouble he'd get into if he was caught helping. *A lot.* Chaltask was well aware his large friend, Beltrandt, was present during the capture, and a man certainly able to assist Carrie and Loyd. He knew how tight of a corner in which he'd be by just arranging a meeting between Beltrandt, Carrie and Loyd. Just being associated posed dire consequences. He was on the fence the entire time gathering the waters— an easy task rarely performed slower.

Finally, he came to his decision vis-à-vis whether he was going to help them with their dilemma, or do something else about the events transpiring in his living room. He looked out the window, gestured to his neighbor standing outside, brought the four waters to his patient guests, and explained to them what exactly was going to be done.

HAWK AND LEOPARD had a hard time not laughing any louder than what they did at how long it took the Molisians to get a fire going. They must've fumbled around for a good hour, trying to get the thing lit. It had only taken Dave four minutes to start his fire the day before, and there was only one of him, compared to the four trying to light that fire. When it was finally lit, the four stood and talked, eventually throwing some food onto the available cooking grate. For many hours, they stood around the fire, unknowingly being spied upon. In those hours, they moved away from the fire only occasionally.

The guards never talked about anything extremely important that afternoon for Mick and Dave's eavesdropping. Though, of small interest, it was revealed to Mick and Dave the structure connected to the fort was indeed strictly used for wood storage. They could see only piles of split wood in the building when guards went in to fetch their firewood.

Persuaded by their desires for warmth and changes in scenery, the guards went back into the fort, giving Mick and Dave a chance to talk. "Before we head back to camp today, I think we should wait until nightfall, and quickly investigate the wood storage building."

"You're right. It may be possible to somehow enter it, without anyone noticing," Dave responded.

"I would say there's only about an hour left of daylight."

"When it's dark, I'll run over there and inspect the door. Conveniently, it'll get pretty dark too, because by my calculations, tonight's sky will be bereft moon."

"By my calculations too. While you're doing that, I'll creep a little closer to the forest edge to keep a lookout. If I see one of the main fort doors opening, I'll whistle like a finch."

"Sounds good, but I didn't know you could whistle like a finch, Mick."

"I'm full of surprises."

When the moonless sky was as dark as it was going to be, Dave started to make his way towards the wood building—the "wood building" was what Mick and Dave unoriginally decided to call it. On his approach to the glade encircling the fort, Dave made sure to keep a tree between himself and the fort, while Mick followed close behind.

With Mick in position on standby with his hidden bird-call talent, Dave rushed into the clearing, past the smoldering contents of the firepit, and to the wood building's door. He inspected the door as close as he could. He pulled on the handle and realized it was locked. No such luck. Twitching the door handle in bursts, he tried to listen to the lock mechanism's idiosyncrasies. He pressed his ear against the door to listen, and continued fiddling with the lock, examining as carefully as he could, not that Dave had much experience in studying the lock mechanisms of doors.

Satisfied with the thorough inspection, and thankful he didn't hear any unusual night finches, Dave slipped back to the protective cover of the forest. He began explaining to Mick what he'd seen and heard. "The door is thick, strong, and reinforced with a metal lining, so there's no way of busting through without leaving a trace. The key-activated lock is connected to a metal rod, which slides in and out of a locking position, as the key is turned. Maybe we can get the key somehow. Don't ask me how we'd accomplish that, but it's just a thought."

"We'll sleep on it. Maybe we'll come up with something tomorrow." Just after Mick said that, he thought of something riveting. He looked away, and curled the right side of his lips into a half smile, realizing a certain thing that'd happened in the past could now be truly revenged.

That night, they had to walk back to the comfort of their campsite in the dark, but it wasn't too terrible. They enjoyed the novelty of it. Supper was consumed and a small amount of tidy work was accomplished. Before going to bed, they walked out to their box traps, saw one had ensnared a red squirrel, and brought it back for skinning and gutting.

At the tents, ripping the intestines out of a tasty mammal's midsection, Dave uttered, "Hopefully tomorrow will be as exciting as today."

"Oh, I'm pretty sure it will."

Dave and Mick went to bed a little later than the night before, and slept really well, considering the fact they'd slept in tents with an exterior temperature of five degrees, and an interior temperature of thirty-two degrees. The interior temperature of their tents hardly ever dropped below that because of the tent-ice insulation. Thirty-two degrees was just warm enough for an adept woodsman, wrapped in a quality sleeping bag, to sleep comfortably.

After breakfast, to keep out scavengers, Mick put the meat of the red squirrel in a rock compartment they'd made, along with all the other food. The hillside was full of opportunistic feeders.

Just before departing for the fort, Mick went into his tent and grabbed one last thing needed for the day. He caught up with Dave, who'd already started to walk their trail in the snow to Fort Gravividon.

Their morning reconnaissance yielded only information concerning how much one of the guards had gotten yelled at by his superior the previous day, one grunt ranting to another. It was pretty useless information otherwise, except for the fact they now knew the name of one of the officers running the fort: Captain Huilghenberk.

There was no campfire from the guards that afternoon, but they did learn there was only one other officer at the fort. Although the officer's rank remained a mystery, they did gain knowledge of his name: Agher Schaet.

At dusk, Mick walked over by Dave and said, "Are there any parts of the fort we need to inspect tonight?"

"I didn't see any. I'm pretty sure all the other doors are locked up tighter than the king's treasury."

"Disappointing. I was hoping we'd receive some excitement again this evening."

Dave replied, "Me too."

Mick paused for a few seconds, and put forth, "You know, Leopard, I was thinking. I'll bet you a day's item carrying that I can sneak down to the wood building, and open it without making a sound or causing damage to the door or its frame."

"You've got to be kidding me. There isn't anyone getting in there without waking the dead while doing so."

"Is it a bet then?"

"I'm so certain I'm going to win I desire to double the stakes of the bet."

"Okay you're on. For two days' worth of item carrying, then."

The friends shook on it. At nightfall, Mick and Dave began replaying the events which occurred the night before, but this time with the roles reversed. Just before they reached the edge of their forest hideout, Mick said, "I don't imagine you can whistle like a finch too, huh?"

"No, Bird Master, I can't. I'll just make a coyote sound."

"A coyote call," Mick exclaimed quietly. "I've got to hear that before I begin."

"Oh, no, no, no. First, you open the door, then, I'll make all the sounds you want. I know darn well you know what my coyote call sounds like, so don't give me any, I need to hear it, so I know for what to listen, crap."

Mick chuckled, "Oh, alright," and began tiptoeing to the wood building door for his revenge for the rooftop incident back in Strwin. When he reached it, he studied it, jiggled on it, and inspected the lock itself. Confidence befell him. He looked around one more time to make sure the coast was clear. It was. While Dave wasn't looking, Mick pulled out from under his coat the item he'd grabbed out of his tent before leaving for the fort— the *parabolic, magnetic key*. Mick had a strong suspicion the magnet was so physically powerful he could use it to bypass the lock mechanism and slide the metal bar out from the locked position.

He held the magnet up to the door, and tried to seize the interior metal bar within its clutch. Mick couldn't have been any more right in his postulation, for it worked like a charm. With the slide of his hand, the door had opened silently. He whispered to himself, "One powerful magnet indeed," and entered the room cautiously.

Once inside, all he could see in front of his face were piles and piles of stacked wood. The only light in the room was supplied by starlight sneaking in through the doorway. Mick left the door slightly open for just that purpose. He'd have to bring a candle next time to better see. Eventually, his eyes adjusted to the darkness, and he could distinguish the four walls of the building, confirming the speculation the wood-building wasn't a part of the fort interior, just a part of the facade. Without the ability to see around thoroughly, he didn't spend much time dawdling. He took one final glance, exited, and locked the door back up behind him using the magnet. With this new trick, he was halfway certain when they executed the fort onslaught it would be easier somehow.

Inconspicuously, Mick crept back to Dave, donning a victory smile the whole time.

Noticing Mick's smile, Dave said, "Clever, clever, you sure got me. I assume what you put back into concealment just after closing the door was the magical magnet doohickey. I should've never inanely doubled the bet."

"You're right, you shouldn't have. And, yes, it was the magnet. I was just happy getting you back thoroughly for your little rooftop stunt back at Strwin."

"Well played, my friend, well played. The good news for me, though, is I don't think we'll be traveling again soon, so maybe you'll forget about it when we do."

"Fat chance," replied Mick.

Mick explained everything he saw in the wood-building to Dave on their way back to camp. When the account was over, Dave said, "I absolutely agree with you, the trick you did with the parabolic magnet tonight may potentially augment our foreseeable fort invasion."

BROM WAS NOW so confident in the strength of his knuckles he started to punch the walls with his finger knuckles. A trick that hurt at first, but not after a while. A person could gain a lot of speed with a jab or a power punch, by punching this way. Brom felt strong—not strong enough to punch through walls, but strong enough to fight if the time came. Though, he felt useless in his cell. He just wanted one chance to fight his way out of town, risking his life with every Molisian soldier faced. At least that way he wouldn't go down without a fight.

He covered his third, five-mile stretch of the day, pacing back and forth within his cell. He kept track of distance by counting laps and multiplying by distance—*fourteen feet per lap*—an activity encompassing both the mental and physical, though one of only minimal enjoyment.

He crawled into his bed and contemplated for an hour before falling asleep. His thoughts were a whirlwind, slowly dissipating as the hour went by.

Marooned in inner darkness, Brom closed his eyes. But then, at the mysterious moment just before falling asleep, he heard a clicking sound at his cell door. He didn't think anything of it, playing it off as a hallucination, ignoring it altogether. But the second time he heard it, he forced himself to stop falling asleep. The third time, he was compelled to take a look at the door. What he saw nearly gave him a heart attack, for the entity making the sound was the same large man who'd put the sack over him during his capture.

"Put your shoes on, and follow me," said the large man.

Brom thought for a moment, and asked himself, am I being executed? Having shrugged away the thought, he saw no reason to argue with the mountain of a man. Maybe he was being rescued? He had nothing to lose. He would've attempted anything, no matter how ludicrous, to get out. He slipped on his shoes, and followed the stranger down the corridor.

Their path headed further underground. Looking around nervously as he followed, Brom saw no other guards. Perhaps they were sleeping or something of the sort. Along the way, he realized he was indeed the only prisoner stationed in the underground jail, but had no idea why. Frankly, he didn't care. All he cared about was continuing the search for his son, and whether this large man was leading him to his freedom, or to a death sentence. He wasted no time asking questions, preparing himself for any and all possibilities.

The manmade corridor eventually gave way to a tunnel of earth, an interesting passage very dark most of the way. The darkness only heightened his apprehension.

After walking in the dark for ten minutes, a light could finally be seen in the distance. In his mind, this was the moment of truth.

When the light was almost on top of them, he noticed the tunnel was about to open up. He put his hand on his heart, held his breath, and refocused his eyes entering the brighter expanse.

Finally, a miracle seeped into Brom Quintaga's life, for he saw standing in front of him the very thing he was hoping to see—his granddaughter, Carrie, and her husband Loyd. He also saw them standing next to a wooden chest, a treasure chest it seemed, the one Mick Thraiker and Dave Ghrere had acquired for them during their adventure together.

Beltrandt, the large man whom Brom was following, said to Carrie and Loyd, "As promised, the prisoner, Brom Quintaga."

The day before, Chaltask had arranged a meeting for Loyd and Carrie with Beltrandt. While in his kitchen getting the four glasses of water, Chaltask had decided to go with his heart, and help out the desperate strangers.

At the meeting, an arrangement was agreed upon, where Beltrandt was given one-eighth of the jewels in the chest as a showing of good faith, and the remaining seven-eighths would be given when he safely delivered Brom.

Beltrandt worked out the plan, and executed it to perfection.

Assuming the guard on duty that night in the underground jail would more than likely be soundly sleeping, Beltrandt stole the keys, let Brom out, and led him to the place where they were all currently standing. Coincidentally, the tunnel system had a site-chute leading to the basement of Beltrandt's home. Needless to say, he knew the tunnels well.

Brom finally caught his breath, from having hyperventilated, and embraced his ecstatic family.

Loyd turned to Beltrandt, and said, "And as promised from our end, the remaining seven-eighths of the jewels inside the chest." He opened the chest for Beltrandt to see.

Brom was astonished at what he saw in the chest as Loyd opened it. He wondered how they'd acquired such a bounty. He thought his granddaughter was capable of anything before, now he was sure beyond the shadow of a doubt she was.

Beltrandt took hold of the jewels and erupted, "A pleasure doing business with you. Now, we must act hastily though. We still all need to get out of town before they notice Brom is missing."

Beltrandt carried the chest of jewels—his prize for defying his evil leader—into his basement, while Loyd, Carrie, and Brom escaped the underworld and made their way to Al's house under the cover of darkness.

Upon seeing his friends, and noticing their success, Al was overwhelmed with joy, and said, "Mr. Quintaga, nice to meet you. You have no idea how much you mean to those two people over there."

"Oh, I have a pretty strong idea. I surely feel the same way about them."

Despite Al's urge to dispense more pleasantries, he continued on with serious matters, "We have to get you three out of town, right now, and it's not going to be easy. I have to try and get you through the front gate, while it's still dark. They haven't detected Brom's absence yet, so we'll attempt to get you out the same way I got you in— by talking nicely."

"Okay, we'll swiftly grab all of our things."

Loyd and Carrie filled up a sack with all their clothes and anonymous gear. They also had another sack, already packed and ready to go. Al gave Brom a supply of clothes; his were all lost during the incarceration. They were out the door in no time flat.

Loyd, Carrie, and Brom, each carrying a sack, followed Al to Sarwa's front gate. Unsurprisingly, they wanted to bring weapons with, but knew they couldn't due to the obvious risk the weapons would present if they were discerned.

The quartet was relieved to see only two guards posted at the gate. Al said to the guards, "My friends are done visiting me now. Will you open the gate to allow them to start their long journey back home?"

The guards were suspicious about such a request asked in the middle of the night, and looked a little closer. "Halt right there! I recognize that man. He was the one who brought the armor. We're supposed to be holding him hostage. *You four are under arres—*"

But before the guard was even able to finish his sentence, Brom, with all his pent-up rage, waiting for a moment like this, unleashed a fury so intense his companions didn't even have time to assist in the takedown. In the matter of mere seconds, Brom had driven his finely-tuned finger-knuckles through the guards' temples, knocking them so far out of commission they'd have no memories of what happened, which was convenient, because if they had remembered anything about what had happened, they certainly would've remembered Al's face, and Al would've gotten tied into the breakout.

Without much effort, Al opened the gate. Brom, Carrie, and Loyd stepped foot outside of Sarwa, and just like that, the trio had successfully escaped. They felt enormously alive. Outside the gate, Loyd voiced to Al, "Goodbye, my friend, thank you for everything."

"You're welcome. I hope to see you again, and that the three of you find your uncle and son. Godspeed."

Meanwhile, Beltrandt saw the whole thing happen. Thankfully, he was the only one to see it. Wanting to take advantage of the situation, Beltrandt thought fast. In an instant, he abandoned his erstwhile station in life, and discreetly sauntered out the wide-open front gate, grasping his justly earned treasure. Venturing off to a faraway land, the large man lived a better life, and was never seen nor heard from again.

After running far enough away from town to ensure safety, Loyd, Carrie, and Brom finally communicated words of rejoice. They discussed the entire plan used to free Brom, including all the steps, and people involved. Brom was amazed. "The whole time I was in the cell, I knew you'd be the one to rescue me. I had no idea how you'd do it, but I knew you'd be the one."

Carrie responded, "I had no idea when we got to Sarwa we'd have to pull off a liberation mission. I didn't know at all what to expect. All we knew was you were headed to Sarwa in an attempt to sell your armor."

"It's a crazy world. I just wish I still had my three suits of armor, but more importantly, I wish I had the funds to continue searching for your uncle. We won't get very far without a single giti."

Suddenly, the biggest smile appeared on Carrie's face. "Fear not, my wonderful grandfather. Your wish is granted. You saw the chest of jewels when we were in the tunnel, right?"

"Yes. Too bad you gave it all to Beltrandt."

Streaming high spirits, Carrie nonchalantly opened the sack she was carrying to show Brom what was inside. "We knew the bulk of your story, and we knew what was needed. So, we couldn't resist skimming enough jewels off the top of the chest to fuel the prolongation of your search. Together, we will journey, journey to find uncle." The jewels in the sack were plentiful, shining impressively in the sun, and more than enough in value to support the continuation of a search mission.

"Oh my God, you brilliant, noble souls. I can't believe this is happening," said Brom, as he hugged Loyd and Carrie. "I must tell you, now, how we had escaped unscratched from that poker game so many years ago. The time when that bar-brawl seemingly randomly started. There couldn't be a better occasion to tell you. You earned it."

"It's about time," exclaimed Carrie. "I've been waiting a long time to hear this. Let me have it."

"It's possible you may not like it, but here goes. The bar fight wasn't random, but that's not new to you. I knew you had supposed that."

"From the moment we started winning profusely in the poker game, I could tell our normally profitable ruse was going to get us in trouble. I just had that feeling. We couldn't simply back out of the game that far in, so I had to come up with a plan, and fast. My plan also doubled as a way to play a prank on you. I had owed you a good one. In case you don't remember, that time you tricked me into rolling around in the mud. Funny, yes, but certainly deserving of revenge."

"When I went to take a piss, prior to returning back to the game, I searched out the roughest, toughest hooligans scattered throughout the bar. I told them all separately you had your eye on them, and that you were interested in something physical. Then, I individually told them all that when I gave the signal, my right index finger raised high into the air, to come make their move. So, when things were starting to get precarious at the poker table, I raised my finger. Immediately, from all corners of the bar, men came at you, drooling. When they all took notice of others walking towards you, thinking you'd be tempted by someone else, they instinctively began fighting. In essence, a fight for the opportunity to sleep with you. But what they didn't know was it was just a planned diversion, one we used to get out of the bar, unscathed. I laughed so hard in private that night."

Carrie and Loyd were both staring at Brom at the completion of his tale, but then, all of a sudden, laughed so hard it startled nearby animals. "You were right! There couldn't have been a better time to tell that story. And, yes, I do remember you had owed me one," Carrie said. "I'm just glad we got out of there, not having to stick around to see who turned out to be the winner of the fight."

Barely being able to fashion words, due to incapacitating laughter, Brom replied, "What an astonishing night this is."

CHAPTER 17

THE DARKNESS SURROUNDING Mick and Dave resembled subterranean darkness, making it harder than usual for them to get back to camp. Mick was still in good disposition. It was rare for him to fool Dave the way he did, Dave typically having his mind on pranks more frequently.

They finally stumbled their way through the ghostly terrain and into camp. Mick put the magnet back into his tent, and received much contentment at eyeing the tent's innards, a simple pleasure occurring from time to time. "Ah, yes, happiness is definitely a warm sleeping bag on a cold night."

"Actually," blurted Dave, "H equals LJ *if and only if* LJ equals T to the power of D. H represents happiness; LJ represents life's journey; T represents time; and D represents your dreams. So logically, Mick Thraiker, happiness is not a warm sleeping bag; it's your *life's journey*, *if and only if* your life's journey equates to time to the power of your dreams."

"You just came up with that now." Mick chuckled.

"Maybe."

"Well, technically speaking, you might be close. But for tonight, happiness is a warm and cozy sleeping bag."

Dave followed Mick's chuckle with one of his own, and replied, "I suppose we can defy the laws of nature for one night."

Their nightly routine was performed. Mick slept as well as he thought he would. It was as if he slept on a bed made of clouds, soaring through his dreams uninterrupted.

In the morning and subsequent breakfast they discussed the day, resolving to again enter the wood building. Before trotting off to Fort Gravividon they grabbed their swords, the magnet and a candle for better seeing in the wood building, hoping to attain a firmer grasp on all its facets.

The Molisian soldiers had summoned a fire early that day, probably because it was a relatively warmer day. To some, warmth made the outdoors seem more inviting. They sat by the fire for a long time, loud enough for Mick and Dave to hear the soldiers had talked on the vital subject of reinforcements. Mick and Dave wished they'd talked further, having only gained minimal information on the subject. There was going to be a number of reinforcements, but it wasn't shared how many or when they'd arrive. Hawk and Leopard hoped they would receive specific details on the subject sooner than later, information that would greatly facilitate their future incursion.

The whole day was spent listening. Unfortunately, for the majority of the time, they had to listen to the soldiers' sexual conquests. Boys will be boys.

Just before dark, the assembly at the firepit dispersed, rendering the area mute. Mick and Dave were glad at that, for they were starting to grow tired of listening to the arrogant male boasting indicative of wartime, campfire communications.

Prompted by nightfall and the approaching of optimal break-in time, the pair started to ponder whether they were going to draw straws or continue alternating turns entering the wood building, a job best performed singularly, as opposed to together. An outside lookout was essential. They ultimately concluded to alternating turns, making it Dave's turn to intrude that evening.

Lightness of foot was imperative as Dave made his way to the wood building. He was accompanied by his sword, a candle, the pivotal parabolic magnet, a heightened acumen, and a few other less significant things. Mick stood on guard behind a nearby tree, poised.

Dave maneuvered the magnet the same way Mick had and entered the wood-building. After lighting the candle with his sword and flint, he immediately saw all the wood. There were four stacked rows. Plus, there was a corner with wood thrown into it, unstacked. No windows or doors, besides the enter/exit, were perceived. A workbench cluttered the eastern wall, which appeared to be used to make wooden trinkets. But it seemed to not have been used for many years, being covered by layer upon layer of dust. Empty bins sat next to the workbench, probably at one time used to store miscellaneous pieces of wood for tinkering.

Dave was beginning to think there wasn't anything at all in the wood building that could be of assistance in their future assault, but as soon as he started walking towards the exit, he heard a voice. It took him a while to discern from where it was coming, but eventually he realized it was a male voice coming from behind the western wall, the wall adjacent to the rest of the fort. A song was being sung.

Dave moved some of the unstacked wood out of the way so he could hear better, aiming to cup his ear against the part of the wall where the voice was loudest. The wood was as cold to the touch as anticipated. Along with the wall.

The singing went on for a few minutes, followed by a five-minute pause. Then, Dave heard the stranger talking. Judging by what he heard, Dave drew to the conclusion he was listening to a prisoner. The main giveaway Dave heard was, "Why can't we ever get any more water?" Water was abundant in the area, since the whole area was situated over a giant aquifer. Water was easily obtainable for a free man. But a prisoner would have to beg for it.

Dave listened to the occasional rants of the prisoner through the wall for another twenty minutes. Instead of contacting the potential ally right then and there, he decided to first talk the whole thing over with his partner, Mick.

Dave exited, locked the door back up, and stealthily traversed back to where Mick was standing guard. Dave relayed everything that had transpired as they walked back to the tents.

Mick responded, "This new knowledge can help us out very much indeed. Being my turn tomorrow to enter the wood building, I'll try to have a conversation with him—a *cautious* conversation. Unless you think that'd be a bad idea?"

"No, I was thinking the same thing."

"Tonight, we'll think over in detail how much information regarding our intents we'll share with this prisoner initially. That was the only voice you heard emanating from the main fort, right?"

"Correct."

"We can only hope the prisoner hales from Garobansurov, and isn't just a Molisian civilian locked up for some common crime."

"Even if he is the latter, I think if we promise him his freedom when we take over the fort, we'll receive a lot of cooperation."

"Good point," stated Mick.

The traps were fruitful that evening, each ensnaring a rabbit, each an entire day's worth of food. "We'll have to cook meat again soon; it's starting to amass. No need for the diminishing of the stockpile to scavenging carnivores."

Mick replied, "I think tomorrow one of us can do that, while the other spies for information from the guards. But when nightfall comes, and it's time to go into the wood-building, the person who went off to cook meat should go to the fort to stand guard and help in battle, in case that were to arise by chance."

"Since it's your turn to go into the wood-building, I'll go cook meat tomorrow, and stand guard at nightfall."

The pair ate supper, and slept peacefully through a light snowfall.

Post the usual hearty breakfast, they started their separate missions. Dave adhered to the same routine he performed the last time he went to cook, while Mick executed reconnaissance at the fort.

Dave's day progressed smoothly, for under certain circumstances there were few moments in life more enjoyable than watching the mystical rhythms of a fire. He successfully cooked a large amount of meat, eating some along the way.

On the other hand, Mick advanced through his task a little slower. Standing by a tree, doing nothing but staring and keeping quiet could get awfully boring. But it had to be done.

Nightfall came soon enough, though, and along with it came Dave Ghrere. Mick stopped spying, registered nothing new was learned from the guards that day, said a few things to Dave, and trespassed into the wood-building.

Unlike the first time he'd been in the wood building, it didn't take Mick long to start hearing the voice. It was easier for him to hear something when he knew for what to listen. He sat amongst the wood pile, where the voice was loudest, in virtually the same spot Dave had. He piled a bunch of wood around himself, so he was modestly concealed, just in case a Molisian were to come inside to grab wood.

He listened for a while to make sure no one else was near the prisoner. When he was certain the prisoner was alone, Mick rapped on the wall three times. The prisoner quickly responded with three raps of his own, paused, and spoke through the wall. "Who's there?"

"Your salvation." Mick listened carefully for a response with his ear against the wall.

"Splendid," voiced the stranger, "I was hoping it would be you. I go by the name *Krell-nor the Lucky.*"

"I'm Mick. Why are you locked up?"

"How did you know I was a prisoner?"

"My partner in adventure was here yesterday, and heard you pleading for more water. Since we know water is abundant around here, we assumed you were imprisoned."

"Excellent reasoning. I'm sure the main reason I'm locked in here is because I'm Garobansurovian. The rest of the story is kind of long, but I'm sure not as imperative to my capture as the aforementioned reason."

"Someday, I'll hear that story, fellow countryman. As for now, the plan is to carve through this wall and get you out." Mick would've started the carving right then and there, but first, he intended to talk over his newly devised plan with Dave, as was customary with the respect the duo shared. "We'll probably start on that tomorrow. I'll need to locate a tool perfect for the job."

"I started doing that myself, but there's only so much wall a person can go through with their bare hands—practically none."

Mick murmured to Krell-nor, "Right now, I'm going to head back to camp, and locate the proper tools. Then, tomorrow, my friend Dave will be here to initiate your liberation. He's the one who discovered you yesterday. We've been alternating turns coming to this location. I will see you in two days' time. And by the way, we're also here to retake this fort for Garobansurov."

Krell-nor bade Mick farewell, and said with honesty, "You've just made a lifelong friend."

EVEN THOUGH HE was still irate about it, General Gamald gave up hope of finding those responsible for the escape of Brom Quintaga. He'd spent the last two days questioning everyone in town, but received no leads. He thought it was suspicious one of his better soldiers, Beltrandt, had gone missing. But Gamald couldn't piece together a scenario in which Beltrandt had the means or justification to organize Brom's escape. The variables of the escape were too numerous for anyone to sleuth out. Gamald didn't spend any more time worrying about where Beltrandt had gone and why. He still had the suits of armor, so being content in that, he stopped investigations, and commenced focusing on more urgent matters. The likelihood of invasion of his conquered city, Sarwa, spearheaded by Ulfenkerki and the Nighteagle was forefront in Gamald's mind.

Gamald spoke to Lieutenant Leedle later that day. "We will definitely be ready to hold Sarwa. I've ordered the creation of many new war machines. I just hope the townsfolk can build as well as they say they can. If not, they just won't earn their payment of food. I also hope the assemblage of reinforcements from the homeland arrive on time. I've been told two are supposed to march here, but I haven't been told when. Plus, I've a nice surprise in store for everyone when the battle proceeds, which I intend to keep secret until then."

Discipline unmatched, Leedle listened, and responded, "We also have the finest warriors in all the land: Grunt and Roar. They've been dying for action."

"I bet they are. Speaking of those two, go round them up for me. I would like to discuss the upcoming invasion with them as well."

"Yes, sir," replied Leedle. Post-haste, Leedle set off to locate the giant men, which wasn't exactly a difficult task—their towering statures made them stick out like sore thumbs.

AT THE SETTING of Thraug, Ulfenkerki, the Nighteagle, and Rayton were also discussing the invasion.

Ulfenkerki commented, "As previously expected, the influx of new recruits thirsting to fight for our cause is considerable."

Archery-General Rayton replied, "I'm impressed with the few archers who came. They'll be fine additions."

The Nighteagle remarked, "It's all coming together nicely."

After an hour, Rayton parted, leaving his elder generals behind. Ulfenkerki and the Nighteagle continued discussing plans in an unimportant backroom exuding the pungent odor of decades of folks escaping prying eyes to smoke.

A puzzled look slipping onto his face, the Nighteagle asked, "I've been thinking about this all morning, but I have to ask: why did you order eighteen siege towers for construction? Why such a weird number?"

"I came up with that number, because twelve of the eighteen are for Sarwa's straight northern, southern, and eastern walls—four each. The remaining six towers are for the greatly convex western wall, which houses the main gate. Since that wall bows out, its surface area is larger, so it needs to be attacked with respectively more siege towers."

"Oh, I see now, makes sense. I must confess, your plan to make half of the siege towers dummy, decoy towers was brilliant. We probably would've only been able to man ten or eleven towers. The more towers for what they have to account, the thinner the defense. They'll never see it coming."

"Exactly. The thinner the walls are guarded the better. However, we're going to have to pull a lot more than dummy siege towers out of our butts in order to win this battle."

"You're probably right, old friend."

"Furthermore, I hope Jason and his battalion are back in time. If it turns out he's not back from tracking Anolski, before we determine the best time to strike has arisen, I'm afraid we'll miss out, losing what he and his company bring to the table. Such is war," said Ulfenkerki.

The Nighteagle shook his head. "Such is war."

"I'm sure with some creativity we'll concoct something to increase our odds of winning. But I'm afraid in order for us to win the encounter entirely, reclaiming Sarwa, help will also have to come from elsewhere."

HAVING ALREADY BEEN hidden for some time, like many of the local birds of prey, Mick and Dave relished the utmost confidence their campsite would remain hidden for the duration of their stay. But they were well aware of the adage stating, "Anything can happen," so they resisted the natural human urge of getting sloppy, and continued to play it safe. Trail maintenance, abstaining from making smoke, loud noises, venturing away from the site, and standing guard were all still performed.

Mick and Dave further discussed everything that'd happened since contacting Krell-nor. Both agreed as to the next course of action: tunnel through the wall to release Krell-nor, using the intrusion as the platform to invade the rest of the fort, claiming it for Garobansurov. But they still needed a lot more information before taking on the entire force of Molisians at Fort Gravividon.

They talked a bit of the albescent sky, then, conversation switched to what tools they were going to use to tunnel through the wall. "I think daggers will be the most efficient. Their sharpness will allow us to carve through the stone like butter," proclaimed Dave.

"That's true. But in the darkness, I glimpsed a tool we could utilize that would be just as efficient as the daggers, while still keeping our valuable secondary weapons' edges intact."

"Go on."

"Inside the wood-building, on the decaying workbench, was an old wood-awl that looked to be in decent shape, and reasonably sharp. Along with using it directly, a person could tap it with a rock using sensible force. Aided by Krell-nor watching for guards, I think we can avoid being heard by anyone whom we don't want to hear us."

"That'll work out pretty well. I have to admit I wasn't looking forward to pounding on my dagger with a rock," commented Dave, skillfully spinning his trusty dagger 720-degrees clockwise in the palm of his hand. "Perfect balance. Tomorrow, when I start chipping away at the wall, I'll use the awl. I'll bring my dagger in case the awl isn't as suitable as it seems."

"I'm ninety-eight percent sure the awl will work," replied Mick, as he palm-spun his dagger 1,080- degrees, just to one-up Dave's show of coordination.

Dave laughed and said, "Oh no, we're not starting this again."

"Come on now. Competitively throwing wood scraps into a triangle was loads of fun."

"Yes, but if we keep at this little contest, one of us is bound to eventually stab themselves, or lose a finger."

Mick turned his small laugh into a larger one. "But that's half the fun."

As they continued to strategize, the duo spun daggers in their hands, but only for a few minutes. They wisely held back the urge to do it any longer.

"Since we've hardly been gaining any new information from the guards in the early hours—none seeming morning people—and we have our new nighttime regimen, I think from now on we should start reconnaissance at midday," proposed Mick.

"That makes sense. That way we don't always have to eat such a monstrous breakfast and supper. We can eat lunch, before walking to the fort."

"True."

The next morning, Mick and Dave slept in, a rare luxury. With a few hours to kill before the day's operations began, they opted to spend a little time on recreation. A relaxed mind is a potent mind. Throwing rocks back and forth to each other, the gamesome duo attempted to hit the other in the head. Luckily their reflexes were too great for a rock to connect with an opposing head, but it was still fun trying. Dangerous, maybe, but fun, yes.

Subsequent the good, clean fun and lunch, Hawk and Leopard took their relaxed minds, and walked to the fort, starting the day's mission.

Later that day, they learned from guards performing rounds about the two battalions scheduled to pass through Fort Gravividon. They also overheard how the battalions were on their way to assist General Gamald in keeping Sarwa under Molisian control. Mick and Dave assumed Gamald was well aware the reinforcements were coming. The overall headcount of the reinforcements was never ascertained, nor when exactly they were coming. Hopefully, they'd learn that bit of data soon.

At dark, Dave grabbed a rock from the forest suitable for pounding, stole into the wood-building, and found the awl Mick was talking about sitting on the workbench. He studied it, and concluded it would work just fine. He sat in the same place Mick had sat the night before, and surrounded himself with practically the same wood. Dave also copied Mick's three-knock system. Upon hearing the return knocks, Dave spoke his first words to Krell-nor the Lucky. "Good evening, sir. It's Dave."

"Good evening to you, Dave. I trust Mick relayed my name to you already."

"This is true, Krell-nor."

"I never got the chance to ask yesterday, but where exactly are you?"

"There's a small building next to the fort. It's not technically part of the fort, but it shares this wall through which we're talking. They mainly use it for storing the wood for the firepit outside. We call it the *wood building*. Every night, Mick and I unlock the door, come in, do whatever it is we're going to do for the evening, and lock it back up when we leave, as to not leave a trace."

"Well I'll be! One other thing: how in tarnation do you open up a locked door, and lock it back up without the key?"

"We don't have the actual key for the door, but we do have something just as good—the most powerful magnet you could imagine. It technically seems more powerful than it should be. It's as if the thing is magic, long forgotten magic, like the days of old."

Krell-nor slapped his knees so hard in amazement he had to make sure none of the guards heard. Seeing the coast was clear, he voiced, "You two are quite the spectacle. I can't wait to see the faces behind such marvel."

Dave smiled, and replied, "And that you will, my friend, for I'm starting on the wall carving right now. If you see or hear a guard, let me know by tapping three times."

"That, I will do."

Dave put the awl up to the wall, and started pounding it with his rock—first softly, then harder as he went along. After a while, he was satisfied in the fact the wall was indeed giving way to the method. He calculated he could go through about four inches of wall per night. He couldn't, however, calculate how many days it would take. He didn't know how thick the wall was. But he was certain breaking through the wall wouldn't be the hardest task Mick and he had ever undertaken.

Dave talked with Krell-nor off and on while chipping and hammering at the wall, planning to work on it for four hours that night.

Slightly past the midpoint of Dave's shift, Krell-nor spontaneously emitted, "I sure wish I had, in here, more of these bindings capable of transferring me from the real world to an imaginary one."

Understanding Krell-nor's joke, Dave chuckled. "Yeah, books are pretty great. How many do you have in your cell?"

"Only two. And I've read them both ten times now. I always ask for more, but they insist there aren't any."

When Dave was finished for the evening, he took note that he pounded a hole four inches deep, and as wide as a person. "I'm pretty sure we'll have you out of here in less than a week. Unless this wall is three feet thick or such, but I doubt that, due to the fact we can talk through it pretty easily."

"Spectacle, quite-the-spectacle."

Dave piled some wood against the wall where he'd carved, so the hole wasn't obvious to anyone entering the wood building. He told Krell-nor he was leaving, and that Mick would be back the next day, same time.

Mick and Dave started walking back to their nameless campsite, surrounded by nameless trees and rocks. Along the way, Mick was hit by an uncharacteristic experience. While staring through a hole in the tree canopy above, the starry sky took precedence over his own balance, and he almost tripped over a log. The event would've caused him to break his long-standing no-trip record. He looked back at Dave, knowing his friend had witnessed the slip-up, and said, "It would've been worth it."

Upon reaching it, Dave peered through the same hole in the canopy with the same wonderment, and said, "You're right, it would've been."

At the campsite that night, they talked about a myriad of subjects, including a conversation on tidal locking. They talked of the moons' images created by asteroid bombardments, and discussed the sun's tendencies. But one subject in particular held significant importance, the *black needle swords*.

"I agree, we sure have looked in a lot of places for another black needle pine tree. But have you ever thought maybe when we do find one, we won't be any closer in learning about it?"

"I sometimes think about that. It's also true that maybe we won't even have to find another member of the species to learn everything we want to know," replied Dave.

"True. Maybe we'll get our information by means we couldn't even imagine."

"That's quite possible. All I know is it's a mission of enlightenment that may take us the rest of our lives to reach a final solution."

"That it may, that it may."

Their voice boxes and muscles spent, Mick and Dave concluded the day, and went to sleep.

The next day, disappointingly, they didn't learn anything fresh from the spying of the Molisians.

It being Mick's turn to work on the wall, he went into the wood-building at nightfall to do so.

While chipping away, he talked about many things with Krell-nor. The guards seemed to neglect keeping their eye on Krell-nor, so stories of considerable length were able to be recited. Mick talked about some of the things that had happened to him and Dave, especially things concerning the opening stages of the war. Krell-nor reciprocated with the story of how he was captured and imprisoned, which goes thus:

I got the name Krell-nor the Lucky, not from my father or mother, but from my mining club, a fine establishment which I've been a member of for many years. For no reason other than luck, I've always been able to find the payload, whether it be gold, silver, or even jewels. However, not enough to make me rich, just enough for them to call me Krell-nor the Lucky. Similar to the renowned Horace the Lucky from the ancient stories. The name has stuck ever since.

A long while back, I was mining these very cliffs about half a mile upstream, hanging from a rope and chipping away at the cliffside. Since there used to be no exceptions to my luck, I was finding a good supply of valuables. But seeing as I was at it for a few days, word of my successes had traveled. Unfortunately, word had gotten to the wrong people—the foreigners currently occupying this fort. I shouldn't have been playing with fire by working so close to them. I just couldn't resist. I do love a good smash and grab.

So, on the evening of the third day mining the cliff, I started climbing back up my rope with my bag of the day's findings. Upon reaching the top, I locked eyes with the enemy.

"What do we have here, boys, looks like we got ourselves a new place to mine," said one of the Molisians. "Grab him, and his bag of goodies."

And at that moment, I knew my life's luck had run out. They tied me up, dragged me back to the fort, and locked me away in this cell. I've been in this very spot ever since. I heard they'd found a small amount of precious metals where I was prospecting, but nothing worth locking a man up for. Like I said before, I'm sure the main reason I'm here is because they enjoy torturing the enemy. One thing I do know is I would trade all of my past luck to not have been drowned in the waters of this clandestine tragedy.

Meticulously, Mick had listened to every word of the story, while chipping at the wall. He replied, "Well, my friend, I do believe shortly your nightmare will be over; and you'll regain your freedom—if Dave and I have anything to say about it."

Having contributed another four inches to the hole in the wall, Mick was pleased. His day's execution of physical labor sufficient, he bade farewell to Krell-nor, and exited the wood building.

On his walk, Mick thought about Krell-nor's tragic story. He was glad to have ended up at that exact place at that exact time. If he hadn't, his and Dave's rescue attempt would've never been possible. It was just one of the unpredictable bonuses being a freelance freedom fighter could provide.

They arrived back at camp and Mick told Dave the whole of Krell-nor's capture story.

CHAPTER 18

ANOLSKI WAS PROVING to be more elusive than a fox. But Jason still had confidence the Molisian general would rue being tracked by him. The mission was taking longer than expected but, self-assured, Jason was certain to see it through to the end. Their path took them through deep snow, many times being swallowed up to their chests. Sometimes, Anolski led them in circles—the oldest trick in the book. It didn't fool Jason Thorncat, however. He and his 150 soldiers were unfazed by the trickery.

Walking steadily, currently in a not so taxing environment, Jason conversed with Gregg Hogarty. "I hope you're ready for a good fight. Even though we outnumber them three to two, we'll still have our hands full. Unless we can gain the element of surprise somehow, but I don't see that happening."

"I'm ready," declared Gregg. "My hand has never left my sword handle's side since leaving Thraug."

"I like that. I doubt we'll catch them today, but It's better to be safe than sorry."

"Exactly, lieutenant, my sentiment as well," replied Gregg, reaching out to flick an icicle off a tree branch.

"I do hope we catch them soon though. I have a feeling the epic battle to retake Sarwa is going to start soon, and I really hope we're there to assist the Black Bear and the Nighteagle."

"I hope so too. I've been ready for that battle for a while now."

Jason shook the caking of snow off his boots, and commented, "I wonder what kinds of subterfuges and strategies Ulfenkerki is coming up with right now for the battle."

"I'm sure he's being as creative as one can be for an invasion."

"If we can retake Sarwa, I think the northeast corner of Garobansurov can rest assured for a while. The wound inflicted by Molisia's initial invasion was substantial."

"That it was. There's been underestimations from both sides. I think we're standing our ground pretty effectively."

"Indeed."

Jason and Gregg talked about the upcoming battle for Sarwa a while longer, until they reached deep snow again. High stepping through such an encumbrance no doubt sapped energy for communication. Even with

Anolski's hundred soldiers breaking ground before them, walking through it was arduous.

Jason assumed there would at least be another day of pursuit.

STEADILY COVERING THE north/north-eastern section of Garobansurov, hunting for Brom's son, Loyd, Carrie, and Brom didn't have to deal with snow as deep as what Jason and his party had to. But some pretty deep stuff, nonetheless. Marked with importance, Brom saw a house in the distance. They were in the wilderness, and roofs under which to sleep were rare. Since escaping Sarwa, the trio had been trying to spend nights at anonymous strangers' homes, offering payment. Something they could certainly afford.

They were all tired and yearned for sleep. The haggard three strolled to the isolated cottage, bringing with the quintessential social skills required to bargain with an unfamiliar person. Carrie was their chief negotiator, possessing a knack for it.

Leading the way, Carrie walked up the front door of the cabin and knocked. While waiting for the response, she looked around, admiring the countryside. She took a deep breath, inhaling as much fresh, cool winter air as she could, an indulgence that felt good in the system. She gazed up at the property's lone shade tree. It was so huge, only the one was needed for sufficient shade. Not that it was the time of year to worry about that.

The homeowner answered the door. "Hello ma'am."

"Nice to see you. My name is Carrie, and the two standing behind me are my husband, Loyd, and my grandfather, Brom."

The two made eye contact with the stranger, smiled, and said, "Hello, sir."

The stout homeowner courteously replied, "What can I do for you?"

Carrie responded, "We are weary travelers, and we would love to offer you ten gitis to sleep under your roof tonight."

"I'm not one for company, but I do have an extra room. I'll tell you what: you can have the room for twenty gitis, as long as you promise to be quiet for the duration."

"We have a long way to go, and many more nights to spend. I don't think we can afford twenty. Will you settle for fifteen gitis, and an ironclad promise you won't hear a peep out of us?"

The homeowner replied, "You three look trustworthy enough. It's a deal."

Carrie handed him the fifteen gitis, and the three were shown the room. A cozy, little room with one bed big enough for two people. The husband and wife would sleep in the bed, and Brom would sleep on the floor—the fairest arrangement.

They kept their promise and were quiet as mice for the entire stay, only having a few short, barely audible conversations.

Brom, lying on the floor, just about ready to fall asleep, whispered, "You guys have no idea how much coming with me means to me. I'll cherish these memories forever."

"We wouldn't have it any other way. Goodnight," Carrie whispered back.

"Goodnight."

The trio slept well, successfully negotiated for breakfast, left the cottage, and pressed on, continuing the search mission.

MICK THRAIKER AND Dave Ghrere were about to nestle inside their tents, but it was going to be one of those rare nights when being in a tent wasn't such a pleasurable occasion. It was cold, very cold. Their cold weather sleeping bags supplied ample comfort when temperature dropped to twenty below. But that night, due to a fast-moving cold front, the temperature was at least thirty below.

On such occasions, they had to implement every trick they knew to keep warm: piling snow around the tents, therefore creating their own personal subnivean zones; using two sleeping bags, both the warm and cold weather ones; keeping their heads completely inside the bags; no unnecessary urinations; and lighting a few candles. Not too many candles though, because the fumes would eventually get too intoxicating, which is also why they never lit fires inside their tents. But even after all the precautions, it'd still get unpleasantly cold inside the tents. If it wasn't for their best trick, the sleeping on heated rocks trick, their night would surely be miserable.

While Dave was putting snow around the tents, Mick played no guts no glory with their fates, and made a fire relatively close. He started the fire a quarter of the way to where they usually made their cooking fires, assuming he was safe, because the cold would force everyone at the fort to hunker down.

He began heating a huge supply of rocks and food. When the food was fit to be eaten, he walked back by Dave with it, while leaving the rocks behind to continue to be heated. After the meal, he went back to gather the rocks, and brought them all back to the campsite. The risk-taking paid off, for the smoke from the fire was never spotted. There wasn't anyone at Fort Gravividon wanting to sit outside in the cold, and meticulously watch the horizon.

The heated rocks were set underneath their tents where they slept. The heat from them would rise onto Mick and Dave's bodies throughout the night, allowing the night to pass tolerably. The rocks made for an unpleasant surface on which to lie, but the ends justified the means.

It was more comfortable for the first half of the night, when the rocks contained the most heat. The second half wasn't as comfortable, throughout which they tossed and turned. But they slept well enough to wake and face the pressures of the day.

Bundled with almost every layer they had, the pair sat, shivering at their spy stations, trying to gather treasured intel. It was still cold because the front hadn't yet passed. That day, they learned how many soldiers in total were currently stationed at the fort: 200. It was information well worth suffering in the cold.

Since it was so cold, Hawk and Leopard threw caution to the wind, and decided to both go into the wood-building that evening. Because of the heat emanating from the main part of the fort, the wood building was a good twenty degrees warmer than it was outside.

Only one worked on the wall at a time, figuring two people chipping on the wall would make too much noise.

Krell-nor was in good spirits. It was his first time in ages being a part of a three-way conversation. He beamed for no one to see. "I've heard many things so far about your most recent activities, Mick, Dave, but you've yet to tell me anything about the events leading up to your immersion into the war."

While excavating a stone chip from the wall, Dave looked over at Mick with a nostalgia driven smile, and said to Krell-nor, "Very well, brother Krell-nor, that is indeed a story worth telling."

And so Dave began telling the story of the actions that led them to their current adventure:

If our hometown of Chalatore is famous for anything, it's famous for the annual arm-wrestling tournament. People come from far and wide to try and win the substantial winner's pot. The tournament has been an annual event for as long as I can remember. Mick and I, since we've been old enough to enter, have taken second and first place respectively every year in our weight division. But this year, Mick got so sick of losing to me in the championship round he decided to enter a heavier weight class, there being always three weight classes.

Mick entering the heavy-weight division generally meant stiffer competition for him. Those in that division were typically built like mountains. He couldn't resist, and entered the heavy-weight class anyways. He figured he had a better chance of beating the mountains than beating me.

Of course, I was the odds-on favorite in my weight class, middle weights, but Mick was far from it in his class. In arm-wrestling, and the same for real life, I am the stronger, and he has always been the quicker. He uses his speed optimally, gaining much ground off the start. Though, usually he can't gain enough of an advantage from the start to beat me.

Because the payoff would be much greater, due to the odds, we bet all of our money on Mick. There's a guy in town, a friend of ours, who arranges and executes a superb betting system every tournament. Needless to say, everyone likes him. His services are impeccable. If both Mick and I won, we'd receive two winners' pots, and the bet money—a huge payday.

I recall what I said to Mick, after making the bet. "I don't know what we're going to do with the money if we win, but I do know there'll be a lot of it."

"Oh, I'm sure we'll find something to do with it," he replied.

This year, the tournament had drawn a bigger crowd than normal. The greater turnout added much to the overall ambiance. Over the years, the event has increasingly become more like a carnival. The people of Chalatore love it, and so do we.

For us, the opening rounds went quickly, having beaten most of our opponents in the past at various taverns. My last opponent before reaching finals, I beat in four seconds. Mick took nine.

Ecstatic to have reached the finals, Mick said to me, "I hope I didn't pull too hard that last match. I'm going to need all the strength I can get, if I intend to get through finals. There's a new-comer I'll have to face built like a brick shithouse—a real tower of a man."

"Yeah, I saw him. I'm glad he's not in my weight class," I admitted.

There was an hour break between finals and qualifying. We spent the time trying to keep limber.

The arm-wrestling table for finals was better than those used for qualifying rounds, sturdier and more aesthetically pleasing. The audience grandstands during finals were all focused on that one table. The stands were packed, barely elbow room.

Mick and I were ready. The roar of the crowd was exhilarating, priming us for action.

For each weight division, finals consisted of the championship match, plus two semi-final matches. Three of the nation's most respected referees were to watch over the match, keeping it honest.

"Good luck, Mick! Tear his arms off," I said figuratively, eyeing the final's table.

"Good luck to you as well."

My semi-finals match was against a guy, whom I've beaten in the tournament in the past, so I faced him with all the confidence in the world. I prevailed as easily as I thought I would.

Mick's semi-finals match on the other hand was not so easy. Though, it was favorable for him he didn't have to face the brick shithouse right away.

There were no issues at the onset of the match. There usually were in big matches, everyone trying to get the best grip possible, nobody wanting to give. Relinquishing the perfect hold in armwrestling feels like being stripped of your clothes.

At the sound of the whistle, Mick power drove, characteristically gaining six inches from neutral. But lost the advantage soon enough, since his opponent wielded a strong countermove. But, over time, the counter from Mick's opponent proved to be too taxing on the man. Mick was able to slowly bring the man's hand closer and closer to winning position. With only three inches left to gain for the win, Mick could taste victory. I know this because he told me after the match. Mick slacked off, losing ground—a technique used for the reserving of energy—and slammed his opponent's hand vehemently to the table, punching his ticket to the championship round.

Happy that we were both destined for the championship round, I said to Mick, "I was impressed with your finishing move, it seems as if you gained a little speed with it. The augmentation is a fine addition to your repertoire."

"I thought so too. I wasn't sure if it was faster, but having you also notice it, makes me believe it's true."

"Good thing you gained in that department. You're going to need all the help you can get, for whom you're pitted against in the title match."

"I most certainly do," replied Mick, before taking a huge gulp from his cup containing some sort of fruity beverage dispensed by the event organizers. To this day, we've no idea what that fruity beverage actually was. "I feel good though. I think I can win," proclaimed Mick.

"That's the spirit. Just imagine how great tonight will be, if we both win. My drinking hand is already starting to curl its fingers, as if it were already clutching the handle of my beer mug."

Mick laughed, and returned, "It will be a good night indeed."

Every competitor of the championship round—six in total, two for each weight class—was introduced to the audience, and received an ovation. Home towners, of course, were bestowed greater applause, Mick and I included.

We six converged on the designated chairs. Four of us sat, while two approached the competition table. The lightweight division's championship would go first, followed by my division's championship, the middleweights. Mick had to go last.

I had won the tournament in my division 6 times before, so I saw no reason for me not to win again. My mind was actually more concentrated on Mick's match. I wanted him to win more than I wanted myself to win.

Post an entertaining lightweight title match, I stood proudly at the firm four-legged table. Five minutes' worth of annoying grip and re-gripping procedure went by before my match began. I wasn't surrendering my clothes, and neither was he.

From the onset, I had the match under control for the most part. But my opponent kept releasing my hand, right when he was about to lose. Because of this, the referees implemented the straps. The straps were a way of bonding our hands together, so no one could let go anymore. Now, I was able to top roll him. An advanced armwrestling technique that involves riding your opponent's hand higher up, closer to their fingers. With a deep breath, I easily finished the match, winning my seventh championship.

The crowd roared tumultuously, while I raised my arms in victory. I didn't loiter in the limelight very long, for I wanted to spend my time encouraging Mick. Unfortunately, I only had time enough to say one thing to him before he had to approach the table. "Remember, big guys have power, but not endurance."

Mick marched up to the table, and grabbed the ergonomic handle with his anchor hand, getting a good feel for the stability it provided. Mick and the man standing across from him were poles apart. Mick is somewhat muscular, but not in an overwhelming fashion, like the brick shithouse, Horace. Mick still thought he could win. Or so I assumed.

Grip procedure finished, the match began.

Like always, Mick gained a fair amount of ground at the sound of the whistle. With a moment's advantage, he tried a series of violent slack and drives, but gained nothing more in the process. Following Mick's fifth slack and drive, Horace loosed a bellow, and surged his adrenaline. This enabled him to bring the match back over the top. For me, it was slow motion; bit by bit, Mick's hand was forced closer and closer to the losing position of the table.

A trouncing drew near. However, a glimmer of hope remained. The speed at which Mick's hand was nearing the point of no return gradually diminished. Eventually, their hands halted just above the table. This was Mick's chance, and he knew it. He closed his eyes, thought of what I told him at the start of the match—at least, that's what I envisioned he did—and held the position with all his might. Big guys really do tend to lack endurance on the arm-wrestling table.

Suffering, Mick grit his teeth, and held his position for many minutes. After agony on both ends, Horace finally broke. With a bellow of his own, Mick slowly brought the locked hands back over the top to his side of the table, covering almost the entire arc. Victory in history's most epic of all armwrestling matches was near for my friend. Channeling all of his adrenalin, Mick fought through the pain. When in the perfect position, Mick attempted one of his famous slack and drives. As a result, Horace's hand contacted the table, and Mick won his first ever Chalatore

Armwrestling Tournament. And in case you're wondering, it's sort of a big deal.

I joined Mick in his moment of glory, and said, "Now, that was a battle."

"Good thing I had that match last. I can't lift my arm right now."

The post-tournament traditions began. Horace—who Mick and I learned enjoyed being called the brick shit-house—was magnanimous in defeat, and congratulated Mick on his victory. The VIPs handed out the trophies, and award money. The hired band started to play, and the beer flowed like water. In no time, Chalatore became raucous.

Jubilantly, we went to collect our massive payday from the bookie, who was glad to pay his friends the substantial amount. The odds were eight to one against Mick winning, yielding our 250 giti bet a generous 2,000 gitis. It was twice as much as what Mick and I had gotten combined from the winners' pots. Our pockets were worth 3,000 gitis between the two of us.

"Well, fellow champion, shall we go get drunk, partake in the festivities, and have a fantastic night?" I asked.

"Yes, we shall."

What happened next, however, caught us totally off-guard.

I looked up and noticed everyone trickling out of the drinking tents. A congregation had formed around a group of people speaking emphatically. Mick and I joined, and heard them talking about how Molisia had declared war, and that an army led by a General Anolski snuck into Garobansurov, desiring to capture our cities. Luckily, Anolski was headed off by General Ulfenkerki and his army. They went on to say how the whole thing happened five miles north of Chalatore, during the first rounds of the tournament. It was probable Anolski had intended to invade Chalatore. How they made it that far into Garobansurov unnoticed remains to be seen. Those doing the bulk of the talking were well known and well respected, so nobody denied the validity of what was being said, including Mick and I.

Conversations went on all night concerning the news, but when they started to debate superfluously, we parted.

To Mick I said, "Good thing we've already spent hours upon hours discussing what we'd do in a situation like this."

Mick replied, "Yes, good thing. Now we can respond in haste. There's one downfall, though."

"What's that?"

"I don't think we're going to have that marvelous night of victory-soaked revelry anymore."

"A real disappointment, but I'm okay with it. I'm definitely in the mood for a quest. We certainly have the funds for one."

"That we do."

Mick and I had always talked about what we'd do if our freedom—or the freedom of those we loved—was ever in jeopardy. In every discussion, we resolved to risk our lives and fight for what's right. But we would fight the good fight our way. The armies of Garobansurov and Hawk' n' Leopard may travel different paths, but our shared common denominator has always been preserving freedom.

So, aiming to do things our way, we grabbed all our money—armwrestling winnings converted to traveling funds—all our traveling gear, and all of our fighting equipment. Firmly strapped to all of our adventure paraphernalia, we headed out of town, towards where it was said the armies were last seen. All in all, we each carry around ninety pounds of integral equipment on long quests, a weight that's increased over the years.

We traveled far that first day. When we were near the action we stopped and slept in an abandoned cabin of which we were aware. A stopover bereft clear water, by the way.

And as you know, we eventually made our way to Strwin and partook of the battle therein.

So that, my friend, was the story of the launch of our current adventure. I couldn't say how many days exactly we've been on it, but it sure has been exciting so far, that's for sure.

After concluding the telling, Dave took a deep breath, and added one more thing. "I think we've made a difference so far as well."

Krell-nor was lost in his imagination, out of which took him a few moments to snap. He too liked armwrestling. When he finally came back to reality, he said, "Made a difference, eh? I'm certain this whole war is going to be won because of you two."

Mick and Dave supplied a slight chuckle. "I doubt that," said Dave.

Realizing he'd gotten a little loud with his last few utterances, Krell-nor peered down the hall to check for guards. He perceived all was well, but made sure to quiet his voice. "There is one thing I have to say, though."

"What's that?"

"I hope you don't think you're the best arm-wrestlers in the country. As soon as I'm out of here, I'll beat the both of you."

Mick and Dave let out another chuckle. Dave replied, "In your dreams, old man."

Krell-nor returned a laugh. "We shall see."

"That we shall."

The wall initiative for the day reached completion, upon which Hawk and Leopard began making their way back to their tented refuge. Fortunately, by then, the cold front had moved through, rendering a much more pleasant night than the one previous. They slept comfortably, and woke the next morning to a curious coyote snooping around.

"He probably smells our meat."

"Sure is a brave fellow," declared Mick.

Just before leaving for the fort, they threw some meat into the trees down the hill for the coyote. They could spare a bit. On many occasions, bravery deserved reward.

That afternoon, listening to the guards rambling to each other, Mick and Dave heard the most valuable information they'd heard yet. One of the reinforcement squads dispatched to aid Gamald had arrived at the fort. The squad intended to leave for Sarwa shortly, stealing half the fort's guard crew. The officers at the fort had made the decision to add to the force assisting Gamald. They thought since the second squad of reinforcements would arrive soon, they could then buttress the skeleton crew with the new influx. Gamald holding Sarwa was vital for their campaign. They were taking a chance, but in their minds, they could afford to. Besides, there were no fighting forces even close to Gravividon. Or so they thought.

After hearing this priceless information, Mick said to Dave, "The window of opportunity is definitely upon us."

"It's all coming together. We must make sure we attack after the first squad leaves, and before the second squad arrives. At that point, there will be only a hundred soldiers defending the fort. It still sounds like a lot, but it can be done."

"I think we've the hole in Krell-nor's wall almost finished, so hopefully we can use the inside positioning as a platform for a surprise attack. We'll have to bust open his cell door, but I don't see that being a problem. We'll find a rock, or something, suitable for such a task. Ill-supplied, nature usually isn't. Hopefully we're not too loud when we do it, and we can still catch them off guard."

"So, we'll plan on going through the last of Krell-nor's wall for the rescue and offensive, as soon as the first squad leaves. I do believe it'll work."

"We'll inform Krell-nor of all this when we see him tonight."

Luckily," Dave commented, "we both don't have to go into the wood building avoiding the cold. One can stand guard."

"True."

Despite it technically being Mick's turn, Dave greeted Krell-nor and explained to him everything they'd learned, and the fact the break-out and fort capture would occur soon. Dave voiced, "I'm pretty sure there are only six or eight inches of seemingly cooperative wall left through which to go."

"That'd be my guess too," Krell-nor emitted. "In case you were wondering, when it happens, I plan on seeing your plan through to the end, assisting you with the fort offensive. I've a score to settle with these guys, but more importantly, my honor outweighs all, so I intend to do everything in my power to help keep you and Mick alive throughout the entirety of this ordeal. Rest assured, I'm pretty competent with a weapon in my hand."

"Krell-nor the Lucky, you are to be sure a staunch man, one of great admiration. We'd be honored to invade this fort with you."

"Wonderful," said Krell-nor. "There has actually been something else I wanted to tell you. So, I was thinking about the assault on the fort, how we could break open this cell door of mine, and continue on into the rest of the fort from here."

"Go on."

"At first, I just assumed you could use something heavy to force the door open. But of course, that'd make a lot of noise, risking losing the element of surprise. I continued to think about a way to get the door open quietly. Then, like a bolt from the blue it came to me. I remembered how you guys told me that the way you get into the wood building is by using a parabola shaped, magic magnet. If it's as strong as you say it is, I bet we could use it to open the cell door. The lock's mechanics are just like the ones described to me of the door to the wood-building."

"That is good news. I can't wait to inform Mick of this intelligence. He will be thrilled. The quieter we can be for the takeover, the better."

At the exact moment Dave had said that, Mick was witnessing danger unfold at the door of the wood building. He had to devise a plan. Two Molisian guards were about to unlock the wood-building's door, and go inside. Mick's instincts at that second were to charge out of the forest, and kill the guards before they were even able to spot Dave inside. But implored by common sense, Mick held back, figuring they were just going in for wood, and they wouldn't even see Dave hidden behind his wood barrier. They'd leave with their wood, clueless. If it came down to the fact Dave was noticed, he'd hear the commotion, and go charging in then.

Meanwhile, Dave could hear the jostling at the door. As fast as he could, Dave blurted to Krell-nor, "Keep quiet, there's somebody entering the wood building."

Dave sat motionless, while the guards came into the building. He thought to himself, *Why does this have to happen now when we're so close to the end? If I end up having to kill these men, their absence would be noticed, and our whole plan will be ruined.* He could feel his heart race and the sweat pouring out of his forehead. His core body temperature and blood pressure were no doubt elevated. He heard the men move around some of the wood pieces. Dave's heart beat faster and faster, his hand motioning towards his sword. Slowly, he started inching his sword out of its scabbard. *Removing my sword is louder than I remember. Figures.*

But just as suddenly as the dilemma started, the guards had for what they came, and exited the wood building, each with armfuls of wood. Dave and Mick sighed relief, wiping sweat from their brows. They were especially relieved to learn the wood wasn't for the firepit just outside the wood building. That would've surely complicated things.

"That was a close one," Dave told Krell-nor, a stutter in his voice. "I think that's enough wall chipping for tonight. It's almost done anyways. Be prepared. The offensive could happen any time now. As soon as the squadron heading for Sarwa leaves the fort, the action from our end will commence."

"The sooner the better. I'm ready to wreak havoc all over this place," responded Krell-nor.

"I'm sure you are."

On their way back to the tents, Mick and Dave talked of the near-peril in the wood-building.

Stating the obvious, Dave said, "Being discovered would've definitely been disastrous for our plan."

"It sure would've."

"Tomorrow, one of us can get up early to check if the soldiers depart for Sarwa."

"Sounds good. I'll do it." Mick started to say something else, but hesitated before resuming. "Please don't construe what I'm about to say as me being afraid of what we're about to do, but I do have to state we've never tried to capture a fort before. Even though luck has been on our sides for pretty much everything we've done, our destinies may not lie on the plane of survival this time."

"You're right. Our tapestries have been woven with strands of prosperity as of late. And there won't be any construing on my part. But I will say it's been more than luck facilitating our continued existence."

"Yeah, it's probably been the swords," replied Mick.

Dave laughed, and responded, "Probably."

The next day, Dave was eating breakfast when Mick appeared from the fort trail. He had woken three hours before Dave to stand watch at the fort. "They've left, about 400 of them. An hour and a half ago, they all started to trickle out of the doors, and march for Sarwa."

"That is good news indeed. Tonight is the night then. I don't think my heart can take another experience like last night's."

"I don't think mine can either. Krell-nor probably knows too, by all the commotion the soldiers made. They weren't exactly quiet in their exodus. I'm surprised you didn't hear them here."

"Nope, I didn't. Just birds and wind," said Dave. "I'm sure Krell-nor will be ready and waiting."

"I'm sure he's also aware darkness will be our ally, and that our onslaught won't commence until it arrives."

"True." Dave pumped his fist. "What a rush!"

"It sure is. I can practically taste the adrenalin. I suppose we can start getting all of our battle gear together."

"And let us not forget to bring the invaluable magnet."

"I doubt we'll ever forget that blessing from above."

CHAPTER 19

MICK THRAIKER AND Dave Ghrere began walking towards Fort Gravividon with full battle gear, the magnet, and handfuls of anxiety. But just before they were completely out of sight of the campsite, they turned around to look at it. Mick said, "You know, Dave, it's kind of sad last night was more than likely our last night at our little wilderness retreat. Either we'll capture the fort tonight, and in effect, sleep within its wind-resistant walls, or we'll be too dead to return."

"Let's hope it's the former."

"At least one of us will get to come back. Someone will have to retrieve the tents and the rest of the gear."

"That's true," said Dave. "I'll regret leaving the handmade tables and box traps behind, but I'm not about to add that much weight to the travel load."

"Me neither. The snowy wayside on the rocky tor has definitely been a fun and interesting part of our lives."

"We will miss it indeed."

Mick and Dave walked the mile stretch to the fort for one last day of recon, towing all their personal battle supplies. Scarcely necessary to wear the armor while idly spying, they propped it all against a tree, and covered it with branches and snow.

While conducting recon and waiting patiently for nightfall, they played out many battle situations in their heads. A myriad of unpredictable circumstances could transpire once inside the fort. They concluded they'd more or less have to play things by ear, since uncertainty would no doubt increase as the fight progressed further and further inside the fort. Who knew what was lurking?

Hawk and Leopard learned no new information that day, other than what two guards who appeared planned on having for supper—hardly valuable information. Dave and Mick were confident in the quality of all previously gathered intel. Their faith in success was high. If it wasn't, they wouldn't be on the verge of mounting an offensive, being the sort who rarely rushed into danger foolishly.

Nightfall finally came, and the duo slipped into all of their battle armor. As he slid his perfectly-fitting helm onto his head, Dave said, "Well Mick, are you ready to get some blood on the *black needles*?"

"That, and maybe some face parts and intestines."

"Gruesome, Hawk, just gruesome."

Mick put on his last remaining piece of armor, and replied, "I'm as ready as I'll ever be. Let's go rescue a friend, and capture ourselves a fort."

"Let's."

The pair took a few deep breaths, forced all the welled-up adrenaline to flow like a surging river, and headed towards the wood building with dignity. Using the magnet, they opened the door and locked it back up behind them. For hopefully one last time, they began working on the wall with the wood-awl.

Mick initiated conversation with Krell-nor. "I'm sure you're aware tonight is the night?"

"Certainly. I heard them all leaving, and I can definitely tell the numbers here at the fort are greatly diminished."

"Splendid. In about thirty minutes from now, there'll be a hole running all the way through for the first time, so be extra vigilant. Try to not let any guards see it from your end."

"Not a problem. For the last few days I've been setting my blanket where I anticipate the hole will be, so the guards got used to it being there."

"Brilliant."

A half hour passed, and Krell-nor saw the first beam of moonlight pioneer its way into his cell. He never felt more alive than what he did at that moment.

The blanket of concealment didn't even get the opportunity to do its job, for a mere twenty minutes after Krell-nor saw the first light beam, the opening had expanded large enough to allow a grown man to crawl through. Not one, but two grown men crawled through, single file.

Krell-nor saw his rescuers for the first time, and quickly shook their hands. "A spectacle indeed. It's funny how you guys look similar to what I imagined."

Dave replied, "Same here."

"I haven't seen a guard in a while," Krell-nor observed. "One may appear at any moment, though."

"We will hurry."

Mick pulled the magnet out of his pocket, and upon seeing it, Krell-nor gasped. "You weren't kidding. That is the most powerful magnet in the universe, and it actually is parabolically shaped."

"That it is. Quite the anomaly," Dave said, as Mick went to work on the cell door.

Krell-nor ended up being correct about his cell door and the wood building's door-lock mechanisms being similar. Mick had it jimmied open in a jiffy with the magnet.

Before the assault got underway, Dave and Mick proudly gave up their daggers to Krell-nor. "You can use these," said Dave, "but if you'd rather use a sword, just grab one from the wreckage along the way. Or if you're more proficient with daggers, go ahead and use them for the duration."

"We'll see how my first kill feels," Krell-nor replied, running one of the daggers through his hands to feel its weight and features.

Accentually and gracefully, Mick and Dave ripped their swords out of their scabbards. One could really feel the power of a sword by such a ripping. Having made sure all of their armor was secure, they were ready.

Mick slapped Dave and Krell-nor on their shoulders, and said, "Shall we go pierce the veil of Gravividon?"

Krell-nor answered, "Yup, I'm set. When we reach the intersection ahead, the guards always come from the left side. They hardly ever go down the right. I was able to see that much from my cell. I think the right side contains empty cells, or something of the sort."

The trio crept up to the intersection. Dave peered inconspicuously around the corner, and observed a small room containing five guards sitting at a table. "Five men sitting around a table. No hands near weapons. An easy conquest, if we rush them."

Mick and Krell-nor nodded their heads in agreement. They followed Dave's lead down the corridor, running quickly at the stationary targets. Each of the three Molisians sitting closest the door ended up with either a sword or dagger shoved through a vital organ, before they were even able to stand. The remaining two suffered the same fate, but did so standing and reaching for a weapon.

The victory was fast, but more importantly it was silent. The threesome still had the element of surprise on their side.

"Hopefully they're all this effortless."

Krell-nor handed the daggers back, grabbed a sword resting at the side of the table, and said, "The daggers worked wonderfully, but I like the added reach a sword can provide."

"As do we."

The three of them, having executed such a flawless victory, were now convinced they could conquer the entire fort without casualty. They set off further into the bowels of the fort.

They reached a point fifty yards from the room with a table and five dead men, and hid behind a stack of barrels in a dark hallway. There, they thought about the next stratagem. At first, they couldn't see nor hear any adversaries while behind the barrels. But when they placed their ears to the ground, they could hear voices in the distance.

Mick whispered, "I say we wait a few more moments to continue on. Maybe the sources of the voices will come into view."

"Right. I suggest giving it five more minutes." To ease tension, Dave went off in tangent, "The cooper who fashioned these barrels sure was a fine craftsman."

Mick and Krell-nor smiled, and chuckled softly at Dave's randomness. Dave was glad to have succeeded in easing nervousness.

Eventually, two armor-less soldiers came into view. When the ill-fated, unsuspecting Molisians walked close enough to the barrels, they were ambushed by the trio lurking behind. It was a swift and soundless kill. The bodies were dragged behind the barrels, so they were somewhat out of sight. The blood, on the other hand, which stained the floor could not be hidden.

Before leaving the cover of the barrels, Mick stated, "If I were a betting man, which I sometimes am, I would bet the sleeping quarters are on the next level up, along with the majority of the soldiers. Plus, I'm sure many soldiers are standing guard topside, probably huddled together, talking, instead of watching the horizon for movement."

Dave replied, "I won't bet, because I agree. I just hope we can get to the sleeping quarters on the second level before we're noticed. That way, we can dispose of all of those who happen to be sleeping without a fight. Not very sporting, but war is war."

Krell-nor added, "I'll keep my eyes open for a stairwell."

The three of them left their temporary safe haven, and tip-toed further down the corridor. As they crept along, they heard no sounds emanating from the level they were on, the ground level, other than the soft sounds of their own feet hitting the cement floor—a floor painted green for some reason.

Every time they were met by a door, they'd either peer in its window, or open it just enough to look inside. They found nothing of interest inside any of them, until Krell-nor found the doorway with the stairwell behind. "Here's the stairs, guys."

Dave returned, "Perfect. It looks like we have this level pretty much cleared of enemies." He pointed at the wall in front of him. "I think we've reached the end of the hall."

"I think so too."

Before ascending the stairs, the trio made absolute certain the echelon was free from Molisians; they didn't need anyone sneaking up from behind. They also made sure the stairs themselves were free from traffic, before proceeding up them.

At the small corridor at the top of the stairs, they noticed there were two paths: one path continued upstairs, and the other led to the second level of the fort. They opened the door leading to the second level, peered down the hallway, saw no one, and quietly closed the door back up to discuss the next scheme.

The three spent a handful of seconds in deep, strategizing thought, from which Mick emerged to speak first. "I have a strong hunch this moment right here is where the battle is going to be won or lost. We have a decision to make—whether we're going to be conservative or liberal the rest of the way. We can be conservative by staying together and sweeping through the sleeping quarters, eliminating with relative ease. But I'm afraid our biggest obstacle waits for us once we're one flight up. Those on night-watch won't be sleeping. Therein lies the second option—we take a chance and split up; two of us annihilate the sleeping foes and whatever else waits on this floor; while the lone third member of our party goes upstairs to the rooftop to seek out the perfect location to gain a flanking advantage for when we come back together. Ultimately, the Molisians will start scrambling upon realizing they're under attack. Amongst their confusion, having one of us hide waiting to jump out from behind might benefit us. Both plans rely on speed of delivery. Time is against us."

Dave replied, "You're the strategy master, you decide which one. I'm behind your decision a hundred percent."

"As am I," added Krell-nor.

Mick wasted no time in deciding, his mind completely focused. "Okay then, you two clear this floor as fast as you can, and I'll go topside and hide somewhere on the western edge. When you start the attack topside, they'll no doubt band together. At this point, their backsides will be vulnerable to the tip of my sword."

"Good plan, let's put it into action," said Dave eagerly.

The trio split up. Mick continued up the stairs to do his thing, while Dave and Krell-nor inched their way through the door to the second floor.

The coast was clear for the pair, so they proceeded down the corridor, swords in hands. Seventy-five feet away from where they emerged from the stairs, they made contact with a door leading to soldiers' quarters. There were three other doors arranged symmetrically down the hall, which more than likely opened to additional soldiers' quarters.

Dave slowly pulled open the door in front of him, and could see twenty-four beds, two rows of twelve. One third of the beds were occupied. They figured the other three rooms were similar, and decided to go through each room one by one, together.

"At all cost, if any are to wake, don't let them get to the top floor to warn their compatriots," Dave told Krell-nor, who nodded in understanding.

The pair snuck into the first room, got into position, and non-verbally agreed who would kill whom—four for each. Killing defenseless adversaries wasn't exactly something either of them wanted to do, it was human life after all. But it needed to be done in the name of freedom.

With the dexterity of an adept sculptor, the pair eliminated all Molisians in the first room, without making a sound. They nodded to each other, and went to the next room seeking to do the same.

Meanwhile, Mick had reached the rooftop. Peering around a door left ajar, he observed approximately thirty sentries standing watch in the dark. Some were positioned on the outthrust river precipice, some were staring through battlements, but most were huddled together, talking, just like he'd previously thought they'd be doing. His job wasn't going to be an easy one, but he figured it was doable.

Before he set off to locate the perfect ambush point, he couldn't help but laugh to himself. *Some of the sentries are looking in the direction of our tents, and have no idea we're here.*

After his little moment and waiting for the most opportune time, Mick slithered out the door, and tiptoed parallel the southern battlement towards the west side of the fort. He moved as stealthily as a hungry carnivore stalking an unsuspecting rabbit. The guards had no idea he was there. They just kept doing their thing, even though a man who'd soon attempt to kill them was sneaking past in the dark.

As Hawk got closer to the western side, he tried to spot the perfect place to hide and wait. He needed a place that was isolated, but not so much so that he couldn't mount an effective demonstration. Mick opted not to hide in the nearby lookout spire, by chance a guard decided to use it. He selected a refuse pile sitting in the south-west corner, consisting mainly of rubble. It wasn't pretty, but it was big enough for concealment, and close enough to where he anticipated the action would occur. He figured the chance was small anyone would notice him amongst it, even if they added to the pile. By skilled, nocturnal navigation, he won his way to the pile, established his post within, and waited to strike.

In the time it took Mick to locate and get to his ambush point, Dave and Krell-nor had completed two more rooms, adding seventeen unfortunate souls to the body count.

Just about to begin work in the final soldiers' quarters, Dave commented, "When we finish this room, there are three more doors at the end of the hall, which I'm almost positive lead to officer's quarters."

Krell-nor replied, "How can you tell?"

"The tags on the doors say the names of the known officers: *Huilghenberk* and *Schaet*."

"You sure have good eyes."

"If you think mine are good, you ought to see Mick's in action. There's a reason we called him Hawk when we were kids." Krell-nor smiled, scrunched his lips, raised his eyebrows, and nodded. Ready to proceed, Dave said, "This room is bigger and probably has more soldiers in it. Hopefully none escape."

They crept into the room, got into position, and began carrying out the procedure. The room contained a dozen soldiers. Eight died in their sleep, two reaching for their weapons. The final two were a nuisance, for one managed to yell out.

Krell-nor and Dave each targeted one Molisian.

Seeing an opening, Dave swung at his opponent's neck, but missed. A return swing came Dave's way, but he dodged it with a quick, agile snap of his torso.

Battling ten feet from Dave, Krell-nor tried to jab his adversary in the head, but was blocked. Krell-nor's challenger tried to push his sword out of the way with his own sword, but only succeeded minimally.

Because one of the Molisians had yelled out, an officer sleeping down the corridor woke up and reacted. Luckily for Dave, Mick, and Krell-nor, he was the only one sleeping in the officer's quarters at the time. Intelligently, officer Schaet noticed how quickly he would've gotten killed by joining the fight against the obvious masters, and chose another course of action. Dave, Mick, and Krell-nor were considered weapons masters by Taraosk standards. The exact reason for this would take far too much time to explain now. The Molisian officer decided to turn around and try to make it up the rooftop, where he knew at least thirty other Molisians were stationed.

Dave spotted the dilemma, and swiftly knocked his immediate opponent off balance, so he could respond to the outlying threat. Instead of reaching for his dagger to throw at the escaping enemy, Dave decided to grab something else. He was decent at throwing daggers, but he figured the success rate of the blade penetrating was only fifty percent at his current skill-level. Having gotten in touch with a shield lying on a nearby bed, Dave hurled the weighty item at the fleeing officer. For Dave, a shield had a ninety percent success rate of causing damage.

He scored a direct hit square in the back, effectively breaking it, causing the man to lose both his ability to walk and yell out in agony.

By this time, Dave's initial opponent had regained his balance and re-engaged. But now, Leopard was just getting warmed up, and easily finished off the foe with a flurry of sword strikes. Dave, then, eradicated officer Schaet before he could crawl up the stairs.

Krell-nor's rival made a last effort for survival by imitating Dave and throwing a shield. But it was his undoing, for he missed terribly and spent too much energy. Krell-nor took advantage of the winded man, slaying him while sluggish.

All threats at hand subdued, Krell-nor said to Dave, "Now that was what I call the definitive shield throw. You made it look too easy."

"I aim to please."

"Somebody has to." Krell-nor observed, "This floor looks to be all clear."

"Excellent. The faster we get to Mick, the better."

The two of them checked behind the remaining officer quarter's doors to make sure they were empty. They were, besides a huge bed and ornate decorations in each. Dave and Krell-nor hurried up the stairs to initiate the final and what was sure to be most challenging stage of the fort capturing mission.

There were exactly thirty-two armed soldiers topside, who, if guided by a tactician as skilled as Mick Thraiker or General Ulfenkerki, could easily defeat a force of three. But they weren't, so there wasn't going to be anything easy about the battle atop Fort Gravividon. Not only was the darkness going to limit visibility, but it was beginning to snow as well. Minimal visibility was an advantage for the smaller force, because it made archery more difficult.

With an ability to ignore shapeless fears, Dave was barely nervous before going into the highly lopsided battle. Krell-nor was similar. Mick was probably the most apprehensive of the three.

Gazing out the door to the top level, Dave calculated both the best time to emerge into battle, and the best path to take once committed. He assessed the two of them could maybe take out three or four Molisians before the rest of the topside platoon would be alerted of their presence.

Dave whispered to Krell-nor, "At the point when the majority of the platoon becomes aware of the attack, Mick will jump out of concealment, putting his plan into action."

"Sounds good." Krell-nor joined Dave in sticking his head out the door.

Dave pointed to four of the guards close by, and said, "I think we can probably take those four guards out silently enough. After that, we'll go after the next few, but we'll probably be bombarded by the horde by then."

"I agree."

The pair looked each other in the eyes, shared unspoken words of brotherhood, and went through the door.

As was premeditated, they eliminated four marks before being noticed. When engaging the fifth and sixth targets pandemonium began. As Mick had previously thought, when the Molisians were stressed they banded together like a school of fish being attacked by voracious sharks, huddling in a state of uneasiness.

The Molisians had no idea at first who and how many were attacking them. And to no surprise to Mick, they congregated near his post. Another bonus for the heroic trio's operation was two of the Molisians decided to go to the underlying floors to procure more sword-hands. But what they didn't know was every other Molisian in the fort had already been immobilized. By the time they'd realize it, it'd be too late for them to help in the fight.

There was only one way to get to the rooftop, so the squad of Molisians all faced Dave and Krell-nor, and whatever else they thought might come through the door.

Dave and Krell-nor knew Mick was on the verge of springing the trap. The pair held their positions, and hid their smirks in anticipation of the moment.

Behind the pile of rubble, Mick had watched everything unfold. He'd seen his compatriots battle with superlative skillfulness. He'd witnessed the two Molisians wastefully run down the stairs. He'd perceived the enemy mass together, and turn their backs on him. It was the perfect time to strike.

As cunningly as he could, Mick drew his sword, rose out of concealment, and began sneaking up behind the unwary pack. The ducks were on the pond. When he was close, he made his charge.

Stabbing as many as he could in the back, Mick aimed for the heart and backbone. A well-placed sword tip in the backbone could immediately paralyze a foe. Mick was unleashed. Dave and Krell-nor took advantage. They each easily defeated another two opponents during the perfect diversion. Before the Molisians even knew what hit them, their initial rooftop headcount of thirty-two went down to twelve. A number in which Mick and Dave had confidence, even though they were still outnumbered four to one—confidence in part because they still possessed the edges, the Molisians were too stupid to break their huddled formation.

Mick, Dave, and Krell-nor kept the battle confusing by not spending too much time on a single opponent. They bobbed and weaved around the periphery of the battlefield with extreme agility, wounding and killing.

In the space of only a few minutes, the Molisian force had whittled down to three. The three Garobansurovians were pitted against the three best Molisian fighters that'd been stationed at Fort Gravividon, three head to head clashes.

Krell-nor's challenger was the only one of the six not using a sword as his primary weapon—a mace. Before his fight began, Krell-nor saw the last opponent he'd have to face wielded a mace, so he'd quickly grabbed a shield out of the battle debris. Maces were particularly deadly against non-shield-wielding opponents, and Krell-nor knew it.

With his borrowed shield, he absorbed powerful mace blows—blows that couldn't have been absorbed by a sword. At the right time, he turned offensive. He swung his sword with great accuracy, cutting his adversary's shoulder. Then, channeling all his might, Krell-nor clobbered his foe in the leg with his shield.

Foreshadowed by a stumble and a grabbing of the injury, the Molisian was doomed. With a broken leg caused by the shield blow, he fell to the ground, and was terminated.

Mick's man was tall, strong, and proficient with a sword, but his fight against Mick wasn't his best fight ever. He'd lost energy during the earlier stages, trying to work his way into the fight around his own allies. Mick on the other hand was not yet out of breath. The initial exchanging of sword strikes was fierce—fierce by both combatants. But, because the Molisian had already been in a state of lethargy, he couldn't keep up the pace, and eventually bled out from multiple stab wounds.

Of the three, Dave's last skirmish was the most arduous. It was one of those struggles, about which the winner could really feel good. The fight was brutally intense, but somewhat short, only lasting thirty seconds longer than Mick and Krell-nor's. So, there wasn't enough time at the end for Dave to receive help from his friends. The pair of combatants went at each other with no reserve.

Of the two, Dave was the last man standing, but he wasn't doing so without his own blood strewn all over his body. He suffered many cuts, some rather deep, but none that would immobilize him for a long period of time.

Before the victorious trio could say anything to each other, they spotted the two who'd gone to the lower levels to get help running at them. But when the two got close enough to see the only three people left standing were the Garobansurovians, they immediately stopped running. They dropped their swords, and kneeled to the ground out of sheer intimidation. One of them said, "We would be stupid not to surrender. The three of you just conquered the entire fort for crying out loud."

Mick responded, "We accept your surrender."

The prisoners' hands were bound, and the trio was able to take in the moment. "Look, fellows, we're now in possession of a fort," Dave emitted.

"Pretty exciting isn't it."

"If a month ago someone had told me instead of being locked in the fort, I'd be standing atop it victoriously with two others, having completely taken it over, I would've assumed that person completely insane."

"I think most people would assume that in a similar situation, Krell-nor the Lucky. It's not every day three people capture an entire fort, especially one as large and important as this one."

"I will definitely be telling my grandchildren about this one." With a humorous undertone, Dave said, "We didn't take this fort by virtue of only your tactics, Mick. Only mostly your tactics, this time."

Mick laughed, and replied, "You're something else alright. Come, my cronies, let's walk out onto the river precipice and survey the distant landscape in euphoria."

"Good plan," responded Krell-nor. The trio walked out on the manmade precipice, and looked down at the river below. "It's practically impossible for the human mind to be as creative as nature, but today you two came pretty close."

"The only way to win a fight is by creativity. Not strength, not speed. Creativity," returned Mick.

"To compare our exploits to the power of nature is indeed a compliment," Dave added.

Standing on the protruding walkway, the trio looked out at the river and beyond. They inhaled the cool air, striving to remember the moment.

"You can really see far into Molisia from up here, as opposed to how far you can see into Garobansurov," emitted Krell-nor.

"Advantageous for we Garobansurovians, being able to spot far off approaching enemy battalions. We'll know far in advance when the second wave of reinforcements is near. We'll have to defeat them, which shouldn't be as hard as what we just did."

Responding to Dave's comment, Mick said, "True. They'll have no idea the fort is no longer under Molisian control. With our high-ground advantage, and maybe a few volunteers, we should have no problem defending it, and preventing Gamald from receiving further reinforcements for his campaign."

"I agree. When they're on the bridge, waiting to get let in, we'll rain arrows upon them."

Krell-nor added, "There's definitely no shortage of bows and arrows up here for that."

"Excellent. The more, the better."

For the next half hour, the trio still high from excitement stared out at the icy river, talking of their triumphant invasion, and of future protocol.

CHAPTER 20

TWILIGHT BROKE OVER the pristine scene. Another long day of searching and traveling behind them, Brom, Loyd, and Carrie needed to find a place to sojourn the night.

"I think we should go back to that farm we passed ten minutes ago," suggested Carrie. "There might not be another place to try for miles."

The rest of the party agreed with Carrie, so they all backtracked the distance to the farmhouse. Upon arrival to the front door, like always, Carrie was set to do the talking.

A farmer, dark with the tan of a lifetime of fieldwork answered the door, and extended a pleasant hello. After pleasantries, Carrie began her negotiation routine.

"I have no room in the house," the farmer replied, "but if the three of you can negotiate for some space in the barn with the party already spending the night therein, that's fine by me. They're a group of travelers as well, and had already paid me. I think there's ten to the party."

"Thank you so much, sir, we'll try that."

With the new initiative established, Carrie led her family to the barn, and knocked on the main door. A man she'd never seen before answered, "Hiya ma'am. What can I do for you?"

"I understand you and your group have already paid for the use of this barn?"

"Correct."

"By chance, would you be willing to share this fine barn with the three of us, for an agreed upon price?"

The man opened the door a little wider, and turned to ask those in his party if what Carrie had requested was doable. With the door opened wider, Carrie could peer inside, and was able to see who else was in the barn. Dropping her jaw in astonishment at whom she saw, Carrie exclaimed, "Uncle Tom! I thought you were on the other side of the country?"

Tom gleamed as much surprise and happiness as Carrie. "We were on that side for the longest time, but we received information which led us here. There's more to the story, but let me introduce everyone first."

Tom's party comprised of Tom, Tom's three sons, Tom's two friends (one who'd answered the door), and Tom's friends' four sons. Everyone was greeted cheerfully. Brom hugged his son, Tom, and his grandsons. Carrie and Loyd joined in on the hugging.

"Have you had any luck in your search? I definitely haven't, but not because of a lack of trying by the three of us," Brom insisted.

Before Brom was able to narrate his tragic story, Tom began telling his far more upbeat one. "As you know, we began searching for my brother west of the Capital, but because of the information we gathered there, we ended up here. And once here, we got even more valuable information. You actually couldn't have arrived at a better time, for we believe my brother is being held captive only a day's journey from here. The ten of us intend to leave in the morning and do whatever it takes to get him back, including risking our lives. But now it seems there will be thirteen of us making that journey, risking our lives."

"Thirteen brave souls indeed," replied Brom. "This is good news. It means he's still alive—well, optimistically speaking at least."

"For all we were told, he's still alive, but we're uncertain of the details of the exact situation."

Succeeding a little more discussion on Tom's news, Brom communicated the disastrous chronicle of how he'd been imprisoned and lost his armor, to which everyone new to the story listened intently. A descriptive account he would've had a harder time reciting, if he hadn't just been infused by hope. Many questions followed Brom's telling.

By the time everyone fell asleep in the hay, the thirteen were all well acquainted, and well prepared for the morrow's journey, Brom especially. *This is my moment, my chance to prove my worth. I love my family, all of them.*

MICK, DAVE AND Krell-nor were now pretty tired. The battle to reclaim the fort had lasted most of the night. Before succumbing to the lethargy and going to bed, the three of them escorted the two prisoners of war to their cells, close to where Krell-nor's was.

"Tomorrow, we'll have to make sure we patch the hole back up in Krell-nor's old cell. We can't have anyone repeating our plan, now can we."

First, Dave replied to Mick, "That would be a shame." Then, Dave addressed the prisoners, "If you guys are good to us, we'll be good to you. There's probably plenty of food in the pantry to go around, so keep that in mind."

The trio of Garobansurovians took turns sleeping in the officer's quarters, making sure one of them stood guard, while the other two slept. Guard duty consisted of laps from the prisoners' cells to topside.

By late morning the next day, the three of them were all able to get five hours of sleep—not enough to feel effervescent, but enough to get by. Coincidentally, Krell-nor was like Dave and Mick in being an eight-hour sleeper.

Upon inspection of the pantry in the lower level, they realized there was a lot of food available, as previously thought. The prisoners ended up being well-behaved and generously fed. The threesome also ended up eating generously. Hardy, diverse meals weren't exactly abundant in the world of an adventurer.

Post pantry inspection, the three sat at a table in the mess hall and talked. Dave said, "Unless you guys can think of anything else, I say there are three or four main things we have to do today. First thing is one of us needs to comb the countryside for volunteers to help keep the fort. I don't think it'll be much of a problem to find a few, because I'm sure the locals will see the value of the fort being in our hands once again. Second thing is to repair the hole in Krell-nor's cell, which I'm sure is something Krell-nor himself doesn't want to do, he being sick of that particular spot and all. Third thing is to bury the dead, and go topside to make sure we have a vast and varied arsenal of weapons ready to go in case the second wave of Molisians arrives soon. And possibly the fourth thing to do today is go get our tents."

Krell-nor replied, "You're right, Insightful Dave, I certainly don't want to spend any more time in that hell-hole. I'll volunteer for burial and topside weapons arrangement."

Mick spoke next. "Since you're still ailing from your battle-sustained injuries, Dave, I'll travel the countryside to muster help, making sure the proclamation goes far and wide."

"Which leaves hole repair for me. And if I have enough time left over, I'll retrieve the tents and the rest of the gear."

"Sounds good, Dave."

After breakfast, and with clear mandates, the trio split up, setting out to perform their designated tasks.

The three worked efficiently, and met back up later in the day to discuss their conducive to the cause jobs.

"I stopped at thirty different residences on my big loop of the countryside," said Mick. "Almost everyone to whom I talked was ecstatic at hearing the news we recaptured the fort. They knew all too well the undesirable situation here. However, most of them didn't want to risk their lives to help in the safeguarding of the fort, except for two brave lads, likable gents who said they'd be here tonight. The countryfolk did promise to spread the word about the victory, and the fact volunteers are needed. Overall, I'd say my day was a success."

"Splendid. Even just two more here will greatly help. In having the high-ground advantage, extra arrow power is paramount," declared Dave. "I managed to patch up the hole in Krell-nor's old cell without difficulty, and was also able to retrieve our tents and gear from the old campsite. It sure was nice being there, and thinking about our good times."

Krell-nor put forth, "One of these days, I'd like to walk up to where you guys had spent all that time to get a feel."

"No problem. Next time we get a chance, one of us will show you where it was."

"I would appreciate that. Thank you," extended the Lucky. "Today, the first thing I did was bury all the unfortunate, supplying proper prayers. Then, I perambulated through the armory, systematizing. I stockpiled the rooftop with every arrow I could find, and about forty bows. It was too bad, though, there wasn't much armor stowed away—only a few inferior pieces here and there. But I was able to scrounge together a couple of near complete suits, neither being spectacular. You two can take a look and use them if you want, but they're certainly no better than the ones you already have."

"We'll take your word for it. Go ahead and take one for yourself, and give the other to one of the volunteers when they come." Mick asked Krell-nor, "How many arrows were you able to find?"

"I'd have to say at least 800 or 900."

"That should be enough. I'm guessing there'll be between 200 and 300 Molisians arriving in the next wave, so that'll give us one arrow each with which to hit them, and two or three arrows to miss."

Krell-nor laughed. "I don't plan on missing."

Dave and Mick joined in on the laugh. "We'll just see about that."

Later that night, the two volunteers, Aaron, and George, who promised Mick they'd help defend the fort, arrived. They were greeted kindly and shown the ropes. The pair were green but exuded a willingness to learn and were glad to be there. They both told Mick, Dave and Krell-nor they wouldn't let them down. Young, eager and confident, Aaron and George were ready to help defend the fort.

George possessed a decent suit of armor, but Aaron's left much to be desired. It was so dilapidated that by looking at it one would've thought the thing had been donned in every battle in Garobansurov's history. There were holes where there really shouldn't have been holes. Not even thinking twice about it, Krell-nor handed the extra suit over to Aaron, who accepted it graciously.

Aaron and George both slept in the soldiers' barracks, while Dave, Mick, and Krell-nor slept in the three officer's quarters, which all had interior doors connecting themselves to each other. A design serving some military purpose unknown to Mick and Dave. There were now five to take turns for watch duty, so each enjoyed a smaller watch-turn and a longer sleep time than the night previous. The newcomers were informed of the expected wave of Molisians, and to especially keep an eye out for them. Krell-nor took first watch duty, George volunteered for second. All but Krell-nor fell asleep quickly.

THE THIRTEEN COMPANIONS traveled all day, and at nightfall reached their destination. Staring at the objective, Brom said, "Sure is an imposing building. Who knows what's inside waiting for us? As long as my other son is inside, I really don't care what else is in there. I'll deal with it."

Loyd asked, "So what's the plan?"

Brom Quintaga couldn't help but want to act impulsively, he'd waited a long time for this moment. He was having a hard time controlling himself—a volcano just waiting to erupt. To Loyd's question, he replied, "There is no plan. I'm just going to smash open a door and we're all going to rush inside like water through a busted dam."

Tom Quintaga chuckled, and said, "I guess sometimes that's just as good a plan as any. Lead the way, old man."

In a pleasant manner all her own, Carrie laughed at the exchange, and said, "We're right behind you, you old man you."

Brom and Loyd searched the area for the biggest rock they could find, and brought it over to the nearest door. Each having grabbed a side of the massive grey boulder, they picked it up over their heads, and smashed it into the door with all their might. The door wouldn't budge at first, but by the fifth time they performed the procedure the door splintered. By the sixth time they were able to reach inside and open it.

Sword up, Brom charged inside. He was prepared to confront anything, knowing he wouldn't stop until his son was found. Carrie and Loyd followed close behind, and the rest of the crew behind them, all streaming productive rage.

May today be the day, thought Brom Quintaga.

KRELL-NOR HAD JUST finished his guard shift and the new guy, George (who didn't mind guard duty so much), took over. He felt it was a noble pursuit. George executed his rounds as accurately as he knew how. When topside, wielding decent vision, he looked to the distance, trying to spot movement in the dark. He spent the majority of guard duty on the top level, looking for Molisians on the horizon. Mick, Dave, Krell-nor, and Aaron did the same.

Mick Thraiker, Dave Ghrere, and Krell-nor the Lucky each slept soundly in the officer's rooms. For some reason, maybe because he was used to sleeping in a tent, Mick uncovered himself in his sleep, and kicked his blanket to the floor.

BROM RAN THROUGH the large building with a single function. No obstructions waited for him at first. He climbed the stairs aggressively, squeezing tighter and tighter onto his sword handle with every step. Each space was examined, all rooms looked into. One of the rooms had a man sleeping in a bed but it wasn't his son so he didn't waste much time on him. Brom shot the man with a single arrow and led by his sword's keen edge, continued the fierce rampage through the rest of the building. There wasn't much that could stop his momentum now, perhaps only a mountain falling out of the sky and crashing directly upon him. A virtual impossibility, but the truth.

Loyd tried his hardest to keep up with Brom, running three steps to the rear. The rest of the crew were much further behind, trying to catch their breath. Unlike Loyd, they weren't able to match Brom's adrenaline fueled high cadence. The thirteen had basically split, Brom and Loyd on point.

Brom Quintaga was a dangerous man with a dangerous mission. Loyd saw it.

WOKEN BY A loud thud, Mick sat up. Still half asleep, he heard another thud. Dave was also awakened by the commotion, and stumbled into Mick's room through the interconnecting door, of which they now realized the advantage.

"What could that sound be?" Mick asked Dave, wondering how his blanket got on floor.

"I have no idea. I don't think the Molisian battalion could've breached the fort, without us spotting them first. They would've had to traverse many miles within our line of sight to get here."

"True."

"It's possible we got played by the new guys, the whole thing being an elaborate setup."

"I doubt that happened. I talked to their families personally. They're Garobansurovian through and through," Mick stated.

Just then, another extremely loud thump echoed. "Whatever it is, I don't like the sound of it."

"Neither do I," Mick nervously returned, prior to grabbing the tightly strung bow sitting on the nightstand. He loaded it with the sharpest arrow he owned, and hid behind the bed with Dave, who already had his arrow aimed. Arrow nocked, Mick drew his bowstring all the way back and pointed the arrow at the door, ready to unleash fury at first sight of it opening.

But just before all hell broke loose, something happened that made Dave think quickly. Soon to realize he was proficient at thinking quickly under pressure, he mentally voiced, *I hear a clicking sound coming from down the hall. Where have I heard such a sound before?* Dave put all his focus into remembering where he'd heard the sound. Then, like a bolt from the blue, it came to him. It's the clicking sound made by the metal strap attached to the bottom of a boot—Loyd's boot. Upon the revelation, Dave whispered to Mick, "I think I hear Loyd coming down the hall. Refrain from any immediate shooting."

A man came violently ripping through the door. Since Mick was instructed by Dave to wait, he didn't let his arrow fly right away. The hesitation supplied them enough time to recognize the older gentleman who'd just ripped through their door. It was the man they'd met at the onset of their journey traveling through Garobansurov trying to sell his three suits of armor. Dave was right, for following close behind was Loyd and his unconventional boot clicking.

Mick and Dave stood up from behind the bed and faced the dangerous Brom Quintaga. "Please, please, guys, it's us!" shouted Dave.

Loyd and Brom immediately recognized Mick and Dave and lowered their swords.

Brom voiced, "I remember you two—" but before he was able to finish his sentence looked out of the corner of his eye, and his jaw dropped—his sword also dropped, hitting the floor loudly. A tear rolled out of his eye, for Brom was now standing before his long-lost son, a man who'd just recently walked through the interconnecting doors of the officer's quarters, a man who'd just recently recaptured Fort Gravividon with Mick Thraiker and Dave Ghrere, a man known to some as *Krell-nor the Lucky*. Father and son were now finally reunited.

Brom took the deepest, most meaningful breath he'd ever taken, then swept Krell-nor into the biggest, most meaningful hug he'd ever given.

Before the hug was over, the rest of the Quintaga contingent came rushing into the room, astonished at the sight they were facing. Brom was just about to speak to Krell-nor for the first time in years, but then, he remembered something imperative. He turned to Mick and Dave. "I shot your man with an arrow on the way in, but I'm pretty sure he's all right. He has an arrow in his shoulder that'll need attention."

Mick and Dave were about to check on Aaron, but stopped in their tracks as Aaron and George came into the room. George had missed all the action because he was topside the entire time, watching for Molisians. Aaron was bloodied, but he'd already pulled out the arrow, and bandaged the wound. He would be fine. "What did we miss?" Aaron said.

After the moment everyone realized Aaron was okay, the excitement of finding Brom's son snowballed, and didn't end up climaxing for a very long time. Brom was finally able to speak with Krell-nor. The two shared immeasurable euphoria, as did the rest of the Quintaga family. Absolutely nothing could've ruined the moment. It was the new best day of Brom's life by far.

Everyone had a story to share, and eventually each story was imparted, each voiced as eloquently as the last.

After hearing the account of how Krell-nor was rescued, Brom said to Mick and Dave, "If not for you two and your incredible fort-capturing scheme, my family and I surely would've been killed by the massive force stationed here. Our fly-by-night operation would've unquestionably been our undoing. I owe you my life, *even more than that.*"

Carrie smiled so wide her dimples formed dimples.

Brom continued, "Furthermore, this incredible moment wouldn't have happened if it weren't for Mick and Dave being responsible for acquiring the chest of jewels, with which we used to bribe for Brom's freedom. Mick Thraiker and Dave Ghrere are indeed the nucleus of this joyous cosmic-righting."

Mick put forth, "We're just honored to have helped."

Dave added, "We would do it again in a heartbeat. We just do whatever we see needs to be done."

Brom commented, "Sometimes the chaos sorts itself out harmoniously into the way that benefits the decent."

Dave nodded, "Sometimes it does do that, doesn't it?"

Brom Quintaga, *a new man*, said to all, "Frankly, my friends, I say we rejoice with a drink. Does this place have drinks?"

"Sure does," answered Mick.

So, the entire group enjoyed a drink, or multiple drinks, and for the rest of the day fittingly celebrated the coming together of a family.

FROM THE PERSPECTIVE of the trees, the deep snow was accommodating, for it supplied insulation on a cold winter's day. But for creatures of foot, it was less accommodating, supplying poor traversability. Regardless of the poor traveling conditions, the soldiers sped through the snow, some being the pursued and some being the pursuer.

Jason Thorncat and his men after many long, hard days of tracking had finally caught up to Anolski and were closing in. The tracking took more of a toll than what was hoped, but it was something that needed to be done.

"We almost got them, Gregg," said Jason, excitingly.

"I'm ready to fight," returned Gregg Hogarty, running as hard as he could, trying to keep up with Jason in the snow. "We outnumber them, so hopefully the fight is short."

"As long as we capture Anolski, that's all that matters. There's no use in us risking all of our lives to capture all of his followers. If we have to fight, we'll fight, but hopefully we won't have to."

"I agree."

Jason and his squad switched into their highest running gears. Heavy breathing could be heard all around.

They were now within arrow shot. But just when a battle would've inevitably taken place, Anolski's party split into three. Two groups went into the forest separately, while Anolski's group headed towards the nearby lake. Jason saw this and excogitated the next course of action.

"This seems to be a last chance effort for them to try and flank us. Anolski is heading towards the lake, so we'll continue following him, and hopefully we catch him before his other parties circle back around," announced Thorncat.

"Yes, sir," returned those nearby.

Jason and his entire contingent ran after Anolski, but in doing so, they lost sight of the rest of Anolski's troops in the forest. An inconsequential development they hoped.

Anolski, his notoriously gaping mouth, and his small band picked up their pace and started to gain ground on Jason. General Anolski aimed his crew towards a certain part of the lake, into where a river flowed. A circumstance causing that part of the lake to be ice-free. The warm river also caused the area's shore to be practically snow-free, making for easier running.

Despite being nearly out of breath from running, Jason vocalized to Gregg, "I hope this whole thing wasn't part of some grand, dramatic plot by Anolski. I'm starting to get worried about the rest of the soldiers in the forest. I've no idea where they are."

"Neither do I."

Just then, Jason and Gregg heard a huge commotion by the lake, and a lot of swearing. They both headed towards the sounds.

When Jason drew near the ruckus, he saw a man hanging upside-down in a net. *Wait a second. Could it be? Yes, it is.* "Anolski is in the net," he said. "An older man with some sort of contraption trapped him. And the rest of Anolski's soldiers are running away." Jason approached the older gentleman, while Gregg stared at an inverted Anolski. "I'm Jason Thorncat, and this is my tracking platoon."

The old man replied, "Oh yes, I know. I'm quite read up on Garobansurov's military personnel. Your insignia gives you away."

"And you're aware of whom your net has ensnared, I take it?"

"Quite certain. I know all about Molisian military personnel as well. I spend a lot of time reading on every subject, for I live alone in a cabin in the woods. Some call me the Hermit."

"Good to meet you, sir."

"I've always known of this good fishing spot on the lake, where the water stays open year-round. I built this portable fishing-net apparatus, which I wheel down here every so often when the fishing is slow in my creek back home. So, when a situation arrived of an enemy general being chased by a group clad in my own country's garb, I took advantage. I dropped my net on top of this unsuspecting adversary, an inattentive man who had no idea he was positioned underneath a giant net at the time."

Jason was impressed. "Our country is greatly pleased by your actions here today. Our position was starting to get a little precarious, but you saved the day with your heroic measures. With their leader captured, I'm sure the rest of the soldiers will try to make their way back into Molisia, with lowered heads."

Jason took Anolski out of the net, bound him tight, and to him said, "Don't worry, general, we're not going to kill you. We treat our POWs kindly here."

Once Anolski was secured by Jason's squad, Jason resumed speaking to the Hermit. "I wish we could stay longer, watch this net-contraption in action, and maybe try to catch a fish or two, since this seems a great place for it. But I'm afraid we have to hurry and get back to Thraug. Any day now, the invasion force is to depart. I'm sure you know about Sarwa, and it being controlled by Gamald."

"Yes, I do."

"Then, you know it needs to be recaptured."

"It certainly does. Undeniably, Ulfenkerki, the Nighteagle, and Rayton have a lot on their plates."

"Very true," said Jason, "which is why I'm hoping we can get back in time to assist them with the invasion."

"Don't let me keep you. If I was a few years younger, perhaps I'd come with you and help in the battle, but I don't think my old, withered body could do much in that department anymore."

Jason responded, "You've already done your country a great service, and me one as well. I thank you sincerely. Good luck fishing, and farewell."

"Farewell soldiers of Garobansurov."

Jason's crew, now one head larger in number, headed back to Thraug as fast as their legs would allow. Their bodies had already been pushed to the limit, but Jason and his crew persevered.

Gregg Hogarty asked Jason, "Do you think we'll make it back in time?"

"I'm not sure. But I do know if Ulfenkerki was to start the assault with a diminished force, he'd have a good reason for it. I can't think right now what such a reason could be, I'm too winded to think, but I'm sure one could exist."

"Let's hurry then."

"We are, my friend, we are."

Chapter 21

A JOYOUS WEEK that'll unfortunately never be seen again had passed since Brom was reunited with Krell-nor. Still, there was no sign of the second wave of Molisians. The entire Quintaga clan, Mick, Dave, and the volunteers, which had increased in size from two to five, all took turns standing watch for the enemy. They enjoyed each other's company thoroughly while doing so.

The Quintagas and their lifelong friends yearned to carve a larger piece out of the Molisian army. What the Molisians did to Krell-nor was unforgivable, which the Quintaga party wouldn't soon forget. They all had decided to help Hawk and Leopard with whatever was to come their way. Mick and Dave were pleased for the assistance.

Now at the fort, were 21 sturdy Garobansurovians, who could probably defend it against a pretty sizable force. How sizeable? No way to tell.

Accompanied by Krell-nor, Mick performed topside watch. "I'm surprised it's taking this long for the second squadron of Molisians to arrive. Gamald is probably getting pretty mad waiting for them." Ironically, before Krell-nor even had time to agree, Mick spotted a mass of soldiers appearing on the Molisian horizon. "That certainly is weird. I talk about them, and they show up."

"Why don't you talk about a horde of beautiful women with heaving bosoms next time. Then, maybe we'll get something of merit."

Mick laughed, and responded, "Maybe I will."

It took a handful of minutes for Mick to be able to scope out just how large the approaching detachment was. "I'm afraid they're more numerous than what was expected and hoped. We anticipated 200 or 300, but it seems by my estimate there's at least 400 on their way."

"Do you think we can still defeat them?"

"It's possible, but only with a little luck."

For a short time, Mick studied, watching the soldiers grow taller and taller as they drew nearer and nearer. Having gotten all the information he wanted, he went to the lower levels of the fort to inform everyone else of the news.

Post hearing Mick's report, Dave postulated, "They're probably so late because they wanted to swell up before meeting up with Gamald."

"That's possible," Mick responded.

"It's going to be harder now to repel them than previously expected, but it may be doable. We'll be outnumbered almost twenty-to-one, but we do have other tactical advantages on our side."

"That we do. We have multiple naturally occurring ones thanks to our high-ground situation."

"Another advantage involves our massive number of arrows," added Dave.

The group continued to talk of strategy for a few hours, but couldn't help but feel a diminished confidence in affairs. They were undeniably vulnerable.

Per his observance topside three hours previous, Mick assumed it would take roughly seven hours for the Molisians to reach the fort. The battle was now a mere four hours away.

The 21 of them were engulfed by the mental preparations for battle when a knocking was heard at one of the doors facing Garobansurov. Perplexed, Mick stood up. "Who could that be?"

Dave and a proclivity to answer questions also stood up. "I have no idea. I'm surprised we can even hear the knocking from this far away."

Nervously, the party of 21 all went to the door to investigate the rapping. Brom opened it slowly, sword in hand, and peered. He recognized naught, but Mick and Dave did.

On the other side of the door was indeed a welcome surprise, for it were the Burg, Tyson, and Dearn families. Almost all the people from the mining compound, whom Mick and Dave had recently rescued from the underground.

Dave came forward and spoke: "This sure is an unexpected occurrence. What brings you folks this far north?"

The oldest Dearn responded, "We'd received news from a traveler you and Mick were requesting help to hold Fort Gravividon—an extremely impressive seizure, by the way—so here we are, answering the call, seeking a little revenge on some enemy Molisians."

Mick chimed in. "I had no idea my proclamation for assistance would travel so far, so fast."

"We just got lucky, I guess. In the right place at the right time. We heeded the call and started out immediately—minus the kids and someone to watch them, of course."

"I don't think you realize how indisputably perfect your timing actually is. At this moment, we're under four hours away from being attacked by an overwhelming band of Molisian soldiers. But with your sizable clan added to ours, we shouldn't have any problems keeping them at bay. There's more than enough archery equipment here to do so."

One of the Burgs replied, "We're glad we made haste then. All we need is a moment to catch our breath, maybe something quick to eat."

"Not a problem. Abundant food in the pantry and comfortable chairs everywhere. When you're prepared, meet the rest of us topside. We're glad you came, and it's outstanding to see you again."

"Same here, Dave."

A couple hours later, the miners, having had enough time to gather composure and stave hunger, went topside to join the rest of the crew. Mick welcomed them to the battle arena, and said, "Now, we have thirty-six soldiers ready to fling arrows. Luckily, just thirty minutes ago, we found a hidden cache of arrows, so we have even more now than previously thought. Clansmen, grab a bow and a hand-to-hand weapon of your choosing, if in fact you need either. If you look through the battlements, you can take notice of the opposition."

The newcomers peered through the openings, and saw the hurdle they were facing. They were surprised at how close to the fort the foreigners were. But showed no fear.

Dave sounded off on strategy. "The goal for what to shoot is eight to ten. If each of us can immobilize or kill eight to ten Molisians, before they realize what's going on, the battle will pretty much be over before it even begins. We'll spread out just enough, both here and on the river precipice, so we can all aim at a different eight to ten. There's no point in killing someone twice." Dave elucidated a few more stratagems, and made a few more jokes, before finishing his vocalization.

The Garobansurovians were almost ready. All that remained was getting into positions, which they did next without imperfection. Many had two bows, and all had near a hundred arrows at their disposal. A second bow in case of malfunction. Also, having a second bow nocked and ready meant half a second could be gained. Half a second was quite valuable in warfare.

An integral part of the overall plan was for the Molisians to believe the fort was still in custody of their countrymen. Other than actually being inside the fort to see for themselves, there wasn't a way for the Molisians to ascertain data on any changes in fort ownership. Due to the fact the bridge adjacent the fort was the only way for information to travel from one country to the other for many miles in both directions. The Garobansurovians intended to not do anything out of the ordinary when the Molisians were close, especially refraining from being seen. Although, they still had to present an image of there being routine operations held. Anonymous semi-concealed movements, along with other minor activity, would be performed.

Mick and Dave waited confidently. Their supply of arrows was stacked neatly for easy, quick access. The black needle blades were sharp and shiny.

Four hundred enemy soldiers marching across a wooden bridge spanning a deep, rocky ravine made for an unforgettably ominous soundscape. The echo of each footstep bounced between the cliff faces a thousand times, inviting a thousand different timbres.

From Mick and Dave's perspective, the approaching detachment appeared clueless. They seemed to have no idea the fort had changed hands.

Dave whispered to those nearby, "Start firing when I put my left fist into the air. Pass it along. Let's teach these trespassers a grand understanding of Garobansurovian pride."

The unsuspecting brigade all stood on the bridge, waiting to be let into the fort. They were cold, hungry, tired, and couldn't wait for the sojourn. Some were surprised they weren't granted immediate entry.

A knock from the Molisian side of the fort was heard topside. Summoning perfect timing, Dave put his left fist into the air, signaling the battle to begin. Arrows flew into the mass relentlessly. Each and every member of Hawk and Leopard's platoon released arrows. Some loosed arrows from both their secondary and primary bows in a matter of only seconds.

It took the entirety of 20 seconds for the Molisians to realize what exactly was happening to them. In that time, the fort defenders had each unleashed an average of twelve arrows, resulting in a fifty percent casualty rate. Once the Molisians realized half the soldiers around them had gotten stuck with arrows, they started to panic. The frenzied, unorganized state led them to even further casualty.

The original topside 36 was still 36. The Molisian original 400 was now barely 100—the wily veterans who didn't panic. However, the veterans weren't exactly smart enough to flee altogether—At least they were smart enough to vacate the bottleneck of the bridge, where the archers on the river precipice all had clear shots.

The Molisians managed to get themselves to the area at the base of the fort, but the move was practically anticipated. Led by Mick and Dave, the majority of the defenders quickly repositioned to the lower levels to shoot at the Molisians through the windows. A wise maneuver by Hawk and Leopard which resulted in an almost immediate total victory.

Three Molisians were able to elude the arrows, and hide in the forest. Ironically, they hid in about the same place where Mick and Dave had performed much of their pre-assault recon. The three were eventually captured, and put into cells near the other POWs. They all laughed at each other for getting captured by such small forces.

The battle was over, and the victorious 36 congregated in the mess hall. Celebrating zero casualties, they discussed the win with great exhilaration.

Brom downed a pint and said, "I don't think we averaged your goal of eight to ten kills at the onset, Dave, but we were pretty close."

"Indeed, we were, Brom. Everything definitely came together in the end. That last batch should've retreated back to Molisia."

Mick added, "Yes, that certainly went well. Gamald is going to have a heart attack when he learns about this."

Enjoying the moment and more pints, the group talked of the triumphant achievement for the better part of two hours. When the animation of the group cooled down, Mick and Dave talked, just the two of them.

"I'm positive, Dave, with all looming threats now eliminated, the fort can now be held with a skeleton crew."

"I'm pretty sure it can too."

"So, knowing that, I think it might be possible for us to leave the fort in the hands of those willing, and make it back to help General Ulfenkerki and The Nighteagle in their attempt to retake Sarwa."

Dave responded, "I think making it to Thraug would be cutting it too close. Maybe if we stuck to the snow compaction of the first wave of Gamald's reinforcements, it'd be possible for us to make it to Sarwa, before the battle is over."

"So, go straight to Sarwa, instead of Thraug?"

"Yes," Dave answered. "I have the feeling we'd miss them at Thraug."

"Good thinking. To Sarwa we go."

"Let's inform everyone else of our plan, and see what they say."

Thraiker and Ghrere corralled everyone, and explained to them what they intended to do. The response they received was somewhat unexpected, but certainly patriotic. The entire Quintaga crew plus the entire Tyson/Burg/Dearn contingent expressed they wanted to accompany Dave and Mick to battle. They were all well aware the battle for Sarwa wasn't going to be as easy. There would be no high ground and element of surprise advantages, like they'd just experienced. Nonetheless, they wanted to fight. Mick and Dave were honored to lead such a noble group of warriors to Sarwa.

The next morning, after Mick, Dave, and Krell-nor spent one last night in the relaxing officer's quarters, 31 capable soldiers were ready to leave Fort Gravividon for a trip south. The five volunteers from the countryside stayed behind, certain they could continue holding the fort. Plus, they'd be bolstered by another five volunteers, showing up in the coming days to help.

"Once we get to Ulfenkerki, we'll explain the situation. I'm sure he'll send soldiers here to help defend the fort, as soon as the battle for Sarwa is over," Mick said to the volunteers, before leaving.

"We're not worried, we can handle it," said George. And handle it they did, for there weren't any additional enemy platoons within a hundred-mile radius of the fort. The first wave that had left Fort Gravividon more than a week ago heading in the other direction, was a hundred and one.

Krell-nor said to Mick and Dave, "I guess it doesn't look like I'll get the chance to see your encampment."

"Oh yeah," replied Dave. "We never got around to doing that."

"Some things are better left to the imagination," stated Krell-nor, who made a point to not turn around and look at Gravividon one last time, it being a place he wanted to forget.

As promised, fulfilling a past bet, Dave began the journey carrying Mick's item of choice: his greaves.

A FEW DAYS after Mick, Dave, and their group left Fort Gravividon, Gamald was sitting in his office when he was approached by an unfamiliar face. A scout-soldier from the first wave of reinforcements toted news the lot had gotten terribly sick, and were held up at a makeshift camp. Seventy-five percent had come down with some sort of virus, but they were on the mend and intended to soon begin the last leg to Sarwa.

Lieutenant Leedle was in the office with Gamald when the general received the news. Leedle asked the soldier, "What about the second squad of reinforcements? They were supposed to be coming too. Is there any news on them?"

"No one has heard anything from them, sir," replied the scout.

General Gamald stood up, and yelled sternly, "You get your little butt back to those soldiers in their little makeshift camp, and tell them I don't care how sick they are! They'd better be here on the double or they'll have to answer to me, and the same goes for the second wave. I don't care who does it, and whether or not they have to walk all the way back to Fort Gravividon to do it, someone had better tell that second squad of reinforcements to make haste or they'll also have to answer to *me*. Trust me—you don't want to have to answer to me!"

The nervous messenger took no chances—He left the office right away. As fast as he could, he headed straight back from whence he came to relay Gamald's orders. The poor lad in the process nearly tripped over Gamald's office rug on his way out.

Leedle commented, "The rug almost claims another."

"Almost," replied Gamald. "Do you believe that ineptitude? *They stopped because they were sick.* Those babies! If I lose this town because of their insolence someone is going to suffer," shouted Gamald. He slammed his fist against his desk, knocking off a jar of quills, which rolled onto the tripping rug.

Leedle, alone, continued to listen to his superior rant and rave for half an hour until Grunt and Roar came into the office. Then Gamald settled a bit. The quartet discussed the uselessness of the sick squadron, among other things, for a good long time. Gamald also shared his secret plan with Grunt and Roar, involving a new troop of archers. Like always, they didn't say much, but they were definitely impressed by Gamald's scheme.

Gamald declared, "Ulfenkerki has another thing coming if he thinks he's going to retake *my* city."

Leedle turned to look at the huge men standing next to him and commented, "My opinion is that Grunt and Roar, here, can defend this city, just the two of them. I bet by now you boys sure are extremely thirsty for blood and can't wait to finally be unleashed!"

"Grrrrrr."

"Rooaar."

The general closed the gathering by saying, "I would hate to be the person, or group of people, having to fight either one of you."

The inhabitants of Sarwa were well aware war was coming, and couldn't have been happier. Being starved, physically abused, and raped by a tyrant's army wasn't really on their list of things to do that year.

THE DAY AFTER Gamald learned of the laxity of his sick unit, one of Ulfenkerki's scouts burst into Thraug, having run exhaustingly through deep snow for many miles. The physically fit man informed his leader and the Nighteagle the same news that had aggravated Gamald to a point of boil the day before. The Black Bear immediately saw the importance of this information: "Good job, you did well to speed this data to us."

"Thank you, sir."

"Before you enjoy your well-deserved rest, can you round up Archery-General Rayton for me?"

"Not a problem, sir."

"Afterwards, go ahead and eat something from the mess hall. Tell the cooks I sent you and to prepare for you whatever you're craving."

"Thank you again, but it's not necessary."

Ulfenkerki shrugged his shoulders and smiled.

The scout dutifully left to retrieve Rayton.

To the Nighteagle, Ulfenkerki said, "We need to utilize this valuable information."

"I agree. What are you suggesting?"

"If we start the invasion now, maybe we can get to Sarwa, before their reinforcements do—or at least we can get there fast enough to attack the vulnerable squadron with our higher numbers. A wise man would suggest keeping the reinforcements from getting behind Sarwa's walls."

"Initiating the invasion is actually possible. All the battle towers just got finished a few days ago, and as of now the trail to Sarwa is still traversable," said the Nighteagle.

Ulfenkerki started turning mental wheels but then, the wheels became cumbersome. He realized if he did begin the invasion of Sarwa, he'd be doing it without his first lieutenant. "It's unfortunate we might have to embark before Jason gets back. However, I know he'd understand. This is just too big of an opportunity for us."

The Nighteagle responded, "Right, he will understand. He's well aware of the importance of flawless timing."

"That he is."

Having been just recently informed by the scout his presence was requested, Rayton made his way to the assault discussion.

Joining Ulfenkerki and the Nighteagle, Rayton inquired, "What's the news, gentlemen?"

"The Nighteagle and I have just been notified the reinforcements sent from the Molisian homeland to aid Gamald in his securement of Sarwa have contracted an illness. They're laid up for the time being, many miles away from Sarwa, and the two of us were just agreeing the time to strike is *now.*"

Puzzled, Rayton asked, "Even though Jason and his squadron haven't yet returned from tracking Anolski?"

"Even though, yes. I think this is a chance we need to take. We may not get there fast enough to intercept the reinforcements, but nevertheless, we still must try."

For some reason, it took a while for Rayton to be convinced they needed to depart for Sarwa. But eventually he saw things Ulfenkerki's way. Rayton left Ulfenkerki and the Nighteagle's company and went to tell his archers the battle plan.

"Do you think we should leave tonight, or wait until morning?" the Nighteagle asked Ulfenkerki.

"If all the assault machinery is indeed built and ready to go, I suggest we leave in a few hours."

"Yes, I'm ninety-nine percent positive the towable catapults and crossbow ballistae are primed. I'm a hundred percent positive the siege towers and ladders are ready to go. I saw them myself this morning. And I must say, they are imposing structures—all eighteen of them. I still love the crap out of your idea of making some of them decoys. Twelve are usable, and the remaining six are distractions, if I remember correctly?"

"Yes, that is correct. I just hope we built the wheels large enough to plow through a snow-laden path without holdup."

"I don't think that'll be a problem," noted the Nighteagle. "Though, I'm no expert in the winterizing of war machines."

"As for numbers, last night's count stood thusly: Rayton commands 355 archers; my army is 3,004 strong; and your count was 2,522. So, the total, rounded up slightly, is 5, 900."

The Nighteagle reached into his pockets, pulled out a hundred gitis, and handed it to Ulfenkerki. "It's official. Here you go, grand champion, your winnings from our bet."

"It got interesting for a while, there." Ulfenkerki humbly fisted the money and said, "I'm very pleased so many new recruits answered the call to arms so quickly. Garobansurovians really know how to rally."

"Yes, they show great fervor to fight for their country. For that, I am swollen with pride."

After the two generals made for certain all war machines were operational, they committed to battle and informed the soldiers to prepare to march. The servicemen and women complied without delay, and were lined up at the front gate within the hour.

Upon beholding the amassing of the invasion force most of the townsfolk were in awe. The ones who weren't were certainly sleeping. All the immense battle-towers, catapults, ballistae, carts, ladders, and everything else one could think of that could be used for ground-based assault were lined up, in no apparent pattern. It was indeed a display to remember. Everyone sensed the battle was going to be huge and bloody. Everyone was tense beyond measure.

One and all knew if Sarwa could be retaken, the war with Molisia—at least in their part of the country—would be subdued for a while. If Sarwa was not retaken there would be much suffering, and Molisia would continue its strong military foothold in Garobansurov, both of which just couldn't be allowed.

The war horns sounded off in melodic harmony. The horns mixed with the cacophony of the crowd was undeniably gripping. At the heart of the commotion was the joint army, comprised of three divisions, led by three generals.

At the moment, the soldiers of each division were receiving orders from their respective leaders and making last-minute preparations. Rayton instructed the archers. The Nighteagle spoke to his outfit, who was responsible for the operation of all mechanical weapons—catapults, ballistae, traps and such. And Ulfenkerki directed his regiment, operators of all wall storming equipment—towers, ladders, grappling hooks, etc. It was a finely tuned war machine that wasn't going to stop until its job was complete, or until broken by the opposing war-machine. In their minds, the 5,900 were invincible.

The front gate was opened, and they took to the snowy path like a pack of carnivores prepared to defend their territory at all costs—the defenders of the realm.

A DAY AFTER the army at Thraug was unleashed, Gamald's first wave reinforcements—now feeling better—finally sped away from camp. And a day and a half after that, the very same campsite played host to a whole new set of residents—Hawk, Leopard, and their company. Convenient for them, many fully functional army tents had been abandoned due to the hasty departure. Plus, the setting made for the optimal place to winter sojourn, because all the snow in the area had already been trampled. Nobody had to set up tents for the evening; they all just stayed in the pre-existing ones.

There were six good-sized usable tents, and six good-sized unusable tents. The unusables were ignored, while the usables were designated one each to groups of five, and one group of six.

With a stick Mick poked the contents of the largest of the seemingly dormant fire rings, as Dave stretched out stiff quads. "It seems as if we're gaining ground on the first wave of Molisians. It appears the former tenants of this encampment departed between one and two days ago," said Mick, after noticing a slight warmth in the ashes of the massive cooking ring.

Dave replied, "We might just catch up to them before the battle is over. Not that we'd be able to do anything about it. An open-field battle is an entirely different story than one under the protection of a fort."

"True. My guess is they came down with a sickness, and decided to lay up here for a while. It is the season for that."

"You're probably right. But I bet when Gamald finds out about it, they're going to wish they hadn't decided to stopover."

"Those poor saps."

Some of the fires were relit, which were used to heat up meals, of which everyone partook.

While eating, Mick asked Dave, "Do you think we should post guards tonight? You never know who or what's lurking."

"I think just one would suffice. Who knows, maybe someone will want to do it."

Most went to bed early, the site guarded by a Berg during the first half of the night, and a Dearn the second, both eager volunteers. Luckily, the night ended up being as still as a pool of water nestled at the far end of an immeasurably deep cave.

Endeavoring for a whole day of walking fast, the contingent commenced the trip's next leg at daybreak. They hoped to significantly lessen the gap between themselves and Gamald's reinforcements.

Thraiker and Ghrere were gaining more and more confidence and trust in their entire company with every new day. They were proud to pilot the proven warriors to combat.

Even though it contained only thirty-one soldiers, some would've called Mick and Dave's squadron an elite force, because a little under one-eighth of them were weapons masters: Mick, Dave, Krell-nor and partly Brom. Brom counted as half, because he was a master when he was younger, but at his current age he was a tad slower. Usually a force as large as 400 or 500 would be lucky to have just one weapons master. Mick and Dave's team was a power that could certainly affect the outcome of any battle—a power that no one in Sarwa or Thraug knew was mobilized, a power that ironically took the place of another.

CHAPTER 22

A DAY AFTER the Hawk/Leopard array departed sick camp, the Black Bear was no longer worrying about whether or not his siege towers had large enough wheels to plow through the snow. The army was making good time, the towers weren't holding them back.

To the Nighteagle, Ulfenkerki said, "We're pretty close now. I think we'll be to Sarwa tomorrow. I'll send scouts ahead to ascertain if we'll be able to intercept the reinforcements."

"Sounds good."

The army stretched out across the countryside for a quarter mile, and were patriotically cheered on by every Garobansurovian they encountered. Nightfalls in Garobansurov were especially patriotic. All dwellings within a two-mile radius of the army housed as many soldiers as humanly possible. Everyone had a warm place to sleep during the march. That night was no different.

It usually took an hour for the army to regroup in the mornings, which was technically kind of fast, given the fact they were spread out so much. But this morning, the soldiers must've been anxious to get moving because it only took fifty-five minutes to reassemble. In no time, they were up to speed.

Ulfenkerki continued his on-going battle discussion with the Nighteagle, saying, "I was right yesterday. I'm sure we'll make it to Sarwa today, probably closer to dark though."

The Nighteagle responded, but first he made sure to jump over the inconvenient, pointed branch in his path. "That sounds about right to me."

"You're still in pretty good shape for an old man, jumping over that stick with as much grace and coordination as someone half your age, and not even getting winded in the process."

The Nighteagle laughed, and said in reply, "It must be the water around here."

Joining his long-time friend, Ulfenkerki opened the door and walked into the room of laughter. "The water? You bet!"

The generals continued the march in good spirits for many hours, almost forgetting the fact they were on their way to battle, and possible death. The day went by fast for them.

An hour after a walking supper, the Garobansurovian army reached a point two miles from Sarwa, and halted to assess the situation.

While at a standstill, the two scouts Ulfenkerki had sent the day before finally returned with their observations. "Generals, I know it's not good news, but Gamald's reinforcements beat us here, and are now all within the walls of Sarwa," reported a scout. "They arrived only thirty minutes ago."

Ulfenkerki sighed with disappointment. "So close, so very close."

"Thirty more minutes, and we would've had them," said the Nighteagle.

"It's okay though, only a small bump in the road. We're still going to win."

"That we will, General."

Ulfenkerki addressed the scouts, "Can you two go back to Sarwa's fringe, and try to ascertain as much intel as you can, until the rest of us get there?"

"Yes, sir." The scouts left immediately.

"At least we're no longer in the dark on that piece of information. We now know what we're facing for the most part," Ulfenkerki said to the Nighteagle.

"Yes, we do. We're facing a whole lot of hostile Molisians with deadly weapons."

"That we are. Let's hope ours are more deadly."

Further back in the procession, Rayton discussed battle plans with Chad Loytin. Archers usually discussed different kinds of plans than infantry and such. They agreed upon what they were going to do, and how they were going to do it, and then relayed it to the rest of the bowmen.

Twenty minutes before the sun finalized its scheme to hide behind the distant hills, the army spotted the relatively old, high-walled Garobansurovian City of Sarwa—a Molisian city at the time. In the woods, far out of reach of Sarwa's projectile firing capabilities, the army gathered. Amidst towering red pine trees, Rayton joined up with Ulfenkerki and the Nighteagle. The three stood triangularly, conferring the topic of when to attack.

"We can either use cover of darkness to invade, or wait till morning when we're all fully rested," proposed Ulfenkerki.

The Nighteagle replied, "It's a toss-up really. They know we're coming, so surprising them in the dark is off the table."

Rayton added, "I agree, either way is fine with me."

"I say we wait until morning," put forth Ulfenkerki. "Who knows, maybe Jason will catch up to us by then."

"Good Idea," stated the Nighteagle, just anterior to catching a falling acorn with his hand that would've hit Ulfenkerki on the head.

"I guess the battle has already begun," said Ulfenkerki, upon the realization of what was going on with the acorn. The trio laughed, and walked away from each other to inform their personnel of the plan.

It was an abnormally warm morning for winter, overcast and windless, but no signs of Jason and his troops. Ulfenkerki and the Nighteagle woke at first light, fully rested and muscles yearning for use.

"Even the crows know something brutal is going to happen here today. I haven't seen one all morning," the Black Bear communicated to the Nighteagle.

"They say crows are one of the smartest animals on Taraosk."

"They must be, if they're getting the heck out of here."

"Too bad Gamald and his followers aren't as smart as the crows," voiced the Nighteagle.

Most of the army had slept as well as their generals. Getting into formation, they all rallied in the field between the forest in which they slept and Sarwa.

After battle lines were all organized, Ulfenkerki, the Nighteagle, and Rayton presented inspirational speeches and final orders. Still, not a crow in sight.

Horns were blown, and the army began approaching Sarwa. Even though Garobansurov's army was out of range, Molisian catapult batteries began firing relentlessly—a cloudless thunder.

Ulfenkerki's squad surrounded the city with their siege towers—real and decoy. As planned, they wheeled a higher number of towers to the side of town containing the front gate. The wall's bulge created more surface area, as anyone could see.

The Nighteagle separated the offensive battle machines into four groups and sent each one to a different side of town.

Rayton and his archers congregated by the front gate with the future purpose of softening up Gamald's defenses. For the moment, Rayton and company waited out of range, since the opposing archers enjoyed the high ground.

Communication between commanders on all four sides of the city was done with a series of flag-wavers. Different flags represented different commands. Ironically, the system was created long ago by a blind Garobansurovian.

Suddenly, via signal from Ulfenkerki, any calm existing in the air had turned tail and fled, just like the crows. The tactically astute general had ordered the first in the series of flag wavers to wave the first degree, light attack presentation. The flag system was broken down into two groups, with each group then separated further into three more, making a total of six categories: light and heavy attack and three degrees thereof. First degree, light attack stood for light arrow fire, light catapult fire, no ground troop advancement.

And just like that, the initiating red flags coinciding with the red sun rising, the assault on Sarwa officially began.

Gamald's war machines continued to fire relentlessly. The Garobansurovians had to deal with arrows, rocks, metallic chunks, and everything else that could be shot with a catapult coming at them from many directions. Wounding and death presented themselves, even at the early stages of battle.

Following numerical order, Garobansurov's second degree, light attack flag sequence was started. Firing pace picked up, but still no troop advancement. The arrow cascade from Rayton's archers could be seen from all sides of the city. It resembled a river surging over an obstructing boulder. Arrows from Gamald's archers could also be seen flying everywhere; but theirs weren't as focused, so it wasn't as marvelous a spectacle.

When an object fired from a Garobansurovian catapult would hit the wall, it'd cause a small amount of damage, but not enough to inspire thoughts the wall could be breached by catapult. The catapult fire was more so used to strike nervousness, and hit the occasional individual. Ballistae, the same.

Second-degree, light attack fire went on for a good hour, before the Black Bear ordered the beginning of the third and final degree of his light attack battery. Third-degree, light attack was the full spectrum of the offensive arsenal operating at full speed—but still no troop advancement.

"Fire away," the Nighteagle yelled to the apparatus operators. Surprisingly, at that point in time, none of Garobansurov's catapults had been destroyed yet, so they all continued operating at max capacity. Sadly, that could not be said of the actual people of the army—both armies.

The original 5,900 of Garobansurov was down to 5,800 hundred, and Gamald's original defense force of 5,000 had suffered a few casualties, bringing his number down twenty head. Even though Gamald's numbers were fewer, he still held a considerable advantage over the Garobansurovians. An advantage because he defended the high ground: the top of the wall.

Knowing he held the advantage, Gamald strut around arrogantly, though the Garobansurov military possessed one importance he did not—a greater cleverness, of which Gamald remained ignorant. High-ground advantage versus cleverness, and the prize was a city.

A rock hurled from Sarwa landed ten feet in front of Ulfenkerki. He looked mockingly at it and its surrounding crater. To the nearest soldier, he said, "That'll put hair on the chest."

The soldier laughed a deep chest laugh, and responded, "That it will."

Ulfenkerki gestured for the Nighteagle to come near, so they could talk.

The Nighteagle ran to Ulfenkerki, and put forth, "Things are going expectedly so far."

"Yes, they are." Ulfenkerki signaled a certain posterior soldier to approach, a tall man in charge of a cart loaded with boxes. While the tall, rapier thin man was walking towards them with his cart, Ulfenkerki said to the Nighteagle, "Well, my friend, you said I'd probably have more tricks up my sleeve, and you were right. That cart is one of those tricks." Ulfenkerki pointed.

"Amazing, a cart! I can't wait to see what a cart can do in battle," the Nighteagle said, accompanied with a chuckle.

"You just save your sarcasm for another day. It's what's upon the cart that's the trick, smartass."

The tall man and his cart contacted the generals. The Nighteagle peered inside the boxes on the cart, and was bewildered by the intricate gadgets within. "What do they do?"

"They're noise replicators to go along with the dummy siege towers."

"So, you're saying these things will replicate noise. What kind of noise?"

"The sound of catapults and ballistae going off. Well, not exactly, but close enough."

"You're full of many surprises. And the fact you were able to keep this covert until this very moment—which I have no idea how you did—furthers the notion you're something else. Something else indeed. I'll ask you some other day how they work, but for now, let's see these babies in action."

"That we shall."

The hand-powered noise devices were brought into battle by a team of soldiers. The devices coincided with the dummy siege towers, because they needed them the most.

When all was in place, the Black Bear signaled for the flag wavers to initiate the first-degree, heavy attack flag sequence. "Now is when things are really going to get interesting," said Ulfenkerki. Along with catapults and ballistae still operating at max capacity, the infantry was now mobilized. They were to begin the attempt at breaking into town.

As fast as a crew could roll an extremely heavy object, each siege tower began to be positioned. All eighteen were to surround town. The soldiers doing the rolling had to dodge onslaught from above, but thankfully the towers bore the brunt of the projectiles—but not all. Casualties ensued.

After hearing one of the noise machines for the first time, the Nighteagle was astounded. How could so much noise come from one little contraption, he thought. "Don't get any ideas of slipping one of those things into my tent, while I'm sleeping tonight."

"I wouldn't do that," replied General Ulfenkerki. "We're going to win this battle, so I wouldn't be slipping one into your tent, it'd go into your quarters within town."

"Let's not do that either."

Catapults and ballistae continued to fire vigorously. Sounds of wood creaking, stones thumping, and metal clanging were erupting everywhere. Two hundred Garobansurovian soldiers per wall were set into motion, for first-degree, heavy attack. Like the light attacks, there were three degrees of heavy attacks—each designating more and more of the army to be exercised. If a third-degree, heavy attack failed, the battle was lost.

The generals watched on as the siege towers were almost in place, hoping no problems arose. It was harder to roll the siege towers once they were near Sarwa's walls because there the snow was deeper, having wind drifts. Slowly but surely, they got into position.

"Now we see if your plan works, General," emitted the Nighteagle.

Ulfenkerki pointed to a place at the wall he was facing, a hundred and fifty yards away, and said to the Nighteagle, "That spot right there—concentrate on that with your firepower. That's where their defenses are the weakest, and that's where we'll break into town first."

"They have their soldiers spread way too thin in that spot, I'm assuming?"

"Exactly. As soon as we penetrate town, I'll order second-degree, heavy attack, and lump up soldiers where we've gotten through."

The Nighteagle made haste, relaying the plan to as many machine operators and infantry as he could.

With concentration unfailing, the soldiers began their assault. Resolved to live through the day, the infantrymen worked their way up through the bowels of the siege tower, and faced the enemies at the top. Most had gotten hit with rocks on their way up.

The survivors who made it to the top jumped down from the wall to the other side, into town. The Garobansurov soldiers making it into town first searched out a place to hide so they could wait until more allies were able to join them. Taking on the brunt of the Molisian force with low numbers wouldn't be such a wise undertaking.

Upon seeing what he'd hoped would happen, Ulfenkerki ordered second-degree, heavy attack, and lumped up soldiers at the successful tower. Time wasn't on their side, so it was absolutely crucial the soldiers got to the successful tower before the Molisians could react.

Ulfenkerki pointed and shouted, "Hurry! Hurry! It's imperative you get to that tower and over the wall. We have vulnerable soldiers inside town."

The soldiers who could hear their leader's command ran as fast as they could towards the tower, proudly grasping an unmatched sense of duty.

The Nighteagle again trotted over to the Black Bear. "Opening stages are going pretty well I would say, thanks in part to your decoy towers and noise contrivances."

"They are," returned Ulfenkerki, "but the battle is young, and I'm sure the tides will turn many times, before the victor is identified."

"Stupid tides."

Four hundred soldiers per wall, plus an additional 400 to the successful tower, were unleashed during second-degree, heavy attack. Ulfenkerki didn't want to send too many up through the successful tower at that moment, as to make it obvious to the Molisians scattered throughout town what was going on. But, of course, he didn't want to deploy too little.

Ulfenkerki's timing was impeccable.

When the new batch of warriors reached the successful tower, they scaled it as orderly as humanly achievable. The Molisians reacted to their weak spot, but under-reacted in the long run. Breaking over them relentlessly, the Garobansurovians faced wave upon wave of rocks, arrows, and metal objects of all shapes and sizes, as they climbed up through the tower. Dead bodies had to be removed from the inside of the tower from below, so they could continue the ascension. Carnage was strewn everywhere.

Eventually half of the ascension force made it to the top and hooked up with the force that had made it through during first-degree, heavy attack. There was a decent-sized group of Garobansurovian soldiers fighting on the inside of town now, centralized by the successful tower. There were also Garobansurovians scattered on the other three sides of town, who'd valiantly made it up the not-so successful towers. They all tried to link up with their compatriots.

"Well, old buddy, are you ready to get dirty?" Ulfenkerki asked the Nighteagle as he watched the last of the second-degree, heavy attackers disappear over the wall. "It's time for the rest of us to go in, time to order the big one—third-degree, heavy attack."

"I'm as ready as I'll ever be," replied the General, pulling his sword out of its scabbard.

Ulfenkerki informed everyone around him third-degree, heavy attack was about to commence. The Nighteagle notified the immediate catapult and ballistae operators to keep firing until most of the troops were over the wall and then to join the fray themselves. The machine operators further away were advised beforehand to follow the lead of those nearest. A chain of notification. Everything was thought of. Ulfenkerki and the Nighteagle were no rookies when it came to warfare.

Ulfenkerki signaled for the commencement of the third-degree, heavy attack flag sequence. The rest of the Garobansurovian army, minus the catapult and ballistae operators, ran fiercely towards the Sarwan walls and the siege towers. Most aimed towards the proven tower. Underneath their own projectiles and through their enemy's, they ran, soldiers and officers. Rayton led his archers into siege towers as well.

The third-degree, heavy attack charge drove the crows even further away. It was said it took years for them to return. Those more sensible knew this to be an exaggeration.

"ISN'T A FOOLPROOF plan supposed to be foolproof? How are they getting in?" yelled Gamald.

An unusually astute soldier answered, "There's a spot on the other side of town, where they seem to be breaking our defenses."

"How are they doing that?"

"I have no idea, sir."

Gamald was furious, but he didn't panic. Along with Ulfenkerki, he too had an assortment of tricks up his sleeve. The first thing he implemented wasn't a trick—tricks were to come—more so a particular soldier, two particular soldiers to be exact. Two incredibly talented fighting machines—the best southern Molisia had to offer. "Grunt, Roar," Gamald hollered.

The two aforementioned walked up to their leader. Grunt asked, "What is it?" Yes, Grunt and Roar had the ability to fashion sentences.

Gamald commanded, "Grunt, Roar, I need you two to go to the other side of town, and put an end to this. Kill every Garobansurovian you see!"

"Yes, sir," they said, confidently, in unison.

And just like that, Gamald's temper was subdued. He was certain the problem at the other end of town would be extinguished. His two finest warriors had never failed him. He could now afford to wait until later in the battle to reveal his hidden cards.

THE BLACK BEAR, followed by the Nighteagle, ascended the siege tower, trying to avoid being hit on the head by objects accelerated by gravity. The successful tower was crammed full of bodies in motion, all trying to get to the top as fast as possible.

Despite eerie echoes of death reverberating through the tower, soldiers persisted onwards and upwards. Nobody noticed or were affected by the chilling sounds of misery more than the generals. Nevertheless, they pushed forward and eventually reached the top of the wall alive.

With maximum aggressiveness and no reserve, Ulfenkerki and the Nighteagle drew their swords and searched out the nearest foes. They fought the same way they did when they were twenty years younger, or at least that's what it felt like to them.

By the time all of the surviving third-degree, heavy attack soldiers including catapult and ballistae operators had entered the city, censuses were level. Both retained 4,000 fighters. Garobansurov had been diminished by a greater percentage, but now at least they were fighting on even terms. That is to say, *even* terms, until Grunt and Roar reached the primary battle scene.

Ulfenkerki had defeated three rivals before noticing the gaps in the battlefield Grunt and Roar were creating. No one survived very long near the pair. It was as if they were black holes, devouring as they saw fit. The General pointed to the problem, and yelled out to Rayton, "Focus your arrows on those two."

Rayton yelled back, "Yes, sir!"

To many it seemed once Rayton and his archers got inside the wall, they weren't hitting their marks. They especially couldn't bring down Grunt or Roar. Even Chad Loytin, the best archer in eastern Garobansurov, couldn't do it. Grunt and Roar seemed impervious to arrows. Ulfenkerki was baffled at the development, but fought on.

An aggressor charged the Black Bear from his blindside, attempting a neck stab, but missed. Luckily for Ulfenkerki, he could practically see out of his ears. It took the wily general forty-five seconds to defeat the Molisian, only to have another immediately replace. Good thing the Black Bear possessed remarkable stamina to go along with his excellent peripheral vision.

Meanwhile, the Nighteagle organized those nearby to band up and attempt a flanking maneuver around Grunt and Roar. The pair was only stupid in terms of vocabulary. They were otherwise intelligent in way of mathematics. They knew right away where the Nighteagle would try to gain an edge. Grunt and Roar thwarted the Nighteagle's company by systematizing a counter-move of their own. So instead of gaining an advantage, the Nighteagle gained nothing for his efforts.

The skin of battle was penetrated. Now, it was the muscle's turn to face pressure.

The conflict managed to break up into separate isolated skirmishes, but the battle's hub was still centered around the successful siege tower and Grunt and Roar.

Gamald watched from a distance, like a coward, as did Leedle.

The Nighteagle won against an unusually tenacious adversary, the struggle of endurance being the longest single fight he'd ever faced. He felt like a million gitis with the effort.

Ulfenkerki was faring well too, but the army as a whole was beginning to get overwhelmed by Molisia, namely Grunt and Roar. Every once in a while Ulfenkerki would hear, "grrrr," and "rooaaar," in the distance, over the noise of mêlée. He'd ask himself how they were going to manage to defeat the two beasts, if it was even possible to do so. Soldier after soldier went up against Grunt and Roar, every one of them defeated. And every Garobansurovian killed by Grunt and Roar was laughed at by Gamald. A coward staying out of sight, hidden behind a doorway.

Things were looking grim for Garobansurov. Their numbers had dwindled down to 3,000 soldiers, while Molisia had 3,400.

Ulfenkerki had fought his way to the Nighteagle. Mid sword-swing, he said, "Five hundred giti bet: winner is who kills either of those two monsters over there. Grunt and Roar I believe their compatriots are calling them."

"You're on, but I have no idea how I would do it."

"Neither do I."

Reliably consistent in winning battles right from the start, Ulfenkerki encountered a new feeling—the gloomy possibility of defeat. He began taking chances during his fights he normally wouldn't have. He surveyed the landscape, his opponents, his allies, looking for an advantage—any advantage. He found none.

Then, when hope was fleeting, something tremendous happened. A face was seen exiting the siege tower at the top of the wall—a new face. A face that every Garobansurovian soldier knew well and was happy to see—Jason Thorncat's face. And behind him, the rest of the soldiers who accompanied in the capturing of Anolski.

Jason came down from the wall, and worked his way through the chaos to Ulfenkerki.

Ulfenkerki laid his free hand on Jason's shoulder and said, "Good timing."

"I see we're losing. Hopefully we can do something about that."

"I hope so, too. Our biggest liabilities are those two hulking lugs over there slicing and hacking their way through our lines, as if we're made of butter."

Jason eyed up Grunt and Roar, and sighed. "And our assets?"

"Pretty much only the fact we made it into town." The Black Bear pierced his challenger through the breastbone and into the lung. "And that my sword is still sharp apparently."

"That seems to be so. I guess we could have fewer assets," Jason chuckled.

"True. I'm glad you made it."

"Me too, General," replied Jason, just before leaving his leader's side to search for someone with whom to clash.

The Sarwans knew their town would never be the same. The roads were drifting into a shade of red, the structures were getting badly damaged, and the eyes of the children were losing innocence, becoming irreversibly acquainted with death. As long as Gamald lost power and they got their city back, Sarwa's inhabitants would rejoice. Most of the villagers who couldn't wield a weapon watched from the insides of their homes, hoping and praying for survival.

Jason's muscles were relatively fresh, so he took to battle with utmost energy. In fact, his first opponent barely had the chance to look Jason in the eyes, before his own were closed forever. And another, expecting greatness, fell short of those expectations, by receiving too many sword wounds from the lieutenant.

Even Jason's right-hand man, Gregg Hogarty, was finding his own ways to win quickly—wins that wouldn't have come so easily for a weaker soldier. During one of those fights, Gregg had been pitted against a strong chap with a giant war hammer, but by outmaneuvering him, Hogarty claimed the conquest.

The tides were beginning to turn. The Sarwans regained hope. Twenty minutes of battle time with Jason and his squadron added to the fold was what it took for the Garobansurov army to once again even the numbers.

Gamald didn't like what he was witnessing at all. Jason and his crew emerging into battle wasn't a part of Gamald's plan. The general was determined to undergo only an ephemeral balancing of the scales. "I believe it's now my turn to show my cards," Gamald said to Leedle. "Let's go present our ace in the hole."

Gamald and Leedle rose from their cover and snuck their way into the fight. To where exactly they snuck was unanticipated by almost everyone, for they crept onto the Garobansurov side of the battle, and met with Archer-General Rayton and Chad Loytin.

"Your troop has done an excellent job today of missing their targets," Gamald said to Rayton. "I could see that plain as day from where I was. It's time to reveal your new allegiance."

Secretly for a month, Gamald and Rayton had worked on bartering a deal, using emissaries. Rayton wasn't happy with his financial situation in the Garobansurov army, and Gamald yearned to spring a trap on Ulfenkerki and the Nighteagle. Gamald knew Sarwa would eventually face an assault, and he wanted all the help he could get. The terms of the deal: Rayton and all his archers, including Chad Loytin, would disloyally switch sides in the battle, while Rayton and his crew would gain lands in New Molisia. Rayton and Loytin would also receive ranks and titles. On paper, it was a good deal for both parties, a cold-blooded deal.

"I am ready, sir," voiced Rayton. "I've the perfect plan to catch them all off guard."

"Beautiful, I love it. Let's see it in action."

Gamald and Leedle stood back and watched the unleashing of his secret weapon, his ace in the hole.

Rayton nodded to Chad, then, gave a signal to the rest of his archers.

Inconspicuously, the archers grouped together in a tight pack, and shifted closer to the Molisian side—a coordinated movement they'd practiced several times in Thraug. When close enough to their new associates, they let their arrows fly at their old ones, this time not trying to miss. The Molisian soldiers had all been informed beforehand of the impending side-switching, so they knew to welcome Rayton's company with open arms.

Widespread devastation and panic ran rampant throughout Garobansurov's ranks, because of Gamald's secret plan. A hundred soldiers were stuck by arrows in their backs before anyone even realized what was happening.

When Ulfenkerki saw what had happened he searched out the Nighteagle as quickly as he could for brainstorming.

"That traitorous coward," Ulfenkerki roared to the Nighteagle. "I hope I'm the one to meet him on the battlefield."

The Nighteagle replied, "I hope you are too, for his sake, as I'd show no mercy, probably ripping his eyeballs straight out from their sockets, and feeding them to him. Do you have any ideas on how to slow this unexpected hemorrhaging?"

"None to completely stop it, but I've one idea that'll give us some time, time enough only for a miracle to happen. The best thing to do is isolate the archers from the infantry, and try to kill them separately. We'll organize a fly-by-night platoon, whose function will be to act as a human wedge. Maybe then, we can get some separation. Without the infantry near, protecting them, the archers will be somewhat vulnerable."

"Yes, good thinking. I'll get the platoon together."

Three minutes after the plan was devised, the plan was realized. The platoon formed by the Nighteagle was most competent. Driving a wedge between Rayton's archers and their new Molisian friends wasn't going to be easy, so utmost competence was required. It was an extremely difficult mission, but it was the only thing that could be done in that situation, given the parameters.

Luckily for Garobansurov, Grunt and Roar were on the other side of the battlefield. If they weren't, the plan would've gone sour rather quickly.

At the wedge's point, leading the way, were Jason and Gregg, competence personified.

Thrusting forward, Jason murmured to his fellow point man, "Watch the guy donning the yellow emblem on his sleeve, Gregg. He looks to be baiting you."

"Thank you, Jason."

Jason was correct about the subterfuge, and because Gregg saw it coming, he was able to easily defeat the man and his yellow emblem.

Jason and Gregg conjured every sword maneuver they knew in order to accomplish the task required of them by the generals. They pushed with all their might.

When Jason and Gregg reached the far end of the fray, they realized they'd survived the drive, and that the wedge was doing a decent job of separating the archers from the infantry. Next, Jason and Gregg intended to start work on the vulnerable archers. When the archers noticed the separation, they switched from bows to close-quarter weapons, the usage of which they were no slouches. But the archers were certainly not as proficient with close-range weapons as the close-range specialists they were about to face. Jason and Gregg charged into the archer formation with rage.

Ultimately, the plan was working, the wedge was doing what it was supposed to do—keeping the Garobansurovians from getting annihilated. However, it wasn't designed to keep Garobansurov from losing soldiers faster than their adversary.

Ulfenkerki and the Nighteagle were waging battle near the wedge. They were staying alive—*barely*.

Amidst the panic, Ulfenkerki managed to say a few words: "Looks like you found the right man to lead the wedge platoon."

"I didn't find anything, he found me," responded the Nighteagle

"He tends to do that. A fine soldier, my first lieutenant is."

"Now that we bought some time, hopefully our fortune will be propitious, and we'll think of something to turn the tables again, or better yet, a miracle will happen."

"The bad news is I can't think of anything to turn the tables, plus, it's seeming no beneficial miracles are presenting themselves," noted the Black Bear.

"Neither can I think of anything; and, yes, no miracles within sight," returned the Nighteagle, as he painfully blocked an incoming rock thrown at him from someone, somewhere in the distance.

"I don't think we're going to win this one."

"Seems that way, old friend."

CHAPTER 23

WHEN RAYTON'S ARCHERS were added to the Molisian side, Molisia swelled to 3,000 strong, while Garobansurov sank to 2,500. During the confusion of the Rayton switch-over, Garobansurov had lost another 250. The Thorncat wedge put a halt to immediate substantial depletion, but it didn't keep Garobansurov from losing soldiers at a higher rate than Molisia. Grunt and Roar's presence on the battlefield was too much of an advantage for Molisia.

Gamald was aware of the numbers, and very self-assured the victory would eventually be his. His confidence grew exponentially when he was approached by one of his wall-soldiers and heard what he had to say. "General Gamald, sir, I thought you'd like to know I spotted your second batch of homeland reinforcements emerging from the distant woods line. From what I saw, they were all in full armor, and ready to fight."

"Excellent, excellent. When they arrive at the wall, open the gate for them immediately."

"Yes, sir."

A GAROBANSUROVIAN SOLDIER overheard the information given to Gamald by the wall-soldier, and relayed it directly to Ulfenkerki and the Nighteagle. Upon hearing the news, Ulfenkerki sighed and said, "It appears we're definitely facing defeat now."

"Looks as if that's to be so," agreed the Nighteagle.

GENERAL GAMALD ORNAMENTED by his typical cocky grin, laid back and prepared himself for the show—a show he thought would be nothing but relaxing entertainment. But he and everyone else in Sarwa were unaware that the second wave of reinforcements had been wiped out at Gravividon. Those coming out of the woods were warriors nobody expected.

They say when Gamald learned of this information one could physically see the overflowing fury escaping his body.

TWENTY MINUTES BEFORE the wall-soldier relayed his information to Gamald, Mick and Dave approached Sarwa from the northwest. They halted their team just before leaving the cover of the trees. The thirty-one were excited their long walk from Gravividon was complete, much of which had been run. Having enough energy in reserve to fight with passion and intensity, the battalion was poised.

"Hopefully, because we're clad in many pieces of Molisian armor, they'll mistake us for their homeland reinforcements, and let us promenade right through the front gate, unheeded," said Dave, with a chuckle. He spent a second thinking of how farfetched it'd be for this to happen.

Mick commented, "I guess Plan B will be for us to climb up/through one of the siege towers they have wheeled up to the walls."

Both Mick and Dave stared at Sarwa for a minute, gathering adrenaline, imagining the battle taking place inside. They could hear the fighting transpiring within the walls, but couldn't see any of it, except for high-arching arrows. Mick and Dave were extremely glad to have arrived before the battle was over, hoping they weren't too late to help out.

Hawk and Leopard averted their eyes from Sarwa and looked to their company, whom they undeniably held in high esteem. They pondered some of the memories they'd shared with each—Krell-nor, Brom, Carrie, Loyd, Tom, the rest of the Quintaga clan, and the miners— Tysons, Bergs, and Dearns.

After their moment of pleasant reflection, Dave and Mick's mindsets turned serious, and they called out for all members of their companionship to congregate near. During the last leg of the journey, Mick and Dave had prepared an inspirational speech to deliver to their unit just before their storming of Sarwa. The party gathered and grew in attentiveness.

Mick spoke: "Gather round, gather round, everyone. Fierce warriors! We have traveled far, and have reached our destination. The battle now lies before us." Mick took a deep breath, and passionately began his part of the prepared speech, which he tried his best to speak iambically, and in a melody pleasant to the ears:

"There comes a time in all our lives when you face that one uncertainty.

That one unknown destiny.

You only get one chance—do you take it?

You only get one life—do you trade it?

There is only a single past—will you regret it?

You only have one mind—must you betray it?

Do you stand down—or do you stand proud?

Your fate is what you formulate."

Almost instantaneously, not missing a beat, Dave took over in the same pitch pattern:

"When faced with human adversity, there are three things you can do.

You can flee, you can hide, or you can fight.

A lot of the time it may be better to just flee or hide.

But let this be the hour when we stand and fight!

This is our one chance—let's take it.

It's our life—we ought not trade it.

Undeniably, one past—we won't regret it.

You each have one mind—please trust it.

We only have one destiny, one chance—let's take it.

One chance—let's take it.

The final line was cried out by Mick and Dave in unison:

By God, one chance—let's take it!

Resuming normal speech pattern, but still with much passion, Mick said loudly, "This town is facing oppression and persecution by the hands of a tyrant— let's take it!"

Mick and Dave raised their swords to the sky, while everyone cheered.

Black needles extended, Leopard and Hawk led their crew out of the cover of the forest, and towards Sarwa. They all were ready and fully energized, every single one having reached a profound emotional level because of Mick and Dave's speech, even its deliverers. Hawk and Leopard were glad it was effective.

Because the Molisians thought it was the second group of reinforcements finally arriving, they didn't bother firing any projectiles at them, so it took practically no effort for Mick and Dave's platoon to reach the city gates. When Mick saw the gates opening, he looked at Dave to say, "How about that?"

"I wasn't looking forward to Plan B, so I'll welcome this turn of events."

When the gates were opened just far enough for a person to get in, Mick and Dave looked back at their soldiers, smiled confidently, and to them Dave whispered just loud enough for them to hear, "Let's take it."

Led by Dave, all thirty-one ran through the gates, single file, with their weapon of choice drawn.

With the new addition, the Battle for Sarwa proceeded past muscle and now finally reached its heart.

The Molisians near the gate were all shocked beyond belief when who they thought were their allies started attacking them. The level of disbelief was only trumped by how fast they were being defeated.

Mick, Dave, and their team, after destroying all opposition at the gate, swiftly moved to where the main battle was transpiring, to put surprise on all the faces there.

Those that either grew up watching Mick and Dave's sword-fighting style, or had the apt ability to have recently seen the style, and perfectly memorize it, namely Jason and Ulfenkerki, identified the fact Mick Thraiker and Dave Ghrere had just joined the fray. Ulfenkerki and Jason reacted in accordance.

The Black Bear knew a wake would form by the introduction of Mick and Dave to the battlefield, so he gathered everyone near him to flank that wake from both sides. Happening fast, the stratagem was calculated to perfection, achieved through some luck, because Grunt and Roar weren't in the area to stop it.

Jason was able to work towards Mick and Dave, having switched away from his wedge assignment. Luckily, most of the treasonous archers had already been successfully wiped out. Rayton was still alive, but because of the clear target on his head, he, too, would hopefully be wiped out soon. Same with Chad Loytin.

Ulfenkerki and his newly formed congregation battled hard, supplying potent flanks for Mick, Dave, and their squad. Vigor renewed, Jason also arrived at the scene with a team of his own.

Neither Gamald nor any of his battle advisors had a way to stop the new Garobansurovian offensive rush. Trapped Molisians were panicking everywhere. At the moment, Molisia still had more soldiers, but for the first time since the battle began, Molisia was losing soldiers faster than Garobansurov.

"Amazing, Dave, did you see how fast Ulfenkerki and Jason formed those flanks?" yelled Mick, as he swung his sword.

"I sure did. I've actually come to not be surprised by any mode of brilliance performed by those two."

"Surprised, no. Electrified, yes."

Krell-nor and Brom were close behind Mick and Dave, fighting with as much intensity as they could summon. Even Carrie was doing her share of sword maneuvering, standing beside her husband. She'd grown a lot since the incident with the merchant thieves. Loyd knew his wife was moderately strong with a sword, so he wasn't surprised in the least every time she made a soldier lose his/her life.

Seeming effortlessly, Mick lunged at a foe and eliminated with exactitude. Nearby, Dave took a step backwards to avoid a hammer swing, a deadly arc executed by someone Dave wasn't really fighting himself. He rejoined his enemy in combat, who also had to avoid the swinging hammer.

Jason Thorncat's eyes bugged out when he saw Gregg completely decapitate an adversary, having no idea Gregg's sword was sharp enough and capable of enough momentum for such an act. "I take it you didn't sharpen your sword yourself this time?" Jason shouted to Gregg.

Covered in blood, Gregg yelled back, "Not this time. I split some wood the other night in exchange for the apparently excellent service."

"You'll have to introduce me to this skilled sharpener, if we get out of this alive. I doubt I could get my sword sharp enough to do that."

"Will do."

Brom Quintaga opportunistically grabbed a bow from a fallen soldier, found high ground, and used it to make a few more fallen soldiers. In the interim, Krell-nor watched his back. They couldn't deploy the arrangement for very long, due to the close quarters, but while it was deployed, it sure worked out well—father and son successfully fighting side-by-side. It would've been hard to find a soldier in the middle of battle as happy as Brom. He was relishing an experience that for the longest time he thought he'd never know again.

The numbers were now finally even—1,500 for each country. All the best warriors who'd begun the Battle of Sarwa were still alive, even the powerful Grunt and Roar. General Gamald and Leedle were again hiding like cowards, watching the tides turning against them. It was in Leedle's best interest to not say much about the current affair, he'd known Gamald long enough to know not to speak a whole lot when things were dire.

Darkness was approaching, and so was the understanding of just how epic the struggle had become.

If Sarwa hadn't been the gateway of the Garobansurovian northeast, the lives lost wouldn't have been worth the reward. But it was the gateway, an important step on Molisia's climb to the Capital, so the battle waged on. Many more Garobansurovian lives would be lost, if the gateway wasn't retaken. Both sides were stubborn, neither wanting to relinquish Sarwa.

Standing on a dead someone's back to gain greater vision of the field, the traitor Chad Loytin found a target, notched his arrow, drew back, aimed, and released. His target was well chosen, for his target was none other than the Nighteagle. An unfortunate occurrence for the Nighteagle, one that never would've happened if he hadn't lost sight of Chad, having become entangled with a skilled combatant. Chad wanted the Nighteagle, and was in the right place at the right time. The well-shot arrow pierced the right lung.

"Aaahhh," hollered the wounded legend, falling to the ground.

The sound of his oldest and dearest friend in agony sent Ulfenkerki to the bleeding general's side. Jason in fact saw who loosed the arrow, reacted quickly, and ran after Chad.

The Black Bear gasped at seeing his friend's puncture, bent down, and quickly wrapped the Nighteagle's wound with a bandage he had tucked away for emergencies. "It looks pretty serious. I don't think you'll survive this one, like the time you took that arrow back at Aberglath."

"It was bound to happen sooner or later," murmured the Nighteagle, wincing.

"Not to you though, my friend. You're too ornery to die."

The Nighteagle tried to laugh, but couldn't. "At least I'm going to die a happy man."

"What do you mean, happy? Even though it seems momentum has swung in our favor, the battle isn't won yet."

The Nighteagle took a deep breath, looked to the sky one last time, and then looked Ulfenkerki straight in the eyes. "I'm dying happy, because I know you're not coming with me."

The Black Bear witnessed the Nighteagle's final breath, and held his composure. Grieving would wait. That moment was reserved for a different task—the imperative business of searching out the man responsible for the injustice. Not the person who shot the arrow, the student, but the teacher, Rayton.

Rayton was easy to find, because he was aiding his pupil, Chad Loytin, who currently had his hands full fighting with Jason.

Meanwhile, in the middle of the battlefield was where Mick and Dave were leaving their mark. They battled wildly opponents from all sides. A gap around them suddenly formed. The pair noticed something was different.

Time stood eerily still. Mick, Dave and their swords had just met the clearing that'd existed around Grunt and Roar since they'd been unleashed. The confrontation that would come to be known as the deciding factor for control of Garobansurov's entire eastern half was to begin.

The Garobansurov/Molisia war was boiling.

For the reason of minimizing collateral damage, the four-man battle remained a four-man battle, until it was over. Grunt, Roar, Hawk, and Leopard all knew the fight was pivotal. Each allied pair had been studying the other throughout the battle.

"Grrrrrr."

"Roaaar."

None of the four desired to have to watch their back, so each chose an opponent, and separated just enough so they didn't have to. Mick faced Grunt, as Dave was pitted against Roar.

Mick charged aggressively at the mammoth, but Grunt wasn't stupid—he knew it was more of a false charge, so he waited patiently and calmly.

As Grunt expected, Mick slowed his approach and performed a few more sensible maneuvers. Grunt blocked Mick's offensive effectively and formed a huge swing of his weapon at Mick's head. Mick moved out of the way and while off balance cleverly tried to bash Grunt's leg with his shield. He succeeded in landing the bash, but accomplished nothing beneficial. It was like hitting a large, robust tree with a melon sized rock. All that resulted was the birthing of a solid thud. Regrouping from the failure, Mick crossed his eyes for adrenalin, regathered his stance, and readied himself for the next progression of moves.

Meanwhile, at the onset of his bout, Dave found himself having to duck an airborne sword. Roar had picked one from a stiff and hurled it at his head. The sword missed, opening the door for Dave to run and close the gap, so no further airborne objects came his way.

Staring Roar in the eyes, Leopard sized up his opponent, and concluded it was a complete mismatch in terms of size and strength. Dave hoped his other attributes would be enough.

With maximum force, he swung the black needle at the giant's waist, but it was interrupted by equal force. Grunt countered with an elbow to Dave's face, breaking Dave's nose. Leopard was in agony, but he regained composure, and went back to work.

At a sizable distance from Dave and Mick, Brom and Krell-nor were still fighting side-by-side. "There's a guy coming from your left."

"Let him come, I'm ready. I haven't felt this strong in ages," replied Brom. With grace and power, he ran towards the soldier, of whom Krell-nor was speaking, just as he was able to do ages ago.

Krell-nor looked at Carrie. "I actually don't think I've ever seen him move that fast."

"Neither have I. And we've been in quite a few situations requiring swiftness of foot, that's for sure."

"Oh, don't I know it, Carrie. This is his day, and he recognizes it as so. Let that gentleman shine," said the son with a warm, radiating smile.

"Let him shine indeed," said the granddaughter with a smile to match.

Brom continued to shine, but as for Sarwa, starlight—not Brom—was now supplying the majority of its illumination. Winter chill had finally enveloped town.

Jason Thorncat was still battling Chad Loytin, the latter realizing his opponent was almost as good with a sword as he was with his bow. The pair fought violently for many minutes, but in the end, Jason terminated the traitor's life with a sense of satisfaction. "There'll be no more switching sides for you, only a switch from this side to hell."

Gregg Hogarty barely missed catching up with Jason to help in the fight with Chad. He'd some hard-hitting fights of his own with which to deal before reaching his friend. But he was there in time to hear Jason's words to the dead Chad Loytin. "Well spoken, Mr. Thorncat. A little cornier than I would've gone with, but still effectual."

"Thank you, I guess." Jason smiled, chuckled, and together the two of them searched out the next Molisians to fight.

General Ulfenkerki needed this. He needed to kill Rayton himself to avenge the death of his best friend. The Black Bear met Rayton on the battlefield. "You chose the wrong side. Your life ends here."

"We will see about that."

In the old days, the Black Bear had a few more sword tricks up his sleeve to end a fight quickly, but no longer. He was going to have to fight for every inch of ground in order to gain the upper hand on Rayton.

The clash had begun by it separating greatly from the Jason/Chad skirmish. It also began with a flood of swings and blocks from both, which did nothing more than dull their blades.

Rayton attempted a flurry of sword tip lunges, only nicking flesh once. Ulfenkerki ignored the nick and the ensuing blood.

Recalling a move he remembered seeing the Nighteagle perform once when they were much younger, Kermoy Ulfenkerki aimed to repeat. Before employing the move, he spoke to his opponent. "Just as you betrayed your country, I'm going to betray fighting fair." Ulfenkerki kicked Rayton square in the balls. Rayton laughed upon hearing the Black Bear's boot clanging against his genital armor. But the kick to the groin was just the decoy. All in one fluid movement, and off balance from the kicking, Ulfenkerki chopped off as much of his own sweaty, bloody hair as he could, and threw it into Rayton's eyes, while he was still laughing about the kick to the balls. With his adversary squirming for vision, Ulfenkerki performed the killing blow—a shield to the temple. He was prepared to stab Rayton into the heart next, but the shield blow was enough to eradicate the defector. He sighed in achievement, caught his breath, and joined Jason, who'd just defeated the teacher's student, and Gregg, who'd just joined Jason.

The Tysons, Burgs, and Dearns were also doing well fighting for their country; their losses so far were minimal. A person would've never thought they were ordinary miners.

The Quintaga crew were holding their own as well. Undeniably, they were a family blessed by a cornucopia of physical attributes.

Five minutes were hooked onto Mick Thraiker and Dave Ghrere's epic clash with the Molisian battle masters, Grunt and Roar, with no end in sight. Against their better judgement, some of the other combatants spent a few moments watching the Mick/Dave/Grunt/Roar quartet fight. Witnessing such skill and incongruency in fighting styles was apparently mesmerizing.

Mick hoped biding his time would pay off. In theory, the larger man wearies first, but theory sometimes wasn't fact, and it seemed like this was one of those times. Grunt was an unbreakable machine—a finely tuned and inexhaustible war machine—the barricade blocking the only road. They both had the will, but whose was stronger.

Massive blow upon blow came crashing down on Mick. He escaped them all, barely. Hawk used Black Needle to the best of his abilities, swinging as fast as lighting, practically leaving vapor trails. His swordplay was performed with the utmost precision, the sword staying firm in his hands, thanks to the unconventional sword handle. The black needle grip kept true when it mattered most.

Three more minutes elapsed, and Mick knew what he had to do—nothing complicated, nothing genius. He simply switched into his final gear. He forced half his blood to his face, so he could tense every facial muscle. He gathered all his hate, all his love, intentionally playing with fire. His own fire.

They stared at each other, one's eyes cold as ice, the other burning with rage.

Moments before Mick had switched gears, Dave could see out of the corner of his eye blow upon blow crashing down on Mick, and him narrowly escaping them. He wished he could help, but now had more than he could handle with grace. Much more.

Roar let out his trademark vocalization, and stutter-stepped away from Dave's sword lunge. Roar countered the lunge by kneeing Dave's quadricep. Limping, Leopard backstepped to gain time to walk off the injury. Dave was successful in subduing the injury, and proceeded onto his next series of moves—a swing at the head, a change of levels, and a swing at the waist. Both swings had missed.

Dave ended up on the ground, after dodging a potentially fatal swing from Roar. While struggling to stand up, he couldn't help but eye Roar's legs—great pillars of strength. Seems those things take up as much space as trees, and just as hard to bring down. Due to his observance, Dave decided against a tripping tactic, instead going with a sword slice upon reaching his feet. However, that was just about as successful as a tripping attempt would've been. So rather than attempting another slice, Dave tried an uppercut with his sword, which was slightly more effective, drawing a little blood. It was the last cut made on Roar for what seemed like forever.

After forever, the next piece of Roar Dave managed to remove was a chunk near the eye, stolen by the crosspiece of his sword. A lesser man would've gotten stunned by the hit, but not Roar, it didn't faze him in the slightest. Like Mick, Dave knew in order to win the fight he had to let his mind go to a place where few dared to venture, a place that once visited couldn't be unvisited.

Coincidentally, Hawk and Leopard simultaneously experienced a battle mode they'd not yet known. A mode that heightened their senses, and the minds controlling those senses. For the first time in their lives, Grunt and Roar found themselves backpedaling in avoidance. Mick and Dave's concentration infinite, their blades whirling death. The grips of the black needles held, almost as if by magic.

When Grunt and Roar had no room left to continue backwards, they made their last stands. With their backs against the wall, they fought with dignity, they fought for their country, they fought for their lives.

In the end, Grunt and Roar's final stands failed, and they cried out their last words.

"Grrrrrrr."

"Rooaaar."

The backbone of the Molisian army defending Sarwa was Grunt and Roar, so with them gone, Molisia's stability was lost. They could no longer stand. Gamald knew this. He didn't actually see Grunt and Roar get killed, but he knew they did, feeling the difference in the battle.

Still hiding with Leedle, Gamald spoke. "We must escape, follow me."

General Gamald hadn't realized how cold the night air really was. He and Leedle had been huddled against the warm outer wall of a heated building for a while. Shivering, the two made their attempt at flight.

Mick and Dave were once again fighting side by side. They looked off to the left, and could see the soldiers of their battalion were mostly still alive and battling together.

Soldier and civilian could easily see how much the Molisian army fell apart under Grunt and Roar's absences. In no time, the Molisians were overwhelmed, their numbers dwindling down to the hundreds, at which time most surrendered. When the last Molisian threw down his sword in capitulation, all the Sarwan residents watching from afar cheered.

Ulfenkerki was heartbroken, but proud his friend's last wish was officially realized. The Nighteagle's desire for his friend to make it through the battle hadn't exactly been an easy thing to accomplish.

Jason approached his general, and laid his hand on his shoulder, seeing the hurt in his eyes. "He was a great man, one of the best in Garobansurov."

"That he was. The best." Ulfenkerki related to Jason the Nighteagle's powerful last words, as a result, Jason was struck hard by emotion. The two of them shared a smile, as they walked towards the victorious army.

Both Mick and Dave could tell the other had just fought the toughest fight of their life, but neither felt the need to talk about it, for the eyes already said it all. Maybe some other day they'd talk about it. At that moment, they wanted to search out their battle companions to thank them for fighting so nobly. Conveniently, they were all already standing in a group.

To their platoon, Mick spoke in a joking tone. "Dave and I had only prepared a speech for the beginning of the battle, so if you were expecting one for the victory, you've got another thing coming."

They all roared with laughter. With a smile practically as large as his face, Krell-nor replied, "We'll wait, just go somewhere for a few hours to prepare one, and come back when it's all ready to go."

Dave and Mick laughed along with their squad. "And miss all this?"

When the laughter and additional one-liners died down, Dave spoke more seriously. "Thanks in part to you all, this section of Garobansurov will remain safe for a good long time."

Mick added, "We'd be glad to go into battle with any one of you, again, at any time. It was truly an honor."

Brom raised his hand in salute, and responded for them all. "Same here."

Jason, Gregg, and Ulfenkerki walked up to Mick, Dave, and their group. To Mick and Dave, General Ulfenkerki said, "Never in a million years, would I have anticipated what you two did. Grunt and Roar seemed indestructible. I was certain nobody was going to defeat them. Plus, the perfection in the timing of your squad's appearance was unprecedented. I've also heard just recently you two single-handedly recaptured Fort Gravividon. Is this true?"

"Yes, along with Krell-nor the Lucky, whom we picked up along the way, having rescued him from his cell within Gravividon," replied Mick.

Stitched by a tone of admiration, Ulfenkerki continued, "Unbelievable. Taking Fort Gravividon like you did, destroying their reinforcements, and making it back here in time to save our butts—simply a miracle. We certainly wouldn't have won here today, if it hadn't been for you, your leadership and your company." Ulfenkerki looked respectfully at every member of Dave and Mick's crew and shook their hands, nodding his head with the utmost approval.

Jason fixed his eyes on his childhood friends, Hawk and Leopard, and said, "There was a point in the battle when I thought to myself, of whom do I know that could possibly get around these virtually impassable barriers, Grunt and Roar. I couldn't help but think of you two. Then, coincidentally, out of the middle of nowhere, you showed up. Simply remarkable."

Dave responded, "You almost would've had to think a little harder. Things were a little too close for comfort."

"I bet. They were cutting through our defenses like we were hardly even there."

The Black Bear added, "I wouldn't be surprised if the news of what you two did reached the ears of the king himself. I'm positive it will. I'll tell him myself if I must. I wouldn't be astonished if he wanted to meet you in person, and give you medals or such."

Mick replied, "It would be nice to make the journey to the Capital again."

Gregg Hogarty spoke: "Was the last time you were at the Capital, Myothraces, the time you went to get your swords made?"

"Yup, it was. It's been so long," answered Mick. "Though, we don't need any special treatment. We risked our lives for what we believe. The same as the rest of you did."

"As modest as ever," emitted Jason.

Not really meaning to change the subject, Ulfenkerki said to Jason, "Gamald may have escaped to parts unknown, and normally I'd have you track him. But this time, what's best for Garobansurov is for you to attend the Nighteagle's funeral, along with the rest of the fallen soldiers'. We'll just let Gamald get away, for now."

"If that's your command, I will comply without question, sir."

The group talked of victory for a time; and then, they all helped in woefully moving the dead off the battlefield, and preparing them for funeral/burial.

The memorial service took place the next day, and all Sarwa attended. Ulfenkerki himself gave the eulogy for the Nighteagle. As was his nature, he was stoic in his delivery. The Black Bear tried his best to not shed a tear, speaking about all the fond memories. He succeeded right up until the very last sentence.

The other fallen soldiers, including notable warrior Steve Johnson, were given heartfelt eulogies by their closest friends. Also, the Molisian prisoners were allowed funeral services for their dead friends and family. Even enemies deserved respect.

After all the services, the deceased, Garobansurovian and Molisian, were buried. Each would get their own headstone.

Prepared with care by the thankful residents of Sarwa, the post-funeral/burial meal was consumed by all. It wasn't much, for most of the town's food was devoured by the Molisian army, but it was enough to eliminate grumbling stomachs. The townsfolk were assured food would be brought in from neighboring villages to help them get through the rest of winter.

Transforming away from the despair of interment, the new day began. It was departure day, and all of the town was up in commotion. Ulfenkerki wanted to get the army back to Thraug, before winter set in any further. Ulfenkerki's army was more than likely going to spend the rest of winter in Thraug, before igniting a new campaign—not including the detachment he was going to send to defend Gravividon, relieving the volunteers.

Jason and Gregg walked aimlessly around the army barracks, talking about the battle. They were already packed, and had time to kill before the army's withdrawal. For some reason that day, the pair was embedded by an extreme amount of curiosity, opening every non-residential door they could find. They found nothing of interest once through the doorways, that is until they discovered a certain room with a locked door, strangely far away from any other room.

Jason said, "I suppose we might as well see what's behind here, as long as we've already seen everything else."

"It's locked."

"Maybe it's locked for you, but not for me."

"I've got to see this. I do believe I've never seen you jimmy open a door before, Jason."

"This is an easy one," said Thorncat, as he pulled his sword out of its scabbard.

In no time, Jason had the lock open.

"I guess you were right, that did seem pretty easy."

Jason and Gregg walked into the room, and looked around. At seeing what was stuffed into a corner, Jason's eyes opened wide in astonishment. "I know exactly what this is, and to whom it belongs. If we hurry, we can catch him before he leaves."

Gregg stared at the items in the corner in amazement for quite some time. He touched them. It wasn't his first time seeing the items, but it was his first time touching them. He rushed to catch up with Jason, who was already halfway to his destination.

MICK, DAVE, BROM, and Krell-nor had finished packing for the trip, and were discussing their future plans, which was an exciting conversation, for they now all HAD futures. Dave was on the verge of asking Brom and Krell-nor if they had enough food for their journey home, when Jason Thorncat and Gregg Hogarty came running up, almost out of breath.

"Guys, guys," blurted Jason, "you all have got to come see this, especially you, Brom."

"This must be important, seeing as though you ran all the way here to tell us about it," said Mick.

"It sure is, follow me."

Ensconced in thrill, the quartet began following Jason and Gregg back to the room they'd just left. Even though there was no real reason to, they jogged part of the way.

After everyone had piled into the room, Jason spoke. "Well, here it is, sir. I knew right away what it was, and to whom it belonged."

The six stood in silence for at least ten seconds. The silence was bogged down, as if the awe the six felt was somehow holding it, keeping it from leaving the room.

Brom finally said something. "Sure is odd that nobody wore it into battle."

Mick replied, "Maybe they didn't want to scratch it. It does belong on a pedestal for all to gaze upon."

Dave chuckled. "Where have I heard that before."

"My armor looks like it's barely been touched," said Brom. "Actually, I just misspoke; this armor is no longer my armor. It was meant to be sold, so that I could attempt to rescue my son. But to my surprise, my son had already been rescued. So, it is my honor to present my armor to my son's rescuers: Mick Thraiker and Dave Ghrere. On the condition that you use at least two of them—not placing at least two on a pedestal. These three suits are yours. May they protect you, like you protected Krell-nor. And no being modest; I know that's your way. So, if you refuse, my feelings will be hurt."

Mick responded, "Well, in that case, we proudly accept this great gift. We'll wear them into battle, always thinking of your great mission to rescue your son."

Brom was happy everything had worked out, but at that moment he remembered something very important to him. Without a word, he left the group, to search for this something.

It didn't him take too long to find it, because he remembered right where it was. He was pleased to find it exactly where he last saw it. Brom untied the string holding the big, blue flower with the purple bow to the banister, and put the flower and its bow into his bag. It was his symbol of hope, when everything seemed lost. Even those toughest of character had room for sentiment.

Once Brom returned to the group, Krell-nor said to him, "Where did you hurry off to?"

"I had one last thing to grab before we took off." Brom showed the inside of his bag to his son, and said, "When all else went dark, this flower was the only thing yearning to illuminate."

"I'm happy you found it then."

"Me too." Brom smiled, and was ready to journey home.

Mick and Dave stood at the colorful courtyard adjacent to Sarwa's front gate, discussing their new armor. "I'm pretty sure he'll appreciate the gift. What he did for us was priceless. The man certainly deserves the third suit of armor."

"I'm sure he'll be very happy to receive it," agreed Mick.

Jason and Brom joined Mick and Dave in the pretty but blood-stained courtyard. Dave declared, "It is settled. For Old Man Johnson's contribution to the making of the Black Needles, we plan to present to him the third suit of armor for his collection of weapons and armor."

Brom remarked, "It's no doubt ironic how I nearly backtracked to Old Man Johnson's cabin as you suggested, to sell him the armor. But instead, I foolishly decided to make haste to Sarwa."

"It sure is."

"Funny how things work out," noted Mick.

Dave added, "Although, things may not have worked out if you had gone that route. If he had bought them, then, you wouldn't have gone to Sarwa. And if you hadn't been on that side of the country, you may not have linked up with Carrie and Loyd, then in turn, the rest of your family. Tom's party would've still ended up at Gravividon, but without you, Carrie and Loyd. Had Loyd not been there for me to hear his boot during your family's invasion, we all may've unknowingly killed each other in the dark. Plus, without the aid of the entirety of the Quintaga family, we may've lost the battle against the second wave of reinforcements, in which case Krell-nor wouldn't have been alive for you to successfully utilize your newly received funds in finding him."

Brom was awestruck at Dave's web of complexity. "It seems chaos really does sort out harmoniously in a way benefitting the decent."

"That seems to be so," agreed Dave.

The group stood in silence for a moment, happy in the thought the eastern half of Garobansurov would be safe for a time.

Having decided to go to Chalatore with Dave and Mick for a well-deserved bout of military leave, Jason double-checked his traveling gear.

Heartfelt farewells were said by/to those who cared for the Quintagas. Mick and Dave thanked Brom for the armor sets one final time, just before he and his crew departed Sarwa.

By mere coincidence, when Mick, Dave, and Jason were leaving Sarwa, the compound dwellers were also leaving, heading back to their mining community. The two groups decided to walk together for a while before having to split.

Just prior to stepping through Sarwa's gateway, the Hawk/Leopard/Thorncat trio said their goodbyes to Gregg and the Black Bear.

Ulfenkerki said, "Don't forget, Mick, Dave, at some point in the future, you may deservingly get medals or some other sort of formal recognition from those at the Capital."

"I guess we'll keep our eyes open for messengers," stated Dave.

"And also, before you leave, I'd like to say for one last time how much of a great honor it was to fight alongside the two of you. Not that I hope it happens, but I'll certainly take pleasure in going into battle again with you. And Jason, enjoy your vacation, you earned it, lieutenant."

"I will, sir," replied Jason.

Mick emitted, "The same goes for you, general. Before we part, I must ask, is it true why they call you the Black Bear, that you're as hairy as one?"

Ulfenkerki produced a deep laugh, and took off his shirt to reveal the truth. Dave, Mick, and Jason walked out of town, knowing something they hadn't known before.

CHAPTER 24

A S SARWA FADED in the distance, thoughts of home became more vivid. Jason was especially glad in knowing he was going to see his hometown again. Army life kept him too busy to venture there often.

After walking together for most of the day, another parting of ways was reached. Earnest goodbyes were said between the compound dwellers and Mick and Dave. The last thing said between them was, "I hope to see you again." And it was meant.

The journey back to Chalatore would end up being uneventful for the three of them, which was a good thing. They'd had enough exposure to danger for the time being. However, they did share long, compelling stories and gut-busting jokes the whole way.

Every once in a while, during the journey, Jason caught himself staring mindlessly at the armor from Brom. Who could blame him? The three sets were the finest and most beautiful pieces of handcrafted armaments in the land.

They traveled for many days, catching up on each other's entire lives, for all three had lives worth sharing.

With sore but stronger legs, the trio of friends finally made it back to their hometown, Chalatore. Mick and Dave realized nothing had changed. Even the tables used for the armwrestling tournament were still sitting in the town square, covered in snow. Most of the chairs were seemingly not sat on for weeks.

"Jason, would you like to come with us later to Old Man Johnson's cabin to present to him the armor?" asked Dave.

"Yes, I would. I don't even think I properly apologized for breaking into his house with you two when we were kids."

Dave replied, "He's well aware it was just the innocent endeavor of a child. I don't think an apology would be necessary. Besides, he's acquainted with your honorable service to Garobansurov, and will probably be humbled by your visit."

"I'll probably apologize anyway."

"Very well. We'll meet back here in a few hours, after we all meet up with our families."

Mick and Dave met with their respective families, and took the time to tell them the story of everything that happened while they were away.

At the designated time, Mick and Dave met back up with Jason, and they made the walk through the snow to Old Man Johnson's cabin. When they got there and went inside, the three observed it was as if they were expected. The cabin was neat and tidy, being hardly ever so tidy, and there was a table of refreshments all set up in the living room containing an assortment of nuts, fruits, sweets, and beverages.

"It seems like you're expecting someone," said Mick, as he embraced his friend.

"Oh, I figured the two of you would be stopping by soon," replied Johnson.

"How did you figure that? There are no tracks in the snow, signifying that you went into town and saw us."

"Old men always have their ways."

Dave curled his lips, and let out a half titter, "That they do." Proudly, Dave put his right hand on Jason's left shoulder, and said, "This is Jason Thorncat, second in command of General Ulfenkerki's army."

"I knew that too. I wouldn't forget one of your childhood best friends, and if I'm not mistaken, your cohort that time you broke in here to look at my collection."

"About that," Jason jumped in, "I am truly sorry."

Old Man Johnson let out a laugh. "Don't waste your time with such foolishness. I know you guys meant no disrespect."

Jason sighed relief. "That is true. It's good to see you again, sir."

"The honor is mine. I hear great stories down at the tavern of your accomplishments. I'd also heard you're quite the tracker."

"Thank you. I've been known to track a general or two through the snow."

Mick grabbed a beverage from the convenient table, and said, "You knew we were coming, but did you know why?"

"To visit with an old man in the twilight of his life, of course," replied Johnson.

"That's only half true."

"So, I'm not in the twilight of my life, then?"

Mick laughed, "Oh no, that you certainly are. We've come for another reason than to just visit."

While Mick was speaking, Jason went outside to retrieve the armor. Carrying it into the house, he couldn't help but admire its greatness one last time.

Spirited, Mick continued talking, even though Jason's arrival into the room with the armor was noisy and attention grabbing. Hawk divulged the story of everything that'd transpired since they left after the arm-wrestling tournament. Every detail of the story was told to Old Man Johnson. He spoke of all the battles, all the people they met, all the locales, everything—even the weather was spoken of slightly. Jason added to the story, by speaking of the events in which he was involved. Old Man Johnson laid back and listened closely. He loved a good story. At the end of the telling, Mick picked up the helmet from the armor pile Jason had laid on the corner chair, and said, "Now for the main reason we've come."

Mick handed the helmet to Mr. Johnson.

Johnson felt the exquisiteness of the helmet in his hands, and blurted, "So you didn't just come to tell me a story?"

"Nope," Dave replied, pulled out his black needle sword from its scabbard, and turned it over in his hands. "Remember the great favor you did for us long ago, supplying the means by which our swords were constructed."

"How could I forget? Those things are the hubs of most of *my* stories down at the tavern."

Old Man Johnson, Mick, Jason, and Dave laughed, after which Dave continued. "Anyways, we were bestowed three suits of the most incredible armor imaginable, the ones Mick spoke of in the narration of our travels. We decided it would be our pleasure to give you the third suit to add to your collection as a sort of repayment for what you did for us."

After setting the helmet down, Old Man Johnson eyed the rest of the suit. He truly was taken aback by the great gesture. "This is indeed the most monumental gift anyone has ever laid before me. I've never seen armor to its equal. You two guys are something else, let me tell you. I am blessed to have you in my life."

"Same for us."

"Today though, the card dealer in the sky has presented me with a different hand to play, a better hand. Even though the armor would certainly be the new centerpiece of my collection, I need to do something else with it. Something that will greatly help in ensuring the continuation of my most prized possession: my freedom. The armor needs to be used instead of gathering dust. And it needs to be used and owned by someone of utmost worth, the fine warrior standing over there." Old Man Johnson pointed at Jason Thorncat.

They all turned just in time to see Jason's jaw drop. He had a look on his face of pure astonishment. Never in Jason's wildest dreams did he think Mr. Johnson was going to say such words.

After some time spent shaking away the astonishment, Jason produced, "I don't know what to say. I've never been so surprised in all my life, nor have I heard such emphatic generosity."

Johnson declared, "Your whole life you've thought of everyone but yourself. Your country, your family, and your friends always come first to you. I've heard all the stories about you—more tavern stories naturally. So now, it's your turn to receive. You could call it my biggest contribution to the war effort. I'll feel better knowing you're wearing it into battle. I'll also feel better you're wearing it if and when you again fight alongside the two finest people I've ever known: Mick and Dave."

Jason picked up the helmet, and looked at it as if he was seeing it for the first time. He touched it like a man lost at sea would touch the beach sand of a saving island. He treasured his new armor and would wear it with pride.

"May it protect you, as you have protected me, Jason."

"It seems everybody likes saying that," blurted Dave.

"Right. Brom said something almost identical upon giving us the armor," said Mick.

"That's right, he did," added Jason. "But anyways... Sir, I will continue that protection until my last breath."

"I have no doubt you will."

The group talked more of their latest participations and conquests well into the night. There were no breaks in the conversations, only furthered comradery. They also ate and drank every single item Old Man Johnson had preparatively set onto the table. They never did learn for sure how Johnson knew they were coming, they just assumed he'd gained insight through another tavern story.

After a great time, the trio left the cabin in the dark, Jason toting the greatest gift he had ever received, or would ever.

Frozen in silence, undisturbed by the worries or concerns of man, Chalatore's town square served as host to anyone who might desire its comfort. Mick, Dave, and Jason eagerly stepped into that comfort, as a dusting of peaceful snow began to fall.

As previously noticed, the armwrestling tables were still in the exact same places they were during the tournament, all covered with snow, save one. They thought about why the lone table was cleared of snow. Maybe it was used by a family for a winter picnic—an unlikely scenario be that as it may. It's more plausible it'd been used by inebriated folks after tavern closing for further drinking.

"It seems," commented Mick, "the accumulation of snow outpaced those responsible for packing the tables away."

"That it does," Jason voiced. "I wish I would've seen you guys win the big tournament and receive your ovations and trophies."

Dave responded, nostalgic in his moment of glory, "We wish you were too; it sure was quite the day."

"But you know," Jason erupted, "you wouldn't have won, had I entered the tournament. I think I can beat the both of you."

Mick laughed boisterously. "Oh, you think so eh? Krell-nor said the same thing. Though, we never got around to the matches."

"I certainly do think I can win." Jason beamed.

"Well alright then, you're on."

They all walked up to the only snow-free table, and arm-wrestled with enjoyment. The whole time, Mick and Dave thinking how great it was to spend relaxing, carefree time with childhood friend, Jason Thorncat.

EPILOGUE

A PAIR OF PARTICULAR ADVENTURERS realized they'd been following footprints for a considerable amount of time. They had ascended and descended a handful of mountains and wondered if they should continue following.

They scratched their chins in deliberation and determined to proceed.

ABOUT THE AUTHOR

NICHOLAS WUDTKE, minimalist, naturalist, and ponderer of philosophy, is rarely seen doing otherwise than sitting on a rock or fallen tree somewhere in the still of Wisconsin's vast Chequamegon-Nicolet National Forest, writing. Nicholas is the father of two sons, one who passed away at a young age due to complications of severe brain damage. Nicholas spent the best years of his life caring for this child, whom he named Lifeson, and his current epic fantasy series is being written in honor of him.

Nicholas enjoys trail running, backpacking, bonsai trees, fossil hunting, and last but not least, listening to favorite rock band Rush, his inspiration, insisting one can come nowhere even close to experiencing this rock power-trio enough.

Author of a list of novels—*The Swords: Friendships and Winds of Far-off Places*, and three installments of his seven-novel *Black Needle* series, including: (1) *Parabolic, Magnetic Key*; (2) *Blunt but Imminently Fatal Projectile*; and (3) *Deserved, Contorted Relics*, Nicholas is a free spirit, currently living in a small home surrounded by trees, a swamp, and fresh air. He cherishes his time with his son, his girlfriend, and the rest of his family and friends.

ACKNOWLEDGEMENTS

A great *thank you* to

Jeanne Wudtke

and

Sara Tischauser

for beta reading.

BLUNT BUT IMMINENTLY FATAL PROJECTILE

CHAPTER 1

B ACK IN THE pack, far from lightweight, were Mick and Dave's awkwardly shaped, homemade tents. The burden of the tents was more than compensated by indisputably proving themselves over the years, having outlasted every hazard Mother Nature decided to throw at them. The time-proven tents were the infrequent brand that screamed imperishability so loud that no one could ignore.

Like always, the tents had been the first things shoved inside Mick and Dave's backpacks, followed by tarps, clothes, and food. After this bulky quad of items were levered into the travel packs, the compartments themselves were full. So, everything else needed to be externally strapped onto the backpacks' frames, including: armor (the new armor they'd recently received from Brom Quintaga); sleeping bags; fishing poles and nets; weapons (not the *black needle* swords, for they were sheathed and waist-strapped); and a few other miscellaneous items. This time around, total combined weight was 192 pounds.

Dave and Mick's hometown of Chalatore, if anything, needed its roads repaired, for they were notoriously well-rutted. The traffic lanes saw traders, tourists, vagabonds, and everyone else of whom you could think come and go daily. Town was normally asphyxiated, even during non-armwrestling tournament days. But along with the traffic came a bustling economy.

Chalatore annually hosted a renowned armwrestling tournament, which saw participants from all over eastern Garobansurov. It was an important strength event which Mick and Dave—previous winners—would more than likely have to miss this year because, as it turned out, General Ulfenkerki was right in telling Mick and Dave last winter to expect a medal or such for their heroics at Fort Gravividon and the Battle of Sarwa. A month ago an emissary from the King himself came to Chalatore to inform Mick Thraiker and Dave Ghrere they were each to receive Garobansurov's highest honor: the Knowing Circle.

The award ceremony and presentation for the Knowing Circle was at the Capital. It was a long journey, which was why the bags were packed and the tournament would be missed. Despite disappointment from the event's organizational committee, Mick and Dave expected to leave days before the tournament's opening bouts. Yet again, the distant winds were calling to Mick and Dave, unignorably beckoning.

Overnight, a fog of no consequence had crept into Chalatore and into its town square, where Dave Ghrere stood busy. Including the potatoes he'd just bought, and the rabbit he trapped earlier at first light, Dave threw all the ingredients of his mother's acclaimed rabbit stew recipe into the town square's large, community cooking cauldron. A company-loving, older man named Gadzud watched Dave heave his ingredients into the cauldron. Waiting for an opportunity to help, Gadzud stood poised for conversation.

Dave said to Gadzud, "Remember ten years ago when Old Man Johnson had to patiently wait for two whole months for a wood trader to come into town, so he could buy the wood needed to fix the hole in his barn roof? Had any more moisture gotten into his barn, it surely would've started to rot. Now, from where I'm standing, I can see three separate wood traders lugging plumped full timber wagons, aiming to sell their wares. I'm glad they're here, but three is superfluous to be sure."

Gadzud took a giant sniff from the pot, and responded, "Well, my friend, if you and Mick would stop putting on such outstandingly entertaining shows during the finals of our armwrestling tournament, people would stop flocking to our town like ravenous vultures on fresh carcasses."

After hearing this comment, Dave couldn't help but nearly fall into the cooking pot laughing. "We should halt the apparently entertaining shows, eh? I'll be sure to tell Mick. I think the townsfolk may be a little upset about it, though."

"Tell me what?" Mick snuck into the conversation and the group from behind.

"Evidently, our armwrestling skills," Dave stated, "are responsible for the boom in traffic."

"I bet those skills are accountable for a lot more than that," Mick let out.

Gadzud chuckled at Mick's bold, but obviously wrapped in humor, statement, and said, "And I don't think the two of you bringing back Knowing Circles will help out the traffic matters any further.

"I think you're probably right."

Gadzud voiced, "I don't mean to change the subject, but who exactly is going to eat all this stew you're cooking here?"

"Whoever wants to," replied Dave. "When it's done, anyone can just come right on over here and eat up."

"How will they know to do so?" asked Gadzud.

"Oh, trust me, they'll know. They'll just smell the aroma wafting through town, and they'll know."

It appeared Dave was right. Once the stew was done half the town showed up to partake in the all-around goodness that was both stew and goodwill. The stew wasn't abundant enough to feed everyone, but no one cared. Everyone had the feeling the cookout was Mick and Dave's way of saying goodbye for a while. No one said anything about it, though, because they all knew what'd happened the last time Mick and Dave left town. The villagers just hoped Mick and Dave's path this time would be safer and a little more war-free. They didn't want to jinx anything by mentioning it.

The war with Molisia still waged on. Mick and Dave's audacious retaking of Fort Gravividon at the onset of the past winter had kept battles and any new invading armies out of their corner of the country for the time being.

At the end of the gathering, Mick, Dave, and their longtime friend Gadzud, cleaned everything up, and went to their homes to sleep off the excitement of the night.

The next day, the one leading up to their departure, Mick and Dave ventured to Old Man Johnson's cabin to bid him farewell. They knocked on the door, were greeted, and entered.

"Glad to see you, youngsters," said Johnson.

"Same to you, old timer."

"Now, you guys do know that there are a lot of people—including myself—who can recite by heart all of the receivers of the Knowing Circle."

Mick unleashed a quick grin and a joke, "Does that mean there've been few recipients, or there are many old men attached to a great deal of time on their hands?"

Old Man Johnson was getting old—as his name suggested—and a little slower at quipping, so it took him a few moments to put together the fact he'd just been on the receiving end of a wisecrack. When he finally understood, he loosed his distinctive, nasal laugh. "I guess it's a little of both, but I'll tell you what: one day, you'll be glad all us old men sit around remembering seemingly useless information."

"Maybe we will."

"All kidding aside, hopefully I'm still alive when you return. I want to see them. I've never actually seen a Knowing Circle up close."

"Oh, I'm sure you will be. We aren't going to be gone that long."

"I hope so. I don't think I'd be very good at explaining to the townsfolk why you've been gone so long. And with any luck, you won't have to use that new armor of yours on the trip," said the old timer.

Dave responded, "I don't think we will, but you never know. Speaking of which, I know we've said this a million times already, but you giving the third set of armor to Jason like that was one of the most honorable things I've ever seen done."

"Not honorable… wise. Our army needs all the help it can get, and him possessing it keeps all of us alive just that much longer."

"You and your modesty. It was *honorable* and you know it."

"Hmmmph." Old Man Johnson shrugged. "Have you heard at all where Jason, General Ulfenkerki, and his army are currently stationed? Sometimes their whereabouts are as mysterious as the existence of the Icytryxis."

"I wouldn't go that far; but, nope, nothing new," answered Mick. "All we know is what you know. Before leaving Chalatore, last winter, Jason expressed planning to rendezvous with the army, either at Zant, Thraug or Strwin. The army very well may have already moved westward, since remnants of war are now showing up in all sorts of unexpected niches of Garobansurov."

"Dangerous times indeed," said Mr. Johnson, as he struggled in hoisting an un-split, hulking log into his fireplace. Mick and Dave knew he liked lifting the logs himself, so they didn't help. "I savor the big ones. They're fun to watch burn, if in fact they do decide to burn."

"To each their own," Dave remarked.

"Will the two of you be leaving tomorrow, then?"

"Yes, sir, that's the plan," replied Mick.

"Say hello to Tim Warmane for me," requested Johnson.

For no real reason, Mick poked at the big log in the fireplace with the available fire rod. "We certainly will do that. Had Dave or I ever told you that when Tim was forging our swords all those years ago, he barbecued over the fire more nights than he didn't?"

"Yeah, he sure liked to barbecue," Dave blurted.

Johnson replied, "No, I can't recall you guys ever bringing that up. Good times."

Mick and Dave stayed for half the day at their great friend Old Man Johnson's cabin. Ironically, barbecuing had transpired. They went home only after eating enough to hurt their stomachs.

Later that day, Mick and Dave stopped at their friend Mrezil's house. It was something they did from time to time, since she was a nice, interesting lady. Plus, she maintained a large collection of books they liked to look over. As for this day, she had a book they particularly wanted to peruse. On their way to the Capital, Mick and Dave intended to stop at the Dourinuset Monastery, a place they'd always yearned to visit. They never got around to doing so because it was built on the top of a large, hard-to-navigate hill and once one made the long journey they weren't necessarily allowed admittance.

Because the monastery was along the way to the Capital, and Mick and Dave were feeling extra-adventurous, they decided to leave early to summit the hill and visit the monks—but a visit that would only transpire if they were indeed permitted entrance by the holy dwellers, a chance they were willing to take. The book they wanted to study at Mrezil's house contained a chapter specifically concerning the Dourinuset Monastery. They thought maybe by knowing a decent amount of data on the subject, their chances of being allowed visitation would be slightly enhanced.

Mrezil reached for the book in her bookcase she was kindly asked to retrieve. After handing it to Mick, she said, "Go ahead and take your time reading it. I'll just be over here, peeling potatoes."

"Thank you so much."

Dave emitted, "I'll help you peel, while Mick reads. Only one person can read from it at a time anyways."

Lacking any inefficiency, Dave and Mrezil finished off her two pails of potatoes, coincidentally in the same amount of time it took Mick to finish reading the chapter on Dourinuset—a long chapter.

Mick voiced, "Well, by reading this, I'm certainly not any more informed on how we can increase our chances of being welcomed into the monastery, but I do know a lot more about elements correlated with them, one of them being that although they're generally a silent monastery, they do speak sporadically, between scheduled activities and such. It seems like a good place to leave you at, Dave. Maybe they'll teach you how to be less chatty."

"That very well may be a good idea, but if I get left there for that lesson, we'll also have to stop at Warton's tavern. There, you can learn how to drink properly. Lately, you've been drinking like a lightweight."

Mick laughed, having realized how fast Dave's comeback was, and responded, "Touché."

Mrezil joined in: "I'm just glad we're all working to improve ourselves."

Three people expressing amusement filled the house, drowning out the all-too-familiar sound of citizens in the street arguing about produce prices.

Mick continued speaking on Dourinuset. "Apparently, parts of their living structure and church are thousands of years old."

"Did it mention if their beliefs go back that far on the timeline too?"

"No, it didn't go into detail about that. I was hoping it would, but it didn't. The chapter did discuss some of their specific beliefs. I'll fill you in more on that along the way, Dave. We wouldn't want to bore Mrezil any further."

"The two of you are way too charismatic to ever bore me with anything."

"Oh, Mrezil, you're too much."

Eventually, conversation ran its course. Dave and Mick left Mrezil's abode, knowing it was a day well spent and most edifying. Thankfully, for Mick and Dave's sake, the streets were now free from annoying produce price-debaters.

Twilight approached all but itself. The city didn't exude much animation, so the previous year's Chalatore Arm-Wrestling Tournament champs went home to bed for much needed sleep for traveling. For no doubt, Dave and Mick were going to journey far—unmistakably reminiscent of countless times before.

MANY MILES FROM Chalatore, a man, a monk, coasted through the motions of life. Brother Alfonso Alardo, for the millionth time, found himself having to break the woeful trance induced by the saddest, most powerful memory of his life. It was a memory where he constantly dwelled, and one from which he constantly had to escape. It was the memory of his wife, who inexplicably left him. Before joining the monastery, Alfonso was happily married, for his part, of ten years. He'd put every ounce of his heart and soul into that love, and never foresaw an ending to the great romance. But guided by the unpredictability of love, Alfonso's world came abruptly to an end. Like lightning on a virtually cloudless day, he never saw it coming, no foreshadowing in the slightest.

After a year of the visceral pain caused by the breakup, he found himself being moments away from killing himself from the despair. But he was miraculously saved by the hearing of God's calling, and as a result, joined the Dourinuset Monastery. It was the best place he could be, to find meaning after such a loss.

Brother Alfonso tolerated existence. He found occasional happiness at Dourinuset, but as soon as memories of his wife flooded in, the happiness washed away. He endured a wound that time could not, and would not, heal. An excruciating burden, from which he was never free. The man had a heart of gold, something that most who knew him surely saw. But they also could see the manifestation of pain in his eyes, and couldn't help but feel immense sympathy.

Momentarily free from the trance and mental anguish, Alfonso pulled out a chair from underneath the large table, and joined the other monks for breakfast, bringing along his contagiously wonderful smile.

For no reason, Abbot Ferdinand (the head monk) liked to fashion his three eggs and toast geo-symmetrically on his plate. Next to Alfonso, Ferdinand carefully sat as to not disturb his creation, and addressed all at the breakfast table: "Good morning everyone."

As aforementioned, the monks spoke only rarely—a degree of peace all twelve monks appreciated. They listened as Ferdinand continued.

"I give you all the credit in the world, Brother Dimetriev, for your attempt at negotiating with the Smiths at their farm for water. Much recognition for your effort. I'm afraid, however, our predicament concerning our well running dry last month is more serious than previously expected. Due to either a water shortage everywhere or nobody wanting to contract with us, things are dire. I'm so confused about nobody wanting to help that I'm at a loss for words. If we're unable to procure a water source soon, we may lose our blissful, hilltop existence here. We're unquestionably in great jeopardy."

Brother Dimetriev bowed his head and voiced, "You're welcome, sir. The Smiths gave no reason as to why they didn't want to negotiate. They just seemed to be uncouth and unaccommodating. I wasn't able to figure out why exactly they didn't want to sell us water rights."

"I guess some people are just like that. We have one more chance, of which I'm aware, to get the water. I'm fairly certain Savata Dearer—a young, single man—has a well at his farm." Ferdinand stood up. "And by no means is it implied that if whoever volunteers for this mission were to fail, they'd hold sole responsibility for our demise. Don't think of it as the last chance. So, knowing that, do I have any volunteers to make the journey to Mr.

Dearer's dwelling and parley with the young gentleman?" Brother Ferdinand sat back down and couldn't help but hold his breath.

Even though Brother Ferdinand had just got done saying the volunteer would hold no ultimate way-of-life-ending accountability, the brothers were in no hurry to step forward to bear the enormous load at hand. They all looked at each other with the uncomfortable stare of unanswered request. Time momentarily stood still, the room silent. The high-pitched whistling of wind was heard channeling through the outer monastery walls, a mystical sound. Finally, Brother Alfonso Alardo figuratively stepped forward.

HAWK AND LEOPARD—MICK and Dave's respective childhood nicknames—having started their westerly walk at sunrise, were ecstatic to be on another heartland crossing. These deep runs were what truly gave them identity. Eventually, they would be returning with Knowing Circles, making them the only folks from their town or neighboring towns to ever do so.

By suppertime, they reached a point fifteen miles away from Chalatore, a fairly decent day's walk by their standards. They had crossed one river, two creeks, and many forests and fields along the way.

Dave flipped the poultry burgers and said, "Too bad the creature that was once these burgers wasn't any larger. Then we could've ridden it through the air all the way to the Capital."

"Keep dreaming, but don't dream too hard and burn my burger."

"You'll never let that go, will you? I burn your burger once, and the whole world comes to an end."

Mick emitted, "Ah yes, the incident at Falbasert. Well yeah, anything could've happened after the Falbasert incident."

In a good mood, Dave laughed. "We're just lucky there were no casualties or collateral damage."

Mick laughed, shook his head, and took a deep breath. "Intriguing phenomenon: a lung full of cool, spring air has the ability to bring back countless memories of old."

"Intriguing indeed. And true. Sure is magnificent to be out here in the untamed wilderness again."

"I wonder if it thinks the same of us."

"Of course it does, Mick. I thought it was common knowledge that the untamed wilderness loves us."

"That very well could be."

Mick and Dave chuckled, ate their burgers (un-burnt) and for the first time of the trip, set up their tents. For them, sleeping in tents were cozy experiences, always summoning feelings of utmost gratification.

Gazing at his tent, Dave said, "Maybe we should just live in these things year-round."

"I wouldn't complain."

Early the next morning, Mick and Dave witnessed rain wash away a weak-rooted bush in lamentable surges. "Well, that's sad," produced Dave. "What a big waste of a little bush."

When the rain subsided just enough for comfort they put down the tents and continued walking. The trail was soggy, but not unbearable. Wetness added a few pounds to the total load weight, but a condition that was only temporary.

A few miles from the previous night's campsite, Mick pointed at a dilapidated farmhouse and said, "Remember the time when we were kids, and we spent a couple days at that house?"

"Oh yes. I don't remember why we did it, but I remember doing it."

"I haven't committed to memory exactly why either, but I think it had something to do with a rampant disease in town or something."

"Makes sense," said Dave. "I remember staying up all night, playing hide-and-go-seek with that one guy."

"I think his name was Dan."

"Yup, Dan. Dan was fun. I wonder whatever happened to Dan."

"Me too."

Run of the mill walks and campouts were all that ensued during the few days of the expedition's opening stage. Mick and Dave didn't typically like that sort of boredom in their lives, but they had no choice in the matter. Every now and then, monotony declared itself the winner of the day, and there wasn't any manner of creative thinking, wild imagination, or prudent planning that could say otherwise.

BLAZINGLY FOCUSED, Brother Alfonso Alardo, still wearing full monk garb, advanced to the front door of Savata Dearer's house. Abbot Ferdinand had supplied him the numerical parameters by which to negotiate for water, with a little wiggle room. Alfonso knew precisely what he was going to say to Savata. He knocked and waited patiently.

A man opened the door, looked at Alfonso, and said, "Now here's a surprise. It's not every day one sees a monk at their door. One hailing from Dourinuset, I presume?"

"That is correct. Hello, nice to meet you. My name is Alfonso." The two shook hands.

"And mine is Savata. Very pleasurable to meet you. Welcome to my home on this fine day. Please, please come inside."

Humbly, Brother Alardo went inside the house, and sat in the chair, at which Savata had kindly pointed. "Lovely home you have here."

"Thank you, sir. So what can I do for you?"

"Well, I'm guessing you know, since you live in the area, the Dourinuset Monastery sits atop a barely traversable hilltop. You might as well call it a mountaintop for as isolated as we are. It's arduous to say the least to import anything at all to such heights. Furthermore, we'd been presented the unfortunate occurrence of our aquifer running dry. I guess for as long as we've been dipping into that well, it was bound to happen at some point."

"How long is that?"

"I'm not sure exactly, but I do know it's been longer than anyone else in the area has been dipping into theirs—over a thousand years."

Savata replied, "I once heard the age of the monastery, but the number was so farfetched that I assumed it was a jest."

"Oooh, it is that old, believe me. Our documentation goes back quite a ways. So, anyways, I see you have a well, yourself. Does it work?"

"For the most part, yes. The block and tackle system I use for hoisting jugs doesn't want to cooperate half the time."

"Yes, apparatuses with moving parts can be finicky." Alfonso unintentionally held his breath for a moment, and put forth, "I'm here to make a proposal. The Dourinuset monks are prepared to offer a sum of 300 gitis for every standard load of water delivered to us, more or less, indefinitely."

"That is an extremely generous offer, but I'm afraid I just don't have the time for that, with all my farm work and all."

Brother Alfonso stopped himself from holding his breath again. "I understand, but, respectfully, I must say that what I'm offering you is much, much more than what your crops are worth."

"That may be true, but I didn't make a promise to my deceased father to deliver water to a monastery. I did promise him that I would farm his cherished land to the best of my abilities, for as long as it was my land to farm."

"What if we hired someone else to do the delivering? All we'd need from you is use of the well."

"I wish I could help, but I use most of my water for irrigation," returned Savata. "I'd hate to risk running it dry. And as you said, wells are running dry these days."

"I recognize and honor your wishes and appreciate your time and attention. I wish you all the best, and since we can't come to an agreement, I must bid you farewell."

Savata showed Alfonso the door, and said, "Good luck to you and your quest. I really hope you do get your water."

Forlorn, Alfonso walked away from the Dearer farm, his mission unsuccessful. He was slightly confused about what was said about the irrigation, since all the land in the area was both fertile, and exhibited high moisture retention, rendering any form of irrigation virtually unnecessary.

Just like everything else in my life, a complete failure.

GET YOUR NEXT GREAT READ!

VISIT

<u>WWW.NICHOLASWUDTKE.COM</u>

TODAY!